# Mid-Century Romance

# OXFORD MID-CENTURY STUDIES

The Oxford Mid-Century Studies series publishes monographs in several disciplinary and creative areas in order to create a thick description of culture in the thirty-year period around the Second World War. With a focus on the 1930s through the 1960s, the series concentrates on fiction, poetry, film, photography, theatre, as well as art, architecture, design, and other media. The mid-century is an age of shifting groups and movements, from existentialism through abstract expressionism to confessional, serial, electronic, and pop art styles. The series charts such intellectual movements, even as it aids and abets the very best scholarly thinking about the power of art in a world under new techno-political compulsions, whether nuclear-apocalyptic, Cold War–propagandized, transnational, neo-imperial, superpowered, or postcolonial.

*Series editors*
Allan Hepburn, McGill University
Adam Piette, University of Sheffield
Lyndsey Stonebridge, University of Birmingham

# Mid-Century Romance

*Modernism, Socialist Culture, and the Historical Novel*

JOHN T. CONNOR

# OXFORD
UNIVERSITY PRESS

Great Clarendon Street, Oxford, OX2 6DP,
United Kingdom

Oxford University Press is a department of the University of Oxford.
It furthers the University's objective of excellence in research, scholarship,
and education by publishing worldwide. Oxford is a registered trade mark of
Oxford University Press in the UK and in certain other countries

© John T. Connor 2024

The moral rights of the author have been asserted

All rights reserved. No part of this publication may be reproduced, stored in
a retrieval system, or transmitted, in any form or by any means, without the
prior permission in writing of Oxford University Press, or as expressly permitted
by law, by licence or under terms agreed with the appropriate reprographics
rights organization. Enquiries concerning reproduction outside the scope of the
above should be sent to the Rights Department, Oxford University Press, at the
address above

You must not circulate this work in any other form
and you must impose this same condition on any acquirer

Published in the United States of America by Oxford University Press
198 Madison Avenue, New York, NY 10016, United States of America

British Library Cataloguing in Publication Data

Data available

Library of Congress Control Number: 2024933234

ISBN 9780192859754

DOI: 10.1093/9780191953057.001.0001

Printed and bound by
CPI Group (UK) Ltd, Croydon, CR0 4YY

Links to third party websites are provided by Oxford in good faith and
for information only. Oxford disclaims any responsibility for the materials
contained in any third party website referenced in this work.

# Acknowledgements

This book has travelled with me from graduate school in Philadelphia to jobs in upstate New York and London. It has accrued debts along the way, which it is my pleasure to acknowledge here. US gradschool was a transformative experience, a place of wonder and welcome. I owe this privilege, in the first instance, to Ato Quayson's suggestion and to the generosity of the Thouron family. At the University of Pennsylvania, I was fortunate to have Margreta de Grazia as a mentor, and as a teacher with Sean Keilen on the seminar, 'Renaissance Gothic', that first alerted me to the literature and politics of romance. Stuart Curran and Michael Gamer were my entrée to the romantic-era novel and the post-enlightenment romance revival. Warren Breckman, Vicki Mahaffey, Jean-Michel Rabaté, and Michèle Richman fostered my interests in literary modernism and intellectual history. Heather Love got me thinking about feeling. This book began as a doctoral dissertation and has been through several iterations since. For their patience with this process, Jim English and Jed Esty have my deepest thanks. Both read early drafts with a speed and care that never failed to amaze: Jim with a constant curiosity, humour, and encouragement; Jed with an alchemical ability to translate disorganized thought into nested frameworks and ambitious claims. Jim was the perfect dissertation director, a model teacher, a loyal champion on the market, and during a difficult year in London together a friend.

Colgate University was a magical place to learn and further develop this project. A Hearst Fellowship from its Faculty Research Council paid for a long trip to the National Library of Australia where the papers of Jack Lindsay unlocked the world of mid-century communist commitment; other grants gave me time with archives in England and Wales. But Colgate was also an experiment in living the liberal arts, an inspiring community of teachers and students. My first thanks are to my colleagues in the Department of English, to Peter Balakian, Jennifer Brice, Marjorie Celona, Susan Cerasano, Michael Coyle, Morgan Davies, Constance Harsh, Yohei Igarashi, Linck Johnson, Tess Jones, Deborah Knuth Klenck, Kezia Page, Nimanthi Rajasingham, Max Rayneard, Lynn Staley, Lenora Warren, Sarah Wider, and to Jane Pinchin and Margaret Maurer as also mentors and chairs. For counsel and continuing kindness, Andrew Rotter and Padma Kaimal have my thanks. Mark Stern remains the very best of friends; I have never learned as much or as joyfully as I have with him. On my return to the UK, I was lucky to land at King's College, London, with Anna Snaith a mentor, and Richard Kirkland and Janet Floyd the most supportive of chairs.

Opportunities to present this project at conferences and talks have proven hugely helpful. Kevin Platt's invitations to teach a seminar at Penn and later join a Slavic and East European Literatures panel at the MLA provided early encouragement to embrace the transnational dimension of my research. Invitations from Rebecca Beasley and Matthew Taunton to present at the Anglo-Russian Research Network in London and from Rachel Potter to join a symposium at UEA got me thinking about literary world-systems and the long Cold War. Erin Carlston was my catalyst for thinking of Jack Lindsay as an Australian modernist, with a seminar and panel at the MSA that later found its way to print. I am indebted to Michael Coyle for my introduction to the Raymond Williams Society and for the friends and colleagues I made there, among them David Alderson, Tony Crowley, Emily Cuming, Kristin Ewins, Ben Harker, Philip O'Brien, Stan Smith, and Elinor Taylor. Two conferences in Manchester, 'Raymond Williams Now!' and 'Wars of Position: Marxism and Civil Society', fostered my thinking on late Williams and the cultural politics of Georg Lukács. My thanks as well to Lucy Delap, Ben Harker, Clara Jones, Benjamin Kohlmann, Peter Mandler, and Henry Stead for invitations to share work at the universities of Cambridge, Freiburg, and Manchester, at King's College, London, the British Association of Modernism Studies, and the London Modernism Seminar.

I am deeply grateful to Allan Hepburn, Adam Piette, and Lyndsey Stonebridge for making a home for my manuscript in their Oxford Mid-Century Studies series. Allan shepherded my project at every step with a sharp and sympathetic eye and always exciting ideas for new leads. Jo Spillane brought it to press. I had the most amazing anonymous readers, whose expert criticisms and suggestions for reorganization, expansion, and further reflection improved the book no end. They have my sincere thanks, as does Douglas Mao for his advice and encouragement on an earlier draft.

Archivists and special collections librarians have been unfailingly generous with access and information. Warm thanks to the staff at the National Library of Australia in Canberra; at the Dorset History Centre in Dorchester; at the British Film Institute, British Library, Marx Memorial Library, National Archives, and Victoria and Albert Museum in London; at the Labour History Archive and Study Centre in Manchester and the Working-Class Movement Library in Salford; at the rare books and manuscript collections of the university libraries of Cambridge, Colgate, Durham, Nottingham, Sussex, Swansea, and Yale; and at the archives of King's College and Newnham College, Cambridge. My thanks as well to the Library and Information Centre of the Hungarian Academy of Sciences, and to Anne Cranny-Francis and the University of Technology, Sydney, for making parts of their collections available online.

Quotations from the unpublished correspondence of Nancy Cunard are included with the permission of the executor of the Literary Estate of Nancy Cunard; from the memoirs of Hyman Fagan with the permission of his Estate;

from the unpublished correspondence of Hope Mirrlees with the permission of Faber & Faber Ltd. and the Estate of Hope Mirrlees; from the correspondence of E.P. Thompson with the permission of the Estate of E.P. Thompson; from the papers of Sylvia Townsend Warner with the permission of the Estate of Sylvia Townsend Warner. My quotation from the unpublished correspondence of John Berger comes courtesy of the John Berger Estate. Unpublished writings of E.M. Forster copyright the Provost and Scholars of King's College Cambridge 2024. I am grateful to the copyright holder for permission to quote from two unpublished novels by Harold Heslop. My especial thanks to Helen Lindsay for permission to quote so extensively from her father's papers. Tom McGrath's 'Against the False Magicians' was later collected in *The Movie at the End of the World*. Copyright © 1972. This material is used by permission of Ohio University Press, www.ohioswallow.com. I am grateful to Wise Music Group for the use of two quotations from *Wat Tyler*. Words by Nancy Bush. Music by Alan Bush. Copyright © 1953 (Renewed) by Novello & Company Limited. International Copyright Secured. All Rights Reserved. *Reprinted by Permission of Hal Leonard Europe Ltd.*

Portions of this book grew out of earlier published versions. Parts of chapters two and four appeared previously in 'Jack Lindsay, Socialist Humanism and the Communist Historical Novel', *Review of English Studies*, n.s. 66, no.274 (2014), and 'Fanfrolico and After: The Lindsay Aesthetic in the Cultural Cold War', *Modernist Cultures* 15, no.3 (2020). Some passages in the epilogue first appeared in '*People of the Black Mountains* and the Politics of Theory', *Key Words: A Journal of Cultural Materialism* 13 (2015); some paragraphs in the introduction appeared in 'Anglo-Soviet Literary Relations in the Long 1930s', a chapter in Benjamin Kohlmann and Matthew Taunton's edited collection, *A History of 1930s British Literature* (2019). Thanks to OUP, Edinburgh University Press, Cambridge University Press, and the Raymond Williams Society for permission to reproduce this content here.

Though they may not immediately recognize themselves in *Mid-Century Romance*, my family and friends have all shared in its making. At Penn: Todd Carmody, Ian Cornelius, Adrian Daub, Chris Hunter, Benjy Kahan, Ciara Kehoe, Jane Malcolm, Melanie Micir, Cathy Nicholson, Cristina Pangilinan, Rebecca Sheehan, Greg Steirer, Julie and Cedric Tolliver, the members of my Marx Reading Group, and the activists of GET-UP (1.0); at Colgate, Noah Dauber, Marjorie, Max, and Mark. I owe to my father a first interest in the lives of historians, and to my mother a sense of scholarship and perseverance in the process. This book is for her. My last and happiest acknowledgement is of Julia Guarneri, surest love and constant companion. 'Camerado, I give you my hand!'

# Contents

Introduction: Modernism, Socialist Culture, and the
Mid-Century National Turn     1

1. Hope Mirrlees and Virginia Woolf in the 'footprints of Sir
   Walter Scott'     35

2. Migrations of the Communist Historical Novel     73

3. Memories of Spain in Sylvia Townsend Warner and John
   Cowper Powys     124

4. Jack Lindsay, Socialist Humanism, and the Communist
   Historical Novel     162

   Epilogue: Parables of Survival     196

*Works Cited*     206
*Index*     229

# Introduction
## Modernism, Socialist Culture, and the Mid-Century National Turn

### I. Narratives of Decline

From high above the 'smashed, dreary city of Vienna', Graham Greene delivers a parable of his century's lost illusions. Rollo Martins has learned that Harry Lime—'the third man' of the title and his hero for twenty years—has been running a racket in doctored penicillin. He has been shown the 'small museum' of confiscated samples and the paper trail that leads to Lime. He has contemplated the casualties: the men who lost limbs and the children who died, the others who 'went off their heads'. The information brings his whole 'world' crashing down. Cherished memories of their schooldays together, 'the dreams, the walks, every shared experience was simultaneously tainted, like the soil of an atomised town'.[1] In this moment of epiphany, sin proves original and hell to have lain about us in our infancy. The insight is theological and a confession of faith, but also political, a blanket indictment of the last century's narratives of perfectibility and progress: the liberal complacency that it could temper with good intentions a system it did not determine; the socialist belief that it could plan the common good. The pain Greene's fictions traffic in, the violence they direct, and the evil they dissect, serve justice on a civilization that had tried to dissociate its ideals from the corruption of the world and our all too human nature. As emblems of this artificial separation, Greene selects as targets of his literary retribution the sanctuaries of happy home and fond-remembered childhood. Their innocence conceived as ideological, they share the calamity that overtakes them with the genre in which Greene first tried his talents as a writer.

His critics called it 'Greeneland', that 'strange violent "seedy" region of the mind' from which he spun, or so they charged, his chastened vision of the world. Greene just called it reality, 'carefully and accurately described'. 'I have been a newspaper correspondent as well as a novelist', he wanted to protest. 'I assure you that the dead child lay in the ditch in just that attitude'.[2] Resolutely present-set and

---

[1] Graham Greene, 'The Third Man' [1949], in *The Portable Graham Greene*, edited by Philip Stratford (London: Penguin, 1994), pp.354–5.
[2] Graham Greene, *Ways of Escape* (Harmondsworth: Penguin, 1981), p.60. Arthur Calder-Marshall coined the term: 'Few living English novelists derive more material from the daily newspaper than Graham Greene; yet even fewer reduce everything to so uniform a vision. The setting may be London

rigorous in their realism, Greene's front-line reports from the century's extremity aimed to assail his readers' ignorance, rub their noses in the world. But they were also a rebuke to his younger self and to an author who had once sought safe harbour in the past: in adolescent notebooks filled with 'stories of sixteenth-century Italy or twelfth-century England', in published novels of nineteenth-century smugglers and the Carlist wars in Spain.[3] Suppressed from his collected works, Greene's historical fictions survive today as a bibliographic trace, the literary equivalent of the 'atomized town' that was once a schoolboy romance.[4] Contaminated by its 'youth'—the 'haze of hopes and dreams and false ambitions' in which a child first plays at politics and literature—Greene named the historical novel his place of no return.[5] The only way was on: to Brighton's racetracks and Four-Powers Vienna, 'to Tabasco during the religious persecution, to a *léproserie* in the Congo, to the Kikuyu reserve during the Mau-Mau insurrection, to the emergency in Malaya and to the French War in Vietnam'.[6] Each new destination atoned for a sheltered English childhood when, knowing 'too little of the contemporary world to treat it', he had written instead of the past.[7]

Greene's rejection of his early work points a Catholic and a Cold War moral. It also confirms a common sense of the historical novel's standing in the first and middle decades of the century. This is a fallow time in our histories of the genre, a hiatus framed to either side by moments of critical mass and prestige: in the age of new nations and in the period of postmodernism. Only twice, we are told, have the conditions obtained to propel the historical novel to the centre of the literary field. Two crises of historicity, of the lived experience of historical time, have been taken to explain the genre's romantic-era rise and later return as a privileged literary form of late capitalism. The interim falls from view, a time of aftermath or unpropitious prelude populated by fringe formations and by isolated individual writers and works. Antiquated, outmoded, our interest lies elsewhere. For this is the period

---

or Liberia, Stockholm, Brighton or Tabasco. But they are all in Greeneland.' Calder-Marshall, 'The Works of Graham Greene', *Horizon* 1, no.5 (1940): pp.367–8.

[3] Graham Greene, 'The Lost Childhood' [1947], *Collected Essays* (Harmondsworth: Penguin, 1970), p.16.

[4] Greene' 'Third Man', p.355. Greene suppressed his second novel, *The Name of Action* (1930), and his third, *Rumour at Nightfall* (1931), from the Uniform Edition (1946–52) and from the Heinemann/Bodley Head Collected Edition (1970–94). Only because 'it would be a little absurd to begin a collected edition with my fourth published novel' did he not suppress *The Man Within* (1929) as well. Graham Greene, 'Introduction' to *The Man Within* (London: Heinemann and the Bodley Head, 1976), p. v.

[5] Greene, *Ways of Escape*, p.16.

[6] Graham Greene, *A Sort of Life* (Harmondsworth: Penguin, 1972), pp.95–6.

[7] Greene, *Ways of Escape*, pp.13–14. The itinerary shaped a reputation as the novelist of his generation and a witness to his times. Writing of the British book trade, John Sutherland has called the period 1945–70 'the age of Graham Greene', a time when public libraries subsidized a boom in accessible literary fiction and the growth of the US and wider anglophone export market prompted a 'vogue for works with international themes'. Norman Sherry closes an obituary notice by describing a writer who 'gulped his life down like damnation. For experience of a whole century he was the man within.' Sutherland, *Fiction and the Fiction Industry* (London: Athlone Press, 1978), p. xx; p.56; Sherry, 'Obituary: Graham Greene', *The Independent*, 4 April 1991, Gazette, p.3.

we cede to modernism and to an experimental fiction either culpably ahistorical or brilliantly contemporary, but in either case allergic to the old-fashioned historical novel.

Falling to the wrong side of the modernist 'Great Divide' and of the new century's break with its proximate past, the historical novel barely registers in accounts of a 'modern fiction' ambitious of its craft and to explore the psychic interior unbound by narratives of historical destiny and social subjection.[8] Unflattering or more darkly critical correlations between modernism's technical inwardness and contracting social referent sharpen the contrast with the epic pretension and expansive mimetic range of the national-historical novel. Instead of a 'canvas on which armies manoeuvre and great hills pile themselves upon each other's shoulders', as Robert Louis Stevenson described his favourite novels of Scott, modernism invites us to attend to the 'shower of ... atoms' as they fall on 'an ordinary mind on an ordinary day'.[9] Arraigned in satire by D.H. Lawrence—'"Did I feel a twinge in my little toe, or didn't I?" asks every character of Mr Joyce or of Miss Richardson or M. Proust. "Is my aura a blend of frankincense and orange pekoe and boot-blacking, or is it myrrh and bacon-fat and Shetland tweed?"'— the modernist novel's gathering introspection and narrowing concern with its own technical procedures would seem to preclude the kind of totalizing retrospect that sees the past as the concrete prehistory of the present.[10]

Time was when the historical novel had given shape to a whole society unfolding in historical time, a social totality that was also a unified reading public and the imagined community of a new nation state. This was Sir Walter Scott's achievement, and his critical reputation matched a popularity unrivalled in the nineteenth century both at home and abroad.[11] Time was, but it couldn't last, or so the story goes. For with the expansion of capital and the metastasis of empire in the later decades of the century, this close equivalence of national story, knowable community, and stable civil society collapsed. Writing in the late 1930s, Georg Lukács

---

[8] Andreas Huyssen rehearses a familiar definition of modernism in terms of its 'insistence on the autonomy of the art work, its obsessive hostility to mass culture, its radical separation from the culture of everyday life, and its programmatic distance from political, economic, and social concerns', in *After the Great Divide: Modernism, Mass Culture, Postmodernism* (Bloomington: Indiana University Press, 1986), p. vii. We have Virginia Woolf to thank for the provocation that 'December 1910' marked a watershed in literary and social relations, and for one exemplary statement in praise of 'modern fiction'.

[9] R.L. Stevenson, 'Victor Hugo's Romances' [1874], in *Familiar Studies of Men and Books* (New York: Charles Scribner, 1895), p.23. Virginia Woolf, 'Modern Fiction' [1925], in *The Essays of Virginia Woolf, Volume 4: 1925–1928*, edited by Andrew McNeillie (London: Hogarth Press, 1994), p.160.

[10] D.H. Lawrence, 'The Future of the Novel' [1923], in *Selected Critical Writings*, edited by Michael Herbert (Oxford: Oxford University Press, 1998), pp.142–3.

[11] More recent scholarship on the romantic-era novel has radically expanded our sense of Scott's predecessors and competitors in the field, recasting the Waverley novels not as the invention *ex nihilo* they were later remembered as but as a brilliant recombination of existing narrative options. Cf. Katie Trumpener, *Bardic Nationalism: The Romantic Novel and the British Empire* (Princeton, NJ: Princeton University Press, 1997) and Richard Maxwell, *The Historical Novel in Europe, 1650–1950* (Cambridge: Cambridge University Press, 2009). For non-specialist critics and creative writers in the middle of the twentieth century, however, it was Scott's legacy that counted; his was the only name still current.

dated the historical novel's decline from the revolutions of 1848, his diagnosis of a 'crisis of bourgeois realism' naming an economic reality less knowable because in the imperial era no longer simply national, a reading public fractured by rising literacy and the cheapening of print, and an imagined community increasingly ideological because increasingly class-divided. Where previously the genre had shared with the contemporary novel the ambition to narrate the social whole—the one its present, the other its past, comprising together a unified and dynamic history of capitalist modernity—the historical novel now abandoned its cognitive vocation, indulging instead in an 'orgy of exotic themes' and 'decorative' period settings unmoored from contemporary social life.[12] Its critical integrity diminished, the historical novel joined the proliferating subgenres of *fin-de-siècle* fiction to be consumed thereafter by the wrong kind of readers (women and children) and for the wrong sorts of reason (light entertainment, pleasurable escape). For Lukács, the story did not end there, but for most other commentators the historical novel continued abject and unremarkable through the first two thirds of the twentieth century. 'Historical fiction proper', writes Chris Baldick, 'has only a minor place in the serious literature of this period.'[13] 'If we look at the interwar scene', observes Perry Anderson, 'the historical novel has become déclassé, falling precipitously out of the ranks of serious fiction'. 'At virtually all levels', the genre has become 'a recessive form'. Extending his analysis from the *entre deux guerres* to the mid-1960s, Anderson discerns only 'a few antique jewels on a huge mound of trash.'[14]

My own study rejects this critical equation of modernist ascendancy with generic recession to show the historical novel in fact a major force in the middle decades of the twentieth century, its presence to be read across national literatures and cultural formations. Not all modernists, I will argue, reviled the form, nor was modernism ever the only game in town. An exemplary genre of British late modernism, the historical novel was also a dominant genre in the culture of British and international communism, where I trace its influence in the rise of radical social history and magical realism. This mid-century historical novel was not a radical new beginning, but rather an adaptation and modulation of the national-historical form associated with Scott and his imitators in other countries. For cause, I posit a national turn in world politics that drew both modernism and socialist culture into its field of force. With the rise of National Socialism in Germany, National Bolshevism in the Soviet Union, and the revolutionary nationalisms of the Popular Fronts, with the urgencies of national defence in the Second World War, of national

---

[12] Georg Lukács, *The Historical Novel*, translated by Hannah and Stanley Mitchell (London: Merlin, 1962), pp.171–250.
[13] Chris Baldick, *The Oxford English Literary History, Volume 10. 1910–1940: The Modern Movement* (Oxford: Oxford University Press, 2004), p.219.
[14] Perry Anderson, 'The Historical Novel: From Progress to Catastrophe', *London Review of Books* 33, no.15 (28 July 2011): p.27.

independence in the emerging postcolonial world, and national retrenchment in the erstwhile metropolis, the nation dominated the mid-century political imagination. In these decades, a crisis of authority in such international systems as the balance of power and the gold standard matched crises of faith in the principles of liberal individualism and in socialist theories of world revolution. The result was a parallel retreat from elite cosmopolitanism and proletarian internationalism, and a new attention to the nation as a horizon of collective agency and aspiration. As such it appeared in the command economy and the welfare state, in the politics of national populism and cultural nationalism, and in such literary forms as could register what Mikhail Bakhtin theorized at the time as the representational space-time or 'chronotope' of the nation.

The war of position to defend the nation or to imagine it anew moved the historical novel to the centre of mid-century literary culture, but not all writers responded in kind. In Britain, some of the writers still most associated with this period resisted the nation's appeal. Graham Greene's career is in this respect the opposite of the mid-century type I have in mind: built on a renunciation of the historical novel rather than a turn towards it, a global itinerary that never looked back, a dark vision of our 'diseased erratic world' and the solitary soul's travail with no counterpoint of redemption in national culture and community.[15] For Greene, there was only one story to tell of the England he had known, with its 'vicarage gardens and girls in white frocks and the smell of herbaceous borders and security'.[16] He welcomed the violence and destruction of the Blitz as 'just and poetic', 'the right end to the muddled thought, the sentimentality and selfishness of generations'. 'The world we lived in could not have ended any other way.'[17] But for the writers I study here—including the modernists Hope Mirrlees and Virginia Woolf, the communists Jack Lindsay and Sylvia Townsend Warner, the oddball modernist and some-time fellow traveller John Cowper Powys—a different future was possible, and the pasts they mined pointed the direction it might take.

Like Jed Esty and Alexandra Harris, scholars of the 'late' or 'romantic' modernism of the British 1930s and 1940s, I depart from some of the more canonical literature of the period. Esty locates his 'Anglocentric turn' among a cohort of ageing metropolitan modernists, supplementing a 'tight canonical focus' on the later work of T.S. Eliot, E.M. Forster, and Woolf, with a handful of more eccentric modernist and mid-century figures.[18] Harris curates an eclectic culture of 'national self-discovery' among visual artists, composers, literary figures, even cookery

---

[15] Graham Greene, 'At Home' [1940], in *Collected Essays*, p.335.
[16] Graham Greene, *The Ministry of Fear* [1943] (London: Penguin, 1978), p.11.
[17] Greene, 'At Home', p.334; p.336.
[18] Jed Esty, *A Shrinking Island: Modernism and National Culture in England* (Princeton, NJ: Princeton University Press, 2004), p.12.

writers and garden designers.[19] My own account of the mid-century historical novel pairs a version of late modernism with the professional and plebeian writers of the British Communist Party in the period of the Popular Front and in the decades thereafter. All our versions of the national turn revise a familiar *récit* of 'the thirties' anchored in the poetry of the Auden generation and in novelists like Greene, for whom the lesson of a 'low dishonest decade' was to recognize dark religious truths about human nature, the reality of evil, and the virtue of restraint. For Esty's late modernists, Harris's romantic moderns, and likewise the novelists of the mid-century Communist International, the violence of mid-century history was not without reparative possibility. Its horizon was an image of the nation transformed.

## II. Imperial Realignment and the National Turn

My corpus of mid-century historical fiction is predominantly British, and more particularly English, Scottish, and Welsh, but my frame is comparative. The politics of domestic self-discovery, cultural introversion, historical revivalism, and popular antiquarianism, for which the historical novel supplied a natural home, was never just a national affair. Esty's 'Anglocentric' or 'insular' turn, Harris' provincial neo-romanticism, are local iterations of a general trend, which to explain requires a more systemic perspective than even Esty's artful conception of British late modernism as a moment of cultural retrenchment in the dialectic of decolonization. In 1944, Karl Polanyi reflected on 'the torrent of events' that was now 'pouring down on mankind': 'A social transformation of planetary range is being topped by wars of an entirely new type in which a score of states have crashed, and the contours of new empires are emerging out of a sea of blood.' Polanyi captures vividly the scale and violence of the 'cataclysm', but also how the collapse of the European economic and interstate system, for all its 'awful suddenness' and 'inconceivable rapidity', had been a long time coming.[20] I read this mid-century 'catastrophe' as the climax in a process of imperial realignment, which from the *belle époque* to the early Cold War saw the transfer of economic, military, and political power from the empires of old Europe to the US and USSR. The transfer was asymmetrical, uneven, and incomplete, and it had huge importance for the practice of literature. I understand the salience of the nation at mid-century as a discrete, later phase in this process.

---

[19] Alexandra Harris, *Romantic Moderns: English Writers, Artists and the Imagination from Virginia Woolf to John Piper* (London: Thames & Hudson, 2010).
[20] Karl Polanyi, *The Great Transformation* [1944] (Boston: Beacon, 2001), pp.4–5; p.21.

I take my cue from the historian of capitalism Giovanni Arrighi and from his collaborators in the development of the world-systems paradigm for the study of political economy and international relations. With his theory of systemic cycles of accumulation—long periods when capitalism embeds itself in a particular city- or nation-state, which for a while headquarters the global economy before it then 'jumps' to another—Arrighi invites us to understand the turbulence of mid-century history in terms not just of terminal crisis, as to so many it seemed, but of radical reorganization in the economic world-system.[21] In each cycle, Arrighi explains, there comes a time when capital, having accumulated smoothly and stably in its hegemonic home, can no longer secure sufficient returns on investment through expanded production and trade; as market saturation and capitalist competition depress profits, the locus of accumulation shifts to finance as a temporary fix. Arrighi departs the Marxist tradition in framing the ascendancy of *haute finance* not as a new, singular stage in the development of capitalism, but as a regular recurring feature whose brief window of prosperity is the bellwether of systemic change, a 'sign of autumn' for the existing hegemon and of springtime for its successor.[22]

In the autumn of Arrighi's third systemic cycle, when as factory and trading and financial centre Britain modelled the world economy, this crisis of overaccumulation caused surplus capital to be channelled into aggressive overseas expansion and surplus labour into military-industrial production. Profits boomed amid escalating inter-imperial rivalry and soon 'the "rattling of arms"—which was music to the ears of the European bourgeoisie as long as it inflated profitability by intensifying inter-state competition for mobile capital—turned into a catastrophe from which nineteenth-century capitalism would never recover.'[23] Britain emerged a victor on the battlefields of Europe and even expanded its territory overseas, but the costs of ruling an increasingly fractious empire were rising; the expense of the war had also to be reckoned, not least in debts to Britain's soon-to-be successor atop the world economy. Largely unscathed by the devastation in Europe, the United States had racked up massive war credits from the main belligerents that allowed it to buy back cheaply the foreign investments that had so grown its economy before 1914. With its share of global liquidity increased, the US was now a creditor nation to compare with Britain and its industrial power unrivalled. Throughout the interwar period, the capitalist world-system was gearing up for another 'jump', and to a home that would afford it even greater scale and scope.

---

[21] Giovanni Arrighi, *The Long Twentieth Century: Money, Power and the Origins of our Times* (London: Verso, 1994). Cf. Giovanni Arrighi, 'The Winding Paths of Capital. Interview with David Harvey', *New Left Review*, n.s. no.56 (2009): p.93.

[22] Arrighi, *Long Twentieth Century*, p.6 and *passim*. The autumnal metaphor derives from Fernand Braudel's *Civilization and Capitalism, 15th–18th Century III: The Perspective of the World*, translated by Siân Reynolds (New York: Harper & Row, 1984), p.246.

[23] Arrighi, *Long Twentieth Century*, p.173.

This process of hegemonic transition has also, however, to be told from below.[24] As Beverly Silver and Eric Slater observe, such transitions are always also periods of intensifying class conflict, state breakdown, and social revolution.[25] Britain's autumn was no different, the chaos of the interwar years affording historic opportunity for social movements to challenge the status quo. 'Non-Western peoples and the propertyless masses of the West had always resisted those aspects of free-trade imperialism that most directly impinged on their traditional rights to self-determination and a livelihood', Arrighi observes of the long British century of economic dominance and hegemonic 'peace'. But this resistance had, 'by and large', proved ineffectual until the turn of the twentieth century.[26] Over the next half century, however, and with gathering momentum from 1917, these anti-systemic movements made major gains. They did so by learning two lessons from the failed revolutions of 1848: that to remake 'society and the world' they must organize institutionally and seize state power.[27] This tactical shift from a politics of utopian withdrawal or spontaneous uprising to the fight for command of the state apparatus made the nation the site of struggle for social democrats, communists, and anti-colonial activists alike. The orientation towards the state scrambled their scripts of anti-systemic praxis and forged new connections between the discourse of nationalism and progressive social change. This ideological reorientation was especially acute for communists.

In *The Communist Manifesto*, Friedrich Engels and Karl Marx had cast proletarian class struggle as the engine of revolution, industrial development in the metropolitan core providing the necessary conditions for workers to aggregate, associate, and discover their corporate interests and collective strength en route to the final showdown with capital. In this story, the nation had no positive part to play, for just as capitalism was global, so too was the exploitation of labour; nationalism was only an instrument of bourgeois class rule and the nation-state its proxy. The proletarian struggle would be fought 'independently of all nationality' and after the revolution the nation, like the state, would just wither away.[28]

---

[24] In conversation with David Harvey, Arrighi recalled that '*The Long Twentieth Century* became basically a book about the role of finance capital in the historical development of capitalism', and that to correct its core-centric and top-down account of change in the economic world-system required referencing both his own earlier work and that of Beverly Silver. Arrighi, 'Winding Paths of Capital', p.74.

[25] Beverly J. Silver and Eric Slater, 'The Social Origins of World Hegemonies', in *Chaos and Governance in the Modern World System*, edited by Giovanni Arrighi and Beverly J. Silver (Minneapolis, MN: University of Minnesota Press, 1999), pp.151–216. See also Beverly J. Silver, *Forces of Labor: Workers' Movements and Globalization Since 1870* (Cambridge: Cambridge University Press, 2003).

[26] Arrighi, *Long Twentieth Century*, p.64.

[27] Giovanni Arrighi, Terrence K. Hopkins and Immanuel Wallerstein, *Antisystemic Movements* (London: Verso, 1989), pp.98–100. 'First take state power, then transform society': Wallerstein calls this the 'two-step strategy' in *After Liberalism* (New York: The New Press, 1995), p.214. He dates its demise to 1968 and the revisionism of the new social movements in *Utopistics, or Historical Choices of the Twenty-First Century* (New York: The New Press, 1998), pp.28–33.

[28] Karl Marx and Friedrich Engels, *The Communist Manifesto*, edited by Phil Gasper (Chicago: Haymarket, 2005), p.58.

At mid-century, things played out differently, however, weakening the connection between rising proletarian power and revolutionary propensity while at the same time strengthening the connection between socialist revolution and the politics of nationalism.[29] In the advanced capitalist world, where Marx and Engels had foreseen the first socialist breakthroughs, high levels of industrial militancy after the First World War did not translate into sustained revolutionary praxis but rather into new forms of accommodation with capital under the sign of social democracy and the welfare state. Conversely, when socialist revolution did find its feet, it did so in a country without a concentrated industrial base or a proletariat organically forged in conflict with its bourgeoisie; it did so, moreover, in a massive multi-ethnic empire collapsing under the strain of a global war that would soon bring the European imperial world-system to its knees.

Communist thinking on the relationship between class struggle and national liberation had evolved rapidly during the First World War, building on Lenin's analysis of this autumnal phase of British hegemony, with its ascendancy of finance capital and imperial competition, as a historically new stage of capitalist development.[30] From 1919, after the failure of the Hungarian and German revolutions, the new Soviet regime began organizing on the presumption that any future revolution would 'not be solely, or chiefly, a struggle of the revolutionary proletarians in each country against their bourgeoisie', but that it would also involve 'the struggle of all the imperialist-oppressed colonies and countries, of all dependent countries, against international imperialism'.[31] Vanguard proletarian rhetoric would continue to sound in Europe and the United States through the 1920s and early 1930s, but it now did so alongside a pivot to the East, and to the US and Global South. By the time that Mao Zedong set about the 'adaptation of communism to Chinese conditions' in 1940, the claim that 'the universal truth of Marxism must be combined with specific national characteristics and acquire a definite national form' was no longer the heresy it had been when Austrian Marxists debated the issue with the Second International in the years before the First World War.[32]

It was not only anti-systemic politics that now took a 'national form'. With the appearance in 1917 of a state without precedent, an anti-capitalist actor on

---

[29] Giovanni Arrighi, 'Marxist Century, American Century: The Making and Remaking of the Labour Movement', *New Left Review*, no.179 (1990): p.43.

[30] V.I. Lenin, 'Imperialism, The Highest State of Capitalism', in *Collected Works. Volume 22, December 1915–July 1916* (Moscow: Progress Publishers, 1964), pp.185–304. See also Arno Mayer, *Political Origins of the New Diplomacy, 1917–1919* (New Haven: Yale University Press, 1959), pp.293–312; Jeremy Smith, *The Bolsheviks and the National Question, 1917–23* (London: Macmillan, 1999), pp.7–28.

[31] V.I. Lenin, 'Address to the Second All-Russia Congress of Communist Organisations of the Peoples of the East' [22 November 1919], in *Collected Works. Volume 30, September 1919—April 1920* (Moscow: Progress Publishers, 1965), p.159. Simultaneously, Bolshevik leaders were elaborating an internal nationalities policy to explain the role non-Russian territories, languages, and cultures should play inside the new Soviet Union. Cf. Terry Martin, *The Affirmative Action Empire: Nations and Nationalism in the Soviet Union, 1923–1939* (Ithaca, NY: Cornell University Press, 2001).

[32] Mao Tse-tung, *On New Democracy* (Peking: Foreign Languages Press, 1954), p.61. Cf. Otto Bauer, *The Question of Nationalities and Social Democracy* [1907], edited by Ephraim Nimni, translated by

track to an alternative modernity and intent on recruiting the world to its cause, the leading capitalist countries adopted a range of counterrevolutionary postures either directly or indirectly national in form. Arrighi identifies three. Britain and France led a conservative push to reinstate the pre-war economic system through the resumption of free-trade imperialism and a return to the gold standard.[33] Throughout the 1920s, this attempt to reinstate the old international order not only exacerbated domestic social tensions, with the gold commission in Geneva requiring painful and unpopular structural adjustments in order to maintain convertible currencies, but also encouraged the use of illiberal and protectionist measures. It was these, according to Polanyi, that 'unconsciously' prepared the way for the policies of economic autarchy that followed the Wall Street Crash in 1929 and Britain's departure from the gold standard two years later.[34] Arrighi identifies a second counterrevolutionary trajectory in the rise of the radical Right after the First World War: militantly nationalist, fiercely anti-Bolshevik, and in the case of Germany and Japan eagerly eyeing Soviet territory for their own imperial ambitions.[35]

Arrighi's third trajectory tracks the politics of national self-determination from Wilson's appropriation of the principle in the lead-up to Versailles to the 'remaking of the interstate system' after 1945, when 'global "decolonization" and the formation of the United Nations' stood as 'the most significant correlates' of the new American hegemony.[36] This project of resignification, defusing a communist *cri de guerre* of its revolutionary charge to promote gradualist, rational, and system-stabilizing reform, was far from straightforward. With the short-term goal to isolate the Soviet Union behind a *cordon sanitaire* of small Central European nations and claim a moral high ground in the negotiations at Versailles, statesmen like Woodrow Wilson and David Lloyd George had to reckon with their rhetoric's global appeal. 'The phrase is simply loaded with dynamite', Wilson's Secretary of State complained in the run-up to the peace conference: 'What a calamity the phrase was ever uttered!'[37] It came as a cruel disappointment to the leaders of colonial independence movements when they travelled to Paris in 1919 to learn that the 'Wilsonian moment' was not meant for them. Many, including the Vietnamese 'patriot' Nguyen Ai Quoc, or Ho Chi Minh as he was soon to be known, then chose the Bolshevik model instead.[38]

---

Joseph O'Donnell (Minneapolis, MN: University of Minnesota Press, 2000); and Jakub S. Beneš, *Workers & Nationalism: Czech and German Social Democracy in Habsburg Austria, 1890–1918* (Oxford: Oxford University Press, 2017).

[33] Arrighi, *Long Twentieth Century*, p.65.
[34] Polanyi, *Great Transformation*, pp.28–9.
[35] Arrighi, *Long Twentieth Century*, p.65.
[36] Arrighi, *Long Twentieth Century*, pp.65–6.
[37] Robert Lansing, *The Peace Negotiations: A Personal Narrative* (Boston: Houghton Mifflin, 1921), pp.97–8.
[38] Cf. Erez Manela, *The Wilsonian Moment: Self-Determination and the International Origins of Anticolonial Nationalism* (Oxford: Oxford University Press, 2007), pp.3–4. As Eric Weitz reminds Western historians, 'the "Wilsonian Moment" was also—perhaps more so—the "Bolshevik Moment"'

'We live in an era of vast culminations and beginnings', Samuel Sillen declared in 1938, writing in the US communist weekly *New Masses*. 'The dimensions of our understanding encompass the past and the future, and we are as concerned about the origins of our destiny as we are about its direction.' For Sillen, the recent run of bestselling historical fictions in the United States—Margaret Mitchell's *Gone with the Wind* (1936), Kenneth Roberts' *Northwest Passage* (1937), Harvey Allen's *Anthony Adverse* (1933) and *Action at Aquilla* (1938)—were so many 'symptoms' of the times. 'It is not chauvinism but confusion which now drives the reader to the past', he explained; the impulse is genuine, the difficulty sincere. Whence his instruction to writers on the Left to capitalize on 'the historical-mindedness of their contemporaries' and direct this 'curiosity about our past' 'toward more fruitful purposes'. Now was the time to begin a 'Marxist revaluation of our history' and to 'represent for truth what *Gone with the Wind* represents for reaction'.[39] A few months previously, an official in Hitler's censorship department had written of the recent 'flood of historical fiction', looking forward to a time when it would abate sufficiently to allow other genres a share of the market. Hellmuth Langenbucher acknowledged, however, that the genre had still a vital role to play in helping readers locate their lived experience in the pattern of social change.[40]

Langenbucher could have pointed to Josefa Berens-Totenohl's fourteenth-century peasant fable *Der Femhof* (1934), one of the most popular National-Socialist historical novels, which opens with the bursting of a dam and its heroine about to drown. This is history as the catastrophic breach of everyday life, and the novel proceeds to reassure: a handsome stranger is on hand to rescue Magdlene from the water and a yet more providential force will intervene to save her farm, and the blood and soil for which it stands, as the novel draws to a close.[41] The mid-century coined a number of paradigms to describe this sense of historical emergency—the irruption of 'time filled full by now-time', the 'state of exception' that annuls the status quo—but it also reflected on past precedent.[42] For Georg Lukács, writing from Moscow in the winter of 1936–37, this heightened historical intensity had been felt once before. 'It was the French Revolution, the revolutionary wars and the rise and fall of Napoleon' that first made history a '*mass experience*', characterized not only by the simultaneity and 'quick succession' of 'upheavals' taking place 'all over the world', but also by the novel sense that a

---

too. Weitz, 'Self-Determination: How a German Enlightenment Idea Became the Slogan of National Liberation and a Human Right', *American Historical Review* 120, no.2 (2015): p.485.

[39] Samuel Sillen, 'History and Fiction', *New Masses* 27, no.12 (14 June 1938): p.22.

[40] Hellmuth Langenbucher, 'Deutsches Schrifttum 1937—politisch gesehen', *Nationalsozialistische Bibliographie* 3, no.3 (March 1938), pp. xiv–xv.

[41] Josefa Berens-Totenohl, *Der Femhof* (Jena: Eugen Diederichs Verlag, 1934).

[42] Walter Benjamin, 'On the Concept of History' [1940], *Selected Writings Volume 4, 1938–1940*, edited by Howard Eiland and Michael W. Jennings, translated by Harry Zohn (Boston, MA: Harvard University Press, 2003), p.395. Carl Schmitt, *Political Theology: Four Chapters on the Concept of Sovereignty* [1922], translated by George Schwab (Chicago: University of Chicago Press, 2005).

singular logic underpinned them all, that 'national and world history', 'economic conditions and class struggle', were all somehow connected.[43] The historical novel evolved to validate this experience and clarify these connections. Lukács credited Scott with inventing the form, and he closed his study with a call for its resumption to serve a present conjuncture every bit as eventful and packed with transformative potential. The revolution in Russia and the rise of anti-systemic movements worldwide were for Lukács the heralds of a new order, one that would 'guarantee' once and for all the 'material and cultural conditions' of 'human growth in every respect'.[44] Such hopes were not exceptional: many at mid-century saw their moment not only as a time of crisis and capitulation to world-historical forces, but also as a window of opportunity to redesign or re-embed the world economy, to reinvent community, democratize culture, and dis-alienate work and play. It is in this context, as labour and capital fought for the fate of the nation, that the historical novel resumed the role it had played when the nation was new: inventing traditions, imagining communities, and teasing out tendencies and hoped-for trajectories.

## III. World Republics of Letters

The narrative I have so far told of imperial realignment and the national turn has also to be read against developments in the 'world republic of letters', the literary world-system historically headquartered in Europe. Pascale Casanova has been its influential theorist, positing the existence of what she calls an 'international literary space' with capitals and provinces, a 'parallel territory' that shadows our own.[45] In *La République mondiale des Lettres* (1999), Casanova defends the relative autonomy of this literary world from the world we otherwise know: its geography is not physical, its economy immaterial, politics and grand strategy have no jurisdiction.[46] Any resemblance to the capitalist world-system—with its axial division of labour between core and periphery, its cut-throat competition within and between nations—is, she insists, a coincidence. For much of the modern period, the centre of this literary world-system has been Paris, its long history of aristocratic sophistication and revolutionary élan investing its intellectual elite with the power to confer distinction, to grant admission, to consecrate *as* literature the textual production of the world. It is to Paris writers have travelled, fleeing their provincial backwaters to partake of its patronage and prestige, adapting their art to its metropolitan norms, and at no time more brilliantly than in the moment

---

[43] Lukács, *The Historical Novel*, pp.23–5.
[44] Lukács, *The Historical Novel*, pp.344–5.
[45] Pascale Casanova, 'Literature as a World', *New Left Review*, n.s. no.31 (2005): p.72.
[46] Pascale Casanova, *The World Republic of Letters*, translated by M.B. DeBevoise (Cambridge, MA: Harvard University Press, 2004).

of modernism. For Casanova, exiles like James Joyce and Samuel Beckett hold a mirror to the system, their literary innovations the intimate expression of its zest for modernity, its cosmopolitan welcome, its will to freedom from any and all past tradition, national or other parochial attachment, political pleading, or commercial concern. Casanova concedes that the primacy of Paris has not gone unchallenged; in the late eighteenth and early nineteenth century, both England and Germany established rival literary capitals and canons of value, but none of these developments ever seriously upset Parisian supremacy. Even in the twentieth century, as the European imperial, economic, and interstate system collapsed, literary Paris preserved its privileges intact.

But as new work now shows, the history of imperial realignment and intercyclical churn reorganized Casanova's literary world-system in quite radical ways.[47] Its turbulence sent shockwaves through the republic of letters, shifting its centres of gravity and recoding the relations of power that through the long nineteenth century secured European literary hegemony. Addressing the first Soviet Writers' Congress in 1934, against a backdrop of capitalist-world crisis and the present success of the Soviet economy, Karl Radek observed a widening 'split in world literature'. With rising proletarian and peasant literary movements throughout the industrial metropolitan and colonial world, in light, moreover, of so many bourgeois writers coming 'over to our side', Radek announced that 'the world bourgeoisie' had 'lost its monopoly on world literature'.[48] Europe's monopoly was indeed challenged at mid-century. In these years, Moscow established itself as the lodestar of a parallel literary universe: a publishing centre, translation hub, and seat of judgement and reward for writers and intellectuals from around the world. Briefly and on a more limited, continental scale, Nazi Germany coordinated its own literary system, centred in Weimar with satellites in Italy and Spain, and throughout northern and south-eastern Europe. The history of the cultural Cold War is the story of how the capitalist literary world-system reclaimed its hegemony, gaining strength and purpose through the need to check the spread of Soviet literary space. Taken together, the rise of a Soviet republic of letters and the mutation

---

[47] Cf. Michael Denning, 'The Novelists' International', in *Culture in the Age of Three Worlds* (London: Verso, 2004), pp.51–72; Katerina Clark, *Moscow, the Fourth Rome: Stalinism, Cosmopolitanism and the Evolution of Soviet Culture, 1931–1941* (Cambridge, MA: Harvard University Press, 2011) and *Eurasia without Borders: The Dream of a Leftist World Literature* (Cambridge, MA: Harvard University Press, 2021); Andrew N. Rubin, *Archives of Authority: Empire, Culture and the Cold War* (Princeton: Princeton University Press, 2012); Benjamin G. Martin, *The Nazi-Fascist New Order for European Culture* (Cambridge, MA: Harvard University Press, 2016); Rossen Djagalov, *From Internationalism to Postcolonialism: Literature and Cinema between the Second and Third Worlds* (Montreal: McGill-Queen's University Press, 2020); Monica Popescu, *At Penpoint: African Literatures, Postcolonial Studies, and the Cold War* (Durham, NC: Duke University Press, 2020); Joe Cleary, *Modernism, Empire, World Literature* (Cambridge: Cambridge University Press, 2021); Peter Kalliney, *The Aesthetic Cold War: Decolonization and Global Literature* (Princeton, NJ: Princeton University Press, 2022).

[48] Karl Radek, 'Contemporary World Literature and the Tasks of Proletarian Art', in N. Bukharin, M. Gorky, K. Radek, A. Stetsky, A. Zhdanov, et al., *Problems of Soviet Literature* (London: Martin Lawrence, 1934), pp.94–5.

of a capitalist system bent on its containment changed the meanings and means of humanistic practice.

To contemporary observers, this process of literary-world realignment was first perceptible as a politicization of literature, to be welcomed or condemned. In 1941, George Orwell looked back on 'the whole period between 1890 and 1930' as 'what we might call the golden afternoon of the capitalist age', when comfort and class privilege protected 'intellectual detachment' and fostered a 'main emphasis on technique'; the subsequent decade had seen literature 'become political' and 'even poetry' involve itself in 'pamphleteering'.[49] In fact, the 'frontiers of art and propaganda' had been shifting for a while. At the outbreak of the First World War, Romain Rolland had pleaded in vain for European intellectuals to remain '*au-dessus de la mêlée*'.[50] This was 'the treason of the intellectuals' for which Julien Benda later coined the phrase, indicting writers' dereliction of universal, non-partisan values during the war and in the years since.[51] Though often framed in terms of writerly commitment, of authors taking sides where before they had preferred to float above the fray, this new *littérature engagée* was not simply a question of individual conscience or complicity. The mid-century saw the rise of new national organizations and transnational institutions and networks to encourage and reward writers, disseminate their works, and amplify their literary and political opinions. It did so in the shadow of a 'new diplomacy', directed over the heads of statesmen to the populations wearied by war.[52] With international relations now seen increasingly as susceptible to public opinion, the question of how to pursue the national interest led a succession of states to experiment in mobilizing literature as an adjunct of domestic and foreign policy, the latter with such labels as *rayonnement culturelle*, *auswärtige Kulturpolitik*, and cultural diplomacy.

Techniques of persuasion developed during the First World War proved highly adaptable to the peacetime projection of soft power. In France, the *Bureau des écoles* became the *Service des oeuvres françaises à l'étranger* and active in a range of pursuits for the promotion of 'intellectual and artistic expansion' abroad, from establishing chairs of French literature in foreign universities to organizing

---

[49] George Orwell, 'The Frontiers of Art and Propaganda', *The Complete Works of George Orwell. Volume 12: A Patriot After All, 1940–1941*, edited by Peter Davison (London: Secker and Warburg, 1998), p.485.

[50] Romain Rolland, 'Au-dessus de la mêlée', *Journal de Genève*, 22 September 1914, Supplement, n.p.; included in Rolland, *Au-dessus de la mêlée* (Paris: Librarie Paul Ollendorff, 1915), pp.21–38. An English translation, by the Cambridge linguist C.K. Ogden, appeared in 1916.

[51] Julien Benda, *La trahison des clercs* (Paris: Grasset, 1927), and first translated by Richard Aldington as *The Great Betrayal* in 1928; cf. Ferdinand Tönnies, *Zur Kritik der öffentliche Meinung* (Berlin: Julius Springer, 1922), pp.544–59.

[52] Cf. George Young, *Diplomacy Old and New* (London: Swarthmore Press, 1921); Mayer, *Political Origins of the New Diplomacy*; and Paul Gordon Lauren, *Diplomats and Bureaucrats: The First International Responses to Twentieth-Century Diplomacy in France and Germany* (Stanford, CA: Hoover Institution Press, 1976), pp.34–68.

travelling exhibitions of French books and art.[53] Britain was initially rather embarrassed by its wartime propaganda success, and through the 1920s funding was routed away from Wellington House. It was only in 1934, the same year that Japan launched Kokusai Bunka Shinkokai or the Centre for International Cultural Relations and even Czechoslovakia and Switzerland established cultural missions, that the Foreign Office authorized the British Council to raise its international profile. In 1935, the Council's first patron, the Prince of Wales, observed how 'Of all the Great Powers this country is the last in the field in setting up a proper organisation to spread a knowledge and appreciation of its language, literature, art, science and education.'[54] The US State Department launched a Division of Cultural Affairs in 1938.

Britain and America had come late to the game, but in the cultural Cold War they led the defence of 'the West' against the great pioneer of interwar cultural diplomacy, the USSR.[55] Economically weak and politically isolated, especially in the early 1920s, the Soviet Union channelled significant resources to influencing public opinion abroad, actively exporting Russian revolutionary culture and courting foreign writers and intellectuals to engage in argument on its behalf. Long before Britain or the United States learned to respond in kind, the Soviet Union had built a formidable infrastructure for the production and dissemination of communist writing, with dedicated domestic and foreign party publishing houses, multilingual literary journals, national and international writers' organizations and conferences, its own literary prize system, and a single highly adaptive aesthetic ideology.

The first visions of a Soviet world republic of letters date from the aftermath of the Revolution and the dark days of Civil War. In August 1920, at the Second World Congress of the Communist International (or Comintern, hereafter), a provisional International Bureau of the Proletkult was launched to foster proletarian cultural movements in Europe and to lay the groundwork for a future 'world congress of Proletkults'.[56] At the Comintern's Third Congress the following year, the proposal was again floated to organize 'something like a Litintern'.[57] Its first

---

[53] Cf. Ruth Emily McMurry and Muna Lee, *The Cultural Approach: Another Way in International Relations* (Chapel Hill, NC: University of North Carolina Press, 1947), pp.9–38.

[54] Quoted in Philip M. Taylor, *The Projection of Britain Abroad: British Overseas Publicity and Propaganda 1919–1939* (Cambridge: Cambridge University Press, 1981), p.153.

[55] Cf. Michael David-Fox, *Showcasing the Great Experiment: Cultural Diplomacy and Western Visitors to the Soviet Union, 1921–1941* (Oxford: Oxford University Press, 2012), pp.28–97. In a book of memoirs recalling his friendships with British writers, long-term Soviet diplomat to London Ivan Maisky recalled how in the 1920s the USSR 'half-consciously, half-intuitively' pioneered the 'direct and genuine link between diplomacy and culture' which Western governments later copied. Cited in Ewa Berard, 'The "First Exhibition of Russian Art" in Berlin: The Transnational Origins of Bolshevik Cultural Diplomacy, 1921–1922', *Contemporary European History* 30, no.2 (2021): p.164.

[56] *The Second Congress of the Communist International, as Reported by the Official Newspapers of Soviet Russia* (Washington: Government Printing Office, 1920), pp.110–11.

[57] Anatoly Lunacharsky, cited in David Pike, *German Writers in Soviet Exile, 1933–1945* (Chapel Hill, NC: University of North Carolina Press, 1982), p.28.

conference of writers in 1927 was a small affair, with delegates drawn from visitors already in Moscow for the tenth anniversary celebrations of the Revolution; but the second, in November 1930 in Kharkov, Ukraine, was altogether more purposive, with delegates from twenty-three countries, including not only established leaders in the field of international proletarian literature like Germany, Japan, and the United States, but also those eager to join like Brazil, Britain, and Egypt. At Kharkov, British delegates Bob Ellis and Harold Heslop pledged to organize a national section of what was now the International Union of Revolutionary Writers (IURW, also known by its Russian acronym, MORP), and to draw British literature into the orbit of Moscow. Two early initiatives tried and failed to grain traction; only in 1934, with the British Communist Party at the helm and a cadre of professional writers in charge of its journal *Left Review*, did Britain finally secure affiliation. It did so just as the IURW was being disbanded, to be replaced by an altogether more ingenious formation, a front organization of the kind pioneered by Willi Münzenberg in Germany in the 1920s.

The *Association Internationale des Écrivains pour la Défense de la Culture* premiered in June 1935, its first congress held not in Moscow or the Soviet Ukraine but in Paris, at the very heart of the capitalist literary world-system. Reporting for *Left Review*, Christina Stead waxed lyrical about how the 'spirit of revolutionary France, of red France, returned to her true tradition' at this conference, how it 'breathed in the hall' and 'was incarnated on the platform in the speakers, the French, Americans, Russians, Germans, those from the French Antilles, from Portugal and Tadjikistan'.[58] By the mid-1930s, the Soviet Union had positioned itself as the heir and defender of Europe's revolutionary and progressive cultural traditions. Socialist realism, debuted at the Soviet Writers' Congress the previous year, was likewise a move to appropriate and build upon Europe's cultural heritage, offering communists a way to claim continuity with nineteenth-century realism without continuing along the trajectory of its decline. Binding realistic depictions of work and struggle to a vision of their future transformation, the new Soviet aesthetic set out to redefine the Parisian standard of literary modernity by inviting writers to be modern in content but not modernist in form and radical where it counted. It remained for the forces of anti-communism to consolidate an aesthetic ideology and a literary machinery of their own. This is the story of how New York 'stole the idea of modern art' and the CIA 'paid the piper', incorporating Paris and London as client capitals in the cultural Cold War and modernism as its mascot.[59]

---

[58] Christina Stead, 'The Writers Take Sides. Report on the First International Congress of Writers for the Defence of Culture', *Left Review* 1, no.11 (1935): p.456.

[59] Cf. Serge Guilbaut, *How New York Stole the Idea of Modern Art: Abstract Expressionism, Freedom, and the Cold War*, translated by Arthur Goldhammer (Chicago: University of Chicago Press, 1983) and Frances Stonor Saunders, *Who Paid the Piper? The CIA and the Cultural Cold War* (London: Granta, 1999). Since the first revelations of the role of the CIA and British secret services in funding and coordinating the cultural Cold War (the term coined by Christopher Lasch in 1968), historians have tended to play up 'complexity, contingency and unintended consequences' in the actual, hit-and-miss

The rise of transnational literary institutions like the IURW and the International Association of Writers for the Defence of Culture, the Nazi-fascist *Europäischer Schriftsteller-Vereinigung* and the US Congress for Cultural Freedom, revolutionized the relationship of art to power and of living writers to an ever more global audience. For whether they promoted proletarian or socialist realism, a *völkish*-traditional or modernist-formalist aesthetic, whether they saw literature as a weapon in the struggle or the vehicle for an apolitical politics, these and other mid-century institutions were developing new ways to coordinate and disseminate the kinds of literature they valued.[60] Translation was key. In 1941, the Soviet children's author and translator Kornei Chukovskii described how completely the 'noble art' had changed since 1917: where previously literary translation had been 'the domain of a very narrow circle of writers and philology specialists', it was now 'an issue of the greatest state importance, in which millions of people have a vital interest'.[61] Susanna Witt credits the interwar Soviet translation machine as 'the largest more or less coherent project of translation the world has seen to date'.[62] 'An entirely new phase in the history of literature' is Andrew Rubin's assessment of the United States' belated response.[63] Rubin's examples include the global translation and multimedia adaptation of George Orwell's anti-communist fiction and the periodical diplomacy of the Congress for Cultural Freedom (or CCF), where the synchronized publication of approved writers and works across journals like *Horizon* in Britain, *Preuves* in France, *Cuadernos* and *Mundo Nuevo* in Latin America, *Hiwar* in Lebanon, *Black Orpheus* and *Transition* in sub-Saharan Africa, helped disseminate such North Atlantic orthodoxies as the new liberalism, the end of ideology, and the modernist literary canon.[64] But the pioneers in the field were again the Soviets: at Kharkov in 1930, the IURW had replaced the Russian-language *Herald of Foreign Literature* (1928–30) with a bimonthly, later monthly, periodical in multiple foreign-language editions, first under the title *Literature of the World Revolution*, then from 1933 to the dissolution

management of intellectuals and the arts. Hugh Wilford, 'The Cultural Cold War: Recent Scholarship and Future Directions', *Cahiers Charles V*, no.28 (2000): p.36. Exemplary in this respect is Greg Barnhisel, *Cold War Modernists: Art, Literature and American Cultural Diplomacy* (New York: Columbia University Press, 2015), and Kalliney, *The Aesthetic Cold War*.

[60] On the promotion of 'political apoliticism', cf. David and Cecile Shapiro, 'Abstract Expressionism: The Politics of Apolitical Painting', *Prospects* 3 (1978): pp.175–214; and Guilbaut, *How New York Stole the Idea of Modern Art*, p.2.

[61] Kornei Chukovskii, *Vysokoe iskusstvo* ('A Noble Art'), cited in Brian James Baer, 'From International to Foreign: Packaging Translated Literature in Soviet Russia', *The Slavic and East European Journal* 60, no.1 (2016): p.51. Cf. *The Art of Translation: Kornei Chukovsky's* A High Art, translated by Lauren Leighton (Knoxville, TN: University of Tennessee Press, 1984), pp.6–7.

[62] Susanna Witt, 'Between the Lines: Totalitarianism and Translation in the USSR', in *Contexts, Subtexts, Pretexts: Literary Translation in Eastern Europe and Russia*, edited by Brian James Baer (Amsterdam: John Benjamins, 2011), p.19.

[63] Rubin, *Archives of Authority*, p.45.

[64] Rubin, *Archives of Authority*, Chapters 2 and 3. Cf. *Campaigning Culture and the Global Cold War: The Journals of the Congress for Cultural Freedom*, edited by Giles Scott-Smith and Charlotte Lerg (London: Palgrave Macmillan, 2017).

of the Comintern, *International Literature*. Platforms like these could elevate and explicate exemplary works, standardize styles, and canonize writers at speed and on a scale without precedent. In the case of the historical novel, they could raise its profile and extend its reach, as Nazi-fascist and Soviet-sphere journals did from the mid-1930s, or render it practically invisible, as the CCF stable of journals contrived to do in the 1950s and 60s.

For the Australian-born British communist Jack Lindsay, whom I discuss in chapter four, the effect of these duelling literary world-systems was a kind of split reputation peculiar to this mid-century moment. In a radio profile from 1958, Arthur Calder-Marshall explained how writers like Lindsay, who straddled capitalist and communist literary worlds, could be hard to pin down. Ask a Soviet intellectual to list contemporary British writers in order of importance and Lindsay would appear in their top five. A British intellectual, by contrast, might hesitate to place Lindsay in the top two hundred. But ask the same British intellectual to name the best British communist writer and Lindsay would be their number one.[65] Lindsay has a place in this study as the leading theorist and practitioner of the communist historical novel in Britain. He does so alongside Sylvia Townsend Warner, whom I treat in chapter three, and whose writing inhabited the same two worlds. Read at home as a lady stylist and in America as an English wit, Warner's 1936 historical novel, *Summer Will Show*, was fêted in Moscow as a model of the genre. Working-class historical novelists like Harold Heslop, Charles Poulsen, and Frederick Harper—all touched on in chapter two—enjoyed profiles and print runs east of the Iron Curtain out of all proportion to their domestic circulation and success. The split in these writers' receptions extends to the genre in which they worked: read, reviewed, and later studied and taught in the Soviet sphere, but increasingly sidelined at home.

In the Anglosphere after 1945, a complex of critical narratives came to overwrite, and to write out of account, the literature of the national turn. America had proclaimed itself the leader of a new international order, privileging democratic over national values in its defence of the 'Free World'. It was a 'fateful mutation', Perry Anderson observes, the moment when capital laid down its long historical association with the nation. 'From the noblest ambitions of Enlightenment patriotism to the criminal inhumanities of fascism', the dominant forms of nationalism had been those of the propertied classes, the dominant forms of internationalism those of labour.[66] But the mid-century mobilization of anti-systemic forces under the rubrics of revolutionary, anti-fascist, and anti-colonial nationalism now led America to claim 'the international' as its own. For its ideologues and apologists, such as Stephen Spender and Irving Kristol in the opening editorial of

---

[65] Arthur Calder-Marshall, transcript of a 'General News Talk' given on the European News Service, 17 July 1958. Canberra, National Library of Australia, Jack Lindsay Papers, MS7168 (hereafter NLA, 7168), Box 123, Odds 16.

[66] Perry Anderson, 'Internationalism: A Breviary', *New Left Review*, n.s. no.14 (2002): p.12.

*Encounter*, 'the nation' was now 'plainly an anachronism'.[67] The anachronism was perhaps especially plain for those (Spender and Kristol among them) who had once thought otherwise, vesting faith in visions of radical diremption and national transformation. Theirs was what Daniel Bell called a '"twice-born" generation', trained by the disappointments of the 1930s and 40s to seek 'its wisdom in pessimism, evil, tragedy and despair'.[68] This mid-century morality tale, already met with in Greene, lent itself well to literary study, where it shaped the critical myths that helped legitimate the Cold War study of literature as a bulwark against communism.[69] Literary histories in the 1950s and 60s told of the rise and fall of a 'supranational movement called International Modernism' and proposed a selective symmetry, and line of transmission, between romanticism, modernism, and the new literary criticism.[70]

This critical climate was 'a product of retreat', as Michael Denning describes the US scene. 'As the Cold War restricted the wide-ranging political, social, and cultural debates of the 1930s and 1940s, literary intellectuals turned increasingly inwards, adopting the rarefied, technical modes of literary analysis' developed in Cambridge and the American South.[71] A defensive faith in literature, detached from the matrix of culture and made the measure of a writer's individual talent and the critic's difficult discernment, united the schools of criticism in post-war Britain and America. On both sides of the Atlantic, the prestige of the literary was a reflection not only of new-disciplinary zeal and bleak-liberal conviction but also of the need to outflank the culturalist and nationalist inflection of mid-century communist and late modernist aesthetics.[72] The literature of the national turn could now be marked as foreign, tarred by association with Nazi-fascist notions of the *Volk* and with the socialist realist demand that art exhibit a popular spirit, *narodnost'* the untranslatable term for general accessibility and national particularity, a live

---

[67] [Stephen Spender and Irving Kristol], 'After the Apocalypse', *Encounter* 1, no.1 (1953): p.1.

[68] Daniel Bell, *The End of Ideology: On the Exhaustion of Political Ideas in the Fifties* (Glencoe, IL.: Free Press, 1960), p.287.

[69] On the constitutive 'anti-Marxism' of Cambridge criticism, cf. F.R. Leavis, *Scrutiny. A Retrospect* (Cambridge: Cambridge University Press, 1963), p.4. On the self-styled anti-totalitarian impulse animating the New Criticism, cf. John Crowe Ransom, 'Criticism as Pure Speculation', in *The Intent of the Critic*, edited by Donald Stauffer (Princeton: Princeton University Press, 1941), p.108.

[70] On modernism's 'international' pedigree, cf. Hugh Kenner, *The Pound Era* (1971) and 'The Making of the Modernist Canon', *Chicago Review* 34, no.2 (1984): p.53. For one way of framing the connection between romanticism and modernism, cf. Lionel Trilling on how Wordsworth 'may be said to have discovered and first explored the ground upon which our literature has established itself', to wit 'the concern with being and its problems'. 'Wordsworth and the Rabbis' [1950], in *The Opposing Self: Nine Essays in Criticism* (London: Secker and Warburg, 1955), pp.148–9.

[71] Michael Denning, *The Cultural Front: The Laboring of American Culture in the Twentieth Century* (London: Verso, 1996), p.434.

[72] In 1949, Richard Chase identified 'the new liberalism' as a movement of 'newly invigorated secular thought' which from 'the dark center of the twentieth century ... now begins to ransom liberalism from the ruinous sellouts, failures and defeats of the thirties'. Chase, *Herman Melville: A Critical Study* (New York: Macmillan, 1949), p.vii. For the characteristic 'bleakness' of this formation, cf. Amanda Anderson, 'Character and Ideology: The Case of Cold War Liberalism', *New Literary History* 42, no.2 (2011): pp.209–29.

connection to the idioms and traditions of the people. To make this connection stick, all domestic precedent for a national-popular literature had also to be erased, and so it was: in histories of the novel told in terms of its eighteenth-century 'rise' and high-modernist apotheosis, and in the new accounting of romanticism.[73]

In 1924, the intellectual historian A.O. Lovejoy had proposed a 'really radical remedy' to the fact that romanticism could mean so many different things: 'we should all cease talking about Romanticism'. Failing which, Lovejoy continued, let us at least 'learn to use the word "Romanticism" in the plural'.[74] By 1949, however, this delight in diversity was out. René Wellek led the charge for a singular 'system of norms': 'imagination for the view of poetry, nature for the view of the world, and symbol and myth for poetic style'.[75] Reduced to its poetry and the pursuit of transcendence, Cold War romanticism elected 1791 as its primal scene. 'The great Romantic poems were written not in the mood of revolutionary exaltation but in the later mood of revolutionary disillusionment and despair', M.H. Abrams explained.[76] The mid-century parallel was clear.[77] Abrams, for one, endorsed the English poets' inward turn as their vision of politics became a politics of vision and their faith in 'an apocalypse by revolution ... gave way to faith in an apocalypse by imagination or cognition'.[78] From here, it was but a short step to Harold Bloom's 'Internalization of Quest Romance' and a definition of romanticism as the journey of 'the creative process' from nature to 'the imagination's freedom', 'redemptive in direction but destructive of the social self'.[79] Absent in this celebration of poetic genius and the autotelic artwork was any mention of romantic-era fiction or the wider ambit of romantic historicism and cultural nationalism; absent altogether was Sir Walter Scott. It could seem that F.R. Leavis had said the last word, when in a notorious footnote to *The Great Tradition* (1948) he dismissed Scott 'as 'a kind of inspired folk-lorist, qualified to have done in fiction something analogous

---

[73] Cf. Homer Brown, 'Why the Story of the Origin of the (English) Novel is an American Romance (If Not the Great American Novel)', in *Cultural Institutions of the Novel*, edited by Deidre Lynch and William B. Warner (Durham, NC: Duke University Press, 1996), pp.11–44.

[74] A.O. Lovejoy, 'On the Discrimination of Romanticisms', *PMLA* 39, no.2 (1924): pp.234–5.

[75] René Wellek, 'The Concept of "Romanticism" in Literary History II. The Unity of European Romanticism', *Comparative Literature* 1, no.2 (Spring 1949): p.147. Jerome McGann argues that Wellek's tercet of terms formed 'the bounding horizon' of Cold War romanticism studies in *The Romantic Ideology: A Critical Investigation* (Chicago: University of Chicago Press, 1983), p.18.

[76] M.H. Abrams, 'English Romanticism: The Spirit of the Age', in *Romanticism Reconsidered: Selected Papers from the English Institute*, edited by Northrop Frye (New York: Columbia University Press, 1963), p.53.

[77] M.H. Abrams references W.H. Auden's 1940 'New Year Letter', which draws the same connection, in *Natural Supernaturalism: Tradition and Revolution in Romantic Literature* (New York: W.W. Norton, 1971), pp.333–4. Already by 1969, E.P. Thompson had grown tired of the 'glib comparisons' which rise up, and which 'lie beneath the surface when unstated', between the 1790s and the 1930s. Thompson, 'Disenchantment or Default? A Lay Sermon', in *Power & Consciousness*, edited by Conor Cruise O'Brien and William Dean Vanech (London: University of London Press, 1969), p.178.

[78] Abrams, *Natural Supernaturalism*, p.334.

[79] Harold Bloom, 'The Internalization of Quest Romance', *Yale Review* 58 (1969): pp.526–36; republished in *The Ringers in the Tower: Studies in Romantic Tradition* (Chicago: University of Chicago Press, 1971).

to the ballad opera'. Scott lacked 'the creative writer's interest in literature', Leavis opined, and made 'no serious attempt to work out his own form'. 'Out of Scott a bad tradition came.'[80]

## IV. Mid-Century Romance

Virginia Woolf's love of Scott struck her Bloomsbury friends as odd, a holdover from childhood which she ought to have outgrown.[81] But in *To the Lighthouse* (1927) she argued a more purposive relation, folding the rehabilitation of Scott into an allegory of social repair that points the direction for her own late modernist aesthetics. The novel's famous interlude conjures a house and its contents on the brink of destruction. At the critical moment, however, in that 'hesitation when dawn trembles and night pauses, when if a feather alight in the scale it will be weighed down', and the house, 'sinking, falling', will be 'turned and pitched downwards to the depths of darkness', an obscure 'force' works redemption. With the help of two domestic servants, Woolf contrives to rescue the house and 'all the Waverley novels' along with it.[82] This is her answer to the question 'about fame, about books lasting', that preoccupies the pre-war section of the novel, and it marks her dissent from a mainline of modernist and mid-century critics for whom Scott's books and fame did not.[83] Woolf's conservative social allegory—of the past's preservation in the present, of continuity across the 'corridor' of time—hinges on a reading of Scott, and of one novel in particular: Mr Ramsay's and her own clear favourite, *The Antiquary* (1816).[84] For not all Waverley novels work the same way, replicating the ideological formula and aesthetic effects of the first in their line; it is important to pick and choose, as did Woolf when she singled out Scott's domestic national tale to champion and defend.[85] *The Antiquary* supplies Woolf's narrative

---

[80] F.R. Leavis, *The Great Tradition: George Eliot, Henry James, Joseph Conrad* (London: Chatto & Windus, 1948), pp.5–6 fn.2.

[81] In 1928, Woolf purchased a complete edition of the novels, to the evident mirth of her friends. 'I am thought a sentimental mug—or is it muff?— ... in consequence', she confided to Hugh Walpole. But she rejected her friends' assumption that this investment in Scott was simply 'because he was read aloud by my father when we were children—not altogether, I think.' Virginia Woolf to Hugh Walpole, 20 August 1928; in *A Change of Perspective. The Letters of Virginia Woolf, Volume 3: 1923–1928*, edited by Nigel Nicholson and Joanne Trautmann (London: Hogarth Press, 1977), p.518. In 1932, Walpole dedicated his popular Scott anthology, *The Waverley Pageant*, to 'Virginia Woolf, who does not scorn Sir Walter'.

[82] Virginia Woolf, *To the Lighthouse*, edited by Stella McNichol (London: Penguin, 1992), pp.151–2.

[83] Woolf, *To the Lighthouse*, p.128.

[84] In her notes, Woolf envisioned the novel like a letter H: 'two blocks joined by a corridor'. Virginia Woolf, *To the Lighthouse: The Original Holograph Draft*, edited by Susan Dick (London: Hogarth Press, 1983), p.48. Woolf published a review of *The Antiquary* in *The Nation & Athenaeum* in 1924 and gives it to Mr. Ramsay to read in the novel.

[85] In May 1926, just as she was finishing the 'Time Passes' section of *To the Lighthouse*, Woolf embarked on a long dispute with E.M. Forster about fiction in general and Scott in particular. Earlier that year, Forster had agreed to deliver a course of public lectures on the novel; now, 'a good deal

of great houses restored as well as her agents of redemption, drawn from that 'class of society' who in Scott's 'Advertisement' he defined as 'the last to feel the influence of that general polish which assimilates to each other the manners of different nations'.[86] In Scott as in Woolf, national character resides among 'the lower orders', repositories of a common culture imperilled by the rising wealth of nations and the cosmopolitan traffic of their elites, but capable—or so Woolf had begun to hope—of now turning the tide.

Lurching and leering, clutching and hauling her way through the house as she rolls from room to room, Mrs McNab sings a song.

> A sound issued from her lips—something that had been gay twenty years before on the stage perhaps, had been hummed and danced to, but now, coming from the toothless, bonneted, caretaking woman, was robbed of meaning, was like the voice of witlessness, humour, persistency itself, trodden down but springing up again.[87]

Woolf had tried to hear this song before: in the voice of an 'old blind woman ... singing out loud' in *Jacob's Room* (1922), in a voice 'of no age or sex' singing outside the Regent's Park tube station in *Mrs Dalloway* (1925).[88] These were songs of a vernacular tradition reaching back behind the institution of literature to the organic cultures of early times; they were the stuff of primitive poetry and ancient minstrelsy granted a residual presence in modernity. But in these earlier novels, Woolf had marked her icons of orality as uncanny, something native and familiar—'like the smoke from a country cottage'—grown altogether strange. The tube lady sings of 'love', but it is a love so old and long-lasting—its duration measured in the millions of years—that it conjures the spectre of bad infinity, evacuating time of human history and the cosy cottage scene of any stable ground.[89] The same song sounds differently, however, when the Waverley novels are lying out to dry in

---

hung up' about all the novels he had never read, he reached out to Woolf for advice, inviting himself to tea on 18 May. 'We argued about novel writing', Woolf confided to her sister the following day, declining to 'fret' her 'ears' with the specifics. But the quarrel spilled over into print: in the text of Forster's Clark Lectures (January–March 1927, published in October as *Aspects of the Novel*), in Woolf's review of these lectures (published in the *New York Herald Tribune* in October, and in the *Nation & Athenaeum* the following month), and in an extended essay on Forster's fiction. In his lectures, Forster spoke disparagingly of Scott and singled out *The Antiquary* for scorn. In response, Woolf claimed the student's right 'to disagree', and to 'exercise this right ... at the earliest opportunity, in the first chapter, about the art of story-telling and Sir Walter Scott'. E.M. Forster to Virginia Woolf, 17 May 1926; Papers of Edwin Morgan Forster, Archive Centre, King's College, Cambridge, EMF/18/609. Virginia Woolf to Vanessa Bell, 19 May 1926; in *Letters*, Vol.3, p.266. Virginia Woolf, 'Is Fiction an Art?' [1927], in *Essays*, Vol.4, pp.458–9.

[86] Sir Walter Scott, *The Antiquary*, edited by David Hewitt (Edinburgh: Edinburgh University Press, 1995), p.3.

[87] Woolf, *To the Lighthouse*, p.142.

[88] Virginia Woolf, *Jacob's Room*, edited by Kate Flint (Oxford: Oxford University Press, 1992), p.89. Virginia Woolf, *Mrs Dalloway*, edited by Bonnie Kime Scott (Orlando: Harcourt, 2005), p.79.

[89] Woolf, *Mrs Dalloway*, p.81.

the sun. The mumbled words of Mrs McNab's 'old music hall song' unleash no temporal vertigo or spatial dislocation; the musical accompaniment to a labour of salvage and repair, her song floats the terms on which Woolf will lend her qualified consent to a vision of England made homely in fragments of literature and demotic speech, in proverbs, metaphors, and half-remembered nursery rhymes. For Scott and his fictional self-portrait in *The Antiquary*, the name for these relics is romance.

Romance can mean many things and many of these meanings blur, but in *Mid-Century Romance* I refer to two.[90] The first is as an antiquarian term of art for the archive of a national culture, the raw materials from which we invent our traditions, our myths of origin and tales of national becoming. It takes its name from the corpus of mediaeval metrical romance and Renaissance gothic literature, the vernacular, non-classical heritage of tales recording the chivalrous deeds and derring-do of the feudal aristocracy. From thence the term expanded in the later eighteenth century to include ballads, folklore, collective memory and mentalities, the traditional forms of primitive and popular cultures felt to be vanishing in the onrush of modernity. A prominent example is the 'curious old manuscript', much 'mutilated' and 'sadly torn', that Thomas Percy rescued from the grate and from which he compiled his *Reliques of Ancient English Poetry, Consisting of Old Heroic Ballads, Songs and Other Pieces of our Earlier Poets* (1765).[91] From such fugitive remains, Percy set out to build a national monument, reclaiming these 'first efforts of ancient genius' as the prelude to an English literature now happily refined.[92] But the politics of romance—its allegiance to class or party, its visionary potential as synecdoche for the nation—was never single or stable. Passions could run high, as when the Stockton-born editor and ballad-collector Joseph Ritson blasted Percy for cultural appropriation in writing over the demotic origins of popular song with a figure of polite respectability, the courtly minstrel 'singing verses to the harp at the houses of the great'.[93] Where Percy had prettified his rude remains to suit genteel taste, Ritson insisted on textual fidelity in his *Pieces of Ancient Popular Poetry from Authentic Manuscripts and old Printed Copies* (1791), the terms of his title each polemically charged and the 'popular' pointing his preference for oral tradition and its constituency among 'the illiterate vulgar'.[94] It was from such as these that Ritson compiled his 'Northern Garlands', collections of local song

---

[90] On the 'protean' meanings of 'romance', cf. Ian Duncan, *Modern Romance and Transformations of the Novel: The Gothic, Scott, Dickens* (Cambridge: Cambridge University Press, 1992), pp.10–11.

[91] *Bishop Percy's Folio Manuscript: Ballads and Romances*, edited by John W. Hales and Frederick J. Furnivall (London: Trübner, 1867), Vol.1, p. xii; p. lxxiv.

[92] Thomas Percy, *Reliques of Ancient English Poetry: Consisting of Old Heroic Ballads, Songs, and other Pieces of our earlier Poets* (London: J. Dodsley, 1765), Vol.1, p. vi.

[93] Unsigned review of Joseph Ritson, *Scottish Songs* [1794], *Critical Review, or Annals of Literature* 13 (1795), p.49. Percy, *Reliques*, p. xvi. Joseph Ritson, 'A Historical Essay on the Origin and Progress of National Song', in Ritson, *A Select Collection of English Songs*, 3 vols (London: Joseph Johnson, 1783), Vol.1, pp. li–liii.

[94] Ritson, 'Historical Essay', p. lii.

from his native North-East, and with an eye to their politics that he assembled the collection of ballads about 'the celebrated English outlaw' Robin Hood (1795) for which he is best remembered now.[95] In the class war to claim the banner of romance, it was popular antiquarians like Ritson who returned literature to the field of culture and therein found traditions to rival those of the London literary and ruling-class establishment. Francis Grose titled his compendium of cant and slang *A Classical Dictionary of the Vulgar Tongue* (1785), because even a scurrilous language becomes 'classical by prescription', its terms venerable through 'long uninterrupted usage'.[96]

In all this 'black letter learning', the line between philological scholarship and fresh invention, authentic lay and modern imitation, was fluid and fraught. Ritson, for example, accused Percy of 'forgery' in rendering his *Reliques* more literary, reviving the charge of the earlier *Ossian* and Rowley controversies. But towards the end of the eighteenth century, the pretence fell away or became its own performative game as writers adapted the antiquarian romance revival to their varied modern purpose, at first in new lyrical ballads and longer verse romances, and then, triumphantly, in prose. In the last years of his life, Joseph Strutt had hoped to popularize his knowledge of costume and country sports in a novel of fifteenth-century England; unfinished at his death, Strutt's publisher approached the bestselling poet and ballad-collector Walter Scott to provide 'a hasty conclusion'.[97] Scott's editorial assistance in bringing *Queenhoo-Hall* (1808) to print prompted his own turn to fiction, which six years later produced *Waverley* (1814), an innovative synthesis of Strutt's antiquarian romance with elements of the Irish national tale and the first in a long series, endlessly then copied and contested.[98]

If romance is a name for the rescued remains of premodern and popular cultures, and for the desire that drives their discovery, it can also flag the labour of fiction, its difference from reality and departure from everyday life. In his *Letters on Romance and Chivalry* (1762), Richard Hurd had framed the bourgeois cultural revolution as a victory for 'reason' and 'good sense' over an older world of '*fancy*' and 'fine fabling': the imagination, 'that had wantoned it so long in the world of fiction, was now constrained, against her will, to ally herself with strict truth, if

---

[95] *The Bishopric Garland, or, Durham Minstrel* (1784); *The Yorkshire Garland* (1788); *The Northcountry Chorister* (1792); *The Northumbrian Garland, or, Newcastle Nightingale* (1793). *Robin Hood: a Collection of all the Ancient Poems, Songs, and Ballads, now extant, relative to that Celebrated English Outlaw* (1795).

[96] Francis Grose, *A Classical Dictionary of the Vulgar Tongue* [1785], second edition (London: Hooper, 1788), p. x.

[97] 'Advertisement', to Joseph Strutt, *Queenhoo-Hall, A Romance*, 4 vols. (London: John Murray, 1808), Vol.1, p. iii.

[98] Critical consensus on the genesis of *Waverley* casts doubt on Scott's later recollection that he began work on the novel 'about the year 1805', suggesting instead the year 1808, following the publication of *Marmion* in February and his completion of Strutt in March. See 'Essay on the Text', in Sir Walter Scott, *Waverley*, edited by Peter Garside (Edinburgh: Edinburgh University Press, 2007), pp.367–83.

she would gain admittance into reasonable company'.[99] The English novel made a similar appeal to 'reasonable company' in its eighteenth-century title pages and prefaces, contrasting its realism to a world of romance illusion variously associated with France, feminine feeling, and the politics of the *ancien régime*. Subsequent elevations of the novel replayed the rhetoric, deploying the figure of romance as a foil for their claims to a superior mimetic or aesthetic intention; but far from dispelling the dark magic of suspended disbelief, romance has remained the novel's constant companion. Michael McKeon, writing of the early English novel, remarks 'the persistence of romance, both within the novel and concurrently with its rise'.[100] Marc McGurl, writing of Henry James and the elevation of the modernist 'art novel', notes again 'the persistence of romance': 'Whether as a separate genre or as a minority position within the novel itself, the *persistent persistence* of romance' is what needs to be explained.[101] Ian Duncan's explanation is to recode 'the old commonplace of an antithetical relation between romance and reality, invoked by the novel in its own apologies of origin', as a dialectic, with romance 'the fulcrum against which—positioned on its edge, between inside and out—reality can be turned around'. In this generous conception, romance lets us 'imagine the transformation of life and its conditions, not their mere reproduction'.[102] It can point the way for utopian desire and serve as a summons to politics.

The mid-century historical fiction I discuss in this study draws on both declensions of romance, the antiquarian and the fictive. That the antiquarian was alive and well in the age of automobiles and total war, consider the billboard Clifford and Rosemary Ellis designed for the Shell Mex petroleum company in 1934. 'Antiquaries Prefer Shell' was the tag, the first in a line of advertisements inviting the 'professions' (broadly conceived) to 'see Britain first on Shell'. The poster assembled a surrealist tableau of English material culture—some random old books, a manuscript scroll, some nineteenth-century pottery—against the background of a ruined abbey and snarling gothic gargoyle. Domestic tourism did not, however, exhaust the mid-century antiquarian impulse, nor was it limited to those who could afford motor cars and the time to go antiquing. The study of popular antiquities was as contentious in the 1930s as it had been in the 1790s and its constituency as varied, but with the difference that the Left was now organized and had framed its crusade against fascism as a fight for the soul of the nation. Fascist ideologues, General Secretary Georgi Dimitrov explained at the Comintern's Seventh World Congress in 1935, had been 'rummaging through the entire *history* of every nation so as to be able to pose as the heirs and continuers of all

---

[99] Richard Hurd, *Letters on Chivalry and Romance* (London: A Millar, 1762), pp.119–20.
[100] Michael McKeon, *The Origins of the Eighteenth-Century Novel, 1600–1740* (Baltimore: Johns Hopkins University Press, 1987), p.3.
[101] Mark McGurl, *The Novel Art: Elevations of American Fiction after Henry James* (Princeton: Princeton University Press, 2001), p.49.
[102] Duncan, *Modern Romance*, p.2.

that was heroic and exalted in its past'. It was now for communists and their allies to set the record straight, to 'enlighten the masses on the past of their own people' and bring it to bear on the present.[103] The practice of writing history 'from below', of recuperating peasant and proletarian agency and resistance, has origins in these mid-century history wars to name and claim the people's past.[104] In search of stories of a subaltern class present at its own making and persisting through long setback and defeat, fascist and communist historians and novelists mined the national-popular past, recasting the romance materials of premodern and popular culture as archives of experience and aspiration. It is through the British Left, however, that this mid-century movement culture captured the world's imagination, immortalized in the poetry and practice of E.P. Thompson's *The Making of the English Working Class* (1963), with its call to rescue even 'the losers and lost causes', 'the casualties of history', from the 'condescension of posterity'.[105]

As for the fictive dimension of 'romance', we could do worse than return to the 1934 Soviet Writers' Congress, where Maxim Gorky spoke of the need to 'supplement' the representation of 'a given reality' by opening it up—'by the logic of hypothesis'—to 'the desired' and 'the possible'. To 'provoke a revolutionary attitude to reality, an attitude that changes the world in a practical way', it was necessary to leaven realism with 'romanticism', a dimension of fantasy and desire most potent among 'the unwritten compositions of the people', in folklore and demotic song.[106] Other, less stigmatized, examples of this mid-century thinking about popular culture and the politics of prefiguration might include Ernst Bloch's 'spirit of utopia' and 'principle of hope', Mikhail Bakhtin's theories of carnival and polyphony, and Miguel Abensour's conviction that utopian projection teaches 'desire to desire, to desire better, to desire more, and above all to desire in a different way'.[107]

---

[103] Georgi Dimitrov, *The Working Class against Fascism* (London: Martin Lawrence, 1935), p.69.

[104] Both communist and national-socialist historians and historical novelists privileged the subaltern as the subject, rather than object, of history in the 1930s and 40s. Reviewing the emphasis on peasant agency in German academic history from the 1930s, Jonathan Dewald points the useful reminder that reparative social history 'can as easily derive from authoritarian as from radical or critical political impulses'. Dewald, 'An Alternative Path to Rural History', in *Lost Worlds: The Emergence of French Social History, 1815–1970* (University Park, PA: Penn State University Press, 2006), pp.183–211; p.206.

[105] E.P. Thompson, *The Making of the English Working Class* (London: Victor Gollancz, 1963), pp.12–13.

[106] Maxim Gorky, 'Soviet Literature', in Bukharin et al., *Problems of Soviet Literature*, p.44; p.28.

[107] Ernst Bloch, *The Spirit of Utopia* [1923], translated by Anthony Nassar (Stanford, CA: Stanford University Press, 2000); and *The Principle of Hope* [1959], translated by Neville Plaice, Stephen Plaice, and Paul Knight (Cambridge, MA: MIT Press, 1986). Mikhail Bakhtin, *Rabelais and his World* [1940, published 1965], translated by Hélène Iswolsky (Cambridge, MA: MIT Press, 1968); and *Problems of Dostoevsky's Poetics* [1963], edited and translated by Caryl Emerson (Minneapolis: University of Minnesota Press, 1984). Miguel Abensour, 'Les formes de l'utopie socialiste-communiste: essai sur le communisme critique et l'utopie' [1972, unpublished doctoral dissertation]; cited in E.P. Thompson, 'Romanticism, Moralism and Utopianism: The Case of William Morris', *New Left Review*, no.99 (1976): p.97.

It has become common, in the now naturalized identification of nations with 'imagined communities' and 'invented traditions', to read these fictions as necessarily duplicitous and tending always to transcendence, the mitigation of class conflict in the emollient unity of some popular or national cultural identity. For Benedict Anderson, the 'nationalist imagining' has too much in common with 'religious imaginings' to be politically useful, being more concerned 'with death and immortality' than with the here and now of rational dissensus and radical praxis.[108] But it was Ludwig Feuerbach who taught the Left to value the physiology of religion, and to read from its double movement—the systolic projection of human desire and creative energies away from the self and onto some ideal figure, the diastolic return of those same powers, mystified, alienated, in the form of the god we then worship—a reminder of whose hopes and desires are at stake throughout. However reified or by other means co-opted, the dream remains authentic. Even fascism, Ernst Bloch believed, for all its 'nastiness and speechless brutality', contained an 'element of an older, romantic contradiction to capitalism, which misses things in present-day life and longs for something vaguely different'.[109] It was dangerous for the Left to concede without a fight this kernel of desire, this element of legitimate protest. But to join the fray, Bloch warned, the Left must first confront what was similarly 'irrational' in its own project, its own intimacy with romance.[110] My study looks to resurrect these mid-century fictions, acknowledging the traffic between Right-religious and secular-Left investments in rituals of belonging I call 'romantic' not only to credit the subtlety of romantic-era debates about imagination and identity but also to float a line of descent.

## V. 'Popular national literature'

*Mid-Century Romance* unfolds at the intersection of British late modernism and mid-century communist culture, chronicling a revival of the historical novel in the 'bad tradition' of Sir Walter Scott and the post-Enlightenment romance revival. Its chapters offer case studies of the drawing of a modernist cosmopolitan or international proletarian aesthetic into the forcefield of the 'national-popular'. This is a term I take from Antonio Gramsci, who in the early 1930s reflected at length on the 'national-educative' function of writers and the style and approach necessary for a 'national-popular diffusion' of their works.[111] Gramsci was by no means alone

---

[108] Benedict Anderson, *Imagined Communities: Reflections on the Origin and Spread of Nationalism*, 2nd ed. (London: Verso, 2006), p.10.
[109] Ernst Bloch, *Heritage of Our Times*, translated by Neville and Stephen Plaice (Berkeley, CA: University of California Press, 1990), p.2.
[110] Bloch, *Heritage of Our Times*, p.139.
[111] Antonio Gramsci, 'Concept of "National-Popular"' [Q21 §5], in *Selections from the Cultural Writings*, edited by David Forgacs and Geoffrey Nowell-Smith, translated by William Boelhower (Chicago:

in this mid-century moment in wanting to theorize the abstraction of intellectual labour and the social alienation of art, but the coherence of his thinking on the politics of culture marks it apart. As well as being alert to culture's power to shape and subvert meanings, identities, and political relations, he thought practically about the vehicles and institutions that mediate its work. His target was a 'people' he understood not as 'a homogeneous cultural collectivity' of the kind associated with liberal or nineteenth-century populism but as a potential alliance of 'numerous and variously combined cultural stratifications' of region and class.[112] The 'war of position' was his term for the long, slow work of building a counterhegemonic force out of these nationally specific elements and fractions, an 'egalitarian' rather than 'hierarchical' 'national intellectual and moral bloc' or new 'national-popular collective will'.[113] Well in advance of the Comintern's national turn, Gramsci had concluded that however 'international' one's 'perspective and directives', 'the point of departure' would need to be '"national"', and that it was 'from this point of departure that one must start out'.[114]

Gramsci's model of a 'national-popular' literature was the French 1840s, which he invoked as a time when writers internalized the 'needs, aspirations and feelings' of their readers, elaborating them in accessible fictional form and thereby raising 'the intellect and moral awareness of the people-nation'.[115] Italian intellectuals, by contrast, had largely shunned this task, cleaving to an image of themselves as a caste apart, an aristocratic or cosmopolitan elite 'and not an articulation with organic functions of the people themselves'.[116] Centuries in the making, this breach with the people informed Gramsci's diagnosis of Italy's incomplete national unification in the nineteenth century and the inroads since made by fascism. It also explained why Italy's canonical historical novels had proven so unpopular, and why readers turned *en masse* to the fiction of French social romanticism, to Alexandre Dumas and Eugène Sue, even if that meant submitting to the 'moral and intellectual hegemony' of foreign writers and identifying with a national story not their own. 'Culturally speaking, they are interested in a past that is more French than Italian', Gramsci observed of his countrymen: 'They know the popular figure of Henri IV better than that of Garibaldi, the Revolution of 1789 better

---

Haymarket, 2012) p.207; Antonio Gramsci, 'An Early Note by Pirandello' [Q23 §2], in *Cultural Writings*, p.146.

[112] Antonio Gramsci, 'Folklore: [Popular Songs]' [Q5 §156], in *Cultural Writings*, p.195.

[113] Antonio Gramsci, 'The Transition from the War of Manoeuvre (Frontal Attack) to the War of Position' [Q6 §138], in *Selections from the Prison Notebooks*, edited and translated by Quintin Hoare and Geoffrey Nowell Smith (London: Lawrence & Wishart, 1971), pp.238–9; Gramsci, 'Concept of "National-Popular"', p.209; and Gramsci, 'Brief Notes on Machiavelli's Politics' [Q13 §1], in *Prison Notebooks*, p.131.

[114] Antonio Gramsci, 'Internationalism and National Policy' [Q14 §68], in *Prison Notebooks*, p.240.

[115] Gramsci, 'Concept of "National-Popular"', p.209.

[116] Gramsci, 'Concept of "National-Popular"', p.209.

than the Risorgimento.'[117] The task now urgent was to win them back, to invest Italians in their own progressive storyline; done right, the national-historical novel could become a 'popular epic', inspiring the people with belief in their own transformative potential.[118] To this end, he suggested rehabilitating the one Italian historical novel that was neither proto-fascist (like Bresciani's) nor condescendingly paternalist (like Manzoni's) but that set out to celebrate popular agency and initiative: Raffaello Giovagnoli's *Spartaco* (1873–74). But for *Spartaco* to cut across, Gramsci continued, its text would need to be purged of 'rhetorical and baroque forms' and made 'current' with the 'new feelings and new styles' of the present.[119]

As with old texts, so with new: style and form would need to be 'adapted' or 'translated' to reach a national-popular audience. 'The most common prejudice is this', concludes a note from 1933: 'that the new literature has to identify itself with an artistic school of intellectual origins, as was the case with futurism'. Gramsci held that the opposite was true, that a literature committed to the task 'of moral and intellectual renewal' must 'sink its roots into the humus of popular culture as it is, with its tastes and tendencies and with its moral and intellectual world, even if it is backward and conventional'.[120] His target in the note was the young French communist writer Paul Nizan, whose manifesto for a revolutionary proletarian literature he had read reviewed in *Educazione fascista*.[121] Nizan had been writing on behalf of the French section of the IURW and channelling the divisive class politics of the Comintern's 'Third Period' analysis of the world situation (1928–33), which predicting capitalism's imminent collapse instructed communists to adopt a militant posture within the ranks of labour and to brand as 'social fascists' all who stood in their way. The communist arts in this period adopted a similarly sectarian approach, their agitprop little magazines and revolutionary writers' circles advancing an international workerist aesthetic, experimental and iconoclastic, that looked for readers among the movement's class-conscious political vanguard.[122]

---

[117] Antonio Gramsci, 'Study of the Moral and Intellectual Tendencies Prevalent in Literary Circles' [Q23 §8], in *Cultural Writings*, pp.215–16.
[118] Antonio Gramsci, 'Popular Literature: Manzoni' [Q14 §45], in *Cultural Writings*, p.296.
[119] Antonio Gramsci, 'Raffaello Giovagnoli's "Spartaco"' [Q6 §208], in *Cultural Writings*, pp.352–3. After the war, the Italian Communist Party moved to act on his advice, publishing a version of *Spartaco* 'cleansed' of all 'stylistic and technical idiosyncrasies' in its popular weekly magazine, *Vie Nuove* (twenty-seven instalments, January–June 1952). Cf. 'Ritorna Spartaco eroe popolare', *l'Unità*, 4 January 1952, p.3, which flags the modernized text as a model for a genuinely popular and empowering national-historical fiction.
[120] Antonio Gramsci, 'Literary Criticism. [Paul Nizan]' [Q15 §58], in *Selections from the Cultural Writings*, p.102.
[121] 'Argo', 'Idee d'oltre confine', *Educazione fascista* 11, no.3 (March 1933): pp.264–8; and Paul Nizan, 'Littérature révolutionnaire en France', *La revue des vivants* 6, no.9, (September–October 1932): pp.393–400.
[122] On this 'proletarian avant-garde', cf. Denning, *The Cultural Front*, pp.64–7. On the equivalent phase in Britain, cf. Andy Croft, *Red Letter Days: British Fiction in the 1930s* (London:

Gramsci criticized this phase of communist cultural production for adopting a 'cosmopolitan' posture comparable to those 'literary and artistic schools and clubs' whose 'calligraphic' and 'neological' idioms speak only to themselves and to their peers in other countries.[123] Communist culture must stop emulating the minority aesthetics of modernism and work instead on developing 'a cultural politics of the popular masses'.[124]

In fact, both modernist and socialist writers were beginning to do just that. Events in the Soviet Union—the liquidation of the Russian Association of Revolutionary Writers in April 1932, the debut the following month of socialist realism as the name, as yet untheorized, of the new Soviet aesthetic—were moving towards recognition of the 'national-popular' as an urgent question of content and form. Among British modernists we can observe a similar recalibration of aesthetic means and ends as writers adapted to the national turn. Jed Esty describes his cadre of English late modernists 'modifying some of their most distinctive stylistic and generic choices in the late thirties', inflecting their writing 'with an organic Anglocentrism that had, during the twenties, been buried under ... the language of cosmopolitan subjectivity'.[125] He offers as examples T.S. Eliot, 'eschewing the private reading practices of high modernism in favor of a *völkisch* revival of verse drama', and Virginia Woolf, arriving at a 'prickly rapprochement' with 'the problem of social engagement and the problem of nationalism'.[126] My own first chapter partners Woolf with the Bloomsbury-peripheral writer Hope Mirrlees, whom I introduce as a pioneer of British modernism's national turn and its awkward pursuit of a national-popular address. Between 1919 and 1926, Mirrlees published in quick succession three novels, two of them historical, and her celebrated day-poem *Paris* (1920). Taken together and read in sequence, these texts anticipate and condense in brief the journey from cosmopolitan modernism to national culturalism that her literary friends, Eliot and Woolf, went on to make later.

As early as *Paris*, Mirlees had grappled with the obscurity of her experimental idiom and flirted with the possibility of renouncing it. The poem makes its way at nightfall to Montmartre where, to the 'obscene syncopation' of jazz, we meet

---

Lawrence & Wishart, 1990), pp.37–41; and James Smith, 'The Radical Literary Magazine of the 1930s and British Government Surveillance: The Case of *Storm* Magazine', *Literature & History* 19, no.2 (2010): pp.69–86.

[123] Gramsci found himself thus far in agreement with the fascist critic 'Argo', on what he called 'the "cosmopolitan" dangers of Nizan's conception' and 'the impossibility of going beyond a national and autochthonous stage of the new literature'. Gramsci, 'Literary Criticism. [Paul Nizan]', p.100. On Gramsci's critique of cosmopolitanism, cf. Timothy Brennan, 'Cosmotheory', *South Atlantic Quarterly* 100, no.3 (2001): pp.659–91. For Gramsci's criticisms of '*calligrafismo*' (aesthetic purism) and '*neolalismo*' (vanguard experimentalism), cf. the notes 'Non-National-Popular Characteristics of Italian Literature: ["Contentism" and "Calligraphism"]' [Q15 §20] and 'Neology' [Q23 §7], in *Cultural Writings*, pp.117–19 and pp.122–3.

[124] Gramsci, 'Neology', p.123.
[125] Esty, *Shrinking Island*, pp.10–11; p.223.
[126] Esty, *Shrinking Island*, p.158; p.84.

lesbian night-club '*gurls*', prostitutes 'like lions ... seeking their meat from God', and a chorus-line dancing the 'Masque of the Seven Deadly Sins'. Clients descend 'like a thousand tom-cats in rut' and desire runs amok.[127] Finally, Mirrlees announces:

> DAWN
> Verlaine's bed-time ... Alchemy
> Absynthe,
> Algerian tobacco,
> Talk, talk, talk,
> Manuring the violets of the moon.[128]

The 'Alchemy' that transforms the night's base elements into the gold of the rising sun codes a reference to Verlaine's bedmate, Arthur Rimbaud, whose 'Alchimie du Verbe' had initiated his own ascent from *Une Saison en Enfer* (1873). Our exit from *Paris* tracks with Rimbaud's, who in 'Morning' confessed himself tired of talking, and whose 'Adieu' instructed its poet-protagonist to quit the city for the countryside, there to confront its 'rugged reality' and his obligations to its people.[129] Mirrlees recalls Rimbaud as the poet who famously turned his back on poetry, who called time on the pursuit of a pure but impractical language, on fantastical 'talk, talk, talk', that profits 'the violets of the moon' but accomplishes nothing on earth. His presence in *Paris* confirms for Mirrlees the arguments of her partner, the Cambridge classicist Jane Harrison: that 'art ... is social, not individual', and has its origins and only effectivity in 'the common act, the common or collective emotion', she called ritual.[130]

Harrison had wondered if a 'systematized attempt' might yet be made 'to remind man, by ritual, of that whole of life' of which he is a part.[131] Her studies of ancient Greek religion and her essays on contemporary culture privileged attempts to revive the properly social, mystical essence of religion and art.[132] Mirrlees' major writings of the 1910s and 1920s are similarly motivated; their challenge is to find a

---

[127] Hope Mirrlees, *Paris: A Poem* (London: Hogarth Press, 1919), p.21.
[128] Mirrlees, *Paris*, p.22.
[129] Arthur Rimbaud, 'Une Saison en Enfer', in *Œuvres complètes*, edited by André Guyaux with Aurélia Cervoni (Paris: Bibliothèque de la Pléiade, 2009), pp.245–80. In 'Matin', Rimbaud exclaims: '*Je ne sais plus parler!*' (p.277) and in 'Adieu': 'Moi! moi qui me suis dit mage ou ange, ... je suis rendu au sol, avec un devoir à chercher, et la réalité rugueuse à étreindre! Paysan!' (p.279).
[130] Jane Ellen Harrison, *Ancient Art & Ritual* (London: Williams & Norgate, 1913), p.240; p.126.
[131] Jane Ellen Harrison, *Themis: A Study of the Social Origins of Greek Religion* (Cambridge: Cambridge University Press, 1912), p. xix.
[132] Harrison's histories of Greek religion gave pride of place to the late-stage revival of the Orphic and Dionysiac mystery cults. She also wrote sympathetically of 'The Religion of To-Day', a new 'Immanence in theology' whose practical aspect was a new 'mysticism', or rather the 'resurgence of an instinct very, very old'. Jane Ellen Harrison, *Rationalism and Religious Reaction* (London: Watts & Co., 1919), pp.21–2; cf. 'The Religion of To-Day' in Jane Ellen Harrison, *Epilegomena to the Study of Greek Religion* (Cambridge: Cambridge University Press, 1921), pp.35–6.

language and a framework for this revival to take hold. In *The Counterplot* (1923), Mirrlees confirmed her rejection of modernism's elite idiom and metropolitan location, and in her last and most accomplished work of fiction—the historical fairy-tale, *Lud-in-the-Mist* (1926)—she lays out her solution. The homely parable of an England made whole by the restoration of ritual and romance, *Lud* combines national allegory with a newly accessible, national-popular address. In chapter one, I argue that Virginia Woolf came to share Mirrlees' faith in the nation as a fix for the challenges of modernity. For both writers, a selective reading of Scott and a strong commitment to the salvage of popular speechways, vernacular literature, and demotic song anchors their version of the national turn in the tradition of the eighteenth-century romance revival. I tell this story across three fictions: Mirrlees' historical novel *Madeleine* (1919), her historical fantasy *Lud*, and Woolf's mock-biography *Orlando* (1928). These novels develop a critical history of the bourgeois cultural revolution and the disembedding of the modern individual from the fabric of community; they do so in service to a vision of religious re-enchantment, for Mirrlees, and of class conciliation, for Woolf, made possible by the resources of national culture.

My second chapter pans out and away to locate the revival of the historical novel on the British Left in a wide-angle frame. I begin in the 1930s and write of the role of the historical novel in Hitler's Germany and in the literature, forged in response, of international anti-fascism. Mapping the travels of the genre along the ley lines of socialist sympathy, I survey Soviet-sphere prescriptions for what a 'revolutionary historical novel' should look like. I reconstruct in detail the argument and publication history of Georg Lukács' landmark study, *The Historical Novel* (serialized 1937–38), as well as shorter, but more widely influential, calls to adopt the genre as a weapon in the struggle. I show how writers in Britain rallied to the cause, sketching different lines of approach among the Communist Party's plebeian and middle-class professional writers, and show how integral the genre became to the Party's historical culture, the larger universe of discussion, discovery, and creative appropriation of the radical-popular past. It is this culture that trained the British Marxist historians, among them E.P. Thompson, Christopher Hill, and Eric Hobsbawm. I return their later academic contributions to the study of social and labour history to the spaces and idioms they shared with autodidact worker-historians, ballad collectors, and historical novelists in the 1930s and 40s. The chapter closes by connecting the communist historical project to validate and rehabilitate less legible forms of subaltern consciousness and resistance to emerging definitions of a Latin American 'magical' or 'marvellous' realism in the years leading up to the literary world-historical event that was Gabriel Garcia Marquez' *One Hundred Years of Solitude* (1967).

Where my second chapter looks to establish the geographical, conceptual, and stylistic parameters of the communist historical novel, shuttling, in the process, from Moscow to East London, and from Bahia, Brazil to Bihar in eastern India, my third chapter begins in a small county town in the south-west of England, where in 1937 two quite different novelists briefly shared a Communist Party stage. I ask whether they also shared a genre. Sylvia Townsend Warner was an early-thirties convert to communism, a Soviet loyalist, and as an activist and intellectual deeply committed to the hard graft of everyday organizing in a part of the world overwhelmingly agricultural, with disproportionately low levels of union membership or even Labour Party support, and where conservative clergy, farmers, and gentry dominated the political scene. From their isolated Dorset village, Warner and her partner Valentine Ackland poured huge energy through the 1930s into raising the Party's profile, protesting local labour and living conditions, and later into consciousness-raising for the Civil War in Spain. Her politics were rural and international, but not immediately national; and though fully on board with revolutionary violence, Warner's country-worker perspective made her willing to wait for such time as they would be ready to act. Warner was not an obvious recruit to the national-popular historical novel as theorized and widely written in the wake of Dimitrov's Seventh World Congress address in 1935. Neither was John Cowper Powys, a former communist fellow traveller who would soon opt for an individualist brand of anarchism, albeit distrustful of any propaganda by deed. Briefly united in 1937 by their support for the Second Spanish Republic, Warner and Powys then went their separate ways. But they spent the 1940s working on two major historical fictions: Warner's novel of a mediaeval Norfolk nunnery, *The Corner That Held Them* (1948), and Powys's great 'Dark Age' romance, *Porius* (1951). Two writers with modernist proclivities and uncomfortable, in their different ways, with the nationalist and culturalist inflection of their moment and milieu, Powys and Warner press at the limits of the communist historical novel.

Chapter four reverts to orthodoxy with a study of Jack Lindsay, the leading advocate and writer of the 'revolutionary historical novel' in Britain. But it first approaches Lindsay as a case study, to compare with Woolf and Mirrlees, of the magnetic power of the mid-century national turn. From 1936 a loyal, life-term communist, Jack Lindsay began his career in the early 1920s advocating the art and opinions of his father, the Australian painter Norman Lindsay. They attributed to art and individual consciousness a universality that could subsume such mid-level conceptions as nation and class, and the histories they each compact. Jack Lindsay's later Marxism undid all that, but it preserved an element of this earlier formation. Shorn of its aristocratic radicalism and masculine entitlement, the arcadian pastoral and delight in sexual licence of the Lindsays' 1920s aesthetic fused to form a vision of social justice under communism where equality in all things would transform not only our interpersonal relations but also our relationship with the natural world. This chapter registers the persistence of these early positions in Lindsay's last historical novel, published in 1965 but begun in the late 1950s as a contribution to the debates about the future of socialism that launched the British New Left. *Thunder Underground* is Lindsay's attempt to define a 'socialist humanism' that could correct for the deformities of Stalinism while still keeping the communist project alive. It is Lindsay's last historical novel, and as such a farewell to the genre he helped raise to prominence on the British and international Left.

In an epilogue, I ask whether anything survives today of the 'political-revolutionary-historical novel'.[133] I begin in the 1980s, with Raymond Williams urging intellectuals and writers of the Left to revisit the mid-century, there to 'search out and counterpose an alternative tradition' to the modernism then dominant in the academy and the postmodernism he saw as its heir.[134] Practising what he preached, Williams set out to salvage a communist historical novel by the Welsh writer, Gwyn Thomas, and I trace its influence on Williams' own late-career trilogy, *People of the Black Mountains* (1989–90). Because the nation was no longer a plausible goal of anti-systemic praxis, as it had been at mid-century, Williams' trilogy adopts a different scale of narration and political action, aiming to combine the most local particularity with a sense of systemic imbrication and global flow. In other ways as well, Williams scrambles the genetic code of the mid-century historical novel, its braiding of individual and collective destinies in a singular arc of insurgency, to illustrate his belief in a 'long revolution' to socialism on the back of cultural and educational democratization. Williams' vision of politics has proven generative and has found its way not only into contemporary activism and theory, but into new-millennium historical fictions as well. With the novels of the Italian Luther Blissett/Wu Ming writers' collective, I suggest one place where the mid-century struggle for the past lives on, vindicating in the process Perry Anderson's contention that 'within the huge multiverse of prose fiction' the historical novel has been, and likely remains, 'the most consistently political' genre.[135]

---

[133] The phrase is Truman Nelson's. A working-class autodidact and life-long communist, Nelson wrote a trilogy of novels on US radical history: *The Sin of the Prophet* (1952), about Boston abolitionist Theodore Parker; *The Passion by the Brook* (1953), about the Brook Farm community; and *The Surveyor* (1960), about John Brown in Kansas. He praised the historical novel as 'a prime form of people's art: it is storytelling, it is example, it is an embodiment of our hidden continuities of hope and rage.' Truman Nelson, 'On Creating Revolutionary Art and Going Out of Print', *TriQuarterly* 23 (1972): pp.109–10.

[134] Raymond Williams, 'When was Modernism?', in *The Politics of Modernism: Against the New Conformists*, edited by Tony Pinkney (London: Verso, 1989), p.35.

[135] Anderson, 'From Progress to Catastrophe', p.24.

# 1
# Hope Mirrlees and Virginia Woolf in the 'footprints of Sir Walter Scott'

## I. 'Oh, I see—"historical fiction"'

Within a week of its publication in October 1928, Hope Mirrlees wrote to congratulate Virginia Woolf on her 'exquisite romantic *Orlando*'. She had found its portrait of Vita Sackville-West 'charming', the book itself 'divine', and in a seemingly offhand remark, she credited Woolf with a singular achievement: 'And, incidentally, you have solved the problem of the "historical novel".'[1] Mirrlees does not elaborate, and read as a throwaway, her compliment may mean as much and no more than other early attempts to ascribe a genre to *Orlando*: Desmond MacCarthy, for example, called it 'a wonderful phantasmagoria', Arnold Bennett 'a play of fancy, a wild fantasia, a romance, a high-brow lark', Conrad Aiken 'a jeu d'esprit', a 'colossal pun', 'a kind of inspired joke'.[2] Mirrlees may have meant the phrase as flattery or as an airy *aperçu*. She may have meant to be perverse: subtitled 'A Biography', *Orlando* clearly has other problems-of-genre to solve.[3] But we may also take Mirrlees at her word, defining the 'problem' from *Orlando*'s solution and from Mirrlees' own experiments in the genre, her historical novel *Madeleine: One of Love's Jansenists* (1919) and historical fantasy *Lud-in-the-Mist* (1926). Read together and in sequence, these fictions suggest a role for the historical novel in mediating for modernism the mid-century national turn.

In Jed Esty's influential analysis, the 1930s saw British modernism reconsider its commitment to aesthetic virtuosity and cosmopolitan individualism in favour of 'a new apprehension of a complete national life—an insular romance of wholeness.'[4] This 'nativist cultural turn' Esty reads as a response to imperial decline, whose prospect afforded modernists who had long been critical of empire the opportunity to experiment in their writing with converting the loss of great-power

---

[1] Hope Mirrlees to Virginia Woolf, 17 October 1928. The Keep, University of Sussex Library Special Collections, Monks House Papers, SxMs-18/1/D/95/1.
[2] Desmond MacCarthy, 'Phantasmagoria', *Sunday Times*, 14 October 1928; reprinted in *Virginia Woolf: The Critical Heritage*, edited by Robin Majumdar and Allen McLaurin (London: Routledge & Kegan Paul, 1975), p.222; p.225. Arnold Bennett, 'A Woman's High-Brow Lark', *Evening Standard*, 8 November 1928; reprinted in *The Critical Heritage*, p.232. Conrad Aiken, review of *Orlando*, *Dial*, February 1929; reprinted in *The Critical Heritage*, p.235.
[3] Woolf had called 'the whole problem of biography' 'a stiff one' in an essay from the year before. Virginia Woolf, 'The New Biography' [1927], in *Essays*, Vol.4, p.473.
[4] Esty, *Shrinking Island*, p.8.

supremacy into visions of recovered small-island integrity. J.A. Hobson, writing his critique of *Imperialism* in the aftermath of Britain's Boer War defeat, had urged the substitution of 'an intensive or qualitative for an extensive or quantitative economy'; with 'each step from barbarism to civilization', he argued, it should be possible for a polity to wean itself from overseas expansion and pursue instead 'the qualitative development of national resources'.[5] This, for Esty, was the logic informing not only 'Edwardian Little Englandism' but the 'postimperial conceptions of England' modernists at mid-century so fervently desired.[6] Instrumental in this 'culture of retrenchment' was the 'repatriation' of those technologies that had previously made the colonial periphery available to metropolitan knowledge and narrative: the anthropology that had reported on so-called primitive societies, the imperial romance that had made overseas adventure so seductive to Britain's younger sons.[7] 'Aging high modernists' like Eliot, Forster, and Woolf, as well as cultural workers in other media and popular genres, now turned the exoticizing gaze back on themselves.[8] They discovered that England's history, landscape, and culture was as rich in 'magic and mystery' as was ever the colonial periphery: the nation had all the resources it could need to reenchant modernity and salve its social divides.[9]

Esty acknowledges the difficulty of 'periodizing modernism and imperialism' together and warns against any too neat correlation of literary and geopolitical history.[10] 'High modernism and high imperialism' may or may not quite peak together, but 'late modernism' reports on the aftermath, when imperial contraction inspired a project of national self-discovery that links 'end-stage' modernists like Eliot and Woolf with the domestic anthropology of British Cultural Studies and the reverse ethnography of colonial writers in the 1950s.[11] Esty's 'dialectical switchpoint, where English modernism, projecting the reintegration of art and culture, becomes something else altogether', falls in the late 1930s, his core examples Eliot's *Four Quartets* (1936–42) and Woolf's *Between the Acts* (1941).[12] 'Circa 1940' is his hinge-date for these 'valedictions' to modernist metropolitan style, but as my own case studies will show, this reorientation within modernism had been in train for a while. This chapter presents a version of the Anglocentric turn reaching forward from the 1920s, contemporary with the moment of canonical high modernism in ways that may complicate Esty's chronology but that confirm his central insight: that the mobilization of 'autoethnographic discourses that projected England qua nation as newly representable' reactivated 'concepts

[5] J.A. Hobson, *Imperialism. A Study* (London: James Nisbet, 1902), p.191.
[6] Esty, *Shrinking Island*, pp.25–6.
[7] Esty, *Shrinking Island*, pp.40–1.
[8] Esty, *Shrinking Island*, p.10.
[9] Esty, *Shrinking Island*, p.41.
[10] Esty, *Shrinking Island*, p.29.
[11] Esty, *Shrinking Island*, pp.2–3.
[12] Esty, *Shrinking Island*, p.12.

of community that had been the vain wishes and half-buried utopian kernels of an essentially postlapsarian and cosmopolitan modernism'.[13] This romance of the nation appealed as a solution to 'the originally divided aesthetic ideology of high modernism', with its contrary pulls of excitable urban modernity and nostalgia for lost organic community, of elite cultural address and desire for a more socially integrated art.[14]

The shift from 'high' to 'late' modernism may track with what Esty calls the 'ebb and diffusion' of British imperial power, but it was also attuned to changes in the capitalist world-system and to parallel developments in other literatures.[15] Britain's imperial contraction was only one element, albeit a central one, in the break-up of the European economic and interstate system and the emergence of new hegemons to its East and West. In this expanded frame, the moment of modernism may correspond less precisely to the apex of European imperialism and the metropolitan privilege of its citizens than to the beginning of a more messy and protracted process of realignment, during which the languages of nationalism and internationalism, nativism and cosmopolitanism, were all variously in play. T.S. Eliot's *The Waste Land* (1922), in other ways an exemplary statement of modernism's metropolitan idiom, gives voice to the new topicality of the national question when it invites a German-speaking Lithuanian to protest her identity—'Bin gar keine Russin, stamm' aus Litauen, echt deutsch'—this at a time when the claims of small nations, the politics of self-determination, and the geography of a 'New Europe' hung newly in the balance.[16] I conceive the national turn in British modernism as but one response to the turbulence of this political and economic conjuncture, one that can be read comparatively and in connection with other attempts to revive or reinvent the nation.

In the case of Mirrlees, the significant influence came from the anti-communist Eurasianism that was popular among elements of the Russian exile community in Paris and elsewhere. But this Russian example returned Mirrlees to England, and thence to Sir Walter Scott, the post-Enlightenment romance revival, and the cultural nation of romanticism. For another way to read 'the reversal and repatriation of anthropology' from the colonies, which Esty argues turned mid-century England into 'the object of its own imperial discourse' and 'primitivizing fantasies', is as the reactivation of an earlier moment in its own genealogy, when Scott first combined the discourses of antiquarian and conjectural history to render the nation knowable in fiction as a dynamic social whole, the composite object of its own social forms, institutions, manners, and customs, its elites, middling classes, and

---

[13] Esty, *Shrinking Island*, p.10; p.47.
[14] Esty, *Shrinking Island*, p.12.
[15] Esty, *Shrinking Island*, p.29.
[16] Quoted and discussed in David Ayers, *Modernism, Internationalism and the Russian Revolution* (Edinburgh: Edinburgh University Press, 2020), pp.1–2.

labouring poor.[17] As Mirrlees seems early to have understood, the historical novel could be a powerful resource for rediscovering the nation, if only its 'problem' could be solved.

## II. 'the problem'

Few would dispute that the historical novel had fallen on hard times in the century since Sir Walter Scott first took the world by storm. Mirrlees acknowledges as much in her second novel, *The Counterplot* (1923), when she stages an awkward interaction between its playwright protagonist, Teresa Lane, and her rejected suitor. Guy Cust is a conceited young man, by turns competitive and insecure about his talents as a writer. 'With a little gulp', he musters the courage to ask Teresa what she's been writing. 'It's . . . it's historical', she replies, to which he responds with sneering condescension: 'Oh, I see—"historical fiction".'[18] He is wrong—Teresa is writing a play—but his drawling pause and quibbling quotation marks capture the genre's contemptible state, *c.*1922. Nothing could be more unfashionable in this novel's contemporary moment than historical fiction, and Guy is nothing if not contemporary. He is an experimental poet, enamoured of 'slang, anacoluthons, and lack of meter', all in service to what he calls 'the modern mysticism'—

> that sense, made possible by wireless and cables, of all the different doings of the world happening *simultaneously*: London, music-halls, Broad Street, Proust writing, people picking oranges in California, mysterious processes of growth or decay taking place in the million trees of the myriad forests of the world, a Javanese wife creeping in and stabbing her Dutch rival. One gets the sense a little when at the end of *The Garden of Cyrus* Sir Thomas Browne says: 'The huntsmen are up in America and they are already past their first sleep in Persia.' It's finest expression, he said, was to be found in the *Daily Mirror*.[19]

The parody has a personal valence. It shows Mirrlees distancing herself from her own most celebrated work, the modernist day-poem *Paris*, which Virginia Woolf had published (and typeset by hand) at the Hogarth Press in 1920.[20] The send-up illuminates what was already, in 1923, a set of conventional oppositions between metropolitan modernism and historical fiction, between synchrony and narrative, the present and the past. And it positions Mirrlees, hitherto an exemplary if minor modernist, on the other side of the divide.

---

[17] Esty, *Shrinking Island*, p.44; p.40.
[18] Hope Mirrlees, *The Counterplot* (London: Collins, 1924), p.188.
[19] Mirrlees, *The Counterplot*, pp.32–3.
[20] The poem's evocations of modern synchronicity repeat Browne's turn of phrase exactly. Cf. 'The sun is sinking behind le Petit-Palais. / In the Algerian desert they are shouting the Koran.' Mirrlees, *Paris*, p.20.

Mirrlees is critical of Guy's faddish embrace of synchronicity and the grammatical collapse of meaningful sequence, but she is not unsympathetic to its proximate cause. A product of Eton and Cambridge, Guy had been on track to become a 'King's don' and devote his life to 'a *recherche de l'Absolu*' when he was called up to the Front; the experience strips him of his philosophy, and his compensatory embrace of accidence and contingency carries this memory of trauma.[21] For many of his contemporaries, major modernists among them, the First World War was indeed the dividing line between timeless truths and a disillusioned modern world. Liberal notions of progress took a particular hit. 'Never before', wrote H.G. Wells towards the end of his popular *Outline of History* (1920), 'can there have been so great and so universal an awakening from assumed and accepted things' as there has been since 1914.[22] E.M. Forster added how strange the present now felt, how 'anything but ours: it is as though a dead object, huge and incomprehensible, had fallen across the page, which no historical arts can arrange, and which bewilders us as much by its shapelessness as by its size'.[23] This 'crisis of historicism' registers across a number of post-war contexts and conversations, well beyond the German academic controversy that first gave it its name.

A concern, for example, with the ordinary and everyday marks a familiar stream in the period's thinking, given new immediacy by such literary innovations as stream-of-consciousness narration, the *style indirect libre*, and literary impressionism. It is tempting to associate this quotidian turn with a kind of mental recoil from the tragic eventfulness of total war, to read it as of a piece with the domestication and diminution, the broad cultural displacement, of the categories of public history that had made themselves so much at home in the nineteenth century, in its architecture, interior decoration, and popular historical fiction.[24] For Walter Benjamin, the war shattered the illusion of 'homogeneous empty time' that had allowed the European bourgeoisie to consume their history in comfort, unconcerned by its violence or by their own complicity.[25] For Karl Polanyi, the war did away with the 'Hundred Year's Peace' that had prevailed on the continent from the defeat of Napoleon in 1815, and so to that conception of modernity so central to Scott's scene of narration as a time of accomplished civil society to the far side

---

[21] Mirrlees, *The Counterplot*, p.32.
[22] H.G. Wells, *Outline of History* (London: Cassell, 1920), p.596.
[23] E.M. Forster, 'Mr Wells' "Outline"', *The Athenaeum*, no.4725 (19 November 1920): p.690.
[24] Raphael Samuel describes 'debunking the past' as 'a kind of national sport in the 1920s, a way perhaps of anaesthetizing the pain for those ... who had walked the fields of death, and for others, marking a break with their elders and betters.' Samuel's examples extend from the music hall to Bloomsbury's 'New Biography' and the academic history of Lewis Namier and Herbert Butterfield. Samuel, 'One in the Eye: *1066 And All That*', in *Island Stories: Unravelling Britain. Theatres of Memory, Volume II*, edited by Alison Light (London: Verso, 1998), pp.210–1.
[25] Benjamin, 'On the Concept of History', p.395. Cf. Benjamin's reflections on the nineteenth-century interior, I2,6 and I3,4; in Walter Benjamin, *The Arcades Project*, translated by Howard Eiland and Kevin McLaughlin (Cambridge, MA: Harvard University Press, 1999), p.216; p.218.

of past discord.[26] The most experimental post-war fictions to flirt with the genre reject altogether this notion of historical distance, with its faith in the passage of time ceding prejudice to perspective and in the privilege of the present to know what those in the past could not. Alfred Döblin's *Wallenstein* (1920) rewrites the Thirty Years War as a theatre of cruelty in a perpetual present tense, with text and event, characters and reader, all submerged in the flood. *Finnegans Wake* (1939) recalls its conception as an attempt at universal history, a project that devolved under the logic of 'transaccidentation' into a 'present tense integument', 'a dividual chaos'.[27]

In the later 1930s, Georg Lukács returned to this antithesis between modernism and the historical novel, casting it as the consequence of a more general 'crisis of bourgeois realism'.[28] For Lukács, modernism's reduction to the present was but the flipside of a genre grown decadent and escapist. In the historical and modernist contemporary novel, he observed a parallel retreat from the representation of objective social processes, which he explained with a materialist claim about the recession of the nation—as collective project, knowable community, and available frame for the narration of social change—in the age of capitalist imperialism. Guy's experimental poetry offers an apt analogy for this experience of the world as an endless stream of global commodities, knowledge, and news, and for their absent causality, the fact that life as lived in London or Paris is determined elsewhere in a system unavailable to everyday experience or easy intellection. His fetish of simultaneity calls attention to the difficulty of conjugating cause and effect, of restoring what he himself calls the 'grammar and logic' that would link core and periphery in a global division of labour.[29] This illegibility of the imperial world-system explains for Lukács the connection between a modernist literature that revels in 'the essential unknowability of the present' and a historical fiction that treats the past as 'a collection of exotic anecdotes'.[30] Neither is able to do what the novel once did—in the age of new nations and nation-scaled economies, in the heyday of European realism—narrate the past as the present's prehistory and the present as subject to change.

More recent elaborations of Lukács' history of realism have sought to separate his insight into the representational challenges of an expanded global frame from his censure of modernism as a symptom of late-bourgeois decadence and decline. Rather than castigate modernism's trademark formal innovations and thematic concerns for their failure to narrate the social whole, Fredric Jameson has suggested that we read these new-model fictions as 'in reality so many unwitting

---

[26] Karl Polanyi, *The Great Transformation: The Political and Economic Origins of Our Time* (Boston, MA: Beacon, 2001), pp.3–21.
[27] James Joyce, *Finnegans Wake* (London: Penguin, 1999), pp.185–6.
[28] Lukács, *The Historical Novel*, pp.171–250.
[29] Mirrlees, *The Counterplot*, p.37.
[30] Lukács, *The Historical Novel*, p.235; p.182.

realisms' reporting objectively on conditions in the imperial metropolis.[31] As for the historical novel, it may now be possible to retain Lukács's chronotopic conjectures while relaxing his categorial distinction between a modernism at sea in present-tense subjectivism and a historical fiction in which, because 'nothing is really objectively and organically connected with the objective character of the present', the writer picks a time and a place at random.[32] To do so would clear space for a modernist historical novel that neither writes in praise of the present nor accedes to its meaning loss, that does not flee from the present but confronts it head on. This is how I understand Mirrlees' *Madeleine* and Woolf's *Orlando*: two attempts to penetrate the epistemological haze of Guy's 'modern mysticism' and reposition the present in the continuum of change.

Lukács had hoped that the 'historical novel of our time' would proceed 'in the form of a negation of a negation', liquidating the 'harmful legacies' of the imperial-age historical novel which had in turn so turned its back on Scott.[33] The novels that I discuss in this chapter are no doubt not what he had in mind. But in their search for a solution to the 'problem of the "historical novel"', Mirrlees and Woolf both avail themselves of techniques that Lukács endorsed and that he derived from Scott. *Madeleine* and *Orlando* elect as their protagonists what Lukács calls 'historical-social types', fictional individuals that '*directly* and at the same time typically express the problems of an epoch'.[34] Woolf pegs her mock 'biography' of an English aristocrat to a critical history of capitalist modernity and of the class-privileged individual. Mirrlees' Madeleine is no less typical, though she is a good deal less likeable. All three novels—*Orlando*, *Madeleine*, and *Lud-in-the-Mist*—share the 'felt relationship to the present' that Lukács observed in Scott, the desire to give 'poetic life to those historical, social and human forces which, in the course of a long evolution, have made our present-day life what it is and as we experience it'.[35] Orlando's fantastical longevity, ageing sixteen years across three and a half centuries, renders this 'long evolution' quite literal and deposits the reader in a present that augurs change. In *Lud*, Mirrlees is eager to imagine what this change might look like, pitching her fantasy of national restoration into the maelstrom of mid-century history. Compared with Lukács, of course, Mirrlees and Woolf remain fuzzy about historical process, calling on culture—the stuff of romance and popular antiquities, vernacular language and national literature—to mollify inequalities and dissipate class conflict. In doing so, however, they may reveal themselves better readers of Scott, and his version of Tory-romantic cultural nationalism, than Lukács in Moscow had any mind to be.

---

[31] Fredric Jameson, *A Singular Modernity: Essay on the Ontology of the Present* (London: Verso, 2002), p.124. Cf. also Jed Esty, 'Global Lukács', *Novel* 42, no.3 (2009): pp.366–72.
[32] Lukács, *The Historical Novel*, p.182.
[33] Lukács, *The Historical Novel*, p.349–50.
[34] Lukács, *The Historical Novel*, p.35; p.284.
[35] Lukács, *The Historical Novel*, p.53.

## III. Sources of the Self

Mirrlees sets *Madeleine* in Paris, in the eleven-month interim between the publication of the tenth volume of Mademoiselle de Scudéry's *Artamène, ou le Grand Cyrus* (September 1653) and the first instalment of *Clélie, histoire romaine* (August 1654). It tells of a young girl's desperate desire to meet de Scudéry and be cast as a character in her next novel *à clef*.[36] Madeleine's family move from the provinces to Paris to help further her aim and there she meets three times with de Scudéry. When all three meetings misfire, Madeleine loses her mind. The last we see of her is as an inmate in a Paris asylum where visitors 'in quest of the crotesque' come to delight in her madness (275). This précis of the plot may suggest a simple, if punitive, novel, but there is a twist in its tail and its intellectual conception is anything but. Around this figure of a seventeen-year-old girl, Mirrlees weaves a dense ideological fabric, of which the salon culture of de Scudéry is only one of the threads. The novel makes sophisticated reference to the sceptical materialism of philosophers like Gassendi, Nandé, and La Mothe le Vayer; it flags Arnauldian linguistics, Descartes, and the rise of procedural reason; it elaborates at length the Counter-Reformation theologies of Jansen and the Jesuits. These cultural currents feed into a story of the disarticulation of man from the cosmic order, the entry of nature into the scientific frame, and the redirection of religious meaning from social life to private. The cultures of feeling practised by the *précieuses*, the disciplines of self enjoined by Jesuit and Jansenist, the rigours of reason asserted by libertine and philosopher, all combine to assert the individual as the measure of modernity.

This history of ideas is erudite and impressive, but it does not make for easy reading, nor does the novel's heroine. Madeleine 'is absolutely without redeeming qualities', concludes Michael Swanwick. 'Every petulant snub and self-absorbed vanity ... is heavily underscored by the author, as if she were afraid the reader might miss the inherent unpleasantness of her protagonist.' As explanation, Swanwick suggests that Mirrlees wrote the novel in an attempt at self-analysis, 'exploring, in grotesquely exaggerated form, tendencies she found deplorable in herself'; or perhaps she just spent so many years struggling with the manuscript 'that she unconsciously set out to sabotage it'.[37] Swanwick is right to ask why Mirrlees should elect an unlikeable heroine, but wrong to look for personal reasons. The problem is of the period, a function of the novel's historical argument. Madeleine's defining characteristic is her 'self-love', a translation of Augustine's *amor sui* by way of the French, which as Mirrlees explains was the 'newly-discovered sin' that came 'to dominate the psychology of the seventeenth century' (52).[38] While still in Lyons,

---

[36] Hope Mirrlees, *Madeleine: One of Love's Jansenists* (London: Collins, 1919), p.31. Subsequent references to the novel are to this edition and given parenthetically in the body of the text.
[37] Michael Swanwick, 'Hope-in-the-Mist', *Foundation* 87 (2003): p.25.
[38] The claim is borne out by subsequent scholarship. Cf. Michael Moriarty, *Fallen Nature, Fallen Selves: Early Modern French Thought II* (Oxford: Oxford University Press, 2006), pp.159–275; and

Madeleine attends a Jansenist sermon on self-love and is brought to reflect 'that *she was such a Narcissus and that "amour-propre"* filled every cranny of her heart' (53). As a vehicle for this newly significant sin, Madeleine exemplifies a period struggle over the proper objects of our love, figured in this Augustinian context as a contest between concupiscence and charity, between love of things as ends in themselves and as means to loving God. For the theologians, it began with the Fall, when we lost our innate love of God, and of ourselves and others in His image. Self-love is our fallen attempt to compensate for that loss, a sinful substitute for the righteous love of God; it is also antisocial, leading us to pursue our own interest at others' expense. Taken together, these characteristics help explain self-love's new topicality as a response to a world of economic actors eager to emancipate themselves from obligations that might otherwise constrain. Defined by her *amour-propre*, Madeleine is a figure of this new social type, the modern self-interested individual, and if she is less than fully likeable then so much the better for a critique of the forces remaking her world and making it our own.

This period-specific moral psychology does, however, raise difficult questions about Madeleine's pursuit of de Scudéry, which the novel invites us to read in the language of same-sex desire. *Madeleine* makes repeated reference to Sappho, both to 'the Grecian Sappho' who 'penned amorous odes to diverse damsels' (74) and the 'Paris Sappho' (76) of de Scudéry's self-portrait in the tenth volume of *Le Grand Cyrus* (181). Early readers were quick to draw the connection: Elizabeth Drew, writing in 1926 of 'the new frankness' in contemporary fiction, linked Mirrlees with Clemence Dane in giving 'us careful and direct studies of Lesbians'.[39] In private to Clive Bell, Virginia Woolf saw a more intimate relation, the novel's 'sapphism' a self-portrait of 'Jane [Harrison] and herself'.[40] Thirty-seven years her junior, Mirrlees was the Cambridge classicist's 'favourite pupil', her 'ghostly daughter', and late-life companion.[41] Their relationship was, and remains, a source of speculation.[42] But it is far from clear that the novel endorses Madeleine's attraction, which it explains as a libidinal displacement of her own self-love. Fired by

---

Charles-Olivier Stiker-Métral, *Narcisse contrarié: L'amour propre dans le discours moral en France, 1650–1715* (Paris: Honoré Champion, 2007).

[39] Elizabeth Drew, *The Modern Novel. Some Aspects of Contemporary Fiction* (London: Jonathan Cape, 1926), pp.108–9. Modern critics have followed suit, cf. Ruth Vanita, '"Uncovenanted Joys": Catholicism, Sapphism, and Cambridge Ritualist Theory in Hope Mirrlees' *Madeleine: One of Love's Jansenists*', in *Catholic Figures, Queer Narratives*, edited by Lowell Gallagher, Frederick Roden, and Patricia Juliana Smith (Basingstoke: Palgrave Macmillan, 2006), pp.85–96.

[40] Virginia Woolf to Clive Bell, 24 September 1919; in *The Question of Things Happening. The Letters of Virginia Woolf, Volume 2: 1912–1922*, edited by Nigel Nicolson and Joanne Trautmann (London: Hogarth Press, 1976), p.391. Scholars have since queried the correspondence, Julia Briggs identifying Harrison with *Madeleine*'s kindly Mère Agnes and suggesting the modernist *salonnière* Natalie Barney as a more likely match for its Sappho. Julia Briggs, 'The Wives of Herr Bear', review of *The Invention of Jane Harrison* by Mary Beard, *London Review of Books* 22, no.18 (21 September 2000): p.25.

[41] Virginia Woolf to Margaret Llewelyn Davies, 17 August 1919; in *Letters*, Vol.2, p.385. Jane Ellen Harrison, *Reminiscences of a Student's Life* (London: Hogarth Press, 1925), p.89.

[42] In 1923, Dora Carrington wrote to Lytton Strachey asking for information on 'the Jane-Hope liaison'. She'd been given 'such an interesting account of them' by Boris Anrep and she wanted to know

that Jansenist sermon on the perils of narcissism, which made its 'hearers feel it as a thing loathly, poisonous, parasitic' (52), Madeleine looks to the literature of *préciosité* for a cure. 'Obviously love for some one else was the antidote to *amour-propre*', she reasons, and if the salon style considers sexual love a 'crime' and '*l'amitié tendre* the perfect virtue', then Madeleine will pursue this 'tenderness' where it is least likely to be tempted: she will 'make a woman the object of that friendship', rather than risk lapsing from 'the discrete and shady groves of Plato's Academe' into 'the garden of Epicurus' (57). She settles on de Scudéry to be this decoy as a woman conveniently old and 'very ugly' (105) but also 'famous' and well placed, a point of access to Parisian polite society (57). It is an improbable logic, and wholly concupiscent by the standards of Augustine and his heirs, insofar as it substitutes a love of created things for the love of their creator. It is also cunning in just the ways that seventeenth-century moralists understood self-love to be.[43] As an attempt to outrun the spiritual 'void' of narcissism, it is doomed to fail.[44] Early in the novel, Madeleine compares her love of de Scudéry to a recurring nightmare she calls her 'Dutch dream'. In the dream, Madeleine imagines herself 'surrounded by divers objects, such as cheeses and jugs and strings of onions and lutes and spoons' like in a Golden-Age still life; all of a sudden, one of the items starts to swell—she never knows which it will be—'and it is wont to continue until I feel that if it get any bigger I shall grow mad. And in like manner, I hold it to be out of chance that it was Mademoiselle de Scudéry that took to swelling, it might quite well have been any one else' (29–30). This is hardly a proud defence of lesbian love,

---

more: 'Win their confidences. I am sure they are a fascinating couple.' Dora Carrington to Lytton Strachey, 27 August 1923; in *Carrington: Letters and Extracts from her Diaries*, edited by David Garnett (New York: Holt, Reinhart and Winston, 1970), p.258. Woolf liked to see them 'billing and cooing together'. She gossiped that they 'practically live together', that they kept 'a Sapphic flat' in Paris. Virginia Woolf to Jacques Riverat, 15 February 1925; in *Letters*, Vol.3, p.164. Virginia Woolf to Molly MacCarthy, 22 April 1923, as quoted in Mary Beard, *The Invention of Jane Harrison* (Cambridge, MA: Harvard University Press, 2000), p.313 fn.77. For their part, Harrison and Mirrlees conducted the relationship in a language more antiquated and opaque than that of modern lesbianism, the language of sentimental friendship. Their correspondence records an intimacy hedged about by humour and routed through a fantasy world of stuffed animals and decorative ornaments. In print this intimate code continued, paraded through the dedications, footnotes, epigraphs, and allusions of their works. For a judicious reading of the relationship, see Beard, *Invention of Jane Harrison*, pp.129–60. At the risk of defusing a romantic charge or diminishing the queer Mirrlees, I read the importance of Harrison for her writings of the 1910s and 1920s in terms of a shared investment in the ritual renovation of society.

[43] Pierre Nicole, for example, wrote of 'the marvellous subtlety' of *amour-propre*: finding its own self-love repulsive and knowing it to be offensive in the eyes of others, the self-loving subject learns to dissimulate, to counterfeit 'charity' by seeking out the love and esteem of others while still remaining 'at the bottom but a self-love more intelligent and exact'. Nicole, 'Of Charity and Self-Love' [1674], in Bernard Mandeville, *The Fable of the Bees and Other Writings*, edited by E.J. Hundert (Indianapolis, IN: Hackett, 1997), pp.5–6.

[44] Michael Moriarty glosses Jansen's warning that 'to fall into self-love is to find oneself in a boundless and incomprehensible void, a realm of unlimited lack', in *Fallen Nature, Fallen Selves*, p.178. Both Jansen and Pascal deploy this metaphor of the void, and it feeds into *Madeleine*'s conclusion when disappointed in love she loses her grasp on reality and 'out into the void she danced' (274). For the Pascal connection, cf. Michael Moriarty, *The Age of Suspicion: Early Modern French Thought* (Oxford: Oxford University Press, 2003), pp.138–9; and *Fallen Nature, Fallen Selves*, pp.185–6.

and we may wonder whether Mirrlees intends it as comedy. Certainly, *Madeleine* tacks close to satire and the parodic plot of anti-romance.[45]

Madeleine has been eager to hear in her name the namesake equivalence of Madeleine de Trocqueville and Madeleine de Scudéry, as well as that of their patron saint Mary Magdalene, whose 'particular virtue ... was that she "loved much"' (163). But there is another, less flattering echo in the Magdelon of Molière's *Les Précieuses ridicules* (1659), the provincial young bourgeoise who travels to Paris to rise in the world and whose affectation of the salon style renders her a laughing stock.[46] There are others of her kind: Juliette in Adrien Perdou de Subligny's *La Fausse Clélie* (1671) and Arabella in Charlotte Lennox's *The Female Quixote* (1752), hoodwinked heroines held to account for thinking that life can be lived as a de Scudéry romance. For all its disciplinary violence, however, the anti-romance was always at root a comic genre, reserving for its humiliated heroines a happy marriage and return to the social fold. For Madeleine, there is no such husband waiting in the wings to forgive her extravagant feeling and romance misreading. Her cousin-lover Jacques has given up the chase, leaving Madeleine with only her 'adamant of desire'. Her hopes dashed, 'the cables binding her to reality' snap and off to the madhouse she goes (274). A martyr for unreason and immoderate desire, Madeleine ends up committed, an early victim of the 'Great Confinement' that in Michel Foucault's classic account swept Europe from the 1650s. Its landmark date was the 1656 royal decree establishing the Hôpital Général in Paris. Thus began the mass incarceration of those whose lives affronted Enlightenment rationality and the bourgeois work ethic: the idle and lame, the indigent and insane, all were now marked by their social uselessness, their alienation from the world of profitable labour.[47]

I have so far rehearsed *Madeleine*'s historical argument, its configuration of the French 1650s as a threshold in the making of the secular modern subject. But in this novel, as in all Mirrlees' major works, there is another logic at play that runs athwart its careful historicism and rich representational realism. Mirrlees' second novel gives this logic a name, and it is the presence in *Madeleine* of a 'counter-plot' that blocks the punitive intent of the anti-romance and the parable of lesbian impossibility we might otherwise infer from a heroine left abject and unwanted by the heterosexual marriage plot. The Paris wits who in the epilogue come to visit 'the well-known lunatic asylum—"les petites maisons"'—save the hospital's 'most delicious' exhibit for last: '"And now for the Pseudo-Sappho", cried one'. Here, we meet Madeleine not as we have known her, an annoying egotistical teenager, but as

---

[45] So named after Charles Sorel's parody of Honoré d'Urfé's *L'Astrée*, *Le Berger extravagant* (1627–28), which in 1633 he retitled *L'Anti-roman, ou l'Histoire du Berger Lysis*.

[46] Mirrlees confirms the allusion in an interview from 1970, quoted in Suzanne Henig, 'Queen of Lud: Hope Mirrlees', *Virginia Woolf Quarterly*, no.1 (1972): pp.11–12.

[47] Michel Foucault, *Madness and Civilization: A History of Insanity in the Age of Reason*, translated by Richard Howard (New York: Vintage, 1988), p.40.

a woman 'smiling affably' who greets the 'troupe of wits' like 'a queen her courtiers' (275). Her cell a salon, Madeleine de Trouqueville has become Madeleine de Scudéry, 'the Pseudo-Sappho' to de Scudéry's original. One of the visitors explains the transformation:

> Did not the ancients hold that in time the worshipper became the god? Surely we have here a proof that their belief was well-founded. And if the worshipper becomes the god then should not also the metamorphosis of the lover into his mistress—Celadon into Astrée, Cyrus into Mandane—be a truly gallant ending of a 'roman'? (275-6)

The ancients did indeed believe that the worshipper could become their god, as Jane Harrison had explained at length. Harrison's *Prolegomena to the Study of Greek Religion* (1905) studied the Dionysiac and Orphic mysteries with an eye to just this union with the divine, and her discussion of their rituals as practised at Eleusis provides Mirrlees with the quotation from Sophocles that she uses as an epigraph for the scene (275).[48]

## IV. 'unsatisfied desire'

When Virginia Woolf reviewed *Madeleine* in 1919, she credited 'the little shock of emotion with which one comes to' its 'conclusion' as 'token that one has been led to it rightly'.[49] There is indeed a method to Madeleine's madness and Jane Harrison is its key. 'Man, say the wise Upanishads, is altogether desire', Harrison had written in *Themis* (1912), but we have thwarted desire to thank for all that makes us man: art and religion, our entire human culture.[50] Citing the new behavioural psychology, Harrison instructs us to understand human nature 'not as a bundle of separate faculties'—'reason, the emotions, and the will' each with 'separate existences' like the gods of Roman mythology—'but as a sort of continuous cycle of activities'. The world registers on our senses, and as soon as we perceive it, 'we feel about it, towards it, we have emotion. And, instantly again, that emotion becomes a motive power' and we act.[51] Or we would 'if we were a mass of well contrived instincts' and each 'stage' unfailingly led to the next.[52] More often, there is a break in the loop, a delay in 'reaction' that forces us to pause in the place of 'pent up' perception and bottlenecked desire. The history of human accomplishment derives from the need

---

[48] Sophocles, *Antigone*, 1151-2; translated in Jane Ellen Harrison, *Prolegomena to the Study of Greek Religion* (Cambridge: Cambridge University Press, 1905), p.542.
[49] Virginia Woolf, 'Madeleine' [1919], in *The Essays of Virginia Woolf. Volume 3: 1919-1924*, edited by Andrew McNeillie (London: Hogarth Press, 1988), p.109.
[50] Harrison, *Themis*, p.83.
[51] Harrison, *Ancient Art*, pp.38-9.
[52] Harrison, *Themis*, p.44; *Ancient Art*, p.41.

to discharge this nervous tension, and Harrison elaborates each outlet in turn, from sympathetic magic and the tribal dance to philosophy and modern science. Our generalizations and abstractions, our dreamworlds, mythologies, and theologies, all derive from this 'space between perception and reaction', this uncomfortable 'halt' in the place of emotion.[53] Without it, 'we should have no representations, no memory, no μίμησις, no δρώμενα, no drama. Art and religion alike spring from unsatisfied desire.'[54]

Harrison's ascetic psychology powers *Madeleine*'s counterplot. Upon her arrival in Paris, Madeleine wakes every morning to the sound of street-sellers hawking their wares, 'and above these cries from time to time would rise the wail of an old woman carrying a basket laden with spoons and buttons and old rags, "*Vous désirez quelque cho-o-se?*"' (61). With time, the 'shrill and plaintive' cry (94) resolves to a simple statement of fact. Madeleine desires. She writes the *roman* of her life in what she calls 'the Optative—the mood of wishing' (264). In managing this mood, Madeleine draws on the techniques of a primitive religious. Her life is full of little rituals. She will often suppose 'that things won't fall out as I would wish except something else happens first. As soon as the desire for a thing begins to work on me, all manner of little fantastical things crop up around me, and I am sensible that except I compound with them I shall not compound the big thing' (28). We see several examples (231) of Madeleine's 'gnat-like taboos and duties upon the doing or not doing of which ... seemed to depend her future success' (148). But by far the most important of her 'ghostly weapons' (191) and 'supernatural aids' (219) is the magical dance. Throughout the novel, Madeleine is to be seen 'dancing madly up and down' (34), 'dancing for hours' (58), 'dancing Maenad-like up and down her little room' (63), 'diligent in her dancing' (69), and once 'again dancing' (187). Mirrlees provides a plausible seventeenth-century explanation, recounting how Madeleine had been prescribed 'daily exercise, the more violent the better', following a bout of illness which 'for want of a better name her doctor called a sharp attack of the spleen' (47). When shuttlecock proved impractical for lack of a partner to play with, Madeleine moved on to a form of solitary *Ausdruckstanz*, her movements 'rhythmic but formless' and 'wild' (47).

Originally prescribed for a case of humoral discrasia, Madeleine's fitness cure reverts to roots. Instead of preventing a build-up of bile, the exercise performs a more primitive function, allowing for Harrison's 'discharge of pent-up emotion' first in action—'you dance and leap for fear, for joy, for sheer psychological relief'—and later, in images and words.[55] This was how Harrison explained the origin of myth, as 'words spoken' to accompany the 'things done' of the ritual dance, words which became narrative with time, 'a tale or story told' 'of magical intent and

---

[53] Harrison, *Ancient Art*, p.41.
[54] Harrison, *Themis*, p.44.
[55] Harrison, *Themis*, p.42; p.45.

potency'.⁵⁶ True to form, Madeleine's dancing becomes increasingly ideational. Her physical exertion induces a 'semi-mesmeric condition', a sort of 'semi-dramatic' 'dreaming' (48). Madeleine's mythic elaboration begins as a 'vague foretasting of future triumphs and pleasures, shot through with pictures of wavering outlines and conversations semi-articulate' (58); but the more she dances, the clearer these projections become. By the time that Madeleine and her family have settled in Paris, her dream-dances take the form of whole pages from an imaginary de Scudéry romance. Mirrlees laboriously transcribes these 'magical pre-doings' (246), casting them in small type or italics to mark their grammatical shift from the indicative to the optative mood.

Madeleine's dissociative split follows the failure of this private magic to win de Scudéry's regard. It marks a change in kind from the dreamstates her dancing brought about and a departure from the ceremonial sequence of the mystery religions, with their set rites and stages of initiation. Madeleine's apotheosis as Sappho corresponds rather to 'the sudden invasion' of the 'Mystical State' that Harrison called 'Conversion'. Its characteristic rhythm is twofold: 'a time of depression, a sense of loneliness, of failure, disaster, often amounting to complete desolation and positive despair', followed by 'a time of extraordinary exaltation, of peace and joy unutterable'. The transformation is 'involuntary', unavailable to ritual intervention. And 'who are the subjects' of this 'sudden Conversion', Harrison asks: 'Why, who but the supremely vital egotists, the people in whom self is inordinately strong, who are over individualized?'

> Some shattering blow has been dealt to a man's personality, to his affection or ambition ... If he is weak, he dwindles and dies or lives a half-starved life. If he is strong, all the pent-up forces, all the cut-off reactions surge over from the self-centre into the circumference of other emotions, other lives. He turns to God, theology would say; he learns at last not to desire other men for himself but to love them for themselves ...⁵⁷

Whence, perhaps, Madeleine's 'affable smile', her delight in her courtiers (275). But Madeleine the convert is still mad; a tension between the novel's historical plot and its religious counterplot remains. The reason is not far to find: Madeleine's mystical transformation lacks what Harrison would call a 'collective sanction' or 'social imperative'.⁵⁸ 'The individual is a frail light bark to launch upon a perilous sea', Harrison had observed in *Themis*, as she built her case that religion 'sums up and embodies what we feel together, what we care for together, what we imagine

---

[56] Harrison, *Themis*, p.328; p.330.
[57] Jane Ellen Harrison, *Unanimism: A Study of Conversion and Some Contemporary French Poets* (Cambridge: 'The Heretics', 1913), p.27.
[58] Harrison, *Themis*, p.100; p.118; p.330.

together'.[59] Madeleine's apotheosis as the object of her own desire drives home the absence of the group. A mysticism of one, it represents the problem *Lud-in-the-Mist* sets out to solve.

## V. 'English things'

Reviewing *Lud-in-the-Mist* upon its publication in 1926 in the Newnham College magazine, 'J' expressed a gratitude many readers have since shared at how different it seems from Mirrlees' earlier work. In *Lud*, 'J' told her readers, there is none of 'that all-embracing pedantry', none of that experience of 'being told so much and so often what one either knew, or, not knowing, did not wish to know'.[60] Indeed, *Lud* wears its theology and ritual theory lightly, though it is these that again power its counterplot, this time towards a revival of religion on a scale no longer individual but collective. The novel's fairy-tale or fantasy mode facilitates this solution to the felt deficiencies of modernity and signals a new concern for accessibility. Virginia Woolf had not been wrong when she called *Madeleine* 'difficult' and *Paris* 'obscure'; the audience who sit through Teresa's play in *The Counterplot* are 'all terribly embarrassed' when it ends, having understood nothing of its purpose.[61] However much Mirrlees may have thematized art's social alienation as a problem in these earlier works, may even have signalled—as in *Paris*—the desire to pivot from a dissident but marginal art to a more participatory, ritual culture, she found it hard to part with her own virtuosity and the promise of distinction. *Lud* shows Mirrlees willing to listen at last to Harrison's instruction, that art should speak 'in the vulgar tongue, understood of the people'.[62]

Unlike *Madeleine*, *Lud* tells a simple story of the origins of modernity. The novel's prehistory narrates the triumph of mercantile capitalism over an aristocratic *ancien régime* and the consequent decline of religion and art. Some two hundred years before the action starts, Lud's rising middle class, 'obsessed by a will to wealth', overthrow the feudal nobility of Dorimare; during these same 'three days of bloodshed', the priests are ousted too, so that 'simultaneously' the country loses both 'its Duke and its cult' (19). The years that follow see the dereliction of the old worship, a state religion based on the reverence of fairy fruit. This fruit becomes taboo (19), and the new bourgeoisie forgets its true significance: the mysteries of life and death, the stuff of dreams, 'delusion', 'the proper nourishment' of the soul (247). Science, and the 'science of jurisprudence' in particular (20),

---

[59] Harrison, *Themis*, p.327; p.487.
[60] 'J', 'Lud-in-the-Mist', *Thersites*, no.82 (1926); cited in Sandeep Parmar, 'Introduction' to Hope Mirrlees, *Collected Poems* (Manchester: Carcanet, 2011), pp. xxxiv–xxxv.
[61] Woolf, 'Madeleine', p.109; Virginia Woolf to Margaret Llewelyn Davies, 17 August 1919; in *Letters*, Vol.2, p.385; Mirrlees, *Counterplot*, p.327.
[62] Harrison, *Ancient Art*, p.248.

replaces the fairy-inspired art and literature of the old dispensation, and thanks to the 'sturdy common-sense of [the] burgher-class' (19) in seeing to it that 'tradesmen gave good measure and used standard weights' (20) a world of quantification and market equivalence recodes the old spiritual and lyric intensities.

Mirrlees compacts this allegory of the bourgeois cultural revolution into the grandfather clock she installs at the heart of her bourgeois hero's household: instrument of the rationalization of time, the division and synchronization of labour, the logic of linear history.[63] This shift from natural and theological to modern technological time tracks with a loss in 'what can only be called the tragic sense of life' (19), the temporal attunement to mortality that is the existential burden of all things fairy. Mirrlees gives it a Catholic inflection—Miguel de Unamuno's *Del sentimento trágico de la vida* (1912) is a constant point of reference—but the ground tone remains Harrison's study of primitive ritual and the later Greek mystery gods as attempts 'to express what Professor Bergson calls *durée*, that life which is one, indivisible and yet ceaselessly changing.'[64] Mirrlees' repository of popular wisdom, the 'country-bred' Nurse Hempie, speaks this truth when she says: '"There's no clock like the sun and no calendar like the stars". And why, because it gets one used to the look of Time.' *Lud* would have us learn to see time 'naked, as it were', rather than 'shut up in a clock' (122). And for this we must let fairy back into our lives. As Harrison had written in a related context: 'Man does not live by bread alone, not even by the most wholesome bread punctually served. There is dream-stuff as well as bread-stuff', and *Lud* would give us both.[65]

The novel's crisis begins when 'that foolish, innocent-looking grand-father's clock' is found to be hiding a stash of fairy fruit:

> Vine-like tendrils, studded with bright, menacing berries were twined round the pendulum and the chains of the two leaden weights; and at the bottom of the case stood a gourd of an unknown colour, which had been scooped hollow and filled with what looked like crimson grapes, tawny figs, raspberries of an emerald green, and fruits even stranger than these ... (161)

One of several such returns of the repressed, the discovery of the forbidden fruit inside this emblem of bourgeois respectability precipitates a fall from grace for its owner, merchant and mayor Nathaniel Chanticleer. Stripped of his titles and pronounced a 'dead man in the eyes the law' (165), Chanticleer will embark on an epic journey that takes him first to the district of Swan-on-the-Dapple to solve a long-cold murder mystery and thence, in search of his abducted son, to Fairyland.

---

[63] Hope Mirrlees, *Lud-in-the-Mist* [1926] (Doylestown, PA: Wildside Press, n.d.). Subsequent references are to this edition and given parenthetically in the body of the text.
[64] Harrison, *Themis*, p. viii.
[65] Jane Ellen Harrison, *Aspects, Aorists and the Classical Tripos* (Cambridge: Cambridge University Press, 1919), pp.30–1.

In the process, Chanticleer unwittingly performs a series of ritual acts that initiates him in 'the ancient Mysteries of Dorimare' (176). High in the Debatable Hills on the border with Fairyland, he meets Duke Aubrey, Dorimare's last duke before the revolution and an avatar of Dionysus, who vouchsafes to Chanticleer a mystic's vision of this otherworld, a land 'not unlike Dorimare' but released from time, where 'everything had the serenity and stability of trees, the unchanging peace of pictures' (264). The vision fades, and Aubrey's presence with it, leaving Chanticleer 'standing alone on the edge of a black abyss, while wafted on the wind came the echo of light, mocking laughter'. Perhaps the vision was indeed a 'delusion', as the bourgeois revolutionaries have deemed all things fairy; but rather than turn back, Chanticleer takes the leap of faith 'down into the abyss' (264).

When months later he returns to Dorimare, it is as Duke Aubrey's deputy, riding 'a great white charger' at the rear of a giant fairy procession: 'battalions of mail-clad dead' escort the three 'balsam-eating priests of the moon and the sun' with their ancient tribute of fairy fruit borne in golden coffers on the backs of sumpter mules. To greet their arrival, the citizens of Lud have decked the town in 'wreathes of Duke Aubrey's ivy' (276), a reminder that Dionysus, god of the grape, is also 'Kissos, god of the ivy', 'Anthios, god of all blossoming things', 'Phytalmios, god of growth'.[66] And in the celebration that follows, trees burst into new leaf, ships' masts blossom, and violets and anemones spring up through the snow in the streets. It is a festival of spring, of the death and rebirth of the spirit of the year, as marked in February in ancient Athens by the Anthesteria. Harrison had studied its ceremonies in *Prolegomena* and *Themis*, explaining how its three days of drunken Dionysian revelry overlay a more ancient festival of ghosts, a Feast of All Souls for the placation and revocation of the dead. Mirrlees' spring festival is likewise not only a ceremonial gorging on fairy fruit, though we are told that the 'coffers of wrought gold' were of 'miraculous capacity', but also a celebration of the dead: as the mail-clad army disbands, 'mothers embraced their dead sons, and maids their sweethearts drowned at sea' (277).

Chanticleer has reinstated an ancient Dorimarite ritual, 'the most solemn event' in its calendar, but with a difference. Originally, the annual tribute of fairy fruit had gone only to 'the Duke and the high priest' (19); now it goes to all. Mirrlees' parable of re-enchantment desires no return to the old ducal ways. She reassures her reader that the revival of religion in Dorimare secures a new legitimacy for its republican government (275–6) and respect for 'the law of property' (257). The clearest emblem, however, of the novel's rapprochement between religion and capitalist modernity is the rise of 'a new industry'. A childhood friend of Chanticleer's, a man praised for his 'sound practical sense', pioneers a way to preserve fairy fruit and so turn it into an export commodity. For her part, Mirrlees is less interested in the candied peel than she is in its packaging: the 'pretty fancy boxes' with 'painted

---

[66] Harrison, *Prolegomena*, p.427.

lids' present the first sign that 'art was creeping back to Dorimare'. The full proof of this cultural renovation comes later, when Chanticleer's ransomed son Ranulph grows up to compose 'the loveliest songs that had been heard since the days of Duke Aubrey' (284).

*Lud*'s fantasy of recovered cultural integrity completes the repatriation of subject matter that Mirrlees had begun in *The Counterplot*, with its Spanish mediaeval '*auto sacramentál*' performed on a contemporary 'English lawn'.[67] Whereas *Madeleine* and *Paris* had made France their scene, the culture and topography of *Lud* are recognizably British. Admittedly, the novel's ritual mechanisms draw on comparative anthropology and link back to ancient Greece; *Lud* also lays claim to a secondary world that can accommodate fairies and dragons. But we do not have to look far in Dorimare to find a version of England. The name of its capital recalls the legendary King Lud, who according to Geoffrey of Monmouth renamed Troynovant Kaerlud, corrupting to London with time. Its major waterway supports an inland port and an overseas commercial empire as did the tideway of the Thames. The rest of the country is bucolic, a world of quaint-sounding villages and contented rustics, while on its borders there rise the Elfin Marches and Debatable Hills, a careful echo of England's Celtic fringe. The prime exhibit of Dorimarite folk culture is an old English song. Mirrlees calls it 'Columbine' and adapts it slightly, but its first known appearance is in the chapbook *Robin Good-Fellow, His Mad Prankes and Merry Jests* (1628), a collection of 'Kentish Long-Tayles' about the hobgoblin better known as Puck. In the jestbook, Robin sings this song as he helps a maid at midnight to 'breake hempe' and 'dresse flax', a context Mirrlees recalls when she makes Nurse Hempie the song's main mouthpiece in *Lud*.[68] The novel's romance resolution projects a nation restored to self-knowledge, its cultural heritage no longer disavowed in the name of economic progress and secular, scientific reason.

*Lud* couples a recognizably national topography with a national-popular culture and style, but the inspiration for its Anglocentric turn is cosmopolitan, with one foot still squarely in Paris and its Russian exile community. While Mirrlees was writing the novel, she was also collaborating with Harrison on the translation of a book of Russian bear-themed folktales, also published in 1926, to which she contributed two stories by the avant-garde fabulist Alexei Mikhailovich Remizov.[69] Harrison and Mirrlees had befriended Remizov in Paris in early 1924, around

---

[67] Mirrlees, *Counterplot*, p.216.
[68] *The Mad Pranks and Merry Jests of Robin Goodfellow* [1628], edited by J. Payne Collier (London: The Percy Society, 1841), pp.19–20.
[69] Of 'the twenty-one tales newly translated from the Russian' in *The Book of the Bear* (London: Nonesuch, 1926), four were by Remizov, and of these four we know that Mirrlees translated at least two: in a postcard to Prince Mirsky, Harrison noted that 'Hope has translated two bear-stories by Remizov—they are the purest Remizov & lovely beyond words.' Harrison to Mirsky, 23 January 1925; in G.S. Smith, 'Jane Ellen Harrison: Forty-Seven Letters to D.S. Mirsky', *Oxford Slavonic Papers*, n.s. 28 (1995): p.79.

the same time that they became friends with the literary historian and critic D.S. Mirsky. Mirsky and Remizov were instrumental in their first Russian translation together, *The Life of the Archpriest Avvakum, by Himself*, which the Hogarth Press published in 1924. But the fact that Remizov edited a Russian-language edition of *Avvakum* for the inaugural issue of *Versty* ['Mileposts'] in 1926, the journal which Mirsky co-edited with Petr Petrovich Suvchinskii and which Harrison helped fund, invites us to place these Harrison–Mirrlees translations in a very different context from that of Bloomsbury and British Russophilia: a visionary program of anti-Soviet cultural nationalism and Russian Orthodox revivalism that mobilized under the name of Eurasianism.[70]

Eurasianism was a messy and fractious movement in the émigré community that sought to counter what it saw as Russia's 'cultural and spiritual enslavement by Europe'—ongoing since the early eighteenth century—with a redemptive vision of Eurasian history and identity.[71] Bolshevism was only the latest manifestation of this alien, European ideology, a materialist antireligious worldview antipathetic to the spiritual authority of the Orthodox Church and 'the elemental, national uniqueness of the non-European, half-Asiatic face of Russia-Eurasia'.[72] The movement had roots in Russian Orientalism and in late-imperial anthropology and ethnography. One of its central myths cast the Mongol invasion of Kievan Rus' in the thirteenth century as precedent for a continental civilization that would unite postcolonial Russia and Central Asia. In 1925, Nikolai Sergeyevich Trubetskoy, one of the movement's leading ideologues, observed how this period of Tartar rule gave rise to 'an intense religious orientation of the inner life of Russians which suffused every product of the spirit, especially art, with its colours'.[73] Leading Eurasianists, critical of the Soviet state, looked to the trauma of the Russian Revolution and Civil War to jumpstart a similar revival of religion and art.

---

[70] On the Hogarth Press connection, cf. Jean Mills, 'The Writer, the Prince and the Scholar: Virginia Woolf, D.S. Mirsky, and Jane Harrison's Translation from the Russian of *The Life of the Archpriest Avvakum, by Himself*—a Revaluation of the Radical Politics of the Hogarth Press', in *Leonard and Virginia Woolf, the Hogarth Press and the Networks of Modernism*, edited by Helen Southworth (Edinburgh: Edinburgh University Press, 2010), pp.150–75. Marilyn Schwinn Smith analyses the Mirrlees-Harrison translations in '"Bergsonian Poetics" and the Beast: Jane Harrison's Translations from the Russian', *Translation and Literature* 20 (2011): pp.314–33. G.S. Smith notes the prominence of *Avvakum* in the first issue of *Versty* in *D.S. Mirsky: A Russian-English Life, 1890–1939* (Oxford: Oxford University Press, 2000), pp.152–3; p.343 fn.83. Nikolai Sergeyevich Trubetzkoy discusses the importance of Avvakum as an example of what might have been had not Western modernity overtaken 'Muscovite Rus'' in 'The Ukrainian Problem' [1927], in *The Legacy of Genghis Khan and Other Essays on Russia's Identity*, edited by Anatoly Liberman (Ann Arbor: Michigan Slavic Publications, 1991), p.249. D.S. Mirsky later reviewed all three of Mirrlees' novels in *Versty*, an accolade they received in no English publication.

[71] Trubetzkoy, 'The Legacy of Genghis Khan: A Perspective on Russian History Not from the West but from the East' [1925], in *The Legacy of Genghis Khan*, p.199.

[72] Trubetzkoy, 'The Legacy of Genghis Khan', p.224.

[73] Trubetzkoy, 'The Legacy of Genghis Khan', p.176. Sergey Glebov provides a rich account of the competing currents of Eurasianist thought in *From Empire to Eurasia: Politics, Scholarship and Ideology in Russian Eurasianism, 1920s–1930s* (DeKalb: Northern Illinois University Press, 2017), pp.39–75.

Early in 1926, Mirrlees published an essay on Remizov in a special 'arts and ideas' issue of the *Journal de Psychologie Normale et Pathologique*, introducing him to French readers as a Russian writer-in-exile and modern-day 'antiquarian'.[74] 'Alexei Mikhailovich is, perhaps, best known as a writer of legends, half fairy, half-apocryphal, in which he captures to a marvel the rhythm and intonation of old Russia', she explains, noting the commitment to vernacular speech he shared with the Old Believer Avvakum and the link to the old religious ways. She proceeds to distinguish Remizov's reparative antiquarianism from the merely 'decorative' approach of the aesthete, who rifles the past for pretty things to combine 'according to his plastic needs' (as would a painter assembling a still life, or *nature morte* in French). The antiquarian, by contrast, makes 'dying' things, not 'dead' ones, 'the object of his quest'.

> Treading in the august footprints of Sir Walter Scott, [Remizov] tracks an old tune to a shepherd whistling it in the hidden valley where it was born, chases winged words with his net, listens to old wives' tales, and hastens to catch the last faltered words of the dying gods.[75]

Remizov's investment in the survivals of 'old Russia'—things dying but not yet dead—marks his descent from the post-Enlightenment romance revival. Mirrlees has Scott's anthologies of border songs and studies of popular superstition in mind, the Scott whose fictional self-portrait in *The Antiquary* (1816) reaches 'instinctively' for 'pencil and memorandum-book' the moment he hears a peasant woman 'chanting forth an old ballad'.[76] Scott's career fused antiquarian recovery and literary invention as did Remizov's, and Harrison and Mirrlees note the novelty of Remizov's 'elaborate style and intensely individual fantasy' which he extrapolates from his ancient materials.[77] But it is as a popular antiquarian hastening 'to catch the last faltered words of the dying gods' that Remizov enters *Lud-in-the-Mist*, in the person of Endymion Leer.[78]

In 1871, E.B. Tylor had shown how 'in the midst' of our modernity we are surrounded by 'primeval monuments of barbaric thought and life'; it needed, he argued, 'but a glance into the trivial details of our own daily life' to see how little we

---

[74] Hope Mirrlees, 'Quelques aspects de l'art d'Alexis Mikhailovitch Rémizov', *Le Journal de Psychologie Normale et Pathologique* 23 (1926): pp.148–59; Sandeep Parmar reproduces Mirrlees' original English typescript in her edition of the *Collected Poems*, pp.75–84. As published, Mirrlees' article followed immediately from an essay by Harrison on the Russian language, 'L'imperfectif dans la langue et la literature', adapted from her *Aspects, Aorists and the Classical Tripos* (1919).
[75] Mirrlees, 'Quelques aspects', pp.153–4; *Collected Poems*, pp.79–80.
[76] Sir Walter Scott, *The Antiquary*, edited by David Hewitt (Edinburgh: Edinburgh University Press, 1995), p.310.
[77] Harrison and Mirrlees, 'Preface' to *The Book of the Bear*, p. x.
[78] Mirrlees, 'Quelques aspects', pp.153–4; *Collected Poems*, pp.79–80. The conceit echoes Mirrlees' and Harrison's description of 'the learned folklorist' who 'sees what lies behind his models—what they have forgotten' in the 'Preface' to *The Book of the Bear*, p. xii.

have left our most distant past behind.[79] Endymion Leer's fictional study—'Traces of Fairy in the Inhabitants, Customs, Art, Vegetation and Language of Dorimare'—performs a similar act of defamiliarization, revealing the secular 'Dorimarite, like a Dutchmen of the seventeenth century, smoking his church-warden among his tulips, and eating his dinner off Delft plates', still immersed in the old religious world (22). *Lud* may conjure a wealth of fantastical exotica—decrepit dragons, pigmy Norsemen, indigo sailors, and fairyland itself—but its greatest act of faith hangs on the presence and power of this ancestral cultural heritage. The novel begins with a trip to the Chanticleer family attic, which turns out to be filled with bric-a-brac from the ducal days. It is our first introduction to the spiritual maturity of the old ways: the robes 'tragic' and 'hierophantic', seemingly unsuited 'to the uses of daily life', the trinkets and toys with 'a curious gravity about their colouring and lines' (12). But the striking feature of this cultural inheritance is that it lies so close to hand. During a childhood game with his friends, Chanticleer seizes 'one of the old instruments, a sort of lute ending in the carving of a cock's head', and plucks a note 'so plangent, blood-freezing, and alluring' that he remains forever haunted by its sound (13). It is a fairy lute, and like the sacred words he later speaks that begin his initiation into the mysteries of Dorimare, it is quite by accident that he plays it. Fairy's power to resacralize the modern world requires none of the labour that Madeleine expended in her primitive dancing; it requires no especial thought.

Looking to define for her French readers the 'aspect' of the exiled Remizov that best expressed his distinctive Russianness, Mirrlees paused to explore the analogy of an Englishness likewise at odds with those presently in power. She ventured the term 'Shakespearean' as the closest equivalent. 'Shakespearean', she explains, does not mean 'very English', as might such institutions of public life as *Punch*, the Book of Common Prayer, or the National Anthem; nor is it identical with the works of Shakespeare, in which the 'accents' of his '*own* voice' are 'unmistakable'. 'Shakespearean' speaks rather to something anonymously English: it is 'applied to the gossip of old village women', she explains, 'to "characters", to the humours of old-fashioned provincial life, to a sort of sweet fooling, and to the strains of that shepherd's pipe that, though it may play different tunes, sounds through the life and traditions of every nation'. 'It is a particular aspect of English things—"the still small voice" of England, which, we flatter ourselves, none but natives can hear.'[80] Mirrlees' conceit cuts against the cosmopolitan impulse to rise above or otherwise disparage national ties and privileges the pastoral and provincial against the modernist metropolis. The words from 1 Kings 19:12 suggest a further analogy, between the God who appeared to Elijah not as a wind, an earthquake, or fire but as a 'still small voice' and a nation no longer beholden to its imperial mission to

---

[79] E.B. Tylor, *Primitive Culture: Researches into the Development of Mythology, Philosophy, Religion, Language, Art and Custom* (London: John Murray, 1871), Vol.1, p.16; p.19.
[80] Mirrlees, 'Quelques aspects', pp.157–8; *Collected Poems*, pp.82–3.

conquer and command. In the words of the King James Bible and of the Quaker hymn set to Sir Hubert Parry's Repton, we sense a cultural and specifically linguistic displacement of the politics of national identity, which as it devolves into the gossip of old village women and the sounds of a shepherd's pipe aspires to lose itself in nature.

For Virginia Woolf as well, the figures of Shakespeare and the antiquarian Scott were instrumental in mediating a mid-century embrace of the nation. Woolf shared none of Mirrlees' religious disposition, amplifying her father's 'muscular' agnosticism into a deep hostility towards God and the established Church.[81] She greeted the news of Mirrlees' conversion in 1929 as dismissively as she had done T.S. Eliot's the year before: 'It is said that Hope has become a Roman Catholic on the sly. Certainly she has grown very fat—too fat for a woman in middle age who uses her brains, & so I suspect the rumour is true.'[82] Her anti-clericalism notwithstanding, Woolf was as interested as Mirrlees in finding sources of enchantment to temper the materialism of modern civilization. Her early fiction had looked to find these sources within, in what she called 'the wedge-shaped core of darkness' that is the privacy of each individual soul, and in those 'moments of being' when our experience seems to touch something sacred, sublime: Lilly Briscoe calls them 'daily miracles, illuminations, matches struck unexpectedly in the dark'.[83] But a parallel track, already legible in *Orlando* and argued forcefully in Woolf's late-career fiction and essays, dials down the emphasis on private epiphanies and transcendental symbols, and on the experimental artwork capable of rendering their truth, towards a contingent but collective vision of national identity. Like Mirrlees, Woolf peels apart the cultural nation from the nation state, insular England from imperial Britain; language and literature are again this England's authentic repository.

## VI. 'between two worlds'

As the portrait of a young aristocrat who ages sixteen years across three-and-a-half centuries, *Orlando* has often been read as the exception to the elegiac mode in which, since *Jacob's Room*, Woolf had sought to recast modern fiction.[84] '*Orlando* is the only one of her books with no deaths', writes Hermione Lee.[85] And indeed,

---

[81] Virginia Woolf, 'A Sketch of the Past', in *Moments of Being: Autobiographical Writings*, edited by Jeanne Shulkind (London: Pimlico, 2002), p.123.

[82] *The Diary of Virginia Woolf. Volume 3: 1925–1930*, edited by Anne Oliver Bell with Andrew McNeillie (London: Hogarth Press, 1980), p.268; entry for 30 November 1929.

[83] Woolf, *To the Lighthouse*, p.69; p.176.

[84] 'I have an idea that I will invent a new name for my books to supplant "novel"', Woolf wrote as she contemplated *To the Lighthouse*. 'A new—by Virginia Woolf. But what? Elegy?' *Diary*, Vol.3, p.34; entry for 27 June 1925.

[85] Hermione Lee, *Virginia Woolf* (New York: Vintage, 1999), p.520.

the novel seems to celebrate permanence, troping continuity in the longevity of great houses and the *longue durée* of literary tradition, both matched to a protagonist of fantastically long life whose 'mind grows rings' as slowly as his beloved oak tree.[86] The organicism derives from Burke and from a common law tradition as old, and as English, as Orlando himself.[87] Like the tree whereof he writes, Orlando is 'English root and fibre'; and in Burke's famous description of the 'natural aristocracy' as 'the great Oaks that shade a Country', we sense the degree to which Orlando's interminable ode, 'The Oak Tree', closes a circle of self-regard.[88] Cynosure of an aristocratic estate some fifteen miles in circumference, Orlando's oak seems primed to argue the Burkean defence of entailed inheritance as the model and guarantee of the nation, its ancient rights and slow-grown customs. But what with Burke we might call Woolf's 'powerful prepossession towards antiquity', her conservative tendency towards thinking of civilization as an intergenerational bequest most attractively embodied in the aristocrat's property and fine breeding, exists alongside a more sceptical conception of history not as a continuum of custom and anonymous transmission but as a series of discrete and discontinuous epochs.[89] It is at the transitions between one age and the next that *Orlando* does its best historical thinking, and here that the deaths pile up. Death is this novel's secret sharer, nor is it only the casualties of the Great Frost or Orlando's many domestics who die. 'For Grimsditch, no, Grimsditch was dead; Bartholemew, no, Bartholemew was dead' (221). Two deaths carry especial weight for Woolf's historical and wider social argument. The first, suggested in the haunting image of Shakespeare glimpsed briefly at the start, is what Woolf in a late essay called 'the death of Anon', the voice of a traditional common culture and the world displaced by Orlando's own rise to view; the second, anticipated with mixed emotion, is Orlando's own.

At stake in this otherwise playful fantasy of English history is an archaeology of the alienated modern subject as a product of capitalist property relations and an ambivalent reflection on what it might mean to sacrifice class privilege for the sake of more than formal equality. Two essays from 1932 directly thematize this ambivalence.[90] 'Abbeys and Cathedrals' and 'This is the House of Commons' contrast the distinction bought in a past age by the concentration of wealth and power in the hands of a few with the present state and future prospects of democracy.

---

[86] The image of the mind I take from Bernard's meditation in *The Waves*: 'The mind grows rings; the identity becomes robust; pain is absorbed in growth.' Virginia Woolf, *The Waves*, edited by David Bradshaw (Oxford: Oxford University Press, 2015), p.154.

[87] Cf. J.G.A. Pocock, *The Ancient Constitution and the Feudal Law: A Study of English Historical Thought in the Seventeenth Century* (Cambridge: Cambridge University Press, 1957).

[88] Virginia Woolf, *Orlando*, edited by Maria DiBattista (New York: Harcourt, 2006), p.89. All subsequent references will be given parenthetically in the body of the text. Edmund Burke, *Selected Letters*, edited by Harvey C. Mansfield Jr. (Chicago: University of Chicago Press, 1984), p.184.

[89] Edmund Burke, *Reflections on the Revolution in France*, edited by Conor Cruise O'Brien (Harmondsworth: Penguin, 1986), p.118.

[90] On Woolf's own investment in the term, cf. Clara Jones, *Virginia Woolf: Ambivalent Activist* (Edinburgh: Edinburgh University Press, 2016), pp.5–7.

The contrast is not, at first, very flattering. 'Abbeys and Cathedrals' begins in flight from the 'democratic helter skelter' of the street, with Woolf seeking sanctuary in a city church among its monuments to a departed elite to spare herself the sight of 'a million Mr. Smiths and Miss Browns', all too 'multitudinous' and 'minute', 'too like each other to have each a name, a character, a separate life of their own'.[91] The tropism towards those who 'rise above the flood and waste of average human life' is nothing new in Woolf.[92] It structures, for example, the opening pages of *The Voyage Out* (1915), set again at rush-hour on a London street, where a crowd of 'small agitated figures' all hurrying to work threatens to engulf two characters whose private income, education, and fine feeling mark them very much apart.[93] Recoiling from the labouring mass, Woolf inclined towards the 'single and substantial', the unique attributes and 'spacious' lives of high-class individuals.[94] Whence, in part, Orlando, whose 'shapely legs' (14) prove him to Elizabeth I 'the very image of a noble gentleman' (84) and to the mistress of Charles II a national asset; Sasha will ravish them with praise, as will their biographer on more than one occasion. The legs were lifted from Vita Sackville-West, whose 'ancestors & centuries & silver & gold' had 'bred the perfect body', but however much they signal a queer desire, they also exceed this intimate connection.[95] In *Orlando*, as in these essays on 'The London Scene', Woolf plays with the possibility that her attraction to aristocratic legs and entitled individuals may prove temporary, that it is a 'morbid symptom', to borrow Gramsci's phrase, of a time when an old world is dying and a new one struggles to be born.[96]

'This is the House of Commons' strains to imagine this new world as it guides the reader from Parliament Square to the Victorian Commons Chamber and on to the great mediaeval Westminster Hall. To each it accords a period and a style of government. The statuary of Parliament Square recalls an age of charismatic personal politics, a time when the minister 'dressed to fit his part', 'shook the air' with his 'fulminations and perorations', 'manipulated facts, toyed with them, elaborated

---

[91] Virginia Woolf, 'Abbeys and Cathedrals' [1932] in *The Essays of Virginia Woolf. Volume 5: 1929–1932*, edited by Stuart N. Clarke (London: Hogarth Press, 2009), p.303; p.301.

[92] Woolf, 'Abbeys and Cathedrals', p.304.

[93] Virginia Woolf, *The Voyage Out*, edited by Lorna Sage (Oxford: Oxford University Press, 1992), pp.3–6. The most challenging example remains Woolf's response to walking on Kensington High Street, a week after the General Strike, when the sight of 'innumerable women of incredible mediocrity, drab as ditchwater' 'almost made me vomit with hatred of the human race'. 'One was actually being sick or fainting in the middle of the street.' Virginia Woolf to Vanessa Bell, 19 May 1926; in *Letters*, Vol.3, p.265.

[94] Woolf, 'Abbeys and Cathedrals', p.301.

[95] *The Diary of Virginia Woolf. Volume 2: 1920–1924*, edited by Anne Olivier Bell with Andrew McNeillie (London: Hogarth Press, 1978), p.306; entry for 5 July 1924.

[96] Antonio Gramsci, '"Wave of Materialism" and "Crisis of Authority"', in *Selections from the Prison Notebooks*, p.276. In 'The Leaning Tower', Woolf turns to Matthew Arnold for the image of a present time stationed between two worlds, 'one dying, the other struggling to be born': 'with a foot in both worlds', the Auden Generation expresses itself in a 'curious bastard language' that is neither 'the rich speech of the aristocrat', nor the 'racy speech of the peasant'. 'It is betwixt and between.' Woolf, 'The Leaning Tower' [1940], in *The Essays of Virginia Woolf. Volume 6: 1933–1941*, edited by Stuart N. Clarke (London: Hogarth Press, 2011), p.272; p.274.

them, and used all the resources of art and eloquence to make them appear what he chose that they should appear to the people who had to accept his will'. This time has passed. On the floor of the House of Commons, the modern politician, 'normal, average, decent-looking', tailors his address 'not [to] the small separate ears' of those present in the chamber but to 'men and women in factories, in shops, in farms on the veldt, in Indian villages', to 'all men everywhere'. His words are clear, grave, and impersonal. Power has passed from 'the hands of individuals to the hands of committees' as 'the intricacies and elegancies of personality' submit to the need for bureaucratic efficiency.[97] Though we might miss the old performative mode, this new featureless impersonality is a necessary adaptation to the scale and complexity of imperial statecraft and an expanding electorate.

Woolf accepts this change as progress, but with all large numbers comes the fear of indistinction. Even to contemplate 'the one thousand six hundred and twenty three million human beings who are, according to statistics, at present in existence', is to confront the spectre of bad infinity, that number posed in absolute negation of the precious individual.[98] And although, in her fiction, Woolf rather courts the infinite than not—witness the impersonal perspectives opened up by geological time and by imperial and interstellar space—the terrifying numberlessness of other people poses a rather different problem to the liberal imagination that pictures society as an aggregate of individuals than does the abstract speculation of a world without the self. In Raymond Williams' classic account of Bloomsbury politics, Woolf and her friends could think society only in terms of the free and civilized persons they considered themselves to be: against the acknowledged evils of imperialism, militarism, discrimination, and poverty, Bloomsbury retaliated not with 'any alternative idea of a whole society', but with an appeal 'to the supreme value of the civilized *individual*, whose pluralisation, as more and more civilized individuals, was itself the only acceptable social direction'.[99] A purpose of Woolf's writing was to multiply from among her readers as many such individuals as she could; but that still left the mass, and the question of how to mitigate their number by making the persons they denote more homely, less strange.

The wishful framing of British imperial decline as an opportunity to convert a sprawling global empire, exploitative and undemocratic, into a compact and vital national culture had here its role to play by striking those 'Indian villages' and 'farms on the veldt' from the equation and by drawing on native resources, both material and spiritual, to compensate their loss. Woolf drew on this vision of a post-imperial England, its nation-scaled economy and participatory democracy dressed in the mantle of ancestral culture and tradition, to solve the problem

---

[97] Virginia Woolf, 'This is the House of Commons' [1932], in *Essays*, Vol.5, p.327.

[98] Virginia Woolf, *A Room of One's Own* and *Three Guineas*, edited by Morag Shiach (Oxford: Oxford University Press, 1992), p.147.

[99] Raymond Williams, 'The Bloomsbury Fraction', in *Culture and Materialism: Selected Essays* [1980] (London: Verso, 2005), p.165.

of strangers in the mass. In the Commons chamber, she notes, there had been 'nothing venerable or time-worn, or musical or ceremonious' to beautify the business of democracy; the space was 'as shiny and as ugly as any other moderate-sized public hall'.[100] But what the Victorian Commons lacked in age and authenticity, Westminster Hall enjoys in abundance. Its 'immense dignity' causes all who pass under its 'vast dome' to appear 'minute, perhaps pitiable; but also venerable and beautiful'. The 'little men and women' who on the street had seemed so contemptible strike Woolf as benign as they move 'soundlessly' across the floor like 'small nameless animal[s]'. In 'a vast cathedral' like this, Woolf can almost imagine wanting herself to be thus transformed. 'Let us rebuild the world then as a splendid hall', she moves to conclude, and see 'whether democracy which makes halls' does not 'surpass the aristocracy which carved statues'.[101]

But at this point, envisioning a future 'age of architecture', Woolf's 'dreaming progress' falters. She notices the policemen on guard 'at every door to see that we do not hurry on with our democracy too fast' and recalls the short hours the Hall is open to the public. The perfection of democracy will take time—a hundred years at least—and while she waits, a familiar hesitation returns. Woolf recalls how, under the Hall's hammerbeam roof, stood King Charles 'when they sentenced him to death; here the Earl of Essex; and Guy Fawkes; and Sir Thomas More'. 'The mind, it seems, likes to perch, in its flight through empty space, upon some remarkable nose, some trembling hand; it loves the flashing eye, the arched brow, the abnormal, the particular, the splendid human being.'[102] We may add Orlando's legs and Vita's perfect body to the list as Woolf takes her place alongside David Hume and Sir Walter Scott: pioneers in philosophy and the modern novel of the hesitation between democratic idealism and reactionary sentiment. Hume's explanation of his historical biases—'My views of *things* are conformable to Whig principles; my representations of *people* to Tory prejudices'—applies as easily to Scott; and like much later Woolf, Hume confessed to have 'shed a generous tear for the fate of Charles I and the Earl of Stratford', even as he rejected, at least in principle, the social forms for which they stood.[103] *Orlando* is just such a 'perch', a concession to that 'tendency in our corrupt mind soaked with habit' to honour the 'splendid human being' while we wait for a more fair and just society.[104]

To honour, but also to historicize, for Orlando enters 'the present moment' with a 'shock' which is not simply the sensorium's raw exposure to metropolitan perception. 'Braced and strung up by the present moment she was also strangely afraid' (235), as though 'Nineteen Hundred and Twenty-Eight' (241) promised some

---

[100] Woolf, 'This is the House of Commons', p.324.
[101] Woolf, 'This is the House of Commons', pp.327–8.
[102] Woolf, 'This is the House of Commons', p.328.
[103] David Hume to John Clephane, ?1756; and David Hume, 'My Own Life'; in *The Letters of David Hume. Volume 1: 1727–1765*, edited by J.Y.T. Greig (Oxford: Oxford University Press, 1932), p.237; p.4.
[104] Woolf, 'This is the House of Commons', p.328.

'terrifying revelation' (219). The novel does not disclose of what, but the signs all point towards an end to Orlando's class and way of life, perhaps also to her craft. These were the years, writes Peter Mandler, 'of [the] desertion, demolition and disuse' of the great house.[105] Woolf's sentimental attachment to these houses and to the people that lived in them is a matter of record, but she was not oblivious to the shrinking material base of the British aristocracy. Revenues from the land had long been in decline, with the end of wartime agricultural subsidies further weakening the stream. If this made grand houses increasingly hard to maintain, the doubling of the top rate of death duty in 1919 and its further increase in 1925 put their inheritance very much in question. Stationed at the threshold of the democratic 'age of architecture', Orlando's hyperbolically large, three-hundred-and-sixty-five-bedroom house is shown for the last time, 'as frail as a shell, as iridescent and as empty' (232). Like its owner, the great house enters mid-century no longer fit for purpose. All *Orlando* can do is replicate in its closing motions the same escape—from the modern city, from the ancestral home—that Sackville-West had herself been driven to perform, a private disappearing act into the timeless patterns of 'The Land' (the title of Sackville-West's long poem from 1926 which is the model for Orlando's oak-tree labours.) That the land could no longer support the great house is one of the novel's ironies. And when Orlando's oak tree rejects the poem that she has written it in tribute, the earth being too shallow above the roots to allow her to bury it as intended, we may sense a further cut. In essays contemporary with the writing of *Orlando*, Woolf predicted that poetry, having held herself so long 'aloof in the possession of her priests', would not survive the transition to a 'democratic age'.[106] By this logic, both aristocrats and poets are living, in 1928, on borrowed time. They will join 'the bustard and the wild cat' as species now extinct.[107] And for so long as Whig head and not Tory heart prevail, *Orlando*'s closing strokes of midnight sound a faintly optimistic note. The break-up of the great estates, the mummification of country houses, the end to 'days of single men and personal power', and of poets and their priestcraft: these tendencies call time on an age of 'splendid' individuals and their uncounted social cost.

## VII. 'to enforce the individual'

When first we meet Orlando, swiping with his sword at a severed head in the attic of his 'gigantic' family home (11), he stands where Woolf's two great metaphors of the Elizabethan age converge: a 'lumber room' at the top of a 'great house'.

---

[105] Peter Mandler, *The Fall and Rise of the Stately Home* (New Haven: Yale University Press, 1997), p.253.
[106] Virginia Woolf, 'The Niece of an Earl' [1928], in *Essays*, Vol.4, p.563; Virginia Woolf, 'Poetry, Fiction and the Future' [1927], in *Essays*, Vol.4, p.434.
[107] Woolf, 'Niece of an Earl', p.563.

These locations date the reign of Elizabeth as the beginning of capitalist modernity, forging connections between primitive accumulation and the emergence of the modern subject, colonial expansion and the contraction of social ties. Locations, more particularly, of literary modernity, the great house and the lumber room link the formal developments that will culminate in *Orlando*'s experimental method to originary and ongoing acts of dispossession. Woolf's 'days of the small separate statute' start here, with severed African heads in the attic, Indian peafowl in the garden, and an English country house secured by a great 'ring of wall'.[108]

Woolf's materialist inquiry into the sources of the self comes into focus a few pages later, when Orlando in haste dons 'crimson breeches, lace collar, waistcoat of taffeta, and shoes with rosettes on them as big as double dahlias' to greet a queen 'caparisoned in all sorts of brocades and gems' (16–17). The novel floats a series of mock-philosophical questions about whether clothes wear us or we wear them, whether clothes are 'a symbol of something hid deep beneath' (138–9). In fact, it is the existence of this psychological 'something' that is at stake in the scene, Woolf's costume drama alerting us to the novelty of a self that wants to be seen and heard, to make its presence felt. 'What desire was it', Woolf was later to ask of Elizabethan couture, 'that prompted this extraordinary display?' 'The cost was great; the discomfort appalling; yet the fashion prevailed. Was it perhaps the mark of an anonymous unrecorded age to enforce the individual; to make one's physical body as bright, as definite, as marked as possible?'[109] That this self-display required new and unlovely methods of surplus extraction Woolf is quite ready to admit. It was always her belief that it took a certain amount of psychological and surplus capital to erect and maintain a self, a range of resources (the luxury, for example, of a room of one's own and five hundred pounds) to support an autonomous subjectivity. Nor did she restrict her argument to writers. In the historical long view that *Orlando* lays out, this psychological support fund takes its first instalment from acts of violent expropriation.

Woolf dramatizes the emergence of the modern subject against a history of overseas expansion and, at home, of ruling-class appropriations of church and common land. Thus, we find Elizabethan literature 'strewn with gold and silver; with talk of Guiana's rarities and references to that America—"O my America, my new-found-land"—which was not merely a land on the map, but symbolized new territories of the soul'.[110] Territorial and literary conquests converge upon the self, but not all voyages of discovery can be so romantically sung. Well might Orlando sleep while Elizabeth puts her hand and seal to the parchment that makes over 'the great monastic house that had been the Archbishop's and then the King's to Orlando's father' (18). Only in the twentieth century will the image of a 'cowled

---

[108] Virginia Woolf, 'The Elizabethan Lumber Room' [1925], in *Essays*, Vol.4, pp.53–61; Woolf, 'This is the House of Commons', p.327; Woolf, *The Waves*, p.9.
[109] Virginia Woolf, 'Anon', in *Essays*, Vol.6, p.588.
[110] Woolf, 'The Elizabethan Lumber Room', p.56.

figure, monastic, severe' become visible again, the dissolution of the monasteries revealed as part-prerequisite for the house's subsequent career as a stage for 'splendid dancers', soldiers, poets, and 'great men' (233). The history of enclosure is meanwhile made literal in the image of Orlando's country estate, ringed around its fifteen-mile circumference with a brick wall ten feet high. Lest we miss the point, in Turkey Orlando is made to confront the so-called 'gypsy point of view' that equates an English 'Duke' with 'a profiteer or robber': both '[snatch] land and money from people who [rate] these things of little worth', or who are powerless to protect their customary claims (109).

Woolf's late essay 'Anon' drives home the price of all this Renaissance self-fashioning. Orlando may not dispute the gypsy Rustum's claim that her ancestors had indeed 'accumulated field after field' in such a manner as would brand them 'adventurer[s]' today (109–10).[111] But it is through Hugh Latimer's travels in sixteenth-century England that Woolf draws attention to 'the poor starving without a goose or a pig for the great were enclosing the fields', to 'the peasants ... starving' and 'everywhere the great houses rising'.[112] From his oak tree elevation, Orlando surveys the neighbouring countryside,

> counting, gazing, recognizing. That was his father's house; that his uncle's. His aunt owned those three great turrets among the trees there. The heath was theirs and the forest; the pheasant and the deer, the fox, the badger and the butterfly. (15)

Woolf's history of enclosure, the privatization of resources previously held in common, issues in descriptions of the modern metropolis where each 'long avenue of brick is cut up into boxes, each of which is inhabited by a different human being who has put locks on his doors and bolts on his windows'.[113] A familiar Marxist analysis reads privacy as a record of the legitimation of property, and in the term's migration to describe an autonomous selfhood modelled on the domestic interior, the translation of alienated property into an inalienable property of the universal subject. For Woolf, the alienation of material and psychological resources proceeds in synch, accumulation by dispossession and the history of self-possession indices of each other's progress. Absent in the panorama, the mediaeval serf freed to sell their labour. Absent, likewise, the fabric of feudal community once held together by 'tracks across the fields joining manor house to hovel, and hovel to church'. Such paths once joined together 'the great house and the small' in a common culture.[114]

---

[111] Burke was more comfortable with the idea: 'long usage mellows into legality' tenures that were 'violent in their commencement', he observes in *Reflections on the Revolution in France*, p.276.
[112] Woolf, 'Anon', pp.586–7.
[113] Woolf, 'Poetry, Fiction and the Future', p.432.
[114] Woolf, 'Anon', p.583; Brenda R. Silver, '"Anon" and "The Reader": Virginia Woolf's Last Essays', *Twentieth-Century Literature* 25, nos.3/4 (1979): p.406.

In the beginning, minstrels travelled these paths, 'lifting a song or a story from other people's lips, and letting the audience join in the chorus'. They lived 'a roaming life crossing fields, mounting the hills, lying under the hawthorn to listen to the nightingale'.[115] Later, as dispersed patterns of settlement became nucleated 'and roads, often flooded, often deep in mud, led from the cottage to the Manor, from the Manor to the church', Anon would sing his songs 'at the back door to the farm hands and the maid servants'; he would stage 'his pageant in the churchyard, or later was given a pitch for his drama in the market place'. Finally, he crossed the threshold of the great house. In 'Anon', that honour belongs to Spenser: we meet him 'standing at the threshold of the "gay and sumptuous house"', slowly separating himself and his craft from that of 'the minstrel; from the chronicler; and from his audience'.[116] Woolf credits Spenser as the first writer to become 'word conscious; an artist; aware of his medium'.[117] As literature refined its means, it refined also its mode of production; the writer turned his back on the audience that laboured outdoors and sought instead 'soft pillows, easy chairs, silver forks, private rooms'.[118] And so we meet Spenser 'on the threshold of the great house', 'half in shadow, half in light'. 'Sunk in shadow' is that part of him that still has access to the 'depths' of an immemorial culture, 'those long years of anonymous minstrelsy, folk song, legend and words that had no name attached to them'; cast in the light is the part of him 'aware of his art ... asking for recognition, and bitterly conscious of his relation to the world, of the world's scorn'.[119]

In *Orlando*, that figure on the threshold is Shakespeare. He is still sufficiently shrouded in the anonymity of popular song to admit doubt about his name and function: 'Was this a poet? Was he writing poetry? ... So Orlando stood gazing while the man turned his pen in his fingers, this way and that way; and gazed and mused; and then, very quickly, wrote half-a-dozen lines and looked up' (17). Long Woolf's model of the impersonal author, 'at once the best known and the least known of all writers', the image of 'Sh—k—re' seated at the servants' table has a distinctly historical 'ambiguity'.[120] Orlando's 'earliest, most persistent memory' (121)—a 'fat, shabby man' 'sitting at the table, as I peeped in on my way downstairs' (59)—is of a figure caught in the transition from ancient minstrelsy to a literary modernity that pays for its wordcraft and powers of analysis in its alienation from the people.[121] Shakespeare is present at the passing; he witnesses 'the death of Anon' as the old, outdoor theatre gives way to 'the theatre of the brain', the 'playwright' to 'the man who writes a book', and 'the audience' to 'the reader'.[122]

---

[115] Woolf, 'Anon', pp.581–2.
[116] Woolf, 'Anon', p.589.
[117] Woolf, 'Anon', p.590.
[118] Virginia Woolf, 'Reading' [1919], *Essays*, Vol.3, p.145.
[119] Woolf, 'Anon', pp.590–1.
[120] Silver, '"Anon" and "The Reader"', p.431; Woolf, 'Anon', p.585.
[121] Woolf, 'Anon', p.582; p.599.
[122] Woolf, 'Anon', pp.598–9.

It is as a reader that Orlando walks the corridors and crypts of his enormous house when he retreats from court and from his courtship of Sasha to 'a life of extreme solitude' (51). He takes as his guide Sir Thomas Browne, whom Woolf credited as the first writer to have found his soul an undiscovered country to rival any in the New World, its prodigies as various and every bit as profitable.[123] As the 'first of the autobiographers', Browne had a further distinction: for unlike Shakespeare, everywhere invisible on the page, Browne was the first to stamp his writing 'with his own idiosyncrasies'. With Browne 'we first become conscious of the impurities which hereafter stain literature with so many freakish colours'; with him, the emancipated 'rainbow' of personality first issues in a proprietary style.[124] Woolf regards 'colour' as the hallmark of a capitalist literary culture that cultivates identity through the solicitation of difference and stability though the call to make it new. And she implicates her own experimental method squarely in this history of sartorial and stylistic self-display. For though she held a 'colourless' style, 'like blue skimmed milk at the bottom of the jar', the measure of perfect art and turned for inspiration not only to pre-modern balladry but also the protocols of modern science and philosophy, Woolf was well aware that the pursuit of impersonality might rather issue in a more colourful text than in the transparent work of art capable, like the minstrel's, of shrouding audience and artist in collective anonymity. *Orlando* exhibits Woolf's most famous formal innovations—her 'lyric vein', her trademark descriptions of the multiplicity of the subject and of the world as seen without a self—as signature-bearing techniques. Named in quotation, as when Woolf references the 'Time Passes' section of *To the Lighthouse* in one of Orlando's odes to nature, the hermeticism of high modernism—its fabled difficulty, philosophical rigour, lyrical intensity—stands revealed as a strategy paying for the subtlety of its vision in its social marginality.

Orlando admits himself 'haunted' by the memory of what his own 'disease of reading', his 'scourge' of writing (56), and his pursuit of personal fame displaced. His quest for a privacy adequate to his precocious interiority, the desire to be in 'his private room alone' (82), 'for ever and ever and ever alone' (14), frames as a function of character the same process of enclosure that builds a ten-foot wall around an estate, securing the great house 'in its green island of park' from the pedestrian traffic of peasants and minstrels.[125] As the 'tracks across the fields, joining manor house to hovel', become blocked, the moral economy of paternalism, of feudal obligation and social conciliation, falls apart: where before there had 'always' been 'a warm corner for the old shepherd in the kitchen', 'always food for the hungry' (78), now there is none. Class antagonism, social atomization, cultural specialization, all follow as these paths become impassable, grassed over, and lost to sight.

---

[123] Woolf, 'Reading', p.155; Woolf, 'The Elizabethan Lumber Room', p.58.
[124] Woolf, 'The Elizabethan Lumber Room', p.59.
[125] Woolf, 'Anon', p.587.

But as the 1930s wore on, Woolf came to believe that they could be walked once more. Aerial archaeology had revealed that these lines etched into the landscape by long use, these contours of a common culture, remained visible from above.[126] The airman could see what Woolf now so much desired—the 'world beneath our consciousness; the anonymous world to which we can still return'.[127] Aerial photographs, published in specialist periodicals like *Antiquity* and in full-page spreads in the national press, became a metaphor for the paths a reoriented literary culture might learn to travel again.

## VIII. 'English geese'

When, in *Orlando*'s closing pages, the famous goose takes flight (241), a series of substitutions unfolds in dazzlingly quick succession.[128] Woolf inserts herself into the narrative, displacing Sackville-West, and summons the spirit of Shakespeare one last time. 'Always it flies fast out to sea and always I fling after it words like nets', Orlando reflects, 'which shrivel as I've seen nets shrivel drawn on deck with only sea-weed in them. And sometimes there's an inch of silver—six words—in the bottom of the net. But never the great fish who lives in the coral groves' (229). Woolf's metaphors of the artist's craft and philosopher's quest left Sackville-West confused. 'I simply cannot make out what was in her mind', she confessed to her husband. 'What does the wild goose stand for? Fame? Love? Death? Marriage?'[129] The joke lost on Vita was, at one level, what Hermione Lee calls 'the joke for Vita', the play on her name and its Latin translation and on the V-shaped pattern of a skein of geese.[130] But it was also the joke '*on* Vita', Woolf's 'Dearest Donkey West': proof that however 'perfect' she thought her body, Woolf had doubts about her 'brain'.[131] These doubts extend to Orlando, in the 'effect noble birth has upon the mind and ... how difficult it is for a nobleman to be a writer' (59). But when she cries out into the night, 'The goose!' (241), Orlando peels apart from her character original and the novel, which in its infancy Woolf had promised Vita would be 'all

---

[126] 'From an aeroplane ... you could still see, plainly marked, the scars made by the Britons; by the Romans; by the Elizabethan manor house; and by the plough ...' Bart Oliver observes in *Between the Acts* (Harmondsworth: Penguin, 1972), p.7. On aerial archaeology, see Kitty Hauser, *Shadow Sites: Photography, Archaeology & the British Landscape 1927–1955* (Oxford: Oxford University Press, 2007).

[127] Woolf, 'Anon', pp.583–4.

[128] Virginia Woolf, 'The Royal Academy' [1919], *Essays*, Vol.3, p.92.

[129] Quoted in Victoria Glendinning, *Vita: The Life of V. Sackville-West* (New York: Knopf, 1983), p.204.

[130] Lee, *Virginia Woolf*, p.515. In draft, the 'single wild bird' (241) that flies overhead at Orlando and Shelmerdine's reunion is the last in a flock of 'wild geese' 'flying, in the shape of a v, each with a long neck outstretched'. Virginia Woolf, *Orlando: The Original Holograph Draft*, edited by Stuart Clarke (London: Stuart Nelson Clarke, 1993), pp.283–4.

[131] Of Sackville-West Woolf wrote in her diary: 'She is stag like or race horse like ... & has no very sharp brain.' Woolf, *Diary*, Vol.2, pp.306–7; entry for 5 July 1924.

about you and the lusts of your flesh and the lure of your mind', leaves us with another mind entirely.[132]

'No biographer could possibly guess this important fact about my life in the late summer of 1926; yet biographers pretend they know people'—so Woolf described her vision of 'a fin passing far out', 'a fin rising on a wide blank sea'.[133] First glimpsed when she was finishing *To the Lighthouse*, Woolf would claim it took *The Waves* to finally catch 'that fin in the waste of waters'.[134] A private vision, jealously guarded, the fin would seem to affirm Woolf's injunction as much to the biographer as to the modern novelist to 'Look within' and to symbolize the mystic union of modernist subjectivity and experimental artwork.[135] But we cannot disregard the humour that accounts any such quest a fool's errand. The joke on 'Vita' and the meaning of 'Life' may still direct some readers to Woolf's self-described 'philosophy', 'that behind the cotton wool is hidden a pattern', a model of meaning and connection discoverable through art.[136] But if the first draft of *Orlando* dissolves its answer to the question of life in ellipses, the second eliminates all suggestion.[137] Woolf's early manifesto 'Modern Fiction' (1919/1925) had compared 'two fictions ... immeasurably far apart': the Russian firm in its belief 'that if honestly examined life presents question after question which must be left to sound on and on after the story is over in hopeless interrogation', and the English, whose tendency is to pre-empt any such discovery with a deflationary joke. *Orlando* sits squarely on the English side of the scale, endorsing the 'voice of an ancient civilization which seems to have bred in us the instinct to enjoy and fight rather than to suffer and understand'.[138] It is English to accept that the meaning of life is a goose not worth the chase, and to delight instead in the idiom's literary and popular pedigree: for it was Shakespeare who helped coin the phrase and Burton who accounted the sport, along with other English pastimes, a suitable cure for melancholy.[139]

To land the goose this way is to content ourselves with a very different order of the symbol, a different derivation of the imagination. Rather than gaze, with

---

[132] For Elena Gualtieri, the closing pages 'push aside Sackville-West's literary achievements and substitute for them Woolf's own dazzling performance'. Gualtieri, *Virginia Woolf's Essays: Sketching the Past* (Basingstoke: Palgrave, 2000), p.113. Sean Latham partners the literary and the biographical trajectory, noting how 'Vita Sackville West, after whom Orlando was styled, gradually fell out of Woolf's favor, in part because she failed the ideal of her fictional counterpart'; the Orlando we are left with in the novel is not Sackville-West but 'the "aristocrat in writing" Woolf imagined herself to be'. Latham, *Am I a Snob? Modernism and the Novel* (Ithaca: Cornell University Press, 2003), p.107.

[133] Woolf, *Diary*, Vol.3, p.113 and p.153; entries for 30 September 1926 and 4 September 1927.

[134] *The Diary of Virginia Woolf. Volume 4: 1931–1935*, edited by Anne Olivier Bell with Andrew McNeillie (London: Hogarth Press, 1982), p.10; entry for 7 February 1931.

[135] Woolf, 'Modern Fiction', p.160.

[136] Woolf, 'A Sketch of the Past', p.85.

[137] The manuscript concludes: 'The wild goose is— / "The secret of life is . . . . "' Woolf, *Orlando: The Original Holograph Draft*, p.287.

[138] Woolf, 'Modern Fiction', pp.163–4.

[139] William Shakespeare, *Romeo and Juliet*, Act 2 Sc.3; Robert Burton, *The Anatomy of Melancholy*, edited by Thomas Faulkner, Nicholas Kiessling and Rhonda Blair (Oxford: Clarendon Press, 1990), Vol.2, p.72.

Coleridge, at the 'Translucence of the Eternal through and in the Temporal' or correlate Woolf's 'moments of being' to a world replete with 'symbols, harmonious in themselves and consubstantial with the truths, of which they are the conductors', *Orlando* suggests that we take a page from Hume.[140] Whereas Coleridge's model of the imagination directs us away from the contingency of social arrangements towards the absolute truth of a Logos consubstantial with Christ, Hume instructs us to appreciate the 'customary connexions' that order a community's common sense of the world. It is with Hume that we laugh at the 'whimsical condition of mankind, who must act and reason and believe; though they are not able, by their most diligent inquiry to satisfy themselves concerning the foundation of these operations, or to remove the objections which may be raised against them'; with Hume we embrace the 'folly' of philosophy and determine that, 'If I must be a fool, as all who reason or believe anything certainly are, my follies shall at least be natural and agreeable.'[141]

Recent criticism has indeed shown Hume seated at Woolf's phantom table, placing Woolf within a 'History of English Thought' that encompasses her father's eighteenth-century thinkers and the twentieth-century Apostles G.E. Moore and Bertrand Russell. Ann Banfield, Gillian Beer, Cairns Craig, and Loraine Sim have all shown Woolf engaging Hume's sceptical epistemology, following the path of rational doubt—a path illuminated in her own time by the complementary insights of physics and Cambridge Philosophy—with a 'modern fiction' that withdraws from the world of common sense to a world made strange by reflection.[142] But if the phase of alienating reason delivers Woolf's lyric interludes and critical defamiliarization effects, it is the opposite but equal impulse, in which the imagination reasserts the power of custom and convention, that underwrites Woolf's mid-century reclamation of the nation. Both phases are integral to a Humean conservative scepticism, and to the degree that Woolf's career seems to privilege one and then the other, we may trace the relative emphases of a high and late modernist aesthetic.

Woolf's fictions of the 1920s abound in allegories of the Humean philosopher, doomed to pass between solipsism and social cheer, compelled by turns to inhabit and then surrender their citadel of privacy for the self-forgetful pleasures

---

[140] Samuel Taylor Coleridge, *Lay Sermons*, edited by R.J. White (Princeton: Princeton University Press, 1972), p.49; p.29.

[141] David Hume, *An Enquiry Concerning Human Understanding*, edited by Peter Millican (Oxford: Oxford University Press, 2007), p.117. And Hume, *A Treatise of Human Nature: Being an Attempt to Introduce the Experimental Method of Reasoning into Moral Subjects*, edited by Ernest Campbell Mossner (London: Penguin, 1985), p.317.

[142] Gillian Beer, 'Hume, Stephen, and Elegy in *To the Lighthouse*', in *Arguing with the Past: Essays in Narrative from Woolf to Sydney* (London: Routledge, 1989), pp.183–202; Ann Banfield, *The Phantom Table: Woolf, Fry, Russell and the Epistemology of Modernism* (Cambridge: Cambridge University Press, 2000); Cairns Craig, *Associationism and the Literary Imagination: From the Phantasmal Chaos* (Edinburgh: Edinburgh University Press, 2007), pp.239–84; Loraine Sim, *Virginia Woolf: The Patterns of Ordinary Experience* (Farnham: Ashgate, 2010).

of community. Like Hume before her, Woolf figures the voyage out and the voyage in as alternating phases of subjectivity. The clearest statement of this psychosomatic rhythm comes from Peter Walsh, when he describes a soul 'who fish-like inhabits deep seas and plies among obscurities threading her way between the boles of giant weeds, over sun-flickered spaces and on and on into gloom, cold, deep, inscrutable', but who then 'suddenly ... shoots to the surface and sports on the wind-wrinkled waves; that is, has a positive need to brush, scrape, kindle herself, gossiping'.[143] In gossip, chatter, traffic, and talk, Woolf admits 'a positive need' for absorption in the illusory surfaces of everyday life. The opposite and equal pole of attraction is privacy and therewith a need, no less positive, to retreat from the 'fever of living' into the fastness of the self.[144] To seek out 'the sociability of the streets' after the 'solitude of one's own room' is 'the greatest pleasure', writes Woolf, but it is equally 'comforting', as we return to our rooms, 'to feel the old possessions, the old prejudices, fold us round, and shutter and enclose the self'.[145]

This oscillation between periods of social integration and separation represents the end point of the Humean journey of philosophy, which begins in naive acceptance of the world of appearance and passes through a stage of debilitating scepticism before it arrives at this happy adjustment to the competing claims of reason and belief. Hume's 'true philosophy' requires a compromise between the 'cogitative part of our natures' and the 'sensitive', or between the human tendency to doubt and 'the natural propensity of the imagination' to accede to a customary, common-sense reality.[146] Crucially, the common life to which we return is no longer what it was to the incurious and un-philosophical mind: to the true philosopher who has practised the sceptical interrogation of custom and appearance, the social world we rejoin has its only reality as a 'fiction' of the imagination. But it is a fiction to be welcomed, its philosophical insufficiency no impediment to our enjoyment of it. Only a false philosopher would sacrifice the illusions we share for the private fantasy of an ultimate truth.

Applied to aesthetics, Hume's epistemology underwrites not only an experience of reading in which ironic detachment and sentimental identification hold each other at bay, but also a mode of relation to the invented traditions of romantic cultural nationalism, the period's remarkable mobilization of memory and association to populate the empty term of the new nation state and cement its imagined community. By this Humean derivation, the imaginedness of this community, the inventedness of these traditions, cannot be reckoned as mere cognitive delusion or ideological fraud, though these are the valences of 'fiction' that have come to accompany the terms. A 'true philosopher's' defence of the nation acknowledges it to be a figment of the imagination, one to which we may give our qualified

---

[143] Woolf, *Mrs Dalloway*, p.157.
[144] Woolf, *Mrs Dalloway*, p.56.
[145] Virginia Woolf, 'Street Haunting: A London Adventure' [1927], in *Essays*, Vol.4, p.480; p.491.
[146] Hume, *A Treatise of Human Nature*, p.273; p.243; p.260

consent and in which we may take pleasure, while still reserving the option of critique. For of course 'reason' demurs. Reason reminds Woolf that 'as a woman, I have no country. As a woman, I want no country. As a woman my country is the whole world.' And yet, 'when reason has had its say, still some obstinate emotion remains, some love of England dropped into a child's ears by the cawing of rooks in an elm tree, by the splash of waves on a beach, or by English voices murmuring nursery rhymes'.[147] These associations, a distillate of childhood memories from St Ives, blend nature and nursery with popular poetry and vernacular speech, the materials of romance; they render England a non-transcendent symbol in the best tradition of eighteenth-century associationist psychology.

As Peter has taught us, the soul delights in gossip; and gossip, on the rebound from philosophy, is of a different order, the medium of a common life in which we may take our pleasure but never again quite fully immerse. For we have only to listen to the idioms of our social life with a sentimental ear to begin to think, with Eleanor in *The Years*, 'What a lovely language', and to hear, in the 'commonplace words, spoken by Celia quite simply, but with some indescribable burr in the r's', the sounds of a patriotism more palatable than songs sung in military-imperial or patriarchal unison.[148] In *The Waves*, Bernard acknowledges himself the 'inheritor', the 'continuer', of a tradition that descends in broken phrases, snatches of verse, the nonsense of the nursery: '"Hark, hark, the dogs do bark", "Come away, come away, death", "Let me not to the marriage of true minds" and so on.'[149] It is from this stock of living speech and remembered literature that Woolf creates her Pointz Hall poetry in *Between the Acts*. For its encore, Woolf's pageant of English history has the cast declaim 'some phrase or fragment from their parts': '... *I am not* (said one) *in my perfect mind* ... Another, *Reason am I* ... *And I? I'm the old top hat.... Home is the hunter, home from the hill*', and on until we hear again '*Hark, hark, the dogs do bark*' and the recitation draws to a close.[150] These 'orts, scraps and fragments' come before the audience, as they do the reader, without captions or credits: decontextualized, decanonized, they represent the ancestral remains and living, linguistic matrix of our national life together.

Thus Woolf confessed herself 'divinely happy', during a visit to Dorset in April 1926, 'in a country, at a moment, which really made one feel ashamed of England being so English, and carpeting the woods and putting the cuckoos on trees, and doing exactly what Shakespeare says'.[151] The pleasure is in the palimpsest, of

---

[147] Woolf, *A Room of One's Own* and *Three Guineas*, p.313.
[148] Virginia Woolf, *The Years*, edited by Hermione Lee (Oxford: Oxford University Press, 1999), p.197.
[149] Woolf, *The Waves*, p.152; p.155.
[150] Woolf, *Between the Acts*, p.129.
[151] Virginia Woolf to Raymond Mortimer, 27 April 1926; quoted in Julia Briggs, "'Almost ashamed of England being so English": Woolf and Ideas of Englishness', in *At Home and Abroad in the Empire: British Women Write the 1930s*, edited by Robin Hackett, Freda Hauser and Gay Wachman (Newark: University of Delaware Press, 2009), pp.97–8.

poetry seeming to overlay a landscape, a national literature 'not printed, bound or sewn up, but somehow the product of trees and fields and the hot summer sky'.[152] Implicit in the 1919 essay 'Reading', but by her career's end insistently argued, is a fantasy of literature's emancipation from the libraries where books are chained down and locked up to circulate as the linguistic *combinatoire* of our common life.[153] Words liberated from the printed page become the free indirect discourse of a community of common readers, remaking the nation in its image as a 'common ground' where all may trespass with impunity. No longer the 'private ground' of the privileged, words assert a democratic freedom of association to breach the walls of Orlando's vast estate and of our own, more private, pales of consciousness.[154] They form the *paroles en liberté* of a national culture marked less by a singular agreed-upon content than by labile, lapsable trains of association. In their pure form, they become gossip, as when Woolf describes a group of nurses chatting while they tend to their charges: 'they were talking—not shaping pellets of information or handling ideas from one to another, but rolling words, like sweets on their tongues; which, as they thinned to transparency, gave off pink, green and sweetness.'[155]

Like the combinations of a kaleidoscope, these 'Words without meaning—wonderful words' connote the aesthetic object of associationist psychology, empty in themselves but fillable with personal memories and social values.[156] Thus, to Eleanor, the sound of elm trees suggests 'England' in the episode of *The Years* that Woolf thought 'about the best, in that line, I ever wrote', and to Isa, in *Between the Acts*, 'the burden ... laid on me in the cradle; murmured by waves; breathed by restless elm trees; crooned by singing women; what we must remember; what we would forget'.[157] The injunction to remember, the fear of forgetting, establishes 'England' as a pattern of associations conjured by the imagination's fictive power, associations that may be shared, that can even forge an imagined community, but that will last only as long as they are thus combined in memory. In its first iteration, the fear of erasure explains what Cairns Craig has called 'the anguish that afflicts Romantic nationalisms', 'their desperate effort to maintain the associative power of their common culture' against the violent and all too visible dislocations of modern state formation.[158] But with nationalism resurgent in the 1930s, Woolf's approach to the nation emphasizes rather the ontological humility of the

---

[152] Virginia Woolf, 'Reading', p.142.
[153] Woolf, *A Room of One's Own* and *Three Guineas*, p.244.
[154] Virginia Woolf, 'The Leaning Tower', p.274; pp.276–7.
[155] Woolf, *Between the Acts*, p.11.
[156] Woolf, *Between the Acts*, p.147.
[157] Woolf, *The Years*, p.198. *The Diary of Virginia Woolf. Volume 5: 1936–1941*, edited by Anne Olivier Bell with Andrew McNeillie (London: Hogarth Press, 1984), p.18; entry for 18 March 1936. Woolf, *Between the Acts*, p.109.
[158] Cairns Craig, 'Coleridge, Hume and the Romantic Imagination', in *Scotland and the Borders of Romanticism*, edited by Leith Davis, Ian Duncan and Janet Sorensen (Cambridge: Cambridge University Press, 2004), p.34.

associationist model and its basic unit, the individual train of thought which, while capable of aggregation, retains its discrete, and potentially dissenting, independence. Composed from the trifles to which it returns, Woolf's England is designed to hold at bay the compulsions of fanaticism and the predatory integration of the transcendental imagination.

England's path-marked landscape and living language, its words patinated by prior use, helped Woolf identify with her fellow citizens and with the project of democracy, solving her problem of people in the mass by enchanting the 'million Mr. Smiths and Miss Browns' with the aura of romance. Framed and contained by sceptical reason, Woolf's mid-century reflections on national destiny and identity took a page from Sir Walter Scott. She adored his novels' stock of 'chatter and gossip', the 'images, anecdotes, illustrations drawn from sea, sky and earth', which seem to 'race and bubble' from the 'lips' of his 'common people'. *The Antiquary* was her favourite, a domestic national tale that devotes its pages, not to historical upheaval, but to 'talk—ostlers talking, old beggars talking, gypsies talking, postmistresses talking', all of them talking 'as if they would talk their hearts out'.[159] Scott's ear for the vernacular informed Woolf's fragile faith in the 'world beneath our consciousness' which survives in words and phrases, linguistic fragments of a common culture that binds the present to the past and softens the effects of social change. *The Antiquary*'s celebration of custom and continuity, its narrative suspension of violence and rupture, served her purpose well. This counterrevolutionary Scott was not, however, the Scott that did most service at mid-century. The Scott the organized Left revived, and who features in the following chapters, wrote epics of national becoming, of mass mobilizations and political emergencies. Rather than *The Antiquary*, it was the more eventful and conflict-rich narratives of *Waverley* (1814), *Old Mortality* (1816), and *Ivanhoe* (1819) that furnished the mid-century Marxist reading of Scott as the pioneering chronicler of social development, a critical realist whose reactionary politics could never cancel or conceal the dialectics of historical change.

---

[159] Virginia Woolf, 'The Antiquary' [1924], in *Essays*, Vol.3, pp.455–7.

# 2
# Migrations of the Communist Historical Novel

## I. Between Proletkult and Boom

The mid-century reactivation of the historical novel was a global phenomenon, a response to a national turn in world politics. At a time of systemic instability, as paramountcy passed from the imperial powers of old Europe to the emerging superpowers of the Cold War, capital and labour laid claim to the nation and fought for its control. In the cultural war of position that followed, the historical novel resumed the role it had played when the nation was new: inventing traditions for the communities of nations in change, questioning the meanings of national belonging, and projecting the people's destiny. The embrace of the nation was not socialism's alone, and the historical novel was by no means a proprietary technique of the Left, but it is on the Left that the genre consolidated a culture of lasting importance, one that reaches beyond the decade to which it is sometimes assigned and that in its global reach exceeds any one national literature. This chapter maps the travels of the communist historical novel, pausing on some of its principal theoretical articulations and formal elaborations. It looks to match a sense of the genre's extension in space—its critical mass and geographical spread—with a consideration of the unique qualities and ideological entanglements of particular people and places. Stations in this journey include Paris and Moscow, London's Jewish East End, and the coasts and islands of the Caribbean. From a combination of familiar and forgotten names and texts, this chapter frames the mid-century communist historical novel as a 'vanishing mediator' in the rise of two of the most important critical and creative projects of the second half of the twentieth century: radical social history and magical realism.[1]

This genealogy of magical realism has begun to be mapped, and what follows owes a debt in method and material to Michael Denning's account of 'The Novelists' International' (2001). Denning writes to connect a first generation of writers 'who now constitute the emerging canon of the world novel'—among them Gabriel Garcia Marquez, whose *Cien años de solidad* [*One Hundred Years of Solitude*]

---

[1] The image of a process that 'vanishes in its own result, leaving no trace behind', derives from Marx's analysis of money in the first volume of *Capital*; Fredric Jameson reworks it as a principle of historical analysis in 'The Vanishing Mediator: Narrative Structure in Max Weber', *New German Critique* 1 (1973): pp.52–89.

(1967) often figures as the breakthrough book for this new corpus of fiction—to their 'roots' in the 'international literary movement that emerged in the middle decades of the twentieth century under the slogans of "proletarian literature", "neo-realism", and "progressive", "engaged", or "committed" writing'.[2] The origins of a socialist literary culture predate the Bolshevik Revolution, but after 1917 actions to organize this formation and make of it a movement gathered pace. At the Second Conference of the Communist International in August 1920, delegates moved to establish a 'temporary International Bureau of the Proletkult', and by the early 1930s the infrastructure for a 'Red International of Literature' was firmly in place.[3] Denning describes how this 'international of writers' came to span both 'the globe and the century', and to simplify his story he focuses on two main phases of production: the early tenement and factory novels, often animated by avant-garde aesthetics and the ambition to capture from below the metropolitan perception of canonical modernism; then, the full-scale novels and novel-sequences of the postwar era, narratives of the subaltern subject in national-historical time. His examples here are the great banana trilogy of Miguel Ángel Asturias (1950–60), Naguib Mahfouz's Cairo Trilogy (1956–57), Pramoedya Ananta Toer's Buru Quartet (1980–88), and aslant these epics of postcolonial subject formation and national becoming, the magical realism of the Latin American Boom. Different formal languages, locations, and narrative subjects mark these two phases, but it is an access of historicity that announces 'the moment of fruition, when writers shaped by the radical literary movement produced [their] major works'.[4]

To explain the transformation, Denning adopts a psychoanalytic conceit. Historical content, repressed in the 'often powerful portraits of factories and cities' of the 1920s and early 30s, returned in the marvellous reality of the Boom with all the force and familiarity of the cultural uncanny. As a means of capturing the breathtaking originality of Alejo Carpentier's *El reino de este mundo* [*The Kingdom of this World*] (1949), its folding of metropolitan surrealism into the colonial historicity of the Haitian revolution, the metaphor is indeed fitting. And Denning is

---

[2] Michael Denning, 'The Novelists' International', in *Culture in the Age of Three Worlds* (London: Verso, 2004), pp.51–2. As Denning explains, at stake in the label of 'world literature' that attaches to a novel like *One Hundred Years of Solitude* are two competing histories of global cultural exchange: one, of a market in global cultural commodities and a discourse of elite cosmopolitanism, the other, a history of insurgent social movements, movement cultures, and 'the promise of the old internationalism'; he offers his essay as an 'experiment' in the kind of 'emancipatory transnational cultural studies' that might keep alive the latter (p.11; pp.33–4).

[3] *The Second Congress of the Communist International, as Reported by the Official Newspapers of Soviet Russia* (Washington, D.C.: Government Printing Office, 1920), pp.110–11. For discussion of a '"Literary International" patterned after the Comintern', see David Pike, *German Writers in Soviet Exile, 1933–1945* (Chapel Hill: University of North Carolina Press, 1982), pp.27–8. The reference to a 'Red International of Literature' comes from Johannes Becher, 'The War Danger and the Tasks of Revolutionary Writers', *Second International Conference of Revolutionary Writers. Reports. Resolutions. Debates*, special issue of *Literature of the World Revolution* (n.d.) [1931], pp. 41–2. See, more recently, the studies by Katerina Clark and Rossen Djagalov already cited, and the essays in *Comintern Aesthetics*, edited by Amelia Glaser and Steven Lee (Toronto: University of Toronto Press, 2020).

[4] Denning, *Culture in the Age of Three Worlds*, p.54.

surely right to regard the thematic shift—from the factories and tenements themselves to the rural migrations that populated them—as opening the proletarian novel to a 'larger historical sensibility'.[5] In the psychogeography of the peasant migrations the 'Novelists' International' discovered the shape of a world-historical process, one requiring a new narrative language to describe the violent dislocations of primitive accumulation and to capture the clash of modern and mythic, peasant and proletarian, mentalities. Magical realism supplied a register, both experiential and analytical, for recounting these forced transitions to capitalism. But to explain the return of history in magical realism, and with it, 'the unleashing of desire and utopia' (previously censored under the puritanical regime of proletarian realism), as so many derivatives of the narrative unconscious obscures the extent to which this historical turn was also conscious and coordinated.[6]

## II. 'National in form and socialist in content'

It is here that a return to the Popular Front is in order, which at its convocation in 1935 officially authorized the mobilization of nationalist rhetorics, the mining of national historical resources, radical traditions, and cultural idioms to combat the present threat of fascism in the European and world arenas.[7] Announcing its shift from the largely unsuccessful 'Third Period' policy of sectarian class struggle to one of courted cooperation with mass-based anti-fascist and anti-imperialist movements, the Communist International introduced a new line on nationalism. 'We Communists are the *irreconcilable opponents, in principle*, of bourgeois nationalism in all its forms', General Secretary Georgi Dimitrov instructed delegates at the Comintern's Seventh World Congress in Moscow on 2 August 1935. 'But we *are not supporters of national nihilism*, and should never act as such.' Identifying his own conduct in the Reichstag Fire Trial as motivated by pride in 'being a son of the heroic Bulgarian working class', Dimitrov drew the new Party-line conclusion: '*National forms* of the proletarian class struggle and of the labour movement in the individual countries are in no contradiction to proletarian internationalism; on the contrary, it is precisely in these forms that the *international interests* of the proletariat can successfully be defended.'[8]

This new line on nationalism clarified developments already underway inside the Soviet Union, from Stalin's 'socialism in one country' thesis first aired in 1924 and codified as policy through 1926 to the introduction of socialist realism after 1932. In February 1934, speaking at the Seventeenth Congress of the CPSU, Stalin announced the completion of the Soviet experiment; the First Five Year Plan had

---

[5] Denning, *Culture in the Age of Three Worlds*, p.67.
[6] Denning, *Culture in the Age of Three Worlds*, p.70.
[7] Dimitrov, *The Working Class against Fascism*, p.72.
[8] Dimitrov, *The Working Class against Fascism*, pp.70–1; emphasis in the original.

succeeded in creating a socialist economy purged of all capitalist remainder and the proletarian cultural revolution had run its course. With consolidation the order of the day, the patriotism previously reviled as 'Great Power chauvinism' could now be repurposed as the legitimate love and necessary defence of the communist project. Some contemporary observers registered this ideological reorientation as a sign of compromise or capitulation, an abdication of socialism's properly universal horizon of world revolution. Leon Trotsky bewailed what he called the 'Soviet Thermidor' in his 1936 pamphlet *The Revolution Betrayed*, and for the émigré historian, Nicholas Timasheff, the revival of patriotic sentiment was further proof of Russia's 'Great Retreat' from Marxist principle.[9] But though the promotion of Bolshevik nationalism inside the Soviet Union and of revolutionary nationalism beyond its borders tended to downplay the concept of class struggle in favour of the people's interests and agency, the kinds of identification that came with this shift were not any less anti-capitalist or less committed to the socialist struggles of other nations. Nor was the Marxist canon wholly without precedent for articulating a discourse of radical populism and cross-class alliance.[10] As Dimitrov insisted in 1935, national and class-based identities were not in theory contradictory, and in practice mid-century communists easily combined their allegiances, braiding international proletarian and anti-colonial solidarities with the new language of the nation.

As the 'nation' and the 'people' replaced the 'workers of the world' in the rhetoric of the Communist International, so in the literary culture of the 'Novelists' International' the present-set narratives of factory, farm, and tenement began to make way for novels of the people's histories of struggle. Dimitrov's address was here instrumental, and it had an immediate impact on how communists came to think of the historical novel. Less than six weeks previously, in June 1935, when the celebrated German historical novelist Lion Feuchtwanger addressed the first International Congress for the Defence of Culture in Paris, he had been at pains to defend the genre from the charge of irrelevance, if not outright reaction. Feuchtwanger was willing to admit that the historical novel had fallen on hard times, that it would likely conjure ideas of 'adventure, intrigue, costumes, bright and lurid colours,

---

[9] Nicholas Timasheff, *The Great Retreat: The Growth and Decline of Communism in Russia* (New York: Dutton, 1946), pp.151–91. These criticisms would resurface thirty years later as the European and North American New Lefts sought to establish their difference from the Old. Compare, for example, in the Italian tradition, Alberto Asor Rosa's critique of Gramsci's concept of the national-popular in *Scrittori e popolo* (1965); and in the British context, Perry Anderson's take-down of E.P. Thompson's 'populism' and 'messianic nationalism' in 'Socialism and Pseudo-Empiricism', *New Left Review*, no.35 (1966): pp.33–9.

[10] Lenin, for example, had reflected at length on Marx's description of the 1871 Paris Commune as attempting a 'real people's revolution'. For Lenin, to mobilize 'the mass of the people' meant embracing 'both the proletariat and the peasants. These two classes constituted the "people"', their 'alliance' the 'precondition' for any 'socialist transformation'. V.I. Lenin, 'The State and Revolution', in *Collected Works. Volume 25, June–September 1917*, edited by Stepan Apresyan and Jim Riordan (Moscow: Progress Publishers, 1964), pp.421–2. It was from statements like this that Antonio Gramsci developed his 'concept' of the 'national-popular' in the late 1920s.

silly emotional talk, love and politics all jumbled up and world-historical events made the backdrop for little, personal passions'. But historical fiction did not have to be written and read as escapist light literature; in the right hands, it could be 'a weapon ... to honour past victories and defeats, and to bring to mind our legends'.[11] His speech came with a warning. 'Incidentally', he noted, 'our opponents also know the advantages of this weapon: in line with their ideology, they are forging bloody, sentimental myths out of the history of humanity and reanimating the historical novel with their stale clichés.'[12]

The historical novel was indeed a major genre in Nazi Germany. Bernt von Heiseler observed in 1935 how a 'whole new literature of historical fiction' had 'sprung up' since Hitler's accession to power. As German writers rediscover their 'national and pedagogical purpose', he wrote, the 'old, well-tested and too often obituarised historical novel' is proving its worth as a major 'tool of national education'.[13] This was certainly how Werner Beumelberg approached the genre; he saw in it a means to legitimate Hitler's Third and thousand-year Reich by chronicling its origins and early anticipations. Beumelberg's novels of Bismarck (1932) and Frederick the Great (1938) celebrated the state-makers, but it is the yearning of the soldier and outlaw Jörg for 'the Reich that is to come' that best captures the mood and ambition of the National Socialist historical novel. In the closing decades of the seventeenth century, the peasant hero of Beumelburg's *Mont Royal* (1936), and of the spin-off stories 'Let Our Reich Come' (1941) and 'Jörg' (1943), travels the territories of the Holy Roman Empire; France encroaches from the West, the Ottomans from the East, and 'Germany' is still only an idea, like a 'secret word' known only by initiates. Of the empire that exists, leaderless and weak, Jörg describes it as 'flesh without bones, a house without a frame'. It is the empire of the future that Jörg 'loves', for which he 'longs', and for which all sacrifice, all 'blood and cruelty' will be justified. 'One must be willing to die for this kingdom and for one's faith in it. One's faith must be so strong that nothing can shake it, for only out of such a faith can the kingdom come.'[14]

---

[11] Lion Feuchtwanger, 'Vom Sinn und Unsinn des historischen Romans', in *Paris 1935: Erster internationaler Schriftstellerkongreß zur Verteidigung der Kultur. Reden und Dokumente*, edited by Wolfgang Klein (Berlin: Akademie Verlag, 1982), p.293.

[12] Feuchtwanger, 'Vom Sinn und Unsinn', p.298.

[13] Bernt von Heiseler, 'Segen und Unsegen des historischen Romans', *Das deutsche Wort* 11 (1935): p.6. According to the University of Innsbruck's *Projekt historische Roman*, a searchable online database of all historical fiction published in Germany between 1780 and 1945, the number of historical novels published in the 1930s more than doubled the output of the 1920s. https://webapp.uibk.ac.at/germanistik/histrom/cgi/graph.cgi [accessed 9 August 2023].

[14] Werner Beumelburg, *Mont Royal: Ein Buch von himmlischen und vom irdischen Reich* (Oldenburg: Stalling Verlag, 1936), p.63; p.114; 'Unser Reich komme', in *Geschichten vom Reich*, edited by Karl Plenzat (Leipzig: Hermann Eichblatt Verlag, 1941); *Jörg*, issued by the 'Kraft durch Freude' section of the German Labour Front (Stuttgart: Deutsche Volksbücher, 1943), p.12. In 1933, Beumelburg was elected to the reorganized Preußische Akademie der Künste; he later became its secretary. For the publisher Heinrich Stalling he edited the influential 'Schriften an die Nation' series. Alongside Beumelburg, notable examples of NS historical novelists include: Hans-Friedrich Blunck, first president of Goebbels'

It was to meet the blood-and-soil propaganda of the Right that in 1935 Dimitrov called on communists to set the record straight. 'The fascists are rummaging through the *history* of every nation so as to be able to pose as the heirs and continuators of all that was exalted and heroic in its past', he explained in a widely quoted passage. Communists must therefore seize back the national story and educate the people that they may become heirs to their own revolutionary inheritance. 'Communists', he concluded,

> who do nothing to enlighten the masses on the past of their people in a historically correct fashion, in a genuinely Marxist, a Leninist-Marxist, a Leninist-Stalinist spirit, who do nothing *to link up their present struggle with its revolutionary traditions and past*—voluntarily relinquish to the fascist falsifiers all that is valuable in the historical past of the nation, so that the fascists may bamboozle the masses.[15]

Dimitrov's instruction to join the struggle for the national-popular past was promptly disseminated along the circuits of international communist culture; more detailed suggestions on how to translate this policy prescription into creative practice followed. Here, the five foreign-language editions of the Soviet journal, *International Literature*, were particularly effective. Notwithstanding local variations of content, the combined effect of these journals' editorials, reviews, serializations, and excerpts was to establish the norms and parameters of a progressive national-historical culture. Less subtle in their powers of suggestion were the so-called Soviet 'controversies' that *International Literature* communicated to its audiences abroad. English-language readers were thus brought up to speed on the ban on Demian Bedny's libretto for the comic-opera *The Bogatyrs* (1936) and on the rationale for repudiating the Pokrovskii school of historiography.[16] However unfamiliar the original references, the lessons to be drawn from these Soviet scenes of correction were clear. Meanwhile, prominent critics weighed in on the

---

Reichsschrifttumskammer and the author of a myth-historical trilogy celebrating Germany's Nordic prehistory, *Die Urvätersaga* (1926-28; republished 1934), as well as portraits of *König Geiserich* (1936) and *Wolter von Plettenberg* (1938), anticipatory *Führer*-figures both; Josefa Behrens-Totenohl, whose novels of fourteenth-century peasant life, *Der Femhof* (1934) and *Frau Magdlena* (1935) had sold over half a million copies by 1942; Austrian novelist Mirko Jelusich was also a major contributor to the genre, with novelized biographies of Caesar, Cromwell, and other proto-Hitlers. Come the War, historical novelists like Blunck and the Bulgarian writer Fani Popova-Mutafova played a prominent role in Nazi efforts to organize a *völkisch* pan-European literature.

[15] Dimitrov, *The Working Class against Fascism*, p.70.

[16] Bedny had made the mistake of parodying the *bogatyrs*, the mediaeval knights of popular Russian legend, just when *narodnost'* was emerging as one of the cardinal virtues of Soviet socialist realism. The radically materialist historiography of Pokrovskii and his students, hitherto ascendant, relegated individual agency and the drama of nation state formation to the margins, emphasizing in their stead the impersonal logic of class struggle in a capitalist world-system; in the new climate, Pokrovskii's brilliantly schematic readings of the role of modes and relations of production represented a direct challenge to the call for heroic and human-scaled histories. Cf. Platon Kerzhentsev, 'Falsification of the Historical Past', *International Literature*, no.5 (May 1937): pp.76-83; F. Gorokhov, 'An Anti-Marxist Theory of History', *International Literature*, no.9 (September 1937): pp.73-7.

emerging canon of Soviet historical fiction and debated the qualities that should define a communist historical novel elsewhere.

For anglophone readers, the September 1937 'Writers and History' issue of *International Literature* carried especial weight. The issue led with Stalin's 'Remarks' on the writing of Soviet historical textbooks (co-signed by Kirov and Zhdanov, and first published in *Pravda* in January 1936), and followed with a series of programmatic essays on the historical novel. Through each of these pieces, treating variously of the historical novel of the German writers in exile, the reactivation of the genre by writers associated with the Popular Fronts in Europe, and the embarrassing success of Margaret Mitchell's *Gone with the Wind* (1936) in the US, the outline of a properly communist historical novel can be seen coming into focus. 'Revolutionary writers must create a historical novel that is true to life and will show the workers that in their struggle for freedom they are heirs of everything good that humanity has accomplished.'[17] 'A genuine historical attitude and a genuine folk character, a search for heroes not among humanist solitaries but in mass movements, an eagerness to arouse the great heroic popular tradition that unites the entire struggle of mankind for liberation, a unity of pathos and of knowledge—these are the features of a truly revolutionary historical novel.'[18] The editors listed a number of promising historical novels by writers aligned with the Popular Front movement in Europe: Jean Cassou's 1935 novel of the Paris Commune, *Les massacres de Paris* ['The Massacres of Paris']; Bruno Frank's biographical novel, *Cervantes* (1934; translated 1935 as *A Man Called Cervantes*); Gustav Regler's novel of the German peasants' war, *Die Saat* ['The Seed'] (1936); Ramon Sender's novel of the Spanish Cantonal rebellion, *Míster Witt en el Cantón* (1935; translated in 1937 as *Mister Witt among the Rebels*); and Sylvia Townsend Warner's *Summer Will Show* (1936), whose action culminates in the French revolutions of 1848. But they added that none of these novels had yet perfected the formula; the novel truly adequate to 'the task of lifting the fighting traditions of the popular movement and transforming them into a mighty contemporary weapon' remained to be written. 'We are awaiting a historical novel in which the writer, synthesizing the vast experience of the contemporary struggle of two worlds [Soviet and Western], from the height of this experience shall interpret the past centuries with the wisdom of a Marxist and the enthusiasm of a fighter.'[19]

Refracted, elaborated, and variously triangulated in each local literary context, this call for 'a truly revolutionary historical novel' was enthusiastically received and writers around the world rallied to the cause. In some cases, uptake was

---

[17] A. Startsev, 'The Civil War and the Contemporary American Historical Novel', *International Literature*, no.9 (September 1937): p.72.

[18] E. Knipovich, 'Problems of the Historical Novel', *International Literature*, no.9 (September 1937): p.69.

[19] 'Writers and History', *International Literature*, no.9 (September 1937): p.51; Knipovich, 'Problems of the Historical Novel', p.69.

immediate; in others, the novels took time to write. It is through a logic of combined and uneven development that we must map the diffusion of this communist-aligned genre at mid-century, alert to the tempo of particular political struggles and to local structures of suppression and censorship. But the following names, titles, dates, and places may capture something of the historical novel's place in the culture of the 'Novelists' International' after 1935. In the United States, Howard Fast began his self-styled 'one-man reformation' of the genre with *The Last Frontier* (1941), a return to 1776 and a decisive moment in the American Revolution; he dedicated it to his father, 'who taught me to love not only the America that is past, but the America that will be'.[20] Many more novels followed. In Australia, Katharine Susannah Prichard wrote a trilogy of novels on the history of the Western goldfields.[21] In Brazil, Jorge Amado continued his Cacao cycle with the novel he considered his best, a history of primitive rebellion in the badlands of the North East.[22] In China, the revolutionary historical novel chronicled the years of struggle against nationalist oppression and foreign invasion.[23] In Egypt, Naguib Mahfouz wrote three of a planned forty-book cycle of historical novels on the model of Sir Walter Scott, blending the cultural nationalism of Taha Hussein and the socialism of Salama Moussa.[24] In India, Rahul Sankrityayan, imprisoned for organizing among the peasants in Bihar, wrote his remarkable transtemporal travelogue, *Volgā se Gaṅgā* [*From the Volga to the Ganges*] (1943) and Mulk Raj Anand his 'Punjab' or 'Village' trilogy.[25] In Indonesia, radicalized by his visits to communist China in the late 1950s and participation in the Soviet-sponsored

---

[20] 'Howard Fast', in *Current Biography: Who's News and Why, 1943*, edited by Maxine Bock (New York: The H.W. Wilson Company, 1944), p.200. Fast deserves special mention for his massive international and especially Soviet-world audience; cf. Rossen Djagalov, '"I don't boast about it, but I'm the most widely read author of this century": Howard Fast and International Leftist Literary Culture, ca. Mid-Twentieth Century', *Anthropology of East Europe Review* 27, no.2 (2009): pp.40–55.

[21] Katharine Susannah Prichard, *The Roaring Nineties* (1946); *Golden Miles* (1948); and *Winged Seeds* (1950).

[22] Jorge Amado, *Terras do Sem Fim* [*The Violent Land*] (1943; translated 1945).

[23] Prominent examples include Du Pengchen's *Baowei Yan'an* ['Guarding Yan'an'] (1954), Mo Yang's *Qingchun zhige* ['The Song of Youth'] (1958) and Luo Guangbin and Yang Yiyan's *Hongyan* (1961), translated as *Red Crag* in 1978. Cf. David Der-wei Wang, *The Monster That Is History: History, Violence, and Fictional Writing in Twentieth-Century China* (Berkeley, CA: University of California Press, 2004), pp.163–5.

[24] Naguib Mahfouz, *'Abath al-Aqdar* [*Mocking the Fates*, more recently translated as *Khufu's Wisdom*] (1939); *Radubis* [*Rhadopis of Nubia*] (1943); and *Kifah Tiba* [*Thebes at War*] (1944) all celebrate Egypt's ancient past and rhapsodize her resistance to foreign invaders, the Fifteenth-Dynasty Hyksos inviting comparison with the contemporary British.

[25] The British Marxist historian Victor Kiernan translated Sankrityayan's novel in 1946, but strangely omitted the final episode of this eight-thousand-year odyssey of human migration and social change. *From Volga to Ganga. A Picture in Nineteen Stories of the Historical, Economic and Political Evolution of the Human Society from 6000 b.c. to 1922 A.D* (Bombay: People's Publication House, 1947) ends in 1922, with criticism of Ghandi's politics of non-violence, rather than in 1942, with the decision of that story's protagonist to join the 'people's war' for the defeat of fascism and defence of the Soviet Union. Left World Books have since put out a complete edition (2021), edited by Kanwal Dhaliwal and Maya Joshi. Mulk Raj Anand's trilogy comprises *The Village* (1939), *Across the Black Waters* (1940), and *The Sword and the Sickle* (1942); it chronicles the transformations the British colonial system wrought on the Indian rural economy and concludes with its protagonist, Lal Singh, now a peasant organizer and

Afro-Asian Writers' Conference in Tashkent in 1958, Pramoedya Ananta Toer adapted his new-found version of socialist realism to 'the theme of Indonesia's National Awakening', writing his way 'step by step ... to the roots of its history'.[26] In colonial Korea, the proletarian novelist Kim Namcheon pioneered the Marxist 'family chronology novel' in *Taeha* ['Great River'] (1939) and its unfinished sequel, 'Tongmaek' ['Artery'] (1945–47).[27] In Senegal, the writer and Soviet-trained filmmaker Ousmane Sembène explored the wellsprings of popular resistance in his novel of the 1947–48 railroad strike in French West Africa, *Les bouts de bois de Dieu* [*God's Bits of Wood*] (1960), and later in the films *Emitaï* (1971) and *Ceddo* (1977).

This is a handful of the writers who in the middle decades of the twentieth century took up the historical novel, modulating Soviet prescription and nineteenth-century precedent to their own narrative needs. Their fictions made heroes of past radicals and raised to what E.P. Thompson called 'first-class citizenship of history' the losers and lost causes, the failed insurrections and premature political expressions of the people.[28] Though national in scope, their works travelled widely. Trafficking in a romantic sensibility, they mobilized a politics of historical identification that translated across borders, forging international solidarity with popular struggles present and past. A German translation of British writer Geoffrey Trease's *Bows Against the Barons* (1934), for example, which cast Robin Hood as the leader of a peasant rebellion fighting to build 'the England of equality and freedom', was spotted in Barcelona during the Spanish Civil War.[29] Trease had wanted 'to expose ... the falsity of the romantic Merrie England image' with the novel's grim depiction of mediaeval serfdom and the privations of the outlaw life, and it was this that resonated in the USSR; the novel's Russian translator

---

in prison, but still preaching 'the ways of struggle'. Mulk Raj Anand, *The Sword and the Sickle* (London: Jonathan Cape, 1942), p.368.

[26] Pramoedya Ananta Toer, 'My Apologies, in the Name of Experience', translated by Alex G. Bardsley, *Indonesia* 61 (1996), p.4. Of Pramoedya's 'step by step' recovery of Indonesia's radical history, the tetralogy of novels he composed during his long imprisonment under the Suharto regime is the most famous. First recited to fellow inmates in the early to mid-1970s, and then published (and banned) between 1980 and 1988, the 'Buru Quartet' chronicled Indonesia's National Awakening in the early twentieth century; also composed on Buru were the long historical novels *Arus Balik* ['The Current Turns'] (1995) and *Mata Pusuran* ['The Whirlpool'], about the fall of the Majapahit maritime empire, and *Arok-Dedes* [*Arok of Java*] (1999), which offered the rise to power of Ken Arok in the thirteenth century as a precedent for Suharto's *coup d'état*. Two novels of an earlier trilogy were among the works destroyed at the time of Pramoedya's arrest in 1965; only *Gadis Pantai* [*The Girl from the Coast*] (1962) survived, a fictionalized account of the life of his grandmother.

[27] Kim Namcheon, *Scenes from the Enlightenment: A Novel of Manners*, translated by Charles La Shure (Champaign, IL: Dalkey Archive Press, 2014).

[28] E.P. Thompson, 'Homage to Tom Maguire', in *Making History: Writings on History and Culture* (New York: New Press, 1994), p.54.

[29] Geoffrey Trease, *Bows Against the Barons* (London: Martin Lawrence, 1934) and *Pfeile gegen Barone*, translated by Willi Schulz (Moscow: Verlagsgenossenschaft ausländischer Arbeiter in der UdSSR, 1935); recounted in Trease, *Bows Against the Barons*, revised edition (Leicester: Bockhampton Press, 1966), p.152.

was reminded 'of the conditions his own grandfather had known'.[30] The English translation of Jorge Amado's novel of the 'cacao rush' in Bahia, Brazil reminded the US children's historical novelist Meridel le Sueur of her own country's history of 'gold rushes', 'bonanza wheat farms', and 'bloody fights over timber'; she praised the book for its ability to capture 'the common accent, experience and hope' that links 'North and South America'.[31] On a visit to Poland in 1951, the Australian-born British communist and novelist Jack Lindsay learned that his novel of the persecution of Protestants under Queen Mary had struck a local chord. Lindsay had written *Fires in Smithfield* (1950) to mine the parallel between Catholic Spain's grip on British domestic policy in the 1550s and the UK's post-war submission to the United States, but in Poland, the novel's 'account of the harried protestant underground' tapped raw and recent memories 'of wartime oppression under the Nazis'.[32]

Read and reviewed outside their country of origin, these novels became models for new novels. Mikhail Sholokhov's epic narration of the Cossacks, *And Quiet Flows the Don* (four volumes, 1928–40), inspired Ngũgĩ wa Thiong'o to chronicle Kenya's history of resistance to colonial rule.[33] Ilya Ehrenburg's account of *The Fall of Paris* (1942) inspired the Burmese novelist and politician Thein Pe Myint to write *Ashei-ga nay-wun htwet-thi-pama* ['As Sure as the Sun Rises in the East'] (1958), a revolutionary *Bildungsroman* of the years 1936–42 which revisits his earlier novel, *Thabeik-hmauk kyaung-tha* ['The Student Boycotter'] (1938), to cast its account of the 1936 Rangoon University students' strike in a wider, national-historical perspective. It would be a mistake, therefore, to equate the national-particularism of the communist historical novel with a contraction of literary or political horizons. The national turn did not cancel the internationalism of the 'Novelists' International'. On the contrary, the conviction that the national story could be wrested from those in power and returned to the people inspired a new and no less global literature than the present-set proletarian tales of the 1920s. The communist historical novel mobilized national and regional difference to confront the system and culture of capitalist imperialism, but it did so in the same old name of freedom and more than formal equality. Its writers took Dimitrov at his

---

[30] Geoffrey Trease, *A Whiff of Burnt Boats. An Early Autobiography* (London: Macmillan, 1971), p.164.

[31] Meridel le Sueur, 'Cacao Rush', *New Masses* 56, no.11 (11 September 1945): p.28.

[32] Jack Lindsay, *Fires in Smithfield: A Novel of Mary Tudor's Reign* (London: Bodley Head, 1950); *Łuny nad Smithfield*, translated by Bronisław Zieliński (Warsaw: Czytelnik, 1951). Jack Lindsay, 'The Fullness of Life: The Autobiography of an Idea', undated typescript, p.189; Jack Lindsay Collection, University of Technology Sydney Library.

[33] 'The story of this heroic resistance: who will sing it? Their struggles to defend their land, their wealth, their lives: who'll tell of it?' So wonders the narrator of *Petals of Blood* [1977] (London: Penguin, 2002), p.81. Ngũgĩ completed the novel on a writer's vacation in Yalta while a guest of the Soviet Writers' Union. He recalls 'the spell' Sholokhov cast on the writing of *A Grain of Wheat* (1967) and *Petals of Blood* in a 1984 interview with Maureen Warner-Lewis; collected in *Ngũgĩ wa Thiong'o Speaks: Interviews with the Kenyan Writer*, edited by Reinhard Sander and Bernth Lindfors (Oxford: James Currey, 2006), p.221.

word, that only socialism could 'signify the *saving of the nation*', its opening up 'to loftier heights'.[34]

## III. 'national-historical time'

One text overshadows and has come to obscure this broad cultural formation. Written in Moscow in the winter of 1936–7 and published as articles through the following year, Georg Lukács' *The Historical Novel* has been hailed as 'perhaps the single most monumental realization of the varied program and promises of a Marxist and dialectical literary criticism'.[35] But this dazzling deployment of critical method served a more immediate literary-political aim, that of showing why 'the historical novel can and surely will play an enormous part' in the anti-fascist and anti-colonial struggle.[36] In a famous argument, Lukács pegged the rise of the historical novel to the 'awakening of national sensibility and with it a feeling and understanding for national history' in the wake of the French Revolution (25), and he mapped its decline onto the progressive reification of intellectual life under capitalism, the closeting of bourgeois consciousness within ever more narrow, self-deluding ways of regarding the world. Modernism's fascinations with interiority and formal autonomy signified, for Lukács, a betrayal of the novel's high cognitive vocation to narrate the social whole and so make knowable the direction of history (252). But in surveying the present situation, Lukács saw reason to hope. 'The contradictory tendencies of the age—the decay of the imperialist period and the democratic protest of the masses, literary decadence and the yearning for popular roots—affect the writer in a contradictory and criss-cross fashion' (254), he wrote, but with the right push, that writer may find her way back to Scott and to 'a fruitful assimilation of the classical inheritance' (344).

Lukács' hopes for a revival of the national-historical novel reflected a deep identification with the Comintern's rightward turn after 1935. Isaac Deutscher once described Lukács as elevating 'the Popular Front from the level of tactics to that of ideology', projecting 'its principle into philosophy, literary history and aesthetic criticism'.[37] The description fits, though Deutscher is wrong to read it solely as

---

[34] Dimitrov, *The Working Class against Fascism*, 72.
[35] Fredric Jameson, 'Introduction', to Georg Lukács, *The Historical Novel*, translated by Hannah and Stanley Mitchell (Lincoln: University of Nebraska Press, 1983), p.1.
[36] Georg Lukács, *The Historical Novel* (London: Merlin Press, 1962), p.277. Subsequent references are to this edition and given parenthetically in the body of the text. This is a translation of the 1955 East German edition of Lukács' complete study, not of the essays as they first appeared between July 1937 and December 1938, serialized in the Russian journal, *Literaturnyi kritik* ('Literary Critic') and some of them separately elsewhere. The print and circulation history of Lukács' study is of some importance, and I will return to it shortly.
[37] This was not meant as praise: for Deutscher, the new line introduced a kind of 'ideological shallowness' and 'patriotic-democratic vulgarity' to the communist project, 'jettisoning all the criteria of

a sign of Lukács' 'ideological dependence on Stalinism'.[38] Lukács' conception of politics predated Stalin's consolidation of power and it outlasted the anti-fascist conjuncture. From at least 1926, Lukács had abandoned his early hope for a promptly perfectible proletarian revolution to urge instead the necessity of 'reconciliation' with an imperfect Soviet and world-revolutionary reality. A series of tactical and aesthetic considerations followed: a belief in the importance of alliances between communists and progressive forces to fight fascism and reaction; a conviction that the bourgeois cultural heritage could play a positive role in articulating the idea of democracy that such alliances should defend and extend; a sense of urgency in orienting intellectual work towards building a progressive cultural hegemony through the institutions of civil society. From the 1928 'Blum Theses', in which Lukács recommended cooperation between Hungarian workers and peasants in defence of the republic and democratic liberties, to his activism on behalf of Hungarian popular democracy in the years immediately after the war, through to his late-career reflections on 'the process of democratization' in the wake of Stalin's death and the Prague Spring of 1968, Lukács can be seen grappling with the cultural politics of what he called 'plebeian-radical democracy'.[39]

Lukács' personal popular frontism would pass into and out of alignment with the policy priorities of the Soviet Union, but in the mid- to late 1930s it rode the wave of a historical conjuncture: a confluence of anti-fascist and anti-colonial struggles on the international stage, and at home, in Moscow, a period of new intellectual friendship and collaboration. As Lukács later recalled, 'this was the first period in my life when work and struggle became possible within a community', a reference to the remarkable group of German and Soviet-trained scholars associated with the Institute of Philosophy, Literature and History and with its journal, *Literaturnyi kritik* ('Literary critic').[40] The catalyst for their work had come with the transfer to Moscow of the Marx–Engels archives, as copies or originals, and the preparation for print of many hitherto unpublished papers, including the 1844 *Economic and Philosophical Manuscripts* of Marx. 'You can only imagine my excitement', Lukács later wrote: 'reading these manuscripts changed my whole relation to Marxism and transformed my philosophical outlook'.[41]

---

proletarian interest and class struggle' in favour of 'the vaguest of "democratic" and antifascist slogans and the most insipid "let's all get together" proclamations'. Isaac Deutscher, *Marxism in Our Time* (London: Jonathan Cape, 1972), p.291; p.151.

[38] Deutscher, *Marxism in Our Time*, p.287.

[39] Georg Lukács, *The Process of Democratization* [1968], translated by Susanne Bernhardt and Norman Levine (Albany, NY: SUNY Press, 1991), p.78.

[40] Georg Lukács to Mikhail Lifshits, 17 September 1966; quoted in László Sziklai, *After the Proletarian Revolution: Georg Lukács's Marxist Development 1930–1945*, translated by Iván Sellei (Budapest: Akadémiai Kiadó, 1992), p.209.

[41] Georg Lukács, 'Interview: Lukács on his Life and Work', *New Left Review*, no.68 (1971): p.57. Excerpts from 'The Economic and Philosophical Manuscripts' first appeared in Russian in 1927; in 1932, the third volume of the *Marx-Engels Gesamtausgabe* carried the complete '1844 Manuscripts' in German. David Riazanov showed Lukács the manuscripts in 1930.

Core texts from the 'early', humanist, Marx could now be joined with Marx and Engels' scattered comments on aesthetics to lay the foundation of a combined critical method and new Left cultural politics. And because, for most of the decade, their concerns largely overlapped the official cultural campaigns of the Party—the turn towards aesthetics, the attacks on 'formalism' and 'vulgar sociology', the promulgation of a still somewhat flexible socialist realism—the circle around Lukács enjoyed a fair degree of autonomy. For this they had also to thank the protection of Elena Usievich, likewise a literary critic but also Revolutionary royalty, having travelled with her father in the armoured train that returned Lenin to Russia in 1917, and Pavel Iudin, philosopher and Party functionary, both of whom were on the editorial board of *Literaturnyi kritik* and able, at least for a while, to defend its positions and personnel from rival literary factions more deeply embedded in the state apparatus. They used this autonomy to pioneer a humanist, Marxist-Leninist aesthetics that could accommodate, and indeed celebrate, the best expressions of European bourgeois culture, mixing Left literary theory with German philosophy and the founding example of Hegel.[42] The prominence of Scott in Lukács' theory of 'critical realism' reflects the revaluation of canonical bourgeois writers that the hitherto unpublished interventions of Marx and Engels made possible.[43]

In the mid- to late 1930s, Lukács played a very public role in Soviet debates about the definition and tradition of realism; in private, meanwhile, his ideas found a sympathetic audience in Mikhail Bakhtin. Bakhtin shared Lukács' love of Goethe and his interest in the *Bildungsroman* as a solution to the problem of capturing individual and collective destinies in the process of becoming. Bakhtin's theory of the 'chronotope' can be seen as a summation of his own ideas about the 'novel of human *emergence*' and as a further elaboration of Lukács' published pronouncements on the history of realism and the 'classical form' of the historical novel.[44] The 'chronotope' is Bakhtin's term of art for 'the intrinsic connectedness

---

[42] For more on this cultural formation, cf. Katerina Clark and Galin Tihanov, 'Soviet Literary Theory in the 1930s: Battles Over Genre and the Boundaries of Modernity', in *A History of Russian Literary Theory and Criticism: The Soviet Age and Beyond*, edited by Evgeny Dobrenko and Galin Tihanov (Pittsburgh: University of Pittsburgh Press, 2011), pp.109–43.

[43] The second and third issue of *Literaturnoe nasledstvo* ('Literary heritage', both 1932) carried Engels' correspondence with Margaret Harkness and Marx and Engels' correspondence with Ferdinand Lassale; numbers seven and eight (1933) contained Engels' letters to Minna Kautsky. Franc Schiller curated this material for readers of the English-language *International Literature* in two articles from 1933.

[44] Bakhtin conceives the *Bildungsroman* as fundamentally historical: in it, 'human emergence ... is no longer man's own private affair'; rather, 'he emerges *along with the world* and he reflects the historical emergence of the world itself'. Mikhail Bakhtin, 'The *Bildungsroman* and Its Significance in the History of Realism', in *Speech Genres and Other Late Essays*, edited by Caryl Emerson and Michael Holquist, translated by Vern W. McGee (Austin: University of Texas Press, 1986), p.23. Lukács engages the *Bildungsroman* at length in his essays on *Wilhelm Meister* (1936) and Gottfried Keller (1939), and in contemporaneous reflections on Goethe's *Faust* and Hegel's *Phenomenology*; thanks to Scott, the 'classical form' of the historical novel is also a *Bildungsroman*. Galin Tihanov reconstructs the bibliography of Bakhtin's 'silent dialogue' with Lukács, in *The Master and the Slave: Lukács, Bakhtin and the Ideas of their Time* (Oxford: Oxford University Press, 2000), pp.11–16.

of temporal and spatial relationships' in literature as these relationships determine and differentiate genres.[45] In their 'classical' or romantic-era forms, both the *Bildungsroman* and historical novel tap the chronotope Bakhtin calls 'national-historical time'. And though it is only Lukács who pursues this line of analysis, it is the pressure placed on the chronotope of the nation by the rise of imperialism in the later decades of the nineteenth century that draws the two genres into the crucible of modernist literary experiment.[46] The surrender of the bounded space-time of the early nineteenth-century nation to an open, extending imperial world-system stands in Lukács' account as both the moral and material explanation of the historical novel's decline in the second half of the nineteenth century, while his diagnosis of a national turn in contemporary world politics underlies his belief that the time was now ripe to revive the historical novel of Scott.

Lukács dates the rise of the historical novel to a period of bourgeois revolutionary optimism, when the romantic cultural and emerging industrial nation supplied a limit to inquiry, a progressive social and economic boundary within which the nation could begin to imagine and understand itself. Circumscribed within the frame of the nation, 'objective reality, and therewith history, was knowable'. Even conservative philosophers and novelists could approach the past 'in a materialist fashion' and by portraying the organic interconnection of individuals and society, by telling of 'their complex rise and decline, their inseparable connection with the slow and confused growth of the whole of popular life, the capillary interplay of the great and small, the significant and the insignificant' (126), arouse in their work 'the feeling of the totality of life' (91). It was a small, contained world that was thus described, one of familiarity with 'the types thrown up by popular life', of 'intimacy with the people's historical life' (253). The story that follows is one of decline, as this residue 'of the old epos', with its 'old epic directness' and 'popular character' (35), evaporates after 1848. In 'the June battle of the proletariat', the bourgeoisie 'for the first time' found itself confronted with the massed ranks of labour, forced to fight 'for the naked continuance of its economic and political rule' (171). Hitherto the champion of secular science and universal freedom (against the religious superstition and feudal absolutism of the *ancien régime*), the bourgeoisie now closed ranks behind a reactionary ideology whose 'destruction of reason' was to culminate in fascism.

---

[45] Mikhail Bakhtin, 'Forms of Time and of the Chronotope in the Novel', in *The Dialogic Imagination: Four Essays*, edited by Michael Holquist; translated by Caryl Emerson and Michael Holquist (Austin: University of Texas Press, 1981), p.84. Bakhtin continues: 'In the literary artistic chronotope, spatial and temporal indicators are fused into one carefully thought-out, concrete whole. Time, as it were, thickens, takes on flesh, becomes artistically visible; likewise, space becomes charged and responsive to the movements of time, plot, history.' Bakhtin's essay on the *Bildungsroman* concludes with praise of 'the profound chronotopic nature' of Scott, how he 'overcomes the closed nature of the past and achieves the fullness of time necessary for the historical novel'. Bakhtin, 'The *Bildungsroman*', p.53.

[46] For a brilliant elaboration of Lukács and Bakhtin on the *Bildungsroman* in the age of empire, cf. Jed Esty, *Unseasonable Youth: Modernism, Colonialism and the Fiction of Development* (Oxford: Oxford University Press, 2012).

For Lukács, the historical novel registers these changes at the level of form and content. In the second half of the century, he sees hostility and fear replace the earlier 'intimacy' with the people; a full-scale mystification of historical process and its representative agencies and actors follows. Gone is the integrated social imaginary and collective destiny of the romantic-era nation. In Europe after 1848, 'writers no longer have the power (and often not the will) to experience history as the history of the people, as a process of development in which the people play the chief role actively and passively, in action and suffering' (206). With the writing over of real social relations, 'the idea of progress undergoes a regression' (174). Whereas with Hegel and Scott the inherited Enlightenment teleology supposed the necessity of contradiction and of conflicting political interests, now progress comes to seem to its bourgeois ideologues one with the tempo of technological change and the 'homogeneous empty time' that Walter Benjamin assailed in his contemporaneous critique of nineteenth-century historicism: a groundless temporality, boundless and falsely transcendent.[47] True to the logic of the 'chronotope', a new spatial reality corresponds to this conception of time as 'a smooth straightforward evolution' (174). After 1848, we enter into an age no longer of self-sufficient nations but of expanding imperial powers, whose internal contradictions are solved by the displacement (mitigation, transcendence) of domestic class conflict by the politics of social imperialism.

What Lukács famously calls 'the crisis of bourgeois realism' attends this scalar shift from knowable national community and classic industrial mode of production to the more global matrix of imperial and international finance capitalism. Lukács conceives empire as the extension of economic processes beyond the perceptual limits of the subject. What follows is a straining and stretching out of cause and effect, origin and outcome, beyond the line of sight and understanding. The ever more complex mediation of economic processes abets the social production of moral invisibility and a loss of faith in history as a medium available to human agency: whence, on the one hand, 'an ever greater disbelief in the possibility of knowing social reality, and hence also history' (251), and on the other, 'a simple and straightforward capitulation to the dehumanizing tendencies of capitalism' (195). This perceptual eclipse of historical process explains what Lukács sees as the proliferation of 'exotic themes' and foreign scenes in historical fiction after 1848.[48] Stripped of causal relation to the place and time of writing, the

---

[47] Benjamin, 'On the Concept of History', p.395.
[48] It should be noted, perhaps, that had Lukács read more widely in the works of Scott, he would have found early anticipations of this exoticizing and dehumanizing pressure on the 'classical form' of the historical novel. This is how Ian Duncan describes the cast of characters in Scott's penultimate Waverley Novel, *Count Robert of Paris* (1831), set in Constantinople towards the end of the eleventh century: 'Its specimens include Greeks, Turks, Normans, Varangians, Moors, Scythians, a homicidally irascible warrior-princess, a philosopher nicknamed "the Elephant," a real elephant, a tiger, a mechanical lion, and a giant orangutan named Sylvan.' Duncan, 'The Trouble with Man: Scott, Romance, and World History in the Age of Lamarck', in *Romantic Frictions*, edited by Theresa Kelley

past becomes a screen for fantasies that shadow the hopes and realities of empire. No longer narrating 'the objective prehistory of men's social development', historical novels traffic in 'the innocent and forever lost beauty of childhood' (232) or in scenes of extravagant cruelty. Gustave Flaubert's novel of ancient Carthage, *Salammbô* (1862), exemplifies the trend. For the past that can be made to seem a place of unspoiled social forms, precapitalist lifeworlds cheering to the alienated gaze, can also appear a time of titillating cruelties, tableaux of oriental despotism and human degradation. For Lukács, the post-1848 historical novel tracks the political unconscious of a European high humanism whose rhetoric of individual and artistic freedom exists in direct contradiction with its continuing subjection of the working class and with the broken bodies of the colonized.

With the First World War marking, in Lenin's classic account, the completion of Europe's colonization of the planet ('so that in the future *only* re-division' will be possible, leading of necessity to escalating inter-imperial rivalry, militarization, and war), the historical novel enters a new phase.[49] Lukács maps onto Lenin's prediction of the coming final crisis of capitalism such premonitions of the 'twilight of humanity' as Oswald Spengler's *Decline of the West* (1918–23). But to the worst fears of the Right the Left makes answer with its own arts of prophesy: 'proletarian revolution' (253) and 'the *dawn* of a new democracy' (345). The rise of the Soviet Union as a new world power names the beginning of the end of the imperial world-system and of the capitalist class it served. To be sure, what to Lukács is not yet visible is the answering dawn in America of a Fordism to face off against the Soviet social experiment. The symmetries of the Cold War are not yet clearly in place for Lukács, nor is it immediately easy to read the Soviet Union and the United States as empires of a new order (it would take another world war and a long telegram to formalize their imperial status: sponsoring revolutions, competing for client states and to occupy in the spaces vacated by the contracting colonial presence of Europe). Nevertheless, Lukács understands a geopolitical shift to be underway, transecting the interwar scene in such a way as to cast its competing, 'contradictory and criss-cross' aesthetic ideologies—modernism, socialist realism, and Lukács' own preferred critical realism—as modes of response to what is not only a crisis in and of Europe but of the literary and imperial world-systems headquartered there.

To have urged the writing of national-historical novels against the chronotope of empire or to sing the great collective project when in practice it lay stalled would have been, for Lukács, the height of tendentiousness: 'a (subjectively devised) commandment' without any objective truth.[50] In the context, however, of popular

---

(*Romantic Circles: Praxis Series*, 2011): https://romantic-circles.org/praxis/frictions/HTML/praxis.2011.duncan.html [accessed 17 December 2019].

[49] V.I. Lenin, *Imperialism, The Highest Stage of Capitalism*, in *Collected Works, Volume 22: December 1915–July 1916*, translated by Yuri Sdobnikov (Moscow: Progress Publishers, 1964), p.254.

[50] Georg Lukács, 'Tendency or Partisanship?' [1932], in *Essays on Realism*, edited by Rodney Livingstone, translated by David Fernbach (London: Lawrence and Wishart, 1980), p.37.

struggles to redirect the nation's destiny—the present fight against fascism and imperialism, the fight for socialism—Lukács believed it possible to write again of national becoming. The promise of universal freedom, abandoned by the bourgeoisie after 1848, was now in play and on a global scale. Lukács describes how the anti-fascist struggle of the later 1930s joins with 'the heroic liberation struggles of the Chinese, Indian etc people [;] all these developments flow concretely into the common historical stream of the liberation of mankind' (345).[51] Lukács writes rousingly of the return of the romantic-era hot chronology that first inspired the historical novel. 'It was the French Revolution, the revolutionary wars and the rise and fall of Napoleon, which for the first time made history a mass experience', the scale and frequency of 'upheaval' forcing 'a change from quantity into quality' and radical reconceptualizations of the meaning of cultural difference, human agency, and historical process (23). The 'classic form' of the historical novel had narrated episodes in the transition from feudalism to capitalism, examples as per *Waverley* (1814) of the necessary 'march of development' from the pre-modern poetry of epic and romance to the 'capitalist prose' (344) of the bourgeois novel. Lukács predicts that the coming form of the mid-century historical novel will hand the baton of historical initiative and therewith the subject of its fiction to the national-popular. Already in the 'heroic' struggle of the people for national liberation and revolutionary democracy, Lukács discerns a '*tendency towards epic*' as the artform of a once and future freedom (347).

## IV. The Communist Historical Novel in Britain

Writing the preface for the first complete English translation of *The Historical Novel* in 1961, Lukács had to admit that his 'expectations' for the Popular Front and for a Scott-styled 'renaissance' (344) of the genre had proven 'too optimistic'. His arguments had been 'belied by historical events' (13). In particular, the Nazi–Soviet neutrality pact took a very personal and professional toll. In November 1939, the Soviet authorities commissioned the penitent ex-formalist critic Viktor Shklovskii to write a damning reader's report on the revised manuscript of *The Historical Novel* for the State Publishing House for Literature, Goslitizdat. Such reports were a mainstay of Soviet literary censorship, a means of suppressing work informally without the public display of state power. The purpose of Shklovskii's review was clear, writes Galin Tihanov: 'to put ... Lukács in his place' and 'remind him that the benevolence of the Soviet political and cultural élite was not to be

---

[51] As this telegraphic notation implies ('Chinese, Indian etc'), Lukács was not a close follower of developments on the colonial front, but his argument in *The Historical Novel* shows him more attuned to the imperial dimension of nineteenth- and early twentieth-century European literature than critics have generally credited.

taken for granted.'[52] As the 1930s drew to a close, Lukács' welcome in Moscow had worn thin, his Europhile cosmopolitanism and reluctance to read and praise Soviet writers only adding to his exposure in a climate of ideological retrenchment. In 1940, Aleksandr Fadeev moved to shutter *Literaturnyi kritik* as part of a wider clampdown on literary 'cliques' and free literary-theoretical expression. Lukács was censured for his part in leading 'an anti-Party *faction in literature*' and for helping theorize 'the bourgeois-liberal opposition to Marxism-Leninism.'[53] As colleagues fell victim to charges of 'vulgar humanism' and 'primitive antifascism', Soviet distrust of Lukács' political heterodoxy and cultural elitism culminated in a brief period of imprisonment in 1941. Lukács had again to fall back on his belief in 'reconciliation under duress', his conviction that, whatever the detours and setbacks along the way, the '"rationality" of human progress exist[s] in reality itself', 'and that the greatness of a thinker or poet is to be seen not in the fact that he reads his subjective enthusiasm into reality, but on the contrary, in the fact that he discovers, considers, and gives shape to the rationality inherent in reality.'[54]

By blocking 'The Historical Novel' from becoming a book, Soviet authorities restricted its influence beyond the specialized Russian readership of *Literaturnyi kritik* and the exile communities of Hungarian and German socialism who could encounter its full argument in article form. Significantly, though British readers had access to an abridged version of Lukács' analysis of the romantic-era historical novel, which appeared across two issues of *International Literature* in 1938, they did not know the essay on 'The Historical Novel of Democratic Humanism' in which he made his pitch for a contemporary revival of Scott's 'classical form.'[55] That the two-part article on Scott did not prompt much interest in Scott's exemplarity as

---

[52] Galin Tihanov, 'Viktor Shklovskii and Georg Lukács in the 1930s', *Slavonic and East European Review* 78, no.1 (2000): p.52; p.56. On Lukács' perilous position and partial accommodations in Moscow during and after the Purges, see also Galin Tihanov, 'Cosmopolitans without a Polis: Towards a Hermeneutics of the East-East Exilic Experience (1929–1945)', in *The Exile and Return of Writers from East-Central Europe: A Compendium*, edited by John Neubauer and Borbála Zsuzsanna Török (Berlin: De Gruyter, 2009), pp.123–43.

[53] Soviet Writers' Union secretaries Aleksandr Fadeev and Valery Kirpotin to Stalin and members of the Communist Party Central Committee, 'On the Anti-Party Faction in Soviet Criticism', 10 February 1940; in Katerina Clark and Evgeny Dobrenko, *Soviet Culture and Power: A History in Documents, 1917–1953* (New Haven: Yale University Press, 2007), pp.214–15.

[54] Georg Lukács, 'Die Widersprüche des Fortschritts und die Literatur', in *Moskauer Schriften zur Literaturtheorie und Literaturpolitik 1934–1940*, edited by Frank Benseler (Frankfurt am Main: Sendler, 1981), pp.82–3. Cf. Theodor Adorno, 'Extorted Reconciliation: On Georg Lukács' *Realism in Our Time*' [1958], in *Notes to Literature*, edited by Rolf Tiedemann, translated by Shierry Weber Nicholsen (New York, Columbia University Press, 1991), pp.216–40.

[55] Georg Lukács, 'Walter Scott and the Historical Novel', *International Literature*, no.4 (1938): pp.61–77; and *International Literature*, no.12 (1938): pp.73–84. What English readers will know as the chapter on 'The Historical Novel of Democratic Humanism' appeared in 1938 in two issues of *Literaturnyi kritik* (nos.8 & 12), in the Moscow-based Hungarian journal *Új Hang* (no.1), and in the German-language edition of *Internationale Literatur* (no.5). A Japanese translation of the complete study should also, however, be noted. Lukács, *Rekishi bungakuron*, translated by Fusaji Yamamura (Tokyo: Mikasa Shobo, 1938). Sunyoung Park credits this translation with influencing Korean proletarian writer Kim Namcheon's historical turn. Park, *The Proletarian Wave: Literature and Leftist Culture in Colonial Korea, 1910–1945* (Cambridge, MA: Harvard University Press, 2015), p.243.

a novelist of the nation in change is evident from the published correspondence it prompted. T.A Jackson and Sylvia Townsend Warner both weighed in with minor criticisms (about the correct spelling of proper names and the precise calibration of Scott's social class), but they were more excited to debate the nature of Scott's Scottishness than to think with Lukács about genre.[56]

Only one writer, then living in almost complete isolation from the main centres of British Left literary life, appears to have grasped the normative intention of Lukács' analysis of Scott. 'During the 1930s when I was struggling to develop the historical novel', recalled Jack Lindsay in 1955, 'I came across Lukács' discussion of the work of Walter Scott', and it 'made me realise that one aspect of what I was trying to do was create characters in whom the contradictions of their society met and clashed with a maximum of intensity, to develop the Scott method in a more active way'.[57] But Lindsay was particularly well placed to appreciate Lukács' reading of Scott absent its larger context. A practised historical novelist, Lindsay had already drawn the obvious conclusion from Dimitrov's 1935 Seventh World Congress speech that what the Left now needed was a new historical fiction. 'With fascism raising everywhere demagogic cries of reactionary nationalism', Lindsay had written in January 1937 in the US periodical *New Masses*,

> there is no task more important for the Communists in each country than to make clear that they stand for the true completion of the national destiny. To wrest from the fascist demagogues the great figures of the past national struggles is a pressing need, and what can do it better than adequate historical novels?.

Months before he could have known Lukács' opinion on the matter, Lindsay was extolling Scott as 'the greatest figure', who though 'lacking the materialistic dialectic' was 'nevertheless aware of history as a conflict of old and new forces and conditions of life'. Scott's 'humanistic shrewdness' had turned these 'abstractions'

---

[56] T.A. Jackson, Georg Lukács, and Sylvia Townsend Warner, 'Points from Letters', *International Literature*, no.9 (1938): pp.100–1; and T.A. Jackson, 'Walter Scott and his Historical Significance', *International Literature*, nos.8–9 (1939): pp.68–76. Elinor Taylor situates these criticisms in the context of debates within British communism as to how to reconcile the traditions of Scottish nationalism with the Left's new embrace of the nation; in *The Popular Front Novel in Britain, 1934–1940* (Leiden: Brill, 2018), pp.145–6.

[57] Jack Lindsay, [No Title], in *Georg Lukács zum siebzigsten Geburtstag* (Berlin: Aufbau Verlag, 1955), pp.130–1. Lindsay confirms how, 'in 1948–9', when he first met Lukács in person, 'the only work of his I knew was the section of his *The Historical Novel* dealing with Scott, which had appeared in the late 1930s in *International Literature*'; Jack Lindsay, 'The Part and the Whole: The Achievement of Georg Lukács', in *Decay and Renewal: Critical Essays on Twentieth Century Writing* (London: Lawrence & Wishart, 1976), p.50. When Merlin Press sent Lindsay an advance copy of the complete English translation of *The Historical Novel* in 1962, Lindsay wrote to his friend to say how much he was looking forward to at last reading the study in full. And he recalled again how, 'in the 1930's ... your remarks [on Scott] had a fundamental effect on my whole thinking about the novel and on my own work in the historical novel.' Jack Lindsay to Georg Lukács, n.d. (1962); Lukács Archives, Hungarian Academy of Sciences Library and Information Centre, Budapest, Ms 2867/251.

of the Scottish Enlightenment 'Science of Man' into richly imagined, intimately lived, dynamic social processes.[58]

Rather than treat Lukács as in any way causative or as an authoritative gloss on the communist historical novel in Britain, his intervention may rather be read as just one of the more sophisticated attempts to find fictional form and past precedent for the mid-century national turn. In fact, there were many roads that led to the national-historical novel, with many but not all writers moving in step with the new Party line. Among working-class communist novelists, the transition from Third Period-contemporary to Popular Front-historical can seem particularly pronounced. The Durham-born miner Harold Heslop, for example, was a faithful student in the school of international communist culture, proud of its community, cleaving to the Party line, and changing when it changed. When Anna Elistratova criticized the 'calibre' of 'political insight' in his second novel, *The Gate of a Strange Field* (1929), diagnosing traces of 'petty bourgeois' individualism in its rendering of the 1926 General Strike, Heslop self-corrected with the short story 'Ten Thousand Men' (1933) and the novel *Last Cage Down* (1935), both exemplary Third Period texts with their communist heroes, Joe Trotter and Joe Frost, committing to fight 'class against class, until capitalism is swept from the earth'.[59] With the Popular Front, Heslop pivoted promptly to the past. As he told readers of *International Literature* in 1939, 'Since 1935 I have been engaged on two novels … One deals with the struggles of the miners in 1832 and the other—a very large book—deals with a family across a century of coal production in the North.'[60] Heslop never found a publisher for this first novel, a tale of the Jarrow pitman Will Jobling who died a martyr in the early days of Thomas Hepburn's Durham and Northumberland colliers' association. But the second novel became *The Earth Beneath* (1946), a chronicle of the Akers family as it is driven from the North Yorkshire dales and forced to find work in the coalfields of County Durham; its climax was a grim rendering of the 1862 Hartley Colliery disaster.

This novel's expansive social frame bears comparison with another 'very large book' from this time, James Barke's *The Land of the Leal* (1939). Both narrate the culmination, in the North of England and in Scotland respectively, of the expropriation of the peasants from the land, the great nineteenth-century migrations to

---

[58] Jack Lindsay, 'The Historical Novel', *New Masses* 22, no.3 (12 January 1937): pp.15–16.

[59] E. Elistratova, 'The Work of Harold Heslop', *International Literature*, no.1 (1932): p.100. Harold Heslop, 'Ten Thousand Men', *International Literature*, no.2 (1933): p.38; compare the similar wording in *Last Cage Down* [1935] (London: Lawrence & Wishart, 1984), p.41.

[60] Harold Heslop, introduction to 'Sunnybank', *International Literature*, nos.8–9 (1939): p.28. The first of these was 'To Reach the Slake', several times submitted to publishers, including to Lawrence & Wishart in 1936, and rejected; though substantially revised after the war, it was never published. An excerpt from the second novel appeared as 'Sunnybank' in *International Literature* (nos.8–9, 1939), and the full novel found publishers in both Britain and the US. Heslop later remembered it as 'my one novel that got across'. Harold Heslop, 'From Tyne to Tone: A Journey', unpublished typescript, c.1971, p.286; Papers of Harold Heslop, Durham University Library, Archives and Special Collections, HES/A10.

Britain's cities and centres of industry, and the formation of a new working-class identity. *The Land of the Leal* unfolds across four generations a widening sense of historical possibility, each son inheriting and extending the politics of the father. Crucially, it is the experience of the city—credited, in familiar Marxist terms, as the engine of proletarian class consciousness—that finally converts a family tradition of 'rebellious individuality', constrained by the debilitating, dispiriting conditions of agricultural labour, into a properly collectivist, national, and internationalist politics.[61] Read side by side, Barke's two big novels of the 1930s nicely illustrate Michael Denning's sense of the new 'temporal and spatial sweep' that followed 'the recognition that the new proletarians' of the cities 'were not simply factory workers and tenement dwellers, but were migrants from the countryside'.[62] *Major Operation* (1936) had been inspired by *Ulysses*, its most famous chapter—'Red Music in the Second City'—Britain's best example of a proletarian modernism: urban, cinematic, and present-tense continuous. But *The Land of the Leal* (1939) pans out and back, conjugating country and city in a national-historical frame while linking its saga of working-class struggle to the politics of anti-fascism in Europe. 'The events of our generation are on too vast a scale to come within the organisational scope of our literary artists', Barke explains in an author's note: 'nevertheless we cannot throw down our pens in despair' and wait for some future writer 'to complete the sequel to *War and Peace*'.[63] However provisionally, we must attempt the epic scale today, and with Tolstoy, not Joyce, as our guide.[64]

The early novels of Gwyn Thomas pivot almost as neatly on this Third Period/Popular Front divide. Thomas had submitted the manuscript of *Sorrow For Thy Sons* to a Left Book Club competition advertised in August 1936 for the best 'genuinely Proletarian novel' by a British writer; it was rejected the following year, Victor Gollancz applauding its 'fervour' but describing its 'facts' about contemporary South Wales as so 'raw, its wrath so pitiless', that 'its commercial prospects were nil unless he could issue a free pair of asbestos underdrawers to every reader.'[65] *All Things Betray Thee* (1949, or *Leaves in the Wind* as it was known in the US) is of an altogether gentler conception, mellowed by its historical perspective. Growing up in the Rhondda Valley in the 1910s, Thomas recalled 'a fine

---

[61] James Barke, *The Land of the Leal* [1939] (Edinburgh: Canongate, 1987), p.365.
[62] Denning, 'Novelists' International', p.67.
[63] James Barke, 'Note' to *The Land of the Leal* [1939] (Edinburgh: Canongate, 1987), p. ix.
[64] Elinor Taylor notes the extent to which the Joyceanism in *Major Operation* is both playful and critical, with Barke 'conscious of the limits of modernism', interested to historicize them and ultimately 'to move beyond them'. Taylor, *The Popular Front Novel*, p.155. The turn from Joyce to Tolstoy, a clear instruction at the Soviet Writers' Congress of 1934, suggests an allegiance to socialist realism. In this period, Barke identified closely with Soviet literary debates. Taylor cites an amazing letter from 1935 in which Barke positions himself with Soviet proletarian writers, veterans of RAPP, against the Left critical establishment in Britain: 'We have nobody who can formulate literary theory (say) like Averbakh, Bezimensky, Radek, Libedinsky, Frichte, Brik, P.C. Kogan, Gorbatchev, Shklovsky, Polonsky. Or Pilnak, Fedin, or the very sensible Gladkov'; cited in Taylor, *The Popular Front Novel*, p.150.
[65] Gwyn Thomas, *A Few Selected Exits* (London: Hutchinson, 1968), p.100. The novel was published posthumously in 1986.

ancient worker, a neighbour of ours', who as a child had followed the funeral cortege of Dic Penderyn, the legendary Welsh miner and revolutionary martyr hanged for his part in the Merthyr Rising of 1831. 'He could still recall the songs of wrath and compassion that the people sang. He wept each time he told the tale and he had to tell it often, for there was no leaf of our class tradition that filled us with more pity and wonder.'[66] Thomas's 1949 novel remains beautifully true to that 'pity and wonder' even as it scrambles the facts of the riots, borrowing from Penderyn for the character of John Simon Adams and inventing its central figure, 'the harpist' Alan Hugh Leigh, from scratch. Alan's art supplies the novel's central metaphor of the socialist struggle as a 'chorus' of voices 'practicing for the great anthem'.[67] I shall return to this metaphor and the use to which Raymond Williams later put it in my epilogue.

Not every communist historical novel so neatly postdates Dimitrov's Seventh World Congress instructions, however. Newly married and strapped for cash in 1934, Geoffrey Trease was 'turning over a dozen journalistic possibilities' when he stumbled upon the idea of writing communist historical fiction for children.[68] He wrote to the Party publishers, floating his notion of a historical adventure-story 'with a socialist slant. What about Robin Hood, I asked.'[69] Martin Lawrence leapt at the chance, offering favourable terms for *Bows Against the Barons* and *Comrades for the Charter*, which both appeared within the year.[70] Trease had been inspired by reading M. Ilin's *Moscow Has a Plan* (1931), a primer for young readers about the first Five-Year Plan; it convinced Trease that 'you could stand Henty on his head without taking the kick out of him'. As Marx had done with Hegel, so Trease set out to do with Victorian children's literature: invert its social idealism, turn its class politics 'upside down'.[71] He had grand ambitions: as he told readers of *International Literature* during a visit to the Soviet Union in 1935, he envisioned 'a whole room lined with volumes! Human history waits to be rewritten, episode by episode.'[72] Trease was fêted in the international communist press as a pioneer, to be counted—wrote Ralph and Frederica DeSola in *New Masses*—'among the

---

[66] From a letter to Howard Fast, cited in Michael Parnell, *Laughter from the Dark: A Life of Gwyn Thomas* (London: John Murray, 1988), p.113.

[67] Gwyn Thomas, *All Things Betray Thee* [1949] (London: Lawrence & Wishart, 1986), p.311.

[68] Geoffrey Trease, *A Whiff of Burnt Boats. An Early Autobiography* (Macmillan: London and Basingstoke, 1971), p.144.

[69] Geoffrey Trease, 'A Lifetime of Storytelling: The Author Takes Stock of Writing Books for Children since 1933', in *The Cool Web: The Pattern of Children's Reading*, edited by Margaret Meek, Aidan Warlow, and Griselda Barton (London: The Bodley Head, 1977), p. 146.

[70] International Publishers in New York and the Moscow-based Cooperative Society of Foreign Workers in the USSR resold copies under their own imprints; a German and Russian translation of *Bows Against the Barons* appeared soon after.

[71] Trease, 'A Lifetime', p.146; p.150.

[72] Geoffrey Trease, 'Revolutionary Literature for the Young', *International Literature*, no.7 (1935): p.101.

founders of proletarian children's literature outside of Russia'.[73] Although Trease's instincts as a professional writer later led him to seek a more commercial market for his fiction, the progressive impulse remained. *Cry Treason: A Tale of Shakespearean England* (1940), for example, muscled in on Arthur Ransome territory, reclaiming the Lake District for its locals and for a fight against enclosure.

Of the professional writers who aligned with the communist historical novel, several were historical novelists already: Jack Lindsay, Naomi Mitchison, Iris Morley, and Sylvia Townsend Warner all had form, and Mitchison a major reputation for novels like *The Conquered* (1923) and *The Corn King and the Spring Queen* (1931). Morley, inspired by her childhood love of Dumas, had written *The Proud Paladin* (1936), a historical romance set in fourteenth-century France, before embarking on an English trilogy that laid out a powerful Marxist analysis of the Restoration, Monmouth Rebellion, and Revolution of 1688. Lindsay would later credit his novels on the fall of the Roman republic (1934–35) with clarifying his understanding of historical dialectics, clearing the way for his discovery of Marx in early 1936 and for a deep identification with the Party's national-popular turn. But the impulse, in the first instance, had been financial: his brother Philip Lindsay, a prolific and popular historical novelist himself, had suggested the genre as a safe commercial proposition. Sylvia Townsend Warner made her name as a communist author with *Summer Will Show* (1936), a novel of the 1848 revolutions in Paris. It was not her first foray into historical fiction, but the period location of *The True Heart* (1929) was only ever secondary to its technical conceit of transposing a Roman myth across time. The novel's classical pastiche gave free rein to Warner's wit, and she delighted in engineering so 'efficient' a fit of modern detail to mythic pretext that 'no reviewer saw what I was up to. Only my mother recognised the basis of my story'.[74] The historical 'basis' of Warner's subsequent fiction reflects an altogether more radical conception of historical materialism, and to the extent that novels like *Summer Will Show* (1936), *After the Death of Don Juan* (1938), *The Corner That Held Them* (1948), and *The Flint Anchor* (1954) still invite a matching operation of their readers, it is no longer to line up the literary character with a divine original but with their contingent, socio-historical type.

The desire to tap existing markets for historical fiction and ring variations on familiar themes may explain the handful of Popular Front historical novels not set in England, Scotland, or Wales. Classical antiquity was the most common destination, inspiring a string of contemporary parallels. Phyllis Bentley wrote

---

[73] Ralph and Frederica DeSola, 'For Young Revolutionists', *New Masses* 16, no.8 (20 August 1935): p.24. Jack Lindsay followed in Trease's footsteps, publishing his one Australian historical novel, *Rebels of the Goldfields*, about the Eureka Stockade, with Lawrence & Wishart in 1936; he also published three 'boy's books' with Oxford University Press: *Runaway: A Tale of Ancient Roman Days* (1935), *To Arms: A Story of Ancient Gaul* (1938), and *The Dons Sight Devon: A Story of the Defeat of the Invincible Armada* (1941). *Rebels* and *Runaway* appeared together in a 1956 Russian translation.

[74] Sylvia Townsend Warner, 'Preface' to *The True Heart* (London: Penguin, 2021), pp. vii–viii.

*Freedom, Farewell!* (1936) 'on account of Adolf Hitler'.[75] The novel told the fall of the Roman Republic, casting blame on the society that acquiesced in Julius Caesar's dictatorship—'the arrogance and stupidity of the patricians, the selfishness of the wealthy, the timidity, confusion and delay of the moderate, well-meaning men, the greed and fickleness and stupidity of the people'.[76] Lindsay's *Hannibaal Takes a Hand* (1941) was another parable of appeasement: 'the reader must blame, not me, but the unchanging nature of ruling classes for the way in which Carthage in 196–5 BC suggests Europe in the 1930s', protested Lindsay in a preface.[77] Mitchison's *The Blood of the Martyrs* (1939) worked the analogy between the persecution of Christians under Nero and recent examples of political violence, including the brutal repression of Austrian socialists after the Civil War of 1934 and the terror visited on the Southern Tenant Farmers Union in Arkansas and other sharecropping states from 1935. Events in Spain, meanwhile, inspired Townsend Warner's *After the Death of Don Juan* (1939), 'a parable, if you like the word, or an allegory or what you will, of the political chemistry of the Spanish War, with the Juan—more of Molière than of Mozart—developing as the Fascist of the piece'.[78] John Sommerfield's *The Adversaries* (1952) borrowed the life of the French mathematician and radical republican Evariste Galois to commemorate the British communist intellectuals who went to Spain and likewise died young: his friend and former schoolmate, the poet John Cornford, the mathematician and philosopher David Guest.

Dimitrov's language at the Seventh World Congress of acclimatizing proletarian internationalism in the national culture and striking 'deep roots' in the 'native land' did not preclude comparison, the option of narrating the national turn at one remove. Lindsay's *Light in Italy* (1941) throws its English innocent abroad into the world of the Carbonari, the underground organization leading the fight for national independence in the early decades of the nineteenth century; we follow as for Harry and his Italian friend Colombo the idea of 'Italy' ceases to be 'an abstraction—an heroic voice in the air, a tragedy-queen, Chariteo's *Italia mia*', and comes 'down to bedrock' in connection with the people, the sailors at an osteria, 'the peasants above all'.[79] Lindsay's *Thunder Underground: A Story of Nero's*

---

[75] Phyllis Bentley, *O Dreams, O Destinations* (New York: Macmillan, 1962), p.202.

[76] Phyllis Bentley, *Freedom, Farewell!* (Harmondsworth: Penguin, 1950), p.379. Bentley hoped with her novel to strike 'a blow for freedom' and was disappointed when she learned that 'nobody, nobody at all, had understood' its message; the suggestion in some quarters that she was simply trying to 'cash in' on the success of Robert Graves' fictional autobiographies of Claudius (1934 and 1935) particularly rankled. Bentley, *O Dreams, O Destinations*, p.204. Though at best an ambivalent socialist, Bentley was fiercely anti-fascist and in the mid-1930s her liberal 'creed' of liberty and 'the brotherhood of man' aligned this parable of how a people could 'let freedom slip' with novels of a more materialist and class-conflictual stripe.

[77] Jack Lindsay, *Hannibaal Takes a Hand* (London: Andrew Dakers, 1941), p.7.

[78] Sylvia Townsend Warner to Nancy Cunard, 28 August 1945; in Sylvia Townsend Warner, *Letters*, edited by William Maxwell (London: Chatto & Windus, 1982), p.51 fn.1.

[79] Jack Lindsay, *Light in Italy* (London: Victor Gollancz, 1941), p.239.

*Rome* (1965) narrates a similar discovery of the national-popular for its Spanish protagonist, as we shall see in chapter four. But in the great majority of novels keyed to the national turn, the nation at stake was their own.

In Harold Heslop's timeslip novel 'The Holy Earth' (1948), we learn that 'the Englishman knows one thing above all else, and that is love of his soil', a soil that is soaked with history and 'touched by the sacred past'. Somehow, this 'memory stuff' that clings to the 'Somerset earth' catapults our protagonists out of the present and into the Duking Days of 1685.[80] When Monmouth lands at Lyme in Iris Morley's *We Stood for Freedom* (1942), breathing new life into the Good Old Cause, 'the very earth seemed quick with the ghosts' of the Civil War, with Gerald Winstanley reclaiming the commons and Colonel Rainborough declaring democracy the 'birthright' of every Englishman. Defeat must follow, of course, but Diana Hayes has learned where she stands.

> She saw the grass at her feet, deep and lush, a green twilight under the roof of thick close trees and an ermine-breasted thrush standing motionless beneath the ancient hanging hedge. And not knowing what she did her fingers plunged down into the earth, down into the coolness, bruising the grass, and there was a weight in her heart, a dull, immoveable strength, monstrous and fixed like the foundation of an old, old wall.[81]

Her lover, Saul Flecke, suggests they flee to escape the coming persecution, that they make their way to America 'to be active again, to interfere and plot'.[82] But Diana cannot bear the thought. '"I won't go!"' she almost shouts in his face.

> 'I don't want America, or any liberty that's there ... This [land] is ours, and I'll never leave it. It's my earth—Why should it be theirs? Haven't we fought for it and died for it? [ ... ] It's mine because I love it—mine!'[83]

This conception of a nation not theirs but ours, a nation at one with those who love and work the land and fight its dispossession, returns in novel after novel.

Many of the more class-privileged communist writers found themselves ringing historical variations on the theme of 'going over to socialism', the process foretold in the *Communist Manifesto* when 'finally', as the class struggle 'nears the decisive hour', 'a small section of the ruling class cuts itself adrift and joins the revolutionary class, the class that holds the future in its hands'.[84] Valentine Cunningham identifies this as 'the key metaphor' among his bourgeois 'British writers of the

---

[80] Harold Heslop, 'The Holy Earth' [1948], unpublished typescript, Heslop Papers HES/A5, p.33; p.142.
[81] Iris Morley, *We Stood for Freedom* (New York: William Morrow & Co., 1942), pp.340–1.
[82] Morley, *We Stood for Freedom*, p.334.
[83] Morley, *We Stood for Freedom*, p.341.
[84] Marx and Engels, *The Communist Manifesto*, p.54.

Thirties'.[85] But British fiction was by no means alone in narrating these journeys to the border of commitment or in transposing them to the past. Jean Cassou's novel of the French Commune, *Les Massacres de Paris* (1935), a novel widely reviewed in the international communist press, told of the sentimental education of Théodore Quiche, son of a bankrupt trader, as he rejects the path of prosperity offered him by an uncle and embraces the working-class cause instead. Introducing the novel in *International Literature*, Louis Aragon explained its relevance: 'it is the adventure of a young bourgeois of last century but also it appears in France in the days of the People's Front', where it reflects what has become 'a great contemporary adventure: the passage to the side of the proletariat of [the] French intelligentsia'.[86] For bourgeois British communists, the plot had a similar appeal. The protagonist in Lindsay's *The Barriers Are Down* (1945) is the fifth-century son of a landowner who will find his way to fighting alongside the *Bagudae* or peasant insurgents of the later Roman empire, but there is much he must unlearn first. Early in the novel, Audax watches the peasants on a friend's estate gathering in the harvest; he longs to feel included 'in the simple yet infinitely entangled rhythms of the earth', to 'climb over the drystone wall and join the men and women in the fields'. 'And yet, how could one step across that wall ... ?'[87] It's a question asked and answered in a string of Lindsay's fictions, by Harry Lydcott in *Lost Birthright* (1939), Dick Gibbes in *The Stormy Violence* (1941), Merric in *Fires in Smithfield* (1950), Lucius Cassius Firmus in *Thunder Underground* (1965).

In her analysis of Lindsay's English trilogy—*1649: A Novel of a Year* (1938), *Lost Birthright* (1939), and *Men of Forty-Eight* (1948)—Elinor Taylor observes the same 'emphasis on bourgeois dissidence', how Lindsay 'exaggerates the significance of the atypical bourgeois intellectual over characters more directly conditioned by the central historical forces of the age.'[88] The criticism is well made: the bourgeois hero and his avatar in earlier times is indeed a problematic trope in a literature of popular rebellion. It is nevertheless consistent with the mid-century discourse of 'commitment' and a problem to which writers like Lindsay and Naomi Mitchison gave considerable thought, drawing on contemporary research in comparative anthropology and history of religion to theorize the process. Lindsay elaborates on the 'myth-motive' of perilous passage and painful transition—birth and initiation, religious conversion—in his non-fiction, including his biography of Bunyan (1937), his *Short History of Culture* (1939, revised 1962), and *The Clashing Rocks: A Study of Early Greek Religion and Culture and the Origins of Drama*

---

[85] Valentine Cunningham, *British Writers of the Thirties* (Oxford: Oxford University Press, 1988), p.211.

[86] Louis Aragon, 'About "The Massacres of Paris"', *International Literature*, no.9 (1936): p.107; the review accompanies an excerpt in English translation. A Russian translation of Cassou's novel followed in 1937, and several others thereafter.

[87] Jack Lindsay, *The Barriers Are Down: A Tale of the Collapse of a Civilisation* (London: Victor Gollancz, 1945), p.66.

[88] Taylor, *Popular Front Novel*, p.127.

(1965), all of which profess their debt to Jane Harrison, whose ritual theory we encountered in chapter one. For Mitchison and others of her circle in the early 1930s, it was not Harrison but the philosopher of religion Gerald Heard who was their 'prophet'.[89] His ideas on group consciousness and communion figure prominently in Mitchison's works of political theory, *The Moral Basis of Politics* (1938) and *The Kingdom of Heaven* (1939), as well as in her novel of Neronian Rome, *The Blood of the Martyrs*. In the latter, the son of a conquered British king quits his class to join a beleaguered Christian community of slaves and freemen.

The protagonists of Iris Morley's trilogy of the seventeenth-century Monmouth Rebellion and Glorious Revolution all begin as creatures of the court and maids of honour to Mary, Duchess of York; thence their trajectories diverge, with the historical Henrietta Wentworth (*Cry Treason*, 1940) and fictional Diana Hayes (*We Stood for Freedom*, 1942) crossing over to the politics of the people, and Elizabeth Villiers (*The Mighty Years*, 1943) aligning with William of Orange as the instrument of an expanding merchant capitalism. Elizabeth's trajectory is only at first glance untypical. As William of Orange's mistress and future Countess of Orkney, she stands largely apart from the West Country rebellion and the defeat of the Good Old Cause; her story is linked to the rise of 'the City of London, the merchants of Amsterdam and the new lords of banking and trade'.[90] But *The Mighty Years* is at pains to mourn the 'woman who might have existed' had she too crossed over.[91] We first meet Elizabeth in *Cry Treason* in 1674, interrupting her reading of Spinoza to explain the historical conjuncture: 'Do you see we are living in an amazingly interesting time? Everything is in flux—fluid, uncertain—*anything* can emerge.' Henrietta listens enthralled as Elizabeth channels Morley's analysis—by way of Marx—of the changes transforming British society. Elizabeth, it becomes clear, has 'brains', an appetite for difficult books and academic argument. But when she hands Henrietta a pamphlet, *The Law of Freedom*, 'by an obscure man called Winstanley' who led the Diggers in the years of the Commonwealth, it is Henrietta his ideas inspire to question her class privilege and imagine a world without it. Elizabeth instead retreats, her mood 'running out, like a deep sparkling river, into the broad shallow spaces'. 'She said diffidently: "It could be true. But all is against it".'[92] While Henrietta will hazard everything on this truth and lose, Elizabeth lives to regret the leap she never took, along with the love she let slip.

That love is Richard Wildman, a radical theoretician cut out of whole cloth to counterbalance *The Mighty Years*' close historical focus on William and his circle; his portrait is one of several in communist historical novels to channel their authors' transformative encounter with Marxism. Wildman fascinates from afar

---

[89] Naomi Mitchison, *You May Well Ask: A Memoir 1920–1940* (London: Fontana, 1986), p.107.
[90] Iris Morley, *The Mighty Years* (London: Peter Davies, 1943), p.181.
[91] Morley, *The Mighty Years*, p.235.
[92] Iris Morley, *Cry Treason* (London: Peter Davies, 1940), pp.34–5.

with his shock of red hair and in person by his 'extraordinary outlook', a philosophy of history whose motto—'no man is greater than the movement beneath his feet'—echoes throughout the novel.[93] The last we see of him is as he plans to 'go away', 'Holland to begin with, perhaps afterwards to some German city', there to 'do some thinking, some mental investigation and exploration into that probing, insistent *why?*'

> Why did some causes fail and others prosper? Why do some classes come into power and others go out from it? There were laws which governed the sun and the stars, a science by which their movements might be measured. Suppose human beings were also so governed, moving not haphazardly and chaotically according to a whim, a genius, or the will of God, but following a pattern of behaviour? Suppose there was a science which could explain the history of mankind?[94]

Warner's *Summer Will Show* (1936) paints a similarly enamoured portrait of its revolutionary theoretician Inglebrecht, a fictional composite of the authors of the *Communist Manifesto* which the novel imagines him writing and which it concludes with Sophia Willoughby 'reading, obdurately attentive and by degrees absorbed' amid the wreckage of 1848. Inglebrecht is 'grim and flat, positive without any flavour, a man like plain cold water' and 'everything' Sophia 'desired'.[95] Like Warner's near-contemporary profile of Rosa Luxemburg, Ingelbrecht's portrait privileges the unillusioned intellect and the practical understanding that patience, cunning and violence have each their part to play.[96] Other novels to tell the history of dialectical materialism include Lindsay's fictional biography of the heretic philosopher Giordano Bruno, *Adam of a New World* (1936). He wrote the novel in the first flush of his 'delighted discovery of Marxism', projecting his own process of assimilation onto Bruno's development of 'a dialectical approach that embraces all reality'.[97] At one point, Bruno, feeling the need for 'a new logic which can deal with the coincidence of contraries', recalls the words of Catullus 85—'*odi et amo*'—for there is 'no ultimate division between love and hate. They are one in the unity of the experiencing self. I-love and I-hate merge with the vital totality of I-live, I-move.'[98]

---

[93] Morley, *The Mighty Years*, p.153; p.145; p.181; p.352; p.354.

[94] Morley, *The Mighty Years*, p.247.

[95] Sylvia Townsend Warner, *Summer Will Show* (London: Virago, 1987), p.219; p.329. Glyn Salton-Cox writes brilliantly of Inglebrecht as a key component of this novel's 'Communist élan' in *Queer Communism and the Ministry of Love: Sexual Revolution in British Writing of the 1930s* (Edinburgh: Edinburgh University Press, 2019), pp.95–106.

[96] Sylvia Townsend Warner, 'Women of Yesterday—2: Rosa Luxemburg', *Woman To-Day* (April 1937), p.5; p.12. *Woman To-Day* was the organ of the British section of the *Comité mondial des femmes contre la guerre et le fascisme*, a communist front organization.

[97] Jack Lindsay, *Life Rarely Tells: An Autobiography in Three Volumes* (Penguin: Ringwood, Victoria, 1982), p.761; Jack Lindsay, *Adam of a New World* (London: Ivor Nicholson & Watson, 1936), p.179. Lindsay explains how he used Bruno's 'passionate quest' to 'symbolise ... my own eager and anxious efforts to move ... into the full categories of Marxism' in 'The Fullness of Life', pp.109–10.

[98] Lindsay, *Adam of a New World*, p.66.

In *Brief Light: A Novel of Catullus* (1939) and again in *Thunder Underground* (1965), Lindsay narrates the poet's discovery of a dialectical synthesis 'in which love and hate were merged and surpassed, so that a totally new relationship was born'.[99]

This romance of theory is less a presence in novels by working-class writers, where the emphasis falls more often on local resources and traditions of struggle. Popular memory is the driver of Thomas's novel of the 1831 Merthyr Rising as it is of Heslop's 'To Reach the Slake', about the miner's leader William Jobling, executed in 1832 and the last man gibbeted in England. Heslop has his comrades steal the body from the gibbet, burying him in an unmarked grave: for Jobling, he writes, 'there would be no memorial. Only in the memory of these men and their children, and their children's children, the memory of the common folk, would he find a memorial.'[100] Born into a long line of potters, Frederick Harper dedicated his second novel of Chartism in the Potteries to his father, 'who first lit and passed to me the torch of a great tradition of struggle'. A fictional biography of the preacher and political leader Joseph Capper, Harper's novel told how this Tunstall blacksmith struck his mark 'upon people and the pattern of society' to become 'a great name in North Staffordshire' and 'the dominant figure in the living tradition of the people'.[101] The most sustained venture in this vein is James Barke's 'Immortal Memory' series (1946–54), a five-volume fictional biography of Robert Burns.

In *The Land of the Leal*, Burns had featured as part of the Ramsay family's radical inheritance, but one whose legacy required careful discrimination, with David, like his father, 'the type who preferred the Burns of *Holy Willy's Prayer* and *A Man's a Man* to the Burns of *The Cottar's Saturday Night*'.[102] The 'Immortal Memory' quintet elaborates this distinction, working to establish Burns as the Scottish people's poet and to extenuate and explain any departures from that standard. Each narrative climax across the novel's five volumes adds another song or poem to this canon of national-popular poetry, culminating, in *The Well of the Silent Harp* (1954), in the moment when Burns shares the text of his French Revolutionary hymn, 'A Man's a Man for a That' (1795). 'It's a' in Paine', Burns modestly explains to his blacksmith friend, Geordie Haugh. Barke then has Geordie reply that while the ideas may be there 'in Tammy Paine—nae doubt', it is 'the way you

---

[99] Jack Lindsay, *Brief Light: A Novel of Catullus* (London: Methuen, 1939), p.286.

[100] Harold Heslop, 'To Reach the Slake', unpublished typescript, first begun in the 1930s and revised 1947; Heslop Papers, HES/A4, p.320.

[101] Frederick Harper, *Joseph Capper* (London: Lawrence & Wishart, 1962), pp.7–8. According to a notice in the *Publishers' and Booksellers' Record* (7 March 1959), Harper planned a series of four novels about politics and Primitive Methodism in the North Staffordshire Potteries; only *Joseph Capper* and *Tilewright's Acre* (1959) made it to print. Well received in the British Labour press and selling well locally, the novels were also translated into Russian (1961 and 1966) and Czech (1961).

[102] Barke, *The Land of the Leal*, p.261. Burns's posthumous reputation, influentially mediated by Scott's son-in-law John Gibson Lockhart, had rested largely on this other Burns; 'The Cottar's Saturday Night' presents a pious peasantry contented with their lot.

put it down' that makes the difference.[103] As proof, this poem's idiom and vision is woven through and through Barke's earlier novel, steeling the Ramsay family's faith in what's possible and a testament to the power of the spoken, sung, and written word. This culturalist inflection, of a radical tradition passed down in family memory and community lore, archived in vernacular poetry and popular song, was the defining feature of mid-century communist historical writing.

## V. Hunting the Wren

The British communist historical novel was nurtured by and helped nurture a historical culture that remains one of the movement's lasting achievements. This historical culture has tended to drop from view when scholars filter the cultural history of the British Left through the narrative of a 'low dishonest decade' and a limiting literary fixation on the Party's public-school poets. To the extent, moreover, that some of this culture's leading players became professional historians, our histories of it have tended to restrict themselves to their main idioms and forms of engagement. But though this collective history-making made use of conferences, lectures, study groups, and summer schools, though its print profile included journals, source-anthologies, edited collections, and monographs, these more academic platforms did not exhaust its range of expression. For it also inspired music, from operas and symphonies to singalongs and songbooks; it inspired performance genres, such as plays, street parades, mass spectacles, and pageants; it inspired visual representation in banners, set design, murals, and prints. Not only did it involve academics and extension lecturers, but it also mobilized amateurs and autodidacts, artists, composers, folklorists and filmmakers, novelists, playwrights, poets, and schoolteachers. Though predominantly urban, this culture was not limited to London, and 'comrades who might hesitate to think of themselves as historians' were encouraged to 'make a valuable contribution to Marxist history by studying the past of their own town or of their union'.[104] Its production and performance was collaborative and inclusive, its stated aim to replace the hardening divisions of academic labour with 'collective Socialist forms of work'.[105]

---

[103] James Barke, *The Well of the Silent Harp: A Novel of the Life and Loves of Robert Burns* (London: Collins, 1954), pp.258–62.

[104] A.L. Merson, 'The Writing of Marxist History', *Communist Review* (July 1949): p.596. In the late 1930s, pageants were performed in Durham, Glasgow, Liverpool, Manchester, Newcastle, and South Wales; in the early 1950s, branches of the Historians' Group were set up in Manchester, Nottingham, and Sheffield. In October 1951, the Party published the first instalment of its *Local History Bulletin*; it was renamed *Our History* in 1953.

[105] Cf. Frank Jellinek on the collaborations for the 1948 centenary of the Communist Manifesto: 'the mere bringing together of a very large number of different but related professional workers on a single project provided the experimental basis for a whole new way of approaching the artist's problems today'. Jellinek, 'The Way To Do It. The Albert Hall Murals for the Communist Manifesto Centenary', *Our Time* 7, no.7 (1948): p.175. Or Christopher Hill: 'Agreement in a Marxist approach [to history]

Intensely cross-disciplinary and multi-generic, this was a culture that, for all the dislocations of war service and the demoralizing tensions of Cold War cultural politics, flourished for twenty years inside the Party and in altered circumstances thereafter. For when, in 1956, some of its most prominent historians left the Party, they retained an approach to history that was born of this broadly participatory historical culture. The names of these historians are now famous: the Early Modernist Christopher Hill; the Mediaevalist Rodney Hilton; the historian of empire and Shakespeare scholar, Victor Kiernan; the historian of eighteenth-century popular protest, George Rudé; Raphael Samuel, who although but a schoolboy in the early 1950s went on to co-found the History Workshop and pioneer the history of popular memory; the Thompsons, Edward and Dorothy, historians of the British eighteenth and nineteenth centuries.[106] Of these so-called British Marxist historians, only Eric Hobsbawm, the polymath chronicler of modern history and global banditry, remained. But whether they left the Party or stayed, they continued to practise a politics of listening for the silenced stories of the people, a method pioneered in the mid-century communist historical novel and in other non-scholarly genres.

To sketch in brief the range and vitality of this Party historical culture, this section follows the migrations of a traditional English folk song that the Popular Front made its own: 'The Cutty Wren'. Identified at the turn of the century with J.G. Frazer's studies of totemism and taken to exemplify the preservation in popular culture of primitive ritual practice, the lyrics were routinely mistaken for nonsense or nursery rhyme.[107] By the 1960s, however, 'The Cutty Wren' had come to signify riot and rebellion, a protest song associated not with the time immemorial of the passive English folk but with the active self-making of the English working class. At the time of the Aldermaston marches and the Centre 42 festivals, the song was to be heard on the Ian Campbell Folk Group's 1962 'Songs of Protest' EP, and in the climactic class-confrontation of Arnold Wesker's *Chips with Everything* (also 1962).

Early in Wesker's play, during a Christmas Party showdown between officers and conscripts on an RAF training base, a sneering Wing Commander orders

---

offers the possibility of collective work by a number of historians, the only means by which the vast mass of detailed knowledge now available can be synthesized ... As the number of Marxist historians increases, so the labour-saving convenience and intellectual stimulus of joint work should lead to an increase in the quality as well as the quantity of Marxist work.' Hill, 'Historians on the rise of British Capitalism', *Science and Society* 14, no.4 (1950): pp.320–1.

[106] The classic account is Eric Hobsbawm, 'The Communist Party Historians' Group 1946–1956', in *Rebels and their Causes: Essays in Honour of A.L. Morton*, edited by Maurice Cornforth (London: Lawrence & Wishart, 1978), pp.21–48. Despite a substantial critical literature on the formation and early published work of the British Marxist historians, the tendency has been to ignore the contribution of non-academic writers and the non-scholarly genres in which they worked.

[107] Walter de la Mare's 1923 anthology of rhymes 'for the young of all ages', *Come Hither!*, likely introduced W.H. Auden to the poem, who riffed on its riddled catechistical form in the epilogue to *The Orators* (1932) before including it in his *Oxford Book of Light Verse* (1938).

the young recruits to entertain the room with 'a dirty recitation or a pop song'; they respond instead with a fourteenth-century funeral dirge and then, to music, with 'The Cutty Wren'. Wesker's stage direction identifies it as 'an old peasant revolt song' and instructs the 'boys' to 'join in gradually, menacing the officers'.[108] Reviewing *Chips* for the *Sunday Times*, Harold Hobson called it 'the first anti-establishment play of which the establishment has cause to be afraid. This is something to be discussed and re-discussed, admired; feared.'[109] That menace had everything to do with the transformation of 'The Cutty Wren' from riddling nursery rhyme to contemporary fighting song; and whatever the period polemic that pits folk authenticity against commercial pop, we may pause on a stage effect that presents as real 'The Cutty Wren's' ability to raise again revolt. This radical revaluation of 'The Cutty Wren' reflects the revisionist intent of mid-century communist historiography and it bears the particular stamp of the Party's working-class intellectuals. Their contribution to the intellectual and cultural life of the Popular Front remains largely underappreciated, lacking perhaps the celebrity of the public-school poets who passed through the Party in the 1930s or the prestige of the professional historians who came after. These plebeian intellectuals were products of the public library and the night-class; their education in the movement was one of its great accomplishments and their works a measure of its success.[110] It was their interpretation of this song, and of its original connection to the 1381 Peasants' Revolt, that put 'The Cutty Wren' on the map.

A.L. Lloyd (1908–82) was the son of a sometime dockworker, draper's packer, and poultry farmer.[111] By the age of sixteen he had lost his parents to tuberculosis and taken an assisted passage to New South Wales, where for the next six years he worked as a sheep- and cattle-hand. He educated himself at nights, reading widely in books borrowed from the Sydney Public Library's distance education service and spending his wages on records of classical music bought on spec from the HMV catalogue; it was the songs of the shearers, swagmen, and station-hands, however, that started Lloyd on his career as a folksinger and ethnomusicologist. When he returned to London in 1934, he made fast friends with the Communist historian A.L. Morton, then at work on his landmark *People's History of England*

---

[108] Arnold Wesker, *Chips with Everything and Other Plays* (Harmondsworth: Penguin, 1980), pp.35–8.

[109] Harold Hobson, 'Mr Ustinov, Enchanted', *The Sunday Times*, 29 April 1962, p.41. *Chips* was a major success; it premiered at the Royal Court Theatre in April 1962, transferred to the Vaudeville in June where it ran for nearly a year, and then to the Plymouth Theatre on Broadway in 1963.

[110] I borrow the term 'plebeian' from Michael Denning's analysis of the social composition of the US Cultural Front. Denning identifies three main groups: 'the moderns' were middle-class professional writers who made a turn to the Left in the 1920s or 1930s; 'the émigrés' brought their radical politics with them as they fled the fascisms in Europe, Asia, and Latin America; 'the plebeians' were the children of working-class and often African-American or second-generation immigrant families, whom the communist arts movement enfranchised to become writers, artists, and intellectuals. 'Plebeian' was their preferred term. Denning, *The Cultural Front*, pp.58–62.

[111] Cf. Dave Arthur, *Bert: The Life and Times of A.L. Lloyd* (London: Pluto Press, 2012).

(1938) and a journalist for the *Daily Worker*. It was likely at Morton's suggestion that Lloyd published his first essay on folk song in the paper in 1937, praising it as 'the people's own poetry' and, though presently in retreat, 'a foreshadowing of what the masses will be capable of when they are at last free from the stultifying miseries of capitalist industrialization'.[112] In *The Singing Englishman* (1944), Lloyd expanded his argument and supplied a radical genealogy of the popular origins and allegiance of folk song. Confessedly a 'sketchy book'—'put together mainly in barrack rooms, away from reference works [and] in between tank gunnery courses'—Lloyd's argument in *The Singing Englishman* was simple: that English folk song was an archive of working-class consciousness and a living testament to its history.[113]

'The Cutty Wren' took centre stage, for Lloyd, as evidence that 'what we nowadays call English folksong is something that came out of revolutionary upheaval', that 'it grew up with a class just establishing itself in society with sticks, if necessary, and rusty swords and bows discoloured with smoke and age'.[114] Originally 'a magical song, a totem song', 'The Cutty Wren' took on 'revolutionary meanings' in the experience of, and in resistance to, the Norman Yoke. Writing against the conservative cultural politics of the first English folk song revival, with its 'prancing curate[s] in cricket flannels' and BBC Singers 'cooing quaintly in the accents of Palmers Green and Ealing', Lloyd argued that what made English folk song English was its distinctive performance 'style'.[115] As evidence, he referenced the report of an old shepherd singing 'The Cutty Wren' in the years before the First World War. When Mr Hawkins came to the final line, he 'stamped violently' with his crook, 'declaring that it was a defiant song, that to stamp was "the right way, and it reminds you of the old times"'.[116] With this stamp, English folk song became a vehicle of defiance and 'The Cutty Wren' a record of the 'revolutionary origins of English folksong'.

Recoding the 1381 Peasants' Revolt as a radical insurrection was the work of another working-class autodidact. Born in 1903 in Stepney to Jewish parents who had fled the pogroms in Russia, Hyman Fagan grew up in a political household, but it was after he left school at fourteen and started work in a tailoring factory off the City Road that his 'his real education began'. The factory 'was my university', he recalled, for which he thanked the junior shop steward who directed his reading: 'it was his object to turn me into a trade unionist and a Socialist, and he did so

---

[112] A.L. Lloyd, 'The People's Own Poetry', *Daily Worker*, 10 February 1937, p.7.
[113] A.L. Lloyd, *The Singing Englishman: An Introduction to Folksong* (London: Workers' Music Association, 1945), p.2; A.L. Lloyd, *Folk Song in England* (London: Lawrence & Wishart, 1967), p.6
[114] Lloyd, *The Singing Englishman*, p.4.
[115] A.L. Lloyd, 'The Revolutionary Origins of English Folksong' [1943], reprinted in *Folk: Review of People's Music, Part One*, edited by Max Jones (London: Jazz Music Books, 1945), p.13.
[116] Lloyd, *The Singing Englishman*, p.8.

with finesse'.[117] In 1925, he joined his factory cell of the Communist Party, and when the factory closed down shortly afterwards he continued his studies at the St Pancras branch. There, Ralph Fox taught him Marx and Dona Torr, later the great mentor of the Marxist historians, encouraged his passion for the past. It was with her help and the advice of Christopher Hill and John Morris that he wrote *Nine Days that Shook England*, a popular history of the Peasants' Revolt published by the Left Book Club in 1938.

*Nine Days* is Popular Front history to a tee.[118]

> The theory of Socialism, utopian, unscientific and fantastic as it must have appeared at the time, is as English as the downs over which [John] Ball's agitators must have tramped, and as deeply embedded in the hearts of English men as are the roots of the great elms in the English soil under whose shelter many a rebel gathering took place.[119]

The book's most imaginative feature, however, is the picture it paints of the peasants' revolutionary organization. Though only vaguely mentioned in the chronicles, Fagan's 'Great Society' prefigures the Communist Party, its influence stretching from the South Coast as far North as the Humber, its members 'not regarded as aliens foisted on their area by some outside body with strange ideas', but as local men respected by their fellows for their political intelligence and steadfast integrity.[120] Fagan understood himself to be writing, 'not as an objective historian, but as a partisan, a supporter of the revolt, just as Marx had done when he wrote of the Paris Commune and as Engels had done when he wrote of the revolt of the German peasants, not that my book was anywhere near theirs'. He was determined to show 'how much there was to admire in the rebels', to avow their political rationality and agency. That the book 'put the backs up of many' came as no surprise: 'I had no scholastic record. I had gone straight from school into the factory, and apart from Marxist classes I had received no other education apart from what I had taught myself, yet I had entered the lists against university trained professional historians, challenging their findings.'[121]

Fagan's account of the Peasants' Revolt fired the imagination of the British Left. Randall Swingler's libretto for the 1939 Workers' Music Association pageant, 'Music for the People', stages the Peasants' Revolt as its third episode, and depicts

---

[117] Hyman Fagan, typescript autobiography of the years 1903–45. Communist Party Archives, People's History Museum, Manchester. CP/IND/FAG/1/5.

[118] Hyman Fagan, *Nine Days That Shook England: An Account of the English People's Uprising in 1381* (London: Victor Gollancz, 1938). Ben Harker is right to read in the title's nod to John Reed's classic 1919 account of the Russian October Revolution, *Ten Days That Shook the World*, the ideological pull of an earlier, Third Period Bolshevism, but it is the Popular Front emphasis on the people's agency and accomplishment that predominates. Harker, '"Communism is English"', p. 26.

[119] Fagan, *Nine Days*, p.159.

[120] Fagan, *Nine Days*, p.10

[121] Fagan, 'Autobiography'.

John Ball preaching to the peasants before they all march on London singing 'The Cutty Wren'. A typical Popular Front affair, the pageant mobilized five hundred singers (drawn from twenty-three London Co-operative Choirs and the Rhonddha Valley Male Voice Choir), one hundred dancers, twelve composers, a wind band, and the soloists Paul Robeson and Parry Jones; Alan Bush conducted.[122] Some of the same singers will likely have performed in the 'Pageant of Freedom', a smaller affair organized by the Watford Cooperative Society the following year. While the first part offers a narrative of the centuries-long struggle for freedom, the 'way of hope' paved 'with the songs that men have sung / In the vanguard of the battle / For Liberty, Labour and Life', the second part is a comic review. 'Nothing Ever Happens in Watford?' introduces the audience to Percy, a bored Watfordian who is about to 'pop round to the Red Lion for a quick one' when he is interrupted by a voice on the radio announcing 'the second in our series of plays "England in Revolt"'.

Percy has been complaining that 'nothing—absolutely nothing ... ever happens in Watford', indeed, that nothing 'ever has happened!' 'England in Revolt' corrects him on that score. 'Tonight's episode is based on the Peasants' Revolt of 1381, and is concerned with that section of the Peasant Army led by one William Grindcobbe, who led the men of Watford' against the Abbot of St Albans. 'During the action of the play one of the earliest English songs will be sung—"The Cutty Wren". The words may mean nothing to the listener, but it is believed that they contained a hidden message to those in revolt at the time.' Percy sits down to listen 'in the living room of [his] suburban home', while under a spotlight upstage the events of 1381 unfold, interspersed with verses of 'The Cutty Wren'. When news is heard of the murder of Wat Tyler, an actor addresses us directly: 'Right, good people—remember this day all your lives—remember the song we were but lately singing. And now sing it with all your hearts and with minds set upon vengeance for this foul deed.'[123]

Alan Bush, who organized and conducted the 'Music for the People' pageant in 1939, wrote an 'Introduction and Passacaglia on "The Cutty Wren"' as the third movement of his *English Suite* (1945), which he also scored for brass band. Bush returned to the song in his symphonic suite, *Piers Plowman's Day* (1946–47), but the most powerful adaptation occurs in his Festival of Britain opera, *Wat Tyler* (1951). The Prologue closes with a conversation between a politicized herdsman and a serf fleeing his village in search of wage work, at the end of which the herdsman bids him stay: 'you will see great matters moving. John Trueman doth you to understand, falsehood and guile have ruled too long'. In the words of John

---

[122] For a full description, see Andy Croft, *Comrade Heart: A Life of Randall Swingler* (Manchester: Manchester University Press, 2003), pp.91–3. Later that year, and as an offshoot of the festival, Topic Records pressed a recording of the song in more authentic folk dress, featuring the Topic Singers accompanied on pipe and drum and conducted by Arnold Goldsborough.

[123] Mike Myson, 'Pageant of Freedom', Jack Lindsay Papers, MS7168 Box 71.

Trueman, we hear the coded message of the Great Society, and then from offstage a chorus begins 'The Cutty Wren', the singers unseen to convey the secrecy of the organization and its threat to power and privilege. With the last line, the herdsman joins in the song and the curtain falls. Bush later dedicated *Wat Tyler* to Hymie Fagan 'whose instigation and encouragement led me to write the work.'[124]

Fagan was the inspiration for Charles Poulsen's historical novel, *English Episode: A Tale of the Peasants' Revolt of 1381* (1946). The novel is a perfect example of the communist historical culture that emerged in Britain in the wake of Dimitrov's address. Like Fagan and Wesker, Poulsen (1911–2001) had been born to poor Jewish parents in the East End of London. He left school at thirteen and found work first in a Houndsditch warehouse and then for a while as a fur-nailer. A committed autodidact, he continued his education at the Stepney public library and in evening classes at the Workers' Circle Friendly Society in Whitechapel. From 1931 he was a member of the Young Communist League and from 1933 a member of the Communist Party.[125] In 1935 he took up work as a taxi driver and found himself three years later in an argument.

> We were arguing as taxi-drivers often do while they wait for fares. The other man said the English were different from most people—always ready to compromise and settle things 'constitutionally.' I knew this wasn't right, and I knew history had plenty of examples to show it wasn't right. The peasant revolt and the treachery and bloodshed used in its suppression seemed one of the first examples. I talked about this with other people and eventually decided to try to write a novel about it.[126]

When the war came, Poulsen joined the Fire Service, and wrote the first half of the novel between callouts in the Blitz; drafted in 1944 to accompany the allied invasion with the AFS Overseas Contingent, Poulsen wrote the second half 'in the back of lorries, in broken down, bombed houses and a good many other places' as his column moved through France, Luxemburg, and Germany.[127] *English Episode* was

---

[124] Alan Bush, *Wat Tyler: An Opera in Two Acts with a Prologue* (London: Novello, 1959). Dedication added in 1974, at the time of the opera's only British stage production at Sadler's Wells in London: see *Alan Bush: A Sourcebook*, edited by Stewart R. Craggs (Aldershot: Ashgate, 2007), p.70. Joanna Bullivant discusses this opera in the context of Soviet-sphere aesthetics in *Alan Bush, Modern Music, and the Cold War: The Cultural Left in Britain and the Communist Bloc* (Cambridge: Cambridge University Press, 2017), pp.177–205.

[125] Poulsen recalls his upbringing in 'the Whitechapel Ghetto of the East End of London' and his first engagements with communism in *Scenes from a Stepney Youth* (London: Tower Hamlet Arts Project Books, 1988).

[126] 'New Play is by Taxi Driver', *Daily Worker*, 2 May 1951, p.3.

[127] 'New Play is by Taxi Driver', p.3. In a later interview with Andy Croft, Poulsen told the story a little differently, postdating the novel's inception to his fire-service work in the Blitz. 'There was this bloke in our station who slept in the next bunk to me, and he maintained that Britain by virtue of the pacific nature of its people and their willingness to compromise had escaped the long series of violent revolutions that most continental countries had been through, and through reason and law

published in 1946 by a subsidiary of Lawrence & Wishart and translated widely behind the Iron Curtain; as *The Word of The King* it was dramatized by Unity Theatre in 1951.[128] Poulsen's reasons for writing are exemplary: the desire to situate communism in an *English* episode, the desire to counter the Whig narrative of history as seamless and smooth, the desire to align the British national story with the revolutionary climaxes in France, America, and Russia, and thus to assert domestic precedent for the present possibility of revolution. And in the earnest conversation and its ambitious outcome we have evidence of a Party culture, in Andy Croft's words, 'instinctively argumentative' and fully at ease 'with the impulse to write'.[129]

'The Cutty Wren' returns in Jack Lindsay's Unity Theatre play, *Robin Hood* (1945), and in his pageant for the sixteenth anniversary of *The Daily Worker* (1946). It appears in Alan Gifford's 'song book for children growing up', *If I had a song* (1954). It accompanies the Peasants' Revolt sequence in *Ilford* (1957), a chronicle of local history by the Ilford branch of the communist New Era Film Society.[130] The song's 1962 appearance in Wesker's *Chips with Everything* and in his Centre 42 festival drama from the same year, *The Nottingham Captain* (about Luddism in the East Midlands), almost completes this line of transmission. But there is one last place to look. For these Old and first New Left historical subcultures, amateur and autodidact as we have seen, did ultimately enter the British cultural mainstream and address the nation at large. Early in January 1972, BBC Radio 4 broadcast the sixth instalment in its pioneering people's history of Britain, *The Long March of Everyman*. Created and produced by Michael Mason, the six-month series traced the history of the British people from prehistoric times through to Windrush and beyond. A stunning line-up of historians and scholars, many of them former communists, directed the individual episodes and supplied the voiceover commentary.[131] But the novelty of the series lay in its commitment to letting 'the people of Britain ... speak for themselves'. Mason and his team

---

and constitutional practices had evolved through history to the fine state of popular representative democracy that we enjoy in England today. And so we argued for a bit, and then I thought I'd write a book about this, make it a novel. A bit ambitious perhaps.' Cited in Croft, 'Authors Take Sides', p.88.

[128] Charles Hobday recalls Poulsen's excitement on learning that the Unity Theatre stage adaptation would 'include songs, which a member of the Workers' Music Association, an authority on mediaeval music, had offered to set'; sadly, if only for my purposes, the song chosen for the play's scene of May Day revelry was a 'carole of Robin Hood' and not 'The Cutty Wren'. Hobday, 'Charles Poulsen: A Study in Loyalties', in *Whitechapel Spring: Poems and Stories by Charles Poulsen*, edited by Charles Hobday (Belfast: Lapwing Publications, 2005), p.52. 'The Word of the King', unpublished typescript, Unity Theatre Archive, Victoria and Albert Museum Theatre & Performance Archives, THM/9/7/166.

[129] Croft, 'Authors Take Sides', p.88.

[130] '*If I had a song*': *A Song Book for Children Growing Up*, edited by Alan Gifford (London: Workers' Music Association, 1954), pp.40–1. *Ilford*, directed by William Bland (Ilford New Era Film Society, 1957).

[131] Christopher Hill, Rodney Hilton, Victor Kiernan, George Rudé, and Raphael Samuel directed episodes, as also did Stuart Hall; Raymond Williams was a literary consultant for the series. David Henry discusses Mason's fabulously expensive, ambitious, and ultimately controversial series in *Life on Air: A History of Radio Four* (Oxford: Oxford University Press, 2007), pp.64–7.

commissioned field recordings to catch the accent of recent and remembered history, while for earlier periods they recruited 'contemporary equivalents of the original speakers' to read from the written record.[132]

Mason brought to the series a missionary belief in the power of radio to forge new mental and emotional connections; inspired by the social anthropologist Edmund Leach, he hoped to develop in his programming a counterforce to the kind of analytical thinking 'which *separates*', which gives us conceptual 'mastery' but also 'murders to dissect', leaving us 'isolated, lonely and afraid in a world in which everything is split apart from everything else, and we are split apart from our world and one another'. His programmes were about combination and juxtaposition, the fusing together of ambient noise and radiophonic effects, folk song and art music, poetry and prose, to form what he called 'a total audio', a 'Great Music' of sound. In the past, *'musique concrète'* had been the preserve of avant-garde composers and progressive rock, but radio, Mason believed, made it possible to widen its appeal, to make of it a medium for stories that could help a post-imperial Britain reconnect with its 'roots' and chart a forward course.[133]

The sixth episode of *The Long March of Everyman* tells a history of the mediaeval peasant, and begins by evoking a bucolic, pastoral feudalism. This world is interrupted by a voice reciting the proverb on which John Ball will later base his sermon at Blackheath in 1381: 'When Adam delved and Eve span, who was then the gentleman?' The proverb returns, with more and more voices speaking it in unison; verses of 'The Cutty Wren' intersperse with intimations of peasant discontent and political organization; and then the Revolt is upon us. But in a complicated closing sequence, the episode ends not with the rising's bloody suppression or even with the suggestion (itself remarkable) that the spirit of resistance was not then extinguished but instead went underground to manifest in scattered acts of vandalism through the early fifteenth century. Without warning, Mason catapults the listener to a contemporary field recording of a gardener recalling his experience on an English country estate between the wars serving a 'Lordship and Ladyship' who were 'very very Victorian and very domineering'. Domestic servants had to turn to face the wall whenever their masters went by and garden staff to keep their labour out of sight. 'We gave, they took; that was the complete arrangement.' But there is an ambivalence to the gardener's account: the experience was 'marvellous' as well as 'frightening'; he'd 'feel sort of strange inside, pitying and hating' his employers 'at the same time'. He ends by observing how, 'in a great garden, you

---

[132] 'Daniel Snowman writes about the series as history', *The Listener* 86, no.2225 (18 November 1971): p.685; Theo Barker, 'Appendix', to *The Long March of Everyman 1750–1960*, edited by Theo Barker (Harmondsworth: Penguin, 1978), p.295.

[133] Michael Mason, 'The Long March of Everyman', *The Listener* 86, no.2225 (18 November 1971): pp.683–4.

grow from seed. And then you see the plant grown where it will always grow.'[134] As the credits roll, the listener is left to puzzle out this metaphor of the ineradicable seed, its ambiguous reference to entrenched class power and popular resistance. For *The Long March of Everyman*, both answers are acceptable, a reminder that both conservatism and rebellion are the people's history, to be told 'in their own voices'.

## VI. 'voices from the past'

The transmission of popular song provided historians on the British Left a model to explain the preservation of the people's radical traditions. Lloyd's account of 'The Cutty Wren' captured perfectly this imagined continuity, the class politics of 1381 surviving in the twentieth-century performance style of Mr. Hawkins, who sang the last line 'the right way' (with a stamp of his crook) 'because it reminds you of the old times'. Folk song also supplied the metaphors by which the new social history looked to explain its method. Taking his title from a popular ballad, Christopher Hill's suggestion in *The World Turned Upside Down* (1972) that 'the obscure men and women who figure in this book' may 'speak more directly to us' than those who 'appear as history-makers in the textbooks'—and that this might in itself 'be a satisfactory upside-down thought to come away with'—identifies not only the flipped perspective of history from below but also its characteristic idiom: that of voices overheard and of conversations carried on across time.[135] Hill and his fellow Marxist historians saw themselves as listening to the past rather than reading it, and the restoration of speech to those whom history had silenced was central to their project.

Eric Hobsbawm wanted his *Primitive Rebels* (1958) to speak 'In Their Own Voices', and it was from 'a rather tricky historical source, namely poems and ballads', that in 1969 he set out to recover the 'remembered history' of social banditry.[136] E.P. Thompson was likewise committed to the spoken word of the historical record. There was no such thing, he claimed, as 'inaudible' evidence, no such thing as a 'dead, inert text'. The archive 'has a deafening vitality of its own; voices clamour from the past'.[137] The historian has therefore to be 'listening

---

[134] 'Ploughmen: The Mediaeval Peasant', episode six of *The Long March of Everyman*, first broadcast 2 January 1972 on BBC Radio 4. Barrie Dobson was the program director, at the time a Senior Lecturer in History at York; the archaeologist Jacquetta Hawkes and the demographic and local historian Michael Drake also provided commentary.

[135] Christopher Hill, *The World Turned Upside Down: Radical Ideas during the English Revolution* (London: Temple Smith, 1972), p.15.

[136] Eric Hobsbawm, *Primitive Rebels: Studies in Archaic Forms of Social Movements in the 19th and 20th Centuries* (New York: Norton, 1965), pp.175–93; Eric Hobsbawm, *Bandits* (London: Weidenfeld and Nicholson, 2000), pp.144–5.

[137] E.P. Thompson, *The Poverty of Theory, or An Orrery of Errors* (London: Merlin, 1995), p.25.

all the time'. 'If he listens, then the material will speak through him.'[138] In a less ventriloquist vein, Thompson suggested the historian engage the past in dialogue. In defence of the empiricist bent of British Marxist historiography, he praised the historian's ability to help the facts 'find "their own voices". Not the historian's voice, please observe: *their own voices*, even if what they are able to "say" and some part of their vocabulary is determined by the questions which the historian proposes. They cannot "speak" until they have been asked.'[139] Call and response, active listening, the historian as acoustic medium: these tropes so central to the methodological conception of New Left social history resonate with the contemporaneous rise of Oral History and the Second British Folksong Revival; in fact, all three movements, through their often overlapping personnel, institutional formation, and political orientation, inherit the emphasis on the sung and spoken word of 1930s British communist historical culture.

Jack Lindsay's historical novel *1649* (1938) contains a sequence in which a seasoned revolutionary instructs a new recruit to listen to the people. 'The people know what they want, Ralph. It's in their songs ... That's the people speaking, lad. That's the voice we have to let speak out loud. Storm-loud.'[140] The conversation takes its contemporary cue from the work of artists and intellectuals associated with the Workers' Music Association, the Ralph Fox writer's group, and the Left Book Club's poetry and music groups, to pioneer a renaissance of radical-popular poetry and song.[141] Ben Harker has traced the Popular Front rehabilitation of popular poetry from which the post-war folk revival sprung.[142] Key sites included the popular Left Book Club anthologies *Poems of Freedom* and *The Left Song Book* (both 1938); the promotion of new balladry and the republication of old demotic song in the pages of *Poetry and the People* (1938–40); the development of new performance genres for 'mass recitation' and participation; the speculative reconstruction of the origins of culture in primitive ritual and the rhythms of work put forward in Lindsay's *Short History of Culture* (1938) and George Thomson's *Marxism and Poetry* (1945).

It is within this context of revaluation, as leading Popular Front intellectuals like Lindsay and Lloyd set out to revive a pre-industrial, pre-proletarian art as

---

[138] Michael Merrill, 'An Interview with E.P. Thompson', *Radical History Review* 3, no.4 (1976): p.15.
[139] Thompson, *The Poverty of Theory*, p.41.
[140] Jack Lindsay, *1649: A Novel of a Year* (London: Methuen, 1938), p.134.
[141] Cf. Andy Croft, 'The Ralph Fox (Writers') Group', in *And in Our Time: Vision, Revision, and British Writing of the 1930s*, edited by Anthony Shuttleworth (Cranbury, NJ: Associated University Press, 2003), pp.171–2; and Croft, *Comrade Heart*, pp.77–81. Cf. also Peter Marks, 'Art and Politics in the 1930s: *The European Quarterly* (1934–5), *Left Review* (1934–8), and *Poetry and the People* (1938–40)', in *The Oxford Critical and Cultural History of Modernist Magazines. Volume I, Britain and Ireland 1880–1955*, edited by Peter Brooker and Andrew Thacker (Oxford: Oxford University Press, 2009), pp.641–6.
[142] Ben Harker, '"Workers' Music": Communism and the British Folk Revival', in *Red Strains: Music and Communism Outside the Communist Bloc*, edited by Robert Adlington (Oxford: Oxford University Press, 2013), pp.89–104.

a weapon in the struggle, that English folk song rediscovered its political punch. 'Take the world as it goes', Richard Overton instructs his young apprentice in *1649*:

> it's dark and bloody with guilt; and it goes on, it stamps on without a turn of the head; you think it is foul to everlasting. And then you hear that weak and rambling voice that's singing where a few poor men meet. And you hear something different. You hear this protest against the money-mongers that buy the bread of life and hide it in a private garner; against them that make their dice of poor men's bones ... that unimportant voice is singing where poor men meet. And some day it will speak out louder and louder.[143]

Lindsay's novel positions popular song as a repository of utopian desire and political resistance; it makes hearing the people's 'unimportant voice' the project of a reparative social history; and it frames the affirmation and amplification of these native and vernacular traditions as vital to the present political struggle.

The next novel in Lindsay's English trilogy, *Lost Birthright* (1939), introduces us to an eighteenth-century crowd of the kind George Rudé would later study and suggests we 'listen more closely to that voice of the masses', to 'the things that the people are saying, the things that stirred in their minds'. Lindsay invites a succession of crowd-members to share their experience: 'I was there. I'll give my version', says one. 'Robert Allen, what's your story?' 'Stand out, Dick Nicholl, rope-maker, and have your say.'[144] To a serving-wench and her lover, accidental characters met first and briefly in the very opening of the novel and long since left behind, Lindsay dutifully returns: 'They play no further part in our tale, but we can spare their small lives a glance.' Forced from the country, they have made their way to the city to seek their uncertain fortune, joining

> the crowd struggling for a crust, a bed, in London. Their voices sound among the other voices. *Wilkes and Liberty!* Give them a thought before they drift down Holborn-way, trickles in the great tide surging on ... Good lad, good lass, good luck! Their voice comes back in the other voices. They are not lost; they are part of this story, through and through.[145]

Thus they, with Robert Allen and Dick Nicholl, find a shelter in the crowd, a crowd that was also a movement, for the crowd's political education during the Wilkite protests was for Lindsay, as later for Rudé and E.P. Thompson, a crucial episode in the making of the English working class.

---

[143] Lindsay, *1649*, p.134.
[144] Jack Lindsay, *Lost Birthright* (London: Methuen, 1939), pp.259–65.
[145] Lindsay, *Lost Birthright*, p.413.

*Lost Birthright*'s appeal to these 'faces in the crowd' to share their story and let their voices sound is of a piece with the performance genres of Popular Front historiography. Lindsay's first 'mass declamation' from 1936 had imagined British history as a May Day parade, a 'March of History' of the kind the Communist Party was soon to make a feature: 'Rise up, peasants ... fall in behind us'. 'Come you Anabaptists and you Levellers, / Come you Muggletonians, all you Bedlamites / fall in behind us'.[146] Lindsay's popular prose-pageant, *England My England* (1938), further personalized the appeal, inviting the reader, for example, 'to give a shout across the centuries to John Walker, brave lad, with the rope around his neck for speaking out too clearly the thoughts of Englishmen'. To this forgotten victim of a suppressed sixteenth-century peasant revolt, Lindsay frames the following colloquial address:

> Good day to you, John Walker, standing on the death-cart one bright morning of 1540, looking your last on the world you loved, the English faces and the English earth, till the hangman jerked the planks from under your feet and the ruling class that feared you strangled the good English breath in your throat. But they could not strangle that voice of independence and courage. We're still talking, John Walker.[147]

This continued conversation links the unfulfilled desires of the past to those awaiting fulfilment in the present, privileging collective experience and expanding the object of historical study to encompass not just the actual but the desired and the possible as well.

Matthew Taunton has explored the 'phonocentric' style of British Popular Front communism, its 'tendency to value speech above writing, orality over literacy', tracing the ways Left-wing intellectuals in the late 1930s figured the fight for socialism as also an occasion to remedy the reification of literature, to reunite the written and spoken word, the individual and collective voice.[148] Taunton takes his term from Jacques Derrida, who in his famous study *Of Grammatology* (1967) equated

---

[146] Jack Lindsay, 'not english? a Reminder for May Day', *Left Review* 2, no.8 (1936): p.355. On 20 September 1936, the London District of the Communist Party organized the first 'March of History', with over sixty full-size banners commemorating episodes of English radical history. Kino Films made a short recording of the London March called 'We Are the English'; BFI Identifier 21,436, British Film Institute, London. Other such marches took place in Liverpool, Manchester, Sheffield, and South Wales. See Mick Wallis, 'The Popular Front Pageant: Its Emergence and Decline', *New Theatre Quarterly* 11, no.41 (1995): pp.17–32. Ernie Trory recounts the preparations for and reception of the Sussex People's March of History (Brighton 1938, Eastbourne 1939) in *Between the Wars: Recollections of a Communist Organiser* (Brighton: Crabtree Press, 1974). After the 1938 march, Brighton Unity Theatre performed Lindsay's mass declamation 'not english?' (retitled 'Who are the English?' after its republication as a one-penny Left Review pamphlet); Brighton-based 'People's Newsreels' filmed both marches.

[147] Jack Lindsay, *England My England: A Pageant of the English People* (London: Fore Publications, 1939), p.19.

[148] Matthew Taunton, *Red Britain: The Russian Revolution in Mid-Century Culture* (Oxford: Oxford University Press, 2019), p.233; p.219.

phonocentrism with the metaphysics of presence and the fantasies of self-identity that embed themselves in ordinary, uncritical notions of living speech. Importantly, as Taunton notes, the logic of Derrida's critique of orality came to buttress a powerful post-war reaction against the culture of mid-century communism, a re-privileging of the written word and of a non-deictic, anti-mimetic poetics, a reassertion of reading against listening that found a home both in the Cold War academy and among younger generations of the Left.[149] In the Derridean 'prohibition on voice' we can see the ways in which the imagined positivity and historical identity of the people, of nation, class, and culture, the vocabulary of experience, consciousness, agency, and desire, all key components of mid-century communist historical thought, would falter in the face of post-structuralism and the linguistic turn.

It bears mentioning, however, that the phonocentrism of the British mid-century Left was hardly its alone; communists like Lindsay and Lloyd shared their fantasies of national cultural renewal and of the redemptive possibilities of communal speech with modernists like Woolf and Mirrlees, whose contemporaneous reflections on print and oral culture we met with in chapter one. Late Modernism and the mid-century Left shared the organicist romance of cultural reintegration and replenishment, however differently they imagined the trajectory of Britain's national story in the context of imperial realignment and the long Cold War. Jed Esty's discovery of 'a new and redemptive form of thirties Anglocentrism' in the late-career writing of modernists such as Eliot, Forster, and Woolf, parallels a similar national-cultural revivalism in writers associated with the British Popular Front.[150] But as I have underscored from the start, these insular or national turns were never only a British or parochially English affair. For British communists, though it was Dimitrov's Seventh World Congress address that officially authorized the mining of national-popular histories and cultural resources for the fight against fascism, it was Maxim Gorky who the previous year had established the 'phonocentric' form this recourse would take. In his keynote speech to the First All-Union Congress of Soviet Writers in 1934, Gorky explained socialist realism as an infusion of modern literature with folklore or with what he called 'the unwritten artistic compositions of the working people'.[151]

For my purposes, it matters little whether the new Soviet *byliny* on modern weaponry and the glories of Stalin as recited by Kazakh *akyns* at their annual

---

[149] Taunton, *Red Britain*, p.220.
[150] Esty, *A Shrinking Island*, p.48.
[151] Gorky, 'Soviet Literature', p.52. Felix Oinas recounts how, in the wake of Gorky's speech, significant state resources were directed towards the transcription of these 'unwritten compositions' and the reanimation of traditional folk cultures; Oinas, 'Folklore and Politics in the Soviet Union', *Slavic Review* 32, no.1 (1973): pp.45–58. British communists followed these developments closely, as they did similar moves to archive and revive vernacular traditions in countries like France and the United States. Cf. John Lehmann, *Prometheus and the Bolsheviks* (London: Cresset Press, 1937), pp.97–101; George Thomson, *Marxism and Poetry* (London: Lawrence & Wishart, 1945), pp.56–8.

minstrels' contests were 'folklore or fake lore'.[152] Since the poems of Ossian, the line between antiquarian romance revival and literary new creation had been blurred. Ian Duncan recalls Friedrich Schiller's distinction between 'naïve' and 'sentimental' poetry, 'between a "primitive", mythic or folkloric, oral culture, its forms embedded in an archaic cosmos, and a civilized literary culture which reproduces and recombines those forms as fictions', to insist that the fantasy of lost origins is itself a sentimental 'trope'. It is a symptom of our literary modernity that we desire the authentically pure, that we posit the existence of unalienated modes and relations of production, but there can be no going back: 'for us, romance must always be romance revival, meaning ... an active cultural work of the discovery and invention of ancestral forms'.[153] Socialist realism acknowledged its debt to this problematic when it adopted 'revolutionary romanticism' as a synonym, capturing what might otherwise seem the paradox of a Soviet cultural revolution intent on abolishing illiteracy while drawing from pre-literate societies its criteria of cultural value. Reviving the Russian romantic-era term *narodnost'* to name the new art's desired national specificity, popular accessibility, and traditional folk character, socialist realism marked the transition from an internationalist-elite model of proletarian literature to a national-popular conception of socialist culture.

The elevation of socialist realism after 1932 breathed new life into romantic-era debates about the origins, vestigial forms, and present function of romance. In its heroic intensification of otherwise realistically coded scenes of labour and struggle, socialist realism embraced that definition of romance that sees it as supplementing the record of reality, opening the flat facticity of the present to the possibility of social change. Of course, not all communists embraced this romantic turn. Georg Lukács, for one, preferred his Marxism scientific, his realism critical, and his romantic-era writers 'classical' (whence the value he attached to Scott's 'classical form' of the historical novel in contrast to the countervailing 'Byronism' of the romantic period, Lukács' shorthand for the lyric expressivism and eccentric individualism that blocks recognition of historical dynamics and socially representative types).[154] A similarly critical realism informs Eric Hobsbawm's sceptical interrogation of the modern 'invention of tradition', as well as his detailed

---

[152] Richard Dorson first framed the contrast in 'Folklore or Fake Lore', *The American Mercury* 70, no.315 (1950): pp.335–43.

[153] Duncan, *Modern Romance*, pp.6–7.

[154] In *The Historical Novel*, Lukács observes in Scott what he calls 'a renunciation of Romanticism, a conquest of Romanticism, a higher development of the realist literary traditions of the Enlightenment'. Lukács was writing against a recent effort to rehabilitate Byron as part of a campaign for a new Soviet or 'civic' lyric poetry. Against a backdrop of the Spanish Civil War and of writers serving, and dying, in the International Brigades, Byron's death in the Greek War of Independence had given his reputation a boost in Soviet literary circles. Lukács countered by framing Byron's politics as a weakly romantic anti-capitalism: his heroes represent 'social eccentricity and superfluity'; their protest against the world devolves into 'a lyrical subjectivist absolute'. Notwithstanding Scott's reactionary personal politics, his choice of 'a "middling", merely correct and never heroic "hero" is the clearest proof' of his 'exceptional and revolutionary epic gifts', his superior critical realism (33–4). On the Bolshevik Byron, see Clark, *Moscow: The Fourth Rome*, p.334.

instructions to the historian of mentalities to attend to what is conscious and coherent in people's desires and actions. To reconstruct the life-worlds of the poor and oppressed requires of the historian an active 'discovery of the internal logical cohesion' and 'mutual consistency' of poor people's 'forms of behaviour, of thinking and feeling'. 'Like the hero of Molière', he concludes a commentary from 1978, 'they have been talking prose all the time. Only whereas the man in Molière didn't know it himself, I think they have always known it, but we have not. And I think we ought to.'[155] The preference is for prose, which as Monsieur Jourdain's philosophy instructor insists cannot at the same time be poetry.

But for a mainline of mid-century Marxist thinking forged in the crucible of the Popular Front and the People's War, poetry and prose, romance and realism, utopian desire and political reason, were much more closely compatible. Writing in 1972 of English Civil War's 'lunatic fringe', Christopher Hill warned that what we dismiss as 'lunacy' might, 'like beauty ... be in the eye of the beholder', that 'madness' might be radical and 'foolery' more than just the carnival-play of the Middle Ages. For 'what was new in the seventeenth century was the idea that the world might be *permanently* turned upside down: that the dreamworld of the Land of Cockayne or the kingdom of heaven might be attainable on earth now'.[156] The recovery of such 'poetic insights', ideas 'in advance of their time' as they remain 'in advance of ours', links key texts of later New Left social history to the mid-century communist historical novel: a shared labour of deciphering symbols and figures, orders of meaning in excess of the bourgeois cultural revolution that for Hill won out at the Restoration, when 'the island of Great Bedlam became the island of Great Britain'.[157]

Jack Lindsay's *The Great Oak* tells the story of the 1549 Kett rebellion in East Anglia, and though finally published in 1957, its first impetus came from a two-day session on peasant insurrection conducted by the sixteenth- and seventeenth-century section of the Communist Party Historians' Group in September 1948.[158] Unlike the more scholarly papers that came from this conference, Lindsay keys his novel to what he calls 'a folk note, in idiom and outlook, to bring out the feeling

---

[155] Eric Hobsbawm, 'Comments', on Peter Burke, 'Reflections on the Historical Revolution in France: The *Annales* School and British Social History', *Review (Fernand Braudel Center)* 1, no.3/4 (1978), p.162. Raphael Samuel expands on Hobsbawm's 'commitment to rationalism' in his classic essay, 'British Marxist Historians, 1880–1980: Part One', *New Left Review*, no.120 (1980): pp.92–3.
[156] Hill, *The World Turned Upside Down*, pp.13–14.
[157] Hill, *The World Turned Upside Down*, p.310; p.306.
[158] The sixth meeting of the Communist Party Historians' Group's sixteenth- and seventeenth-century section was held 18–19 September 1948 at the Garibaldi Restaurant in London. Kenneth Andrews, Rodney Hilton, Eric Kerridge, Mervyn James, and Allan Merson presented papers; Jack Lindsay attended. A.L. Morton credits the discussion in his article on Kett's Rebellion, 'The Norfolk Rising', *Communist Review* (July 1949): p.608. See also: Rodney Hilton, 'Peasant Movements in England before 1381', *Economic History Review* 11 (1949): pp.117–36; Eric Kerridge, 'The Revolts in Wiltshire against Charles I', *Wiltshire Archaeological and Natural History Society Magazine* 57 (1958): pp.64–75; and Mervyn James's essays on the 1536 Lincolnshire rebellion and the 1601 Essex revolt in *Society, Politics and Culture: Studies in Early Modern England* (Cambridge: Cambridge University Press, 1986).

of a peasant revolt'; this 'folk note' includes popular song and social ritual, as well as the desires and dissent registered in peasant superstition and witchcraft.[159] An early scene contrasts two kinds of subaltern response to the enclosure of the commons: Jack of the Stile's advice to mobilize around the common cause and organize resistance, and the magical alternative, a hex upon the landlords. Lindsay does not place these two protest forms on parity, but neither does he disparage Nan Towting's malediction; it forms part of an epistemology of the oppressed that extends through to the novel's end, when after the defeat of the peasants at Dussin's Dale, one character consoles another: 'It was a brave business while it lasted. But it wasn't the first time the people have sought to right the wrongs of the world, and it won't be the last.' The battle, though lost, represents

> no more than a blow given for a blow taken. A tale that men will tell at midnightfire in the wintry alehouse or under the red berries of the hedgerow, to hearten them and solace them for the villainies they endure. And when at last the tale grows stale, men will rise again and win another tale that sweetens their hardwrung lives for a dark while.

In an afterword, the novel invites the reader into this peasant community, describing how, 'by the midnight fires and under the hedgerows, we told the story of Robert Kett and many said he would come again to save England'.[160] The translation of history into the prophetic space of legend, the once and future rebel leader surviving in popular memory as a promise of resistance, is no doubt a compensatory fantasy, a forward dreaming that ill comports with the Left's prescribed pessimism of the intellect. But *The Great Oak* shares this plot solution with another novel written in 1948, though this time published the following year in a context seemingly worlds away.

Alejo Carpentier's *The Kingdom of this World* (1949), a historical novel set against the slave rebellions in Haiti of 1757 and 1791 and the subsequent reign of Henri Christophe, is both an exemplary text of mid-century radical romance revival and one of the founding texts of magical realism. The novel's inspiration has itself become lore, told and retold in the essay 'On the Marvellous Real in America' that Carpentier first published in the Caracas newspaper *El Nacional* in 1948; in 1949, he used it as a prologue to *The Kingdom of this World*, and in 1967 he expanded it for inclusion in a collection of his essays. Across each of these editions, Carpentier reflects on a trip he took to Haiti in 1943 which he credits with first opening his eyes to the radical historicity of the New World. In Port-au-Prince, Carpentier had delivered a lecture on the role of the Haitian

---

[159] Jack Lindsay. *A Catalogue of First Editions extensively annotated by the author, together with letters, manuscripts and association items*, edited by Harry Chaplin (Sydney: The Wentworth Press, 1983), p.31.

[160] Jack Lindsay, *The Great Oak: A Story of 1549* (London: Bodley Head, 1957), pp.300–2.

revolution in expanding the definition of 'the people' beyond its white bourgeois, French revolutionary, limits; but then, in touring the 'poetic ruins' of this history—Henri Christophe's palace of Sans-Souci 'and the bulk of the Citadel of La Ferrière, imposingly intact in spite of lightening and earthquakes'—he came to realize that this was all still very much a living history.[161] Carpentier's discovery of the 'presence and vitality' of a past as yet un-surmounted by the stadial logic of Enlightenment historicism came as a revelation. The 'marvellous reality' he found in Haiti and claimed as the 'heritage' of all America was a function of ecology and demography—'the virginity of the land', 'the Faustian presence of the Indian and the black man'—but it derived its temporal dimension from a charged combination of popular memory and collective 'faith'. To be sure, the continent has had its share of eccentric believers, like those who went in search of 'the fount of eternal youth', of 'El Dorado' and 'the enchanted city of the Caesars'. But it is the 'cosmogonies' of the subaltern, their rituals of community and memories of struggle, that most define the marvellous real.[162]

This class allegiance clarifies Carpentier's main point of difference with the European surrealism he had earlier espoused. Two figures exemplify the ostensible similarity and significant political difference in the way the Old and New Worlds access the improbable: Maldoror, the eponymous protagonist of Lautréamont's *Chants* (1868–69) and a hero to the Surrealists who severally and separately 'discovered' him during the First World War, and Mackandal, the *houngán*-magician who inspired and led Haiti's 1757 slave rebellion. Both are shapeshifters and can transform into animals; both use their ability to evade police capture. But Mackandal has an authenticity Maldoror lacks, his power vested in him by the people he serves, the 'thousands of men, anxious for freedom', who believe in him. Lautréamont laughed off his own creation as a 'poetic Rocambole', and Carpentier takes him at his word to disparage as artificial fantasy the aesthetic experiments of surrealism. Mackandal's, by contrast, is a natural magic, guaranteed by custom and belief, potent to the point where it fomented 'one of the strangest and most daring uprisings in history'. Whereas Maldoror left to posterity an 'ephemeral literary school', Mackandal 'leaves behind an entire mythology, preserved by an entire people, and accompanied by magic hymns still sung today during voodoo ceremonies'.[163] It is these rituals of resistance (all the more pointed given the 'antisuperstition campaign' the Catholic Church had waged against them in 1940–42) that gives the radical edge to a 'marvellous reality' powered by the perceived

---

[161] Alejo Carpentier, 'La evolución cultural de América Latina', in *Alejo Carpentier: Crónicas Caribeñas*, edited by Emilio Jorge Rodríguez and translated by Rafael Rodríguez Beltrán (Havana: Instituto Cubano del Libro, 2012), p.111; first published in the *Haïti-Journal*, 23 and 28 December 1943. Alejo Carpentier, 'On the Marvellous Real in America' [1967], in *Magical Realism: Theory, History, Community*, edited by Lois Parkinson Zamora and Wendy B. Faris, translated by Tanya Huntington and Lois Parkinson Zamora (Durham, NC: Duke University Press, 1995), p.84.
[162] Carpentier, 'On the Marvelous Real', pp.87–88.
[163] Carpentier, 'On the Marvelous Real', pp.87–88.

political as well as literary possibilities of 'synchronism', of 'relating' 'this to that' and 'yesterday to today'.[164]

In *The Kingdom of this World*, Mackandal's uprising supplies the first of the novel's four episodes and his execution a critical allegory of the class politics of the Americas' marvellous reality. After months in hiding, terrorizing the white owners of the plantations with poisonous concoctions administered by his followers, Mackandal is at last captured and his 'crusade of extermination' brought to an end. He is to be burned at the stake as a public warning against insurrection. The square in Cap-Haïtien is packed with slaves and their owners line the balconies; all watch on as the one-armed Mackandal is lashed to the post and his pyre set on fire. What follows, however, is a clash of epistemologies, the marvellous and the real apportioned their social locations in the two audiences there present. For the slaves, those whom Mackandal has so regularly visited during his time in hiding disguised as an animal, insect, reptile, or fish, there is nothing to fear: when the time comes, their hero will simply shift shape and escape.[165] As the slaves watch on and the flames rise up around him, Mackandal summons his magic. Waving the stump of his arm, 'howling unknown spells and violently thrusting his body forward', his 'bonds' appear to fall away and his body to rise into the air and to hover overhead 'until it plunged into the black waves of the sea of slaves. A single cry filled the square: Mackandal saved!' In the ensuing chaos, as slaves and soldiers struggle at street level, there is not a single slave to witness what the planter-class has been watching from its balconies and from the raised steps of the main church: the spectacle of Mackandal being 'thrust head first into the fire', the flames 'fed by his burning hair' drowning out his final cry. By the time order is restored and the slaves return their attention to the fire, it is 'burning normally like any fire of good wood'. But the fact that 'there was no longer anything more to see' allows both slave and owner to preserve intact their account of the day: Mackandal's miraculous escape and his total incineration are alike supported by the absence of remains.[166] The reality principle may appear to side with the slave-owners and wishful thinking with the oppressed, but the novel does not adjudicate.

Our vantage on these events has been that of Ti Noël, fellow slave and devoted follower of Mackandal, later rebel ringleader in the sack of Sans-Souci, and a more or less middling hero of the kind Lukács elaborated from Scott. Many years later, it is Ti Noël who on his deathbed revives the memory of Mackandal whose magic served a social movement and who, by channelling 'the power and the fullness of his remote African forebears', first brought Ti Noël to 'believe in the possible germinations the future held'. For however ambivalent Carpentier's portrait of premature political violence—and the novel draws into its fictional space not

---

[164] Carpentier, 'On the Marvelous Real', p.84.
[165] Alejo Carpentier, *The Kingdom of This World*, translated by Harriet B. Onís (Harmondsworth: Penguin, 1975), p.26.
[166] Carpentier, *The Kingdom of This World*, pp.31–2.

only Mackandal's rebellion, but Bouckman's in 1791 and the Aponte Conspiracy of 1812—a powerful socialist humanism informs Ti Noël's last 'lucid moment'. He has come to understand that though he has suffered, hoped, and toiled 'for people he will never know, and who, in turn, will suffer and hope and toil', this ethic of service and social strife is what confers upon man 'his greatness, his fullest measure ... in the Kingdom of This World'.[167] This, then, is the politics Carpentier inferred from his discovery in Haiti of the living presence of the past, from the Voodoo drum and from the 'poetic ruins' of a palace: traces of a once and future possibility he claimed was latent in the marvellous 'synchronisms' and radical 'mythologies' of the New World.

Addressing the first Congress of Black Writers and Artists in Paris in 1956, Jacques Stephen Alexis returned to the question with which Carpentier had ended his essay and prologue to *The Kingdom of this World*: 'What is the entire history of America if not a chronicle of the marvellous real?' 'What is then the marvellous', Alexis asks in antiphon, 'if it is not the imagery in which a people wraps its experience, reflects its conception of the world and of its life, its faith, its hope, its confidence in man, in a great justice, and the explanation it finds for the forces that block its way to progress?'[168] For the communist activist and novelist Alexis, the 'marvellous realism' of Haitian and black African art was a national-popular form of expression whose only adequate 'criterion of judgement' was whether it clarifies 'the nature of man and his collective destiny, his problems in the moment and the hopeful course of his struggle towards liberation'.[169] Whereas scholars have long worried over the precise relation of Carpentier's New World manifesto to the novel it accompanies, Alexis' statement allows no such equivocation. 'Marvellous realism' is for Alexis the 'revolutionary romanticism' of the Black Atlantic. The canonical definitions of socialist realism—Zhdanov's call for a faithful depiction 'of the most stern and sober practical work' in a context of 'magnificent future prospects', Gorky's insistence that the representation of 'life' be infused with a vision of 'mankind, united into a single family' and of a world transformed by its labour—map onto the utopian, prefigurative power of the marvellous.[170]

'Naturally', Alexis continues, we should not rest content with 'whatever is irrational, mystic, and animist' in our 'national patrimony'; 'the combatants of the avant-garde of Haitian culture' know that they must ultimately 'reject the animist garment which still clothes the kernel of realism', but not yet, not while it can still educate desire and inspire with a vision of what's possible in 'this century in which men travel at the speed of sound', 'ideas cross borders without passports',

---

[167] Carpentier, *The Kingdom of This World*, pp.111–12.
[168] Jacques Stephen Alexis, 'Du réalisme merveilleux des Haïtiens' [1956], reprinted in *Présence Africaine*, n.s. nos.165–6 (2002): p.108.
[169] Alexis, 'Du réalisme merveilleux des Haïtiens', p.106.
[170] Andrei Zhdanov, 'Soviet Literature—the Richest in Ideas, the Most Advanced Literature', in Bukharin et al., *Problems of Soviet Literature*, p.22; Gorky, 'Soviet Literature', pp.65–6.

and humanity is on course to finally conquer a basic standard of living.[171] Alexis calls for a 'general programme of work' to serve as the charter for a 'School of Marvellous Realism' that would write the romance of a Red Atlantic, braiding its histories of suffering and of hope, 'its treasure of tales and legends', its deep reserves of 'musical, choreographic and plastic symbolism', to the struggle for socialism. In this sense, 'The necessities of all national work need now to be defined globally.'[172]

Magical realism would indeed become a global school, a 'general programme of work' defined by imaginative proximity to the Haitian and later Cuban revolutions and by an elective affinity to 'the under-developed populations of the world'.[173] But it was also, and from the beginning, enmeshed in the polemics of the Cold War and these have long shaped its critical reception in the West. Compare to Carpentier and Alexis the version of magical realism proposed by Angel Flores to the annual convention of the Modern Languages Association in New York in December 1954.[174] Tailored to his North American and professional, academic audience, this is a magical realism to suit their purpose. 'The magical realists do not cater to a popular taste', Flores reassures the room; 'rather they address themselves to the sophisticated, those not merely initiated in aesthetic mysteries but versed in subtleties'. Their style tends towards the minimal; they are concerned for 'the well-knit plot'. Their greatest achievement has been 'to overhaul and polish the craft of fiction' and to find an 'authentic expression' for the continent, 'one that is uniquely civilized'. This elite cultural formation of 'meticulous craftsmen' and 'brilliant stylists' knows nothing of the national-popular, its only concern is the autonomy of literature.[175]

It has been for recent scholars to restore the anti- and post-coloniality of magical realism and to refigure that part of its pre-history that is European and 'modernist' in terms of surrealism's own self-critique and the heterodox mid-century Marxisms of figures like Georges Bataille, Walter Benjamin, and Ernst Bloch.[176] But a reticence remains to align the magical and the marvellous with the politics of anti-fascism and anti-colonialism during the years of the Popular Front, to place Carpentier as a delegate to the Second International Congress of Writers for the Defence of Culture in Valencia and Madrid in 1937, for example, or to read the rehabilitation of America's marvellous historicity and Haiti's revolutionary modernity as continuous with Dimitrov's Seventh World Congress instructions.[177]

---

[171] Alexis, 'Du réalisme merveilleux des Haïtiens', p.109; p.91.
[172] Alexis, 'Du réalisme merveilleux des Haïtiens', p.92; p.109.
[173] Alexis, 'Du réalisme merveilleux des Haïtiens', p.107.
[174] Angel Flores, 'Magical Realism in Spanish American Fiction', *Hispania* 38, no.2 (1955): pp.187–92.
[175] Flores, 'Magical Realism', pp.189–92.
[176] Cf. Timothy Brennan, 'Postcolonial Studies Between the European Wars: An Intellectual History', in *Marxism, Modernity and Postcolonial Studies*, edited by Crystal Bartolovich and Neil Lazarus (Cambridge: Cambridge University Press, 2002), p.198.
[177] Manuel Aznar Soler describes Carpentier's visit to Spain in 1937 'as, to paraphrase John Reed, a marvellous-real historical event that shook his world', in *República literaria y revolución* (Sevilla:

With the runaway success, some thirty years later, of Gabriel Garcia Marquez' *One Hundred Years of Solitude*, magical realism found its way onto the markets of the West as an exotic cultural commodity laundered of its socialist politics and packaged as a primitivism, however subtle and self-questioning, for the age of neo-colonialism. A part of its genesis, however, lies with the 'Novelists' International' and with a mid-century mode of inquiry into what Carpentier called 'the lives of men who inscribed dates in the history of the continent and who left the names that we still carry: from those who searched for the fountain of eternal youth and the golden city of Manoa to certain early rebels or modern heroes of mythological fame from our wars of independence'.[178]

---

Editorial Renacimiento, 2014), p.666. Not only did Carpentier report on the Congress in four searing 'cronicas' filed with the Cuban magazine *Cartelas* in September and October 1937, but he also returned to it in *La consagración de la primavera* ['The Rite of Spring'] (1978), writing it into his fictional pre-history of the Cuban Revolution. Topics slated for discussion at the conference included 'Nation & Culture', 'Humanism', 'Cultural Inheritance'; in the event, the exigencies of assembling in a country at war placed these cultural-political debates on hold.

[178] Carpentier, 'On the Marvellous Real in America', p.87.

# 3
# Memories of Spain in Sylvia Townsend Warner and John Cowper Powys

### I. Soap for Spain

On 26 July 1937, Sylvia Townsend Warner and John Cowper Powys addressed an audience at the Labour Hall in Dorchester. Their subject was Spain and the wider fight against fascism, and they followed their remarks with an appeal for donations to supply the Republican side with soap. Earlier that month, Warner and her partner Valentine Ackland had defied the British Foreign Office to attend the Second Congress of the International Association of Writers for the Defence of Culture in Barcelona, Valencia, and Madrid. It was a galvanizing experience, and since their return to Dorset ten days previously, the two women had been working tirelessly to publicize the war and their own 'Soap for Spain' campaign. In Valencia, the German physician Max Hodann had alerted them to a shortage of soap and they undertook 'to rub it into the heads of those at home that it must be sent, more and more often, and soap for human consumption too, not just carbolic dog-soap for hospital floors'.[1] Passing through Paris on their way home, Ackland and Warner arranged with the Spanish medical aid coordinating committee to supply it, giving their names as guarantors to a first shipment of £25. To pay for this and for three subsequent consignments, Ackland and Warner set about the 'the odious activity of soliciting [their] friends'.[2] An appeal to women writers drew contributions from Rose Macaulay, Naomi Mitchison, Vita Sackville-West, and Rebecca West.[3] They went door to door in Chaldon Herring, organized a raffle, and called a local meeting of the Left Book Club, recruiting John Cowper Powys, who happened to be holidaying in their village, to join them on the stage.

At the Labour Hall, Warner recounted her impressions of the Congress, praised the determination of the Spanish people and the progress made on their behalf by the Republican government in public services and land reform. She closed with

---

[1] Sylvia Townsend Warner to Steven Clark, 6 November 1937; Sylvia Townsend Warner and Valentine Ackland Collection, Dorset History Centre (hereafter D-TWA) A84; STW.2012.125.5008.
[2] Sylvia Townsend Warner to Naomi Mitchison, 17 July 1937; in *Letters of Sylvia Townsend Warner*, edited by William Maxwell (London: Chatto & Windus, 1982), p.46.
[3] 'Soap for Spain', list of contributions enclosed in Sylvia Townsend Warner to Isabel Brown, 8 September 1937; intercepted letter. PRO KV 2/2338-2. By the time of this letter, Ackland and Warner had sent £58 4s to the *Centrale Sanitaire Internationale d'aide à l'Espagne républicaine* in Paris; the 'Meeting in Dorchester' raised £4 5s 6d.

*Mid-Century Romance*. John T. Connor, Oxford University Press. © John T. Connor (2024).
DOI: 10.1093/9780191953057.003.0004

an anecdote that was fast becoming lore: Corpus Barga reported it for *Hora de España*; Alejo Carpentier relayed it to readers in Cuba.[4] Breaking for lunch on their way from Valencia to Madrid in the small town of Minglanilla, the convoy of writers met survivors of the Badajoz massacre, one of whom—a young mother in mourning for a murdered husband and two brothers killed in battle—attached herself to Warner. Barga describes them walking silently 'back and forth in each other's arms, weeping without tears beneath the implacable sun'. The locals, meanwhile, look on, puzzling to explain this scene of stricken grief and natural sympathy; they speculate that the widow has 'found someone from her own village', a '*paisana*' to share her pain. Barga credits their conclusion, casting it as proof of the international ties that bind.[5] But for Warner the story pointed a less gratifying moral. She presented the widow as an example of 'loyalty' unshaken by loss and as a warning to her Dorchester audience of the struggle to come: 'These people are defending our liberties, fighting our battle as well as their own', and they are 'fighting it better than we do'.[6]

Powys' remarks were more ambiguous. Rather than address Spain directly, he expanded on the importance of independent reading, praising the Left Book Club for making available 'books dealing with Liberal, Socialist and Communist ideas'.[7] Armed with the right books, he told his Dorchester audience, they would put the arguments of fascism to flight; they might even reach to 'that plane of existence, from which proceeds the inexplicable imperative to follow goodness and mercy in a world built upon a different plan'.[8] After a long career on the public lecture circuit extolling his own personal canon of great books, Powys was here in his element; but the event also had him on edge. He had marked it down in his diary as 'this Russian Spanish Left Meeting tonight', and whether because he identified Ackland and Warner as Communist Party members or the Left Book Club as a Party front, the event troubled his growing sense of the Soviet Union as totalitarian, its presence in Spain as malign, and of Marxism as a body of thought hostile to his own pluralist cosmology.[9] He expressed the hope that in time the Club would find its way to making books with 'other ideas' available, and he closed by defending the individual's right to think for themselves against any and all ideologies.[10]

---

[4] Corpus Barga, 'El II Congreso Internacional de Escritores. Su Significacíon', *Hora de España*, no.8 (August 1937): p.9. Excerpted also in Alejo Carpentier, 'España Bajo las Bombas, III', *Carteles*, 10 October 1937; collected in Alejo Carpentier, *Bajo el Signo de la Cibeles: Crónicas sobre España y los españoles, 1925–1937*, edited by Julio Rodríguez Puértolas (Madrid: Editorial Nuestra Cultura, 1979), pp.162–3.

[5] Barga, 'El II Congreso Internacional', p.9.

[6] Sylvia Townsend Warner, notes for a talk on Spain; D-TWA/A26; STW.2012.125.0546 Diary 11 Box C.

[7] 'Three Authors at Dorchester', *Western Gazette*, 30 July 1937, p.16

[8] 'Three Authors at Dorchester', p.16; John Cowper Powys, *The Pleasures of Literature* (London: Cassell, 1938), p.660.

[9] *Petrushka and the Dancer: The Diaries of John Cowper Powys, 1929–1939*, edited by Morine Krissdóttir (Manchester: Carcanet, 1995), p.252; entry for 26 July 1937.

[10] 'Three Authors at Dorchester', p.16.

Such differences of emphasis were perfectly in keeping with the broad inclusivity of the Popular Front, the strategy adopted by the Communist International in 1935 to mobilize all available forces in the fight against fascism. It was this policy that allowed Warner to commandeer a range of support: Sackville-West professed herself 'neutral' on the question of Spain and thought the soap appeal a joke, but she still contributed to the fund; Powys took the stage in Dorchester, for all his reservations about Russia.[11] And it is there, side by side and in the act of speaking on or around the crisis in Spain, that I wish to introduce this chapter's two protagonists, and in the process correct a common misconstruction of their mid-century location. For both Powys and Warner would soon become victims of what Warner's Party comrade Arnold Rattenbury called political 'trivialisation', the Cold War belittling of their mid-century commitments. In the decades after her death in 1978, Rattenbury wrote to reclaim Warner's 'red, loving heart', reminding readers that 'however bewitched her pen, however bewitching, she lived wholly in an unambiguous world where the only dignity [lay] in taking sides'.[12] He insisted that Warner's post-war reputation—as 'a wit, a short story writer who sometimes extended her talents into longer witty works', a woman who was 'Valentine's tragic lover and, except for a short period of aberration, was apolitical'—was a travesty.[13] Feminist recovery work has since placed Warner's long-form fiction front and centre, while critical interventions by Wendy Mulford, Patrick Wright, Maroula Joannou, and Glyn Salton-Cox, have more finely gauged the weight of Warner's commitment to British and international communism.[14] With Powys, the Dorchester Labour Hall is as good a place as any to meet a writer who but forty years later struck George Steiner as seeming to elude all 'placing' in his century. 'There is no writer so complexly out of his time', Steiner opined: Powys simply escapes 'historical location'.[15] David Goodway has since led the way in placing Powys' politics, patiently reconstructing the American radical milieu in which, in the 1910s and

---

[11] Vita Sackville-West gave her opinion on Spain in *Authors Take Sides on the Spanish War*, edited by Nancy Cunard (London: Left Review, 1937), n.p. Though she sent Warner a cheque for £1, she joked that she thought it 'one of the funniest appeals I've ever had! I thought the Spanish need for soap was chronic, and not just due to the war!' Cited in Claire Harman, *Sylvia Townsend Warner: A Biography* (London: Chatto & Windus, 1989), p.170.

[12] Arnold Rattenbury, 'Literature, Lying and Sober Truth: Attitudes to the Work of Patrick Hamilton and Sylvia Townsend Warner', in *Writing and Radicalism*, edited by John Lucas (London: Longman, 1996), p.230; and Arnold Rattenbury, 'Plain Heart, Light Tether', *PN Review* 8, no.3 (1981): p.46.

[13] Rattenbury, 'Literature, Lying and Sober Truth', p.230; p.235.

[14] Wendy Mulford, *This Narrow Place. Sylvia Townsend Warner and Valentine Ackland: Life, Letters and Politics, 1930–1951* (London: Pandora, 1988); Patrick Wright, *The Village That Died for England: The Strange Story of Tyneham*, revised edition (London: Faber, 2002), pp.164–79; Maroula Joannou, 'Sylvia Townsend Warner in the 1930s', in *A Weapon in the Struggle: The Cultural History of the Communist Party in Britain*, edited by Andy Croft (London: Pluto Press, 1998), pp.89–105; Glyn Salton-Cox, *Queer Communism and the Ministry of Love: Sexual Revolution in British Writing of the 1930s* (Edinburgh: Edinburgh University Press, 2019), pp.77–112.

[15] George Steiner, 'The Difficulties of Reading John Cowper Powys', *Powys Review* 1 (Spring 1977): p.9. Cf. Richard Holmes: 'there remains the pressing problem of "placing" Powys in some accessible context'. Holmes, 'A Strange Kingdom', *The Times*, 20 December 1973, p.10.

1920s, he received his mid-life political education and carefully chronicling his passage from fuzzy communist fellow-travelling to a more or less coherent position as a self-described 'anarchistic individualist' or philosophical anarchist.[16] Whatever their separate trajectories, during the Popular Front they shared a platform and a genre.

Warner and Powys turned to the historical novel in the 1930s with an eye to expanding their canvas, following Scott in recounting the 'inundation' of everyday life by the dynamics of social change, representing the forces at play in a time of national crisis and tracing them out across a wide social field.[17] Though only Warner read Lukács on Scott's 'classical form', both writers cast the past as the present's 'prehistory' and saw their fictions as 'giving poetic life to those historical, social, and human forces which, in the course of a long evolution, have made our present-day life what it is and as we experience it'.[18] Although both wrote historical fiction from the Left, neither quite neatly inhabited the national-popular form of the communist historical novel elaborated in the previous chapter as a response to Dimitrov's Seventh World Congress instructions to repossess the national past and wrest a progressive people's history from the forces of reaction. They brought to the genre a bundle of modernist preoccupations—a radical subjectivism in the case of Powys, impersonality in the case of Warner, a fidelity to fleeting states of mind and fugitive sense impressions in both—that could cut against, though not necessarily annul, the solicitations of a more orthodox critical or socialist realism and with it, the large-scale transformations, deep structures, and durable inequalities that power a Marxist philosophy of history. Both writers introduced elements of irony into the otherwise earnest narration of historical change in ways that frame as a question the relationship between experience and abstraction, grand narrative and the wayward particular. Written concurrently through the 1940s, Warner's chronicle of a fourteenth-century Norfolk nunnery *The Corner That Held Them* (1948) and Powys' 'Dark Age' romance *Porius* (1951) probe the limits of the mid-century communist historical novel and the cultural formation that gave rise to it. Supplementing the previous chapter's broad-brush conspectus of the genre, these two examples suggest something of its variety.

*Porius* and *The Corner That Held Them* are both novels of the 1940s and have been rightly read as such. Warner's portrait of a beleaguered women's community mirrors the exigencies of life on the Home Front. Powys' novel mines fifth-century history for a parable of national defence, the Battle of Britain explicitly

---

[16] John Cowper Powys, *Obstinate Cymric: Essays 1935–47* [1947] (London: Village Press, 1973), p.133. Cf. David Goodway, *Anarchist Seeds Beneath the Snow: Left Libertarian Thought and British Writers from William Morris to Colin Ward* (Liverpool: Liverpool University Press, 2006), p.153.

[17] Cf. Richard Maxwell, 'Inundations of Time: A Definition of Scott's Originality', *ELH* 68 (2001): pp.419–68.

[18] 'Points from Letters', responses by Sylvia Townsend Warner and T.A. Jackson to the first of two instalments of Georg Lukacz [sic], 'Walter Scott and the Historical Novel', *International Literature*, no.9 (1938): pp.100–1. Lukács, *The Historical Novel*, p.53.

foreshadowed in its narrative of the Anglo-Saxon Conquest. But Spain remains a presence in both works. Warner spent a sorry afternoon in June 1940 'tidying and throwing away' the piled-up paperwork of her Spanish activism, 'thinking how vainly I had worked' and wishing 'I had worked a hundred times harder', but she never let it go.[19] In *The Corner That Held Them*, the link to Spain resides in Warner's conception of the Civil War as a battle fought over the future of feudalism between a ruling class still recognizably 'mediaeval' and a progressive coalition of urban professionals, proletarians, and peasants. Spain gave a prominence to the politics of land distribution and agricultural labour that chimed with Warner's rural brand of communism. The Soviet agrarian system represented the hoped-for horizon and Warner's vision for Spain was of a country of modern collective farms, rural electrification, and heavy agricultural machinery. The Catholic Church was what stood in its way, galvanizing fascist reaction to the Republican government and blocking the path to a Soviet Spain. With such presumptions in place, it was easy to construe the loyalist resistance as a peasants' revolt against the Church and its secular authorities, as Warner did in her Spanish allegory, *After the Death of Don Juan* (1938). Extending the analogy with earlier insurrections, *The Corner That Held Them* chronicles the break-up of feudalism in Britain and culminates in the Peasants' Revolt of 1381; local details, I will suggest, match even more closely onto Warner's Spanish experience.

For Powys, the war in Spain clarified his conviction that 'the Anarchist Ideal ... is of course the perfect one'.[20] It coincided with a renewed acquaintance with Emma Goldman, then resident in Britain as the London representative of the Spanish anarchist CNT-FAI and head of the English section of the *Solidaridad Internacional Antifascista*. She saw to it that Powys received a steady stream of Spanish 'propaganda-information'.[21] In a letter to his sister Katie, a communist and close friend of Warner's in Dorset, Powys boasted of receiving

> *such* an exciting mass of *Anarchist Literature* sent to me by my old *Emma Goldman* who is *my* Prime Minister & chief Political Philosopher! and every week I get the anarchist paper from *Avenue A* New York City [the 'libertarian

---

[19] *The Diaries of Sylvia Townsend Warner*, edited by Claire Harman (London: Chatto & Windus, 1994), p.106; entry for 20 June 1940. After the war, Warner spent a full five years corresponding with interned Spanish refugees, her 'Cats and Comrades' in Lancashire and the South of France, sending them money and packing food parcels, enquiring anxiously for word of friends left behind in Spain. This was a time when, as Nancy Cunard complained, Spain had been all but forgotten in England, 'a cupboard, when that.' Reflecting on her own efforts to help Republican exiles in France, Cunard declared that 'Spain is the heart.' Her feet might be English ('well-shod, practical, capable') and her 'head', with its 'lucid brain', French; but Spain was her compass, her emotional lodestar. It was a bond she shared with her comrades in Dorset. Nancy Cunard to Valentine Ackland, 8 May and 14 May [1946]; D-TWA/A03; STW.2012.125.5053.

[20] John Cowper Powys to Louis Wilkinson, 13 October 1939; in *The Letters of John Cowper Powys to Louis Wilkinson* (London: Macdonald, 1958), p.54.

[21] John Cowper Powys to Emma Goldman, 9 January 1937; in *The Letters of John Cowper Powys and Emma Goldman*, edited by David Goodway (London: Cecil Woolf, 2008), p.61.

weekly', *Challenge*] and also the 'Bulletin of Information' from the Anarchists of Barcelona. This *latter* pamphlet I am carefully keeping; because it is not so much concerned with the war as with their *experiment in Catalonia* of organizing their life on *Anarchist lines* and getting rid of *all* Dictatorship & of the 'Sovereign State'.[22]

Goldman's propaganda parcels gave Powys a direct line to the Catalan social project, which became his model of 'the desirable state of things', 'a Society that is humane and free'.[23] Revolutionary Spain was the realization of an ideal, 'a *living experience*' of actually existing anarchism.[24] Powys translated its defeat in early 1939 into a pattern that lies at the heart of *Porius*: this is a novel that turns on a depletion of the possible, the becoming-impossible of something desired. But for all the excitement of receiving the Spanish *Boletín de informacíon* direct to his home in North Wales, Powys also struggled with the materialization of his philosophy as a contingent social movement. He feared that the programme of the 'Catalonian Anarchists & Anarchist Syndicalists', though 'the very best we have yet evolved', was still too 'abstract' and 'doctrinaire'.[25] He feared that these 'politicians & builders', 'more idealistic & un-practical than any other group!' were yet too willing to temporize with history and the calculus of means.[26] Whether or not Powys preferred his anarchism 'too good to be true', the dilemma of acting in history, however noble the goal, returns in *Porius* as a 'peculiar kind of uncertainty about the value of all powerful and formidable and persevering efforts' to alter the course of events and intervene in the lives of others.[27]

## II. 'the greatest Romance'

For John Cowper Powys, the impulse to abandon the contemporary frame of his earlier Wessex fiction and fully indulge his 'pedantic mythological archaic mania for the past' came with his retirement to Wales in 1935.[28] He saw his settlement in Corwen 'as the fulfilment of an early and youthful longing—"hiraeth" is the Welsh word for this obscure stirring of some secret destiny—to return to the land of my

---

[22] John Cowper Powys to Philippa [Katie] Powys, 24 September 1938; in *Powys to Sea Eagle: The Letters of John Cowper Powys to Philippa Powys*, edited by Anthony Head (London: Cecil Woolf, 1996), p.106.
[23] Powys, *Petrushka and the Dancer*, p.263; diary entry for 17 January 1938.
[24] John Cowper Powys, 'The Real and the Ideal', *Spain and the World* 2, no.34 Supplement (May 1938): p.3.
[25] John Cowper Powys to Louis Wilkinson, 20 February 1942; in *Letters to Louis Wilkinson*, p.105.
[26] Powys, *Petrushka and the Dancer*, p.263; diary entry for 17 January 1938.
[27] John Cowper Powys to Louis Wilkinson, 28 November 1939; in *Letters to Louis Wilkinson*, p.56. John Cowper Powys, *Porius: A Romance of the Dark Ages*, edited by Judith Bond and Morine Krissdóttir (New York: Overlook Duckworth, 2007), p.741; subsequent references are to this edition and will appear parenthetically in the body of the text.
[28] John Cowper Powys to Louis Wilkinson, 2 August 1945; in *Letters Louis Wilkinson*, p.185.

remote ancestors'.[29] Two years previously, while still in upstate New York, the 'old longing to go to Wales and write something with all those Welsh gods & traditions & magic behind me' had returned; he imagined that with Wales as his 'background' he could write 'the greatest Romance of Modern Times', 'an extraordinary book—a book of wondrous possibilities'.[30] His partner Phyllis Playter's wide reading in new fiction provided further prompts for this 'masterpiece about Wales *in* Wales'.[31] In 1933 they read together the pre-publication 'syllabus' of Harvey Allen's *Anthony Adverse* and Powys 'envied it & longed to write a vast Historical Novel'.[32] In 1935, Playter read to Powys from L.H. Myers' trilogy, *The Root and the Flower* (1929–35). As Powys recounted in his diary, she then spoke 'with great eloquence on the subject of my future writings':

> —how—as in this Indian book, *The Flower & the Root* [sic], I ought to bring in Reality in the more stirring & historic form of large national movements, both political & religious—& no longer be content with vaporous summer-lightning but by getting some historic reality have some real thunder & some dominant subject—[33]

*Owen Glendower* (1941) was Powys' trial run, a novel of the Welsh Revolt; he wrote it at speed between 1937 and 1939, adopting 'humbly the method of Sir Walter Scott': 'fast & bold & free & in large strokes, staking all on the humour & naturalness of the characters & on the descriptions of nature & on the exciting adventures & on the clash between the monks and bards and orthodox churchmen & Lollards and Welsh & English'.[34] But it was *Porius*, written doggedly between 1941 and 1949 with much jobwork interruption, that Powys hailed as his long-awaited 'masterpiece', the 'chief work' of his lifetime, his 'best book of all'.[35]

With its late-fifth-century setting, *Porius* pitches its tale on a time of transition between 'the horrible, delicious, beguiling, fascinating decadences of the dying classical world' and 'the startling, childlike, magical, shocking, crazy beginnings of nobody-then-quite-knew-what kind of a Christian world'.[36] The place is the Valley of Edeyrnion, the time a week towards the end of October 499 CE, seven days

---

[29] Powys, *Obstinate Cymric*, p.55.
[30] Powys, *Petrushka and the Dancer*, pp.132–3; entries for 27 and 29 August 1933. John Cowper Powys to Littleton Powys, 3 September 1933; in *Essays on John Cowper Powys*, edited by Belinda Humfrey (Cardiff: University of Wales Press, 1972), Appendix 1(b), p.338.
[31] Powys, *Petrushka and the Dancer*, p.133; diary entry for 29 August 1933.
[32] Powys, *Petrushka and the Dancer*, p.118; diary entry for 3 February 1933.
[33] Powys, *Petrushka and the Dancer*, p.193; diary entry for 1 September 1935.
[34] John Cowper Powys to Marian Powys, 21 April 1937; cited in Morine Krissdóttir, *Descents of Memory: The Life of John Cowper Powys* (New York: Overlook Duckworth, 2007), p.341.
[35] John Cowper Powys to Louis Wilkinson, 18 August 1949; in *Letters to Louis Wilkinson*, p.267. In a letter to C. Benson Roberts dated 14 November 1951, Powys relates how *Porius* 'beats that Glendower book of mine hollow'; in *Essays on John Cowper Powys*, Appendix 1(c), p.345.
[36] John Cowper Powys, '"Preface" or anything you like to *Porius*', in 'The Matter of *Porius*', edited by R.L. Blackmore, *Powys Newsletter* 4 (1974): p.8.

seemingly selected at 'the heart of this shifty tumultuous chaos of an age' on the grounds that no documentary record survived to constrain Powys from writing as he liked. The novel recruits from Welsh mythology and the Matter of Britain; it is also, as Powys wrote to one of his publishers, highly '"conscious" ... of being written after Dostoievski and of being contemporary with certain exciting and very modern psychological novelists'.[37] But these other plotlines, the mythological and the psychological, all braid with the historical as Powys turns his little window of Dark Age time into a hot chronology of national and even world-historical significance. The novel revels in the complexity of its Dark Age social world, in the 'rich, beautiful, mysterious fusion of so many cults, traditions, races, languages, religions' all condensed in this one tiny corner of North Wales. A confluence of national crises—each with its own mid-century analogue—then throw this 'mass of chaotic and whirling contradictions' into motion.[38] The pressures from without of a 'Germanic' invasion, and from within of Welsh nationalist and proto-communist insurrections, raise the state of emergency and give the novel its historical 'thunder'. As a druid exclaims: 'We certainly live ... in the most exciting times the world has ever seen! What world-shaking events! What settings and risings of zodiacal aeons! What sinkings into irretrievable downfalls! What mountings into unbelievable restitutions!' (239).

In Porius, Powys creates a protagonist almost comically equipped to play his part in this history. He is the 'heroic strong man of the House of Cunedda' (617), heir to Edeyrnion and to the British imperial presence in Wales. Roused to a new sense of patriotic duty by the call of national defence, Porius gladly commits himself to 'clearing Ynys Prydein of the Saeson' (671). 'No longer could he be shut up in the childish feeling that the forests and mountains and pastures and swamps of Edeyrnion were the be-all and end-all of everything' (62). As for fighting the Saxon, Porius has what it takes: at one point, he takes a page from Rabelais and like the giant Pantagruel seizes the corpse of a Saxon he has just slain to club a score more to death.[39] This 'exploit' will become nationwide news before the year is out, and the novel ends with 'our Brythonic Hercules' (516) en route to join Arthur at the Battle of Badon Hill. But there are also counter-logics at play. Powys himself explained his rationale for concentrating the events of *Porius* into the 'brief extent of seven days' as a way of avoiding the pitfalls of historical abstraction:

> nothing so dismally and tediously destroys our interest as when great lumbering weeks and months and years, full of turning-points of history weighing them

---

[37] John Cowper Powys to Yvonne Muller, 16 February 1949; in 'The Matter of *Porius*', p.6.
[38] Powys, '"Preface" or anything you like to *Porius*', pp.7–8.
[39] The incident of 'how Pantagruel discomfited the three hundred giants armed with ... Loupgarou their Captain' makes a passing appearance in John Cowper Powys, *Rabelais: His Life, the Story Told by Him, Selections Therefrom Here Newly Translated, and an Interpretation of His Genius and His Religion* (London: Bodley Head, 1948), p.346.

down and us down with them like so many milestones made of adamant[,] have got to be fumbled and rumbled through somehow while every vivid dramatic personal string ceases to vibrate. History 'in the making' is the beating of *individual* human hearts, the machinations of *individual* human brains, the creations and destructions, the imaginations and aberrations, of *individual* human nerves.[40]

*Porius* allows 'the waves of centuries before and the waves of centuries after' to wash across its pages and for many characters to see beyond the novel's seven-day span, but it always reverts to the present-tense vibrations of each 'personal string'. In a characteristic sequence, the novel joins Porius on his marriage bed as he reflects on the geopolitical changes going on around him and recalls what he has been told 'of the zodiacal signs that rule the world today'. But Porius then dismisses such abstract speculations for an 'orgy of his cherished "cavoseniargizing"' (450), by which 'fantastic name' (92) he has come to call his 'psycho-sensuous trick of ravishing' the smallest details of the phenomenal world (466).

For all his hyperbolic heroism, Porius retains something in common with Scott's 'middling' hero, caught between rival political allegiances, more passive than active, and sufficiently marginal to the main events as to register history for our benefit as the disturbance of everyday life. His own inclination is to heed a 'Nature' that 'was always whispering to him to dodge, evade, avoid, and circumvent' (676). 'How can I take sides', he ponders, 'when I loathe poisoned arrows and, not a bit less, hate tournament lances, Roman horses, stirrup cups, and ladies' favours?' (451). His only 'real pleasure' and his one sure purpose lies apart from such 'human agitations' (366-7) in his practice of 'cavoseniargizing'. Approaching a philosophy of solipsism, Porius comes to wonder if the only thing that truly exists, the one thing he can know to be real, is this 'private experience, shared only very superficially and very casually by others—*of a particular consciousness* with its own particular powers of awareness' (733). The drama of *Porius* and the secret of its style, however, draws from the fact that these domains of historical implication and of 'psycho-sensuous' escape cannot be kept apart. Porius may enjoy a 'curious psychic lacuna' (42, 467) between his actions and his 'secret thoughts' (26), as though 'his Herculean body had a life of its own' (42) and his 'secret game' of 'cavoseniargizing' (93) were only ever private. But the novel shatters this illusion of innocence on a plane of history far removed, and more consequential, than any short-term Saxon invasion.

## III. 'naught but a jest'

When, in 1933, 'it all came over me that old longing to go to Wales and write something with all those Welsh gods & traditions & magic behind me', Powys was still a believer in the 'wondrous possibilities' of romance. The previous year he

---

[40] John Cowper Powys, 'Characters of the Novel', in 'The Matter of *Porius*', p.17.

had summoned the Grail in *A Glastonbury Romance* (1932), not just as a comic anachronism 'contemporaneous with airplanes and "wireless" and the Quantum Theory' or as a transcendent literary symbol, but as a practical ideal capable of galvanizing a radical social project.[41] Holy Sam is vouchsafed a vision of a 'chalice' with 'a shining fish' inside, and the question of its 'authenticity' is said to be settled when he recognizes this '*Ichthus* out of the Absolute' as in fact 'a Tench'.[42] But Sam's vision connects with his labour at the Glastonbury Commune, hauling clay from seven to five, and with the purpose to which this clay is put. For Powys had wanted to put 'some Communist Propaganda' into the novel ('for at heart & at brain I am a Communist', he wrote at the time), and so he engineered for Johnny Geard's Glastonbury Revival—a project to restore the town's mediaeval identity as a pilgrimage site—to catalyse a political alliance of the Left, a municipalization of local industry, and 'a real movement of imaginative art'.[43] It is this practical application of the politics of romance revival that for Ian Duncan marks Powys apart from his 'Modernist precursors in Grail symbolism'. Against 'the esoteric text of a symbolist avant-garde (like *The Waste Land*)', which looks to poetry to preserve the Absolute inviolate, Powys embraces 'romance' in the 'popular, mass-market form' of the modern novel and its equally impure analogues in the novel. It is as iterations of a 'worldly, compromised version of romance revival' that Duncan suggests we read Powys' portrait of the Commune's politics and of the culture it creates, the Arthurian figurines for which Sam Dekker hauls the clay and which, though mass-produced as tourist souvenirs combine something of 'the communal spirit of the town's socialistic rulers' and 'the new religion of Glastonbury's Mayor' with 'the imaginative freshness and childlike appeal of an authentically primitive art'.[44]

Over the course of the 1930s, Powys transferred the hopes which in 1917 he had vested in the Bolshevik Revolution onto the cause of the Spanish anarchists. But the defeat of the Spanish Republic marks a turning point, whether as first or collateral cause, for a reckoning with romance, including the recovery of lost origins that had inspired his return to Wales and the archetypal quest-romance of a transformative politics.[45] It is this reckoning with the positive entailments of romance that Powys' historical fiction records. *Owen Glendower*, written under the shadow of events in Spain and the subsequent slide to war, thematizes what Duncan has called the 'rout of the supernatural narrations of *A Glastonbury Romance*'.[46] Among several allegories of this new conception, the novel turns the long-desired

---

[41] John Cowper Powys, 'The Creation of Romance', *The Modern Thinker and Author's Review* 1, no.1 (1932): p.75.
[42] John Cowper Powys, *A Glastonbury Romance* (New York: Simon and Schuster, 1932), pp.982–3.
[43] Powys, *Petrushka and the Dancer*, p.54; diary entry for 12 September 1930. Powys, *Glastonbury Romance*, p.966.
[44] Ian Duncan, 'Supernatural Narration: *A Glastonbury Romance*, Modernity and the Novel', *Western Humanities Review* 57, no.1 (2003): p.88; p.92. Powys, *Glastonbury Romance*, pp.965–6.
[45] John Cowper Powys to Louis Wilkinson, 28 November 1939; in *Letters to Louis Wilkinson*, p.56.
[46] Ian Duncan, 'The Mythology of Escape: *Owen Glendower* and the Failure of Historical Romance', *Powys Notes* 8 (1992): p.60.

homecoming of its young protagonist Rhisiart, raised in England on stories of his ancient Welsh ancestry, into a set-piece confrontation between historical reality and romance idealism in which the visionary possibility—of recovered potency, plenitude, fairy-tale restitution—is seen to fail, to be 'limned' henceforth 'on those flying cloud-wracks of the mind's horizon that no madness could touch and no burning blacken!'[47] Rhisiart's fantasy of redeeming history in historical time retreats from the encounter in defeat.

Henceforward, negativity will be the master term and Sam Dekker's faith in 'a hope beyond hope, a Something somewhere hid perhaps in the twisted heart of the cruel First Cause and able to break in *from outside* and smash to atoms this torturing chain of Cause and Effect', will give way to the atavistic, anti-epiphanic sensual nihilism of Powys' late fiction.[48] The bleakest articulation of this hollowing out of hope comes in the dirge that haunts *The Brazen Head* (1956):

> Where leaf do fall—there let leaf rest—
> Where no Grail be, there be no quest—
> Be'ee good, be'ee bad, be'ee damned, be'ee blest—
> Be'ee North, be'ee South, be'ee East, be'ee West
> The whole of Existence is naught but a jest—

Rejecting any call to historical agency or collective endeavour, any future purpose beyond the here and now, any solidarity beyond the unit of two, the 'ditty's' unseen singer resolves to 'enjoy [their] hour' while they can. 'A mortal's fate is the same as a mole's' and 'The same as the fishes that leap in shoals': even human exceptionalism the song casts in doubt.[49] Absent the future, there is only the meantime and Powys' egoist injunction to 'enjoy'. 'And what' do we mean by our 'clue-word "enjoy"?' 'Well, it means to approach, to grasp, to seize upon, to embrace something or other ... with all our senses simultaneously.'[50] *Porius* provides this compensatory adjustment—'enjoy to the end', '"cavoseniargize" to the end!' (488)—with an origin story, a place in history from which to date the death of romance.

Porius, whose herculean strength betrays his great-grandmaternal giant's blood, has fantasized that the giantess his ancestor married might not have been the last. 'The underdreams of his entire life' (461) have turned on whether 'it was in the scope of some stretched-out *cantref* of possibility that there were women among the last remnants of the old race of Cewri', as the novel calls these aboriginal Welsh mountain giants,

---

[47] John Cowper Powys, *Owen Glendower* [1941] (London: Picador, 1978), p.261.
[48] Powys, *Glastonbury Romance*, p.983.
[49] John Cowper Powys, *The Brazen Head* [1956] (London: Picador, 1978), p.247.
[50] John Cowper Powys, *In Spite Of: A Philosophy for Everyman* (London: Macdonald, 1953), pp.12–13.

and that sometimes, by some incredible miracle of magnetic attraction, these beautiful children of Eyri and Cader, fairer and larger than the daughters of the ordinary tribes of men, and with all the mists of those mountain chasms, and all the depths and silences of those mountain tarns, and all the sun radiances of those mountain ridges, and all the moon remoteness of those mountain peaks, gathered up into their flesh and blood, might come down into the forest and be seen and known of such as, like himself, had been calling to them for so long. (372)

When a father and daughter, the last of their kind, descend from the mountains, there are many who witness their passage through the forest. However rare and reclusive, giants remain a Dark Age reality as of the morning of 21 October, 499 CE. There is only one witness, however, to their extinction later that day. Moved by his 'youthful mania for the Cewri' (471) and the 'nerve of imaginative romance in his heart' (480), moved also by something darker, 'his manhood's craving to beget a child' on the young giantess (471) and to 'bring forth some world-saving birth' (448), Porius gives them chase. He finds himself 'stalking these Cewri, stalking them like wild beasts' (471), 'whirled by his own will' towards a 'rape' of the young daughter (477, 479). In the event, Powys assures us of the daughter's 'feminine complicity and consent', her 'overpowering passion' (479) in the act, but the violence of Porius's pursuit incriminates what follows.

Interrupted, post-coitus, by the giantess's father, a desperate battle between Porius and the old *cawr* ensues; a mistimed blow from the giant's club strikes the daughter dead instead. Seizing her lifeless body, the father runs to the side of 'the first, and also the secretest and most hidden, of all the mysterious and fathomless lakes or tarns, that from the beginning of Time, at least from an upheaval worked by some planetary catastrophe unrecorded in Time, seem to have been designed by Nature herself to protect the security of her primal offspring' (482) and plunges in. The giants sink 'like a landslide' to the bottom of the tarn, their combined weight forcing them through 'an orifice between two jagged teeth of slaty stone, that had been broken at such an angle by the original upheaval that what once passed through them could never come forth again' (483). Immured in this 'hollow space below the teeth-barrier of this earthquake-sculpted' tarn-bed, 'the last Cewri of the Cader' pass from history into myth. All that remain are their 'two pairs of up-gazing eyes', burning through the green waters to lodge as the 'dark throbbing of a portion of [Porius's] consciousness which he had now to carry with him wherever he went' (483–4).

Powys would sometimes explain his choice of this Dark Age window of time on the grounds that it gave him the freedom to invent: the fact that 499 CE was 'a beautiful, a heavenly, *blank*' in the historical record gave his fiction free rein; the best thing about 'these felicitously darker than dark years' was that '*anything might happen!!*[51] The death of the giants, however, resubmits this free-play of romance to the doom of historical necessity. Jerome McGann rightly marks this episode as 'the foundational catastrophe', 'the disappearance of "the Impossible"'.[52] It stages the disenchantment of the Dark Age lifeworld as the advent of modernity, positioning ours as the Dark Age inaugurated by their death, darkened by this depletion of the possible. If to the modern reader the scene seems implausible—as it famously did for Powys' Bodley Head reader, Norman Denny—that is because we inherit the impoverished world whose origin it narrates, just as we inherit the consequence of the novel's other historical plots.[53]

*Porius* begins with the arrival of 'two disturbing pieces of news' (22), each establishing a possible trajectory for our hero to play his part in history: the first, as Arthur's champion against the invading Saxon; the second, to mount a mission to Constantinople and there 'to reopen the ancient Pelagian controversy' (47). Both plotlines are couched in historical irony. However patriotic the drumbeat to Arthur's victory at Badon Hill, we know that the Saxons will 'come back—back and back and back again' (526), and that they will prevail just as others will prevail after them. The plot to rehabilitate Pelagius would have been yet more consequential, had it ever stood a chance: at stake is the possibility of reversing Church teaching on Original Sin, thereby grounding the new Christian religion on an altogether more humanist, permissive, perhaps even godless, theology. With its transitional temporal location between Classical and Christian worlds, *Porius* appears to position itself in a window of possibility only to then slam that window shut. The Christianity that branded Pelagius a heretic at the Council of Carthage in 418 is the one whose two-thousand-year 'tyranny' (258) has already begun; its representatives—the fanatical priest Minnawc Gorsant and his unnamed successor—model the modern will to power, a totalitarian impulse whose twentieth-century declensions are easy to read. It hardly matters that Porius opts not to accept his invitation to Constantinople or that he elects instead 'to try his strength against these Colgrims and Badulfs and Cheldrics from Germania' (61–2); futility, if not fatality, attends his every historical move.

With his parable of the giants, Powys punishes a naïve belief in the power of romance to right the course of history. Onto his giantess Porius has projected the recovery of lost origins and in that fantasy of a 'world-saving birth' the promise of an end to history, figured as a 'vast upheaving life-and-death struggle' between the 'aboriginals' of 'Ynys Prydein' and its successive 'invaders' (447–8). The irony that he himself is one of these invaders is not lost on us, nor the fact that his

---

[51] Powys, '"Preface" or anything you like to *Porius*', p.8. John Cowper Powys to C. Benson Roberts, 14 November 1951; in *Essays on John Cowper Powys*, Appendix 1(c), p.345.

[52] Jerome McGann, 'Marvels and Wonders: Powys, *Porius* and the Attempt to Revive Romance in the Age of Modernism', *Times Literary Supplement*, 1 December 1995, p.6.

[53] Norman Denny to John Cowper Powys, 4 December 1949; in 'Letters on the Publication of *Porius*', edited by Michael Ballin, *Powys Notes* 7, no.2 (1992): pp.27–8.

actions succeed only too well in their goal. Hot in pursuit of his Creiddylad, Porius had envisioned their procreation in terms of a 'swirling bottomless pool, wherein there whirled round and round a terrible vortex of all the beautiful and horrible waves and eddies and ground swells of black blood and crimson blood, mingled with slime and scum and ooze and seaweedlike hair, that cover the shoals and porches of the threshold of life' (477); the same imagery—'of yellow hair and grey hair swaying like a submerged tangle of weeds amid clots of blood' (483)— accompanies the tragic issue of their encounter. The parallel replays, in a more fantastical vein, Powys' argument in *Owen Glendower* (1941) that history contaminates the romance quest, transforming the object of desire into its antithesis. As Ian Duncan explains, Owen's romantic Welsh Revolt becomes a 'gruesome mirror-image' of its English antagonist, Henry of Lancaster, whose 'regime of history' the novel figures 'as the institutionalized power-sadism of a monotheistic, totalitarian, "modern" state', buttressed by science and theology. Owen may 'dream of a Wales restored to its mythical Saturnian dispensation before the foreign invasions and conquests', but to act on that dream is to temporize with Henry's historical regime: to participate in history only perpetuates its violence. When Porius's world-saving birth devolves into a world-ending death he becomes cousin to those later ends-touting experimentalists, figures like *Owen*'s Gilles de Pirogue who hope to 'cure evil by evil, pain by pain, torture by torture'.[54] But there is then a further dialectical twist, as Powys recuperates the narcissistic injury to the 'nerve of imaginative romance' by a symbolic identification with the subsequent scene of desolation. It is on Porius's precociously sensitive psychology that Powys first registers the modern regime inaugurated by this primal scene.

When we first meet the 'precious cosmogonic art' Porius calls 'cavoseniargizing', his 'secretive psycho-sensuous trick of ravishing the four elements with the five senses, and of doing it with these latter so fused together that it was like making love to the earth-mother herself' (466), it is figured in terms of plenitude. Even Porius's 'intercourse' with a cluster 'of derelict seed vessels' atop an ash tree (104–5) is positively charged, an 'ecstasy of life worship indescribable in words' (494). But with the death of the giants, a 'difference' enters into Porius's 'familiar "cavoseniargizing"' (494), a new feeling 'that embraced the whole world as if it were something under water, something that included not only staring eyes and pieces of bone, but ourselves also, as if we lived under water and saw ourselves, and everyone else, as weeds, stones, reeds, minnows, newts, water-beetles, mud!' (495). Freud's 'creative sense of guilt' has taken root, with death and complicity henceforth the ground for Porius's 'lotus eating' (92); he must now force himself to enjoy the world his own actions have impoverished,

---

[54] Duncan, 'Mythology of Escape', pp.76–7; Powys, *Rabelais*, p.341.

both the outward world, with all its forms and colours, its splintered rocks, jagged spikes, dizzy peaks, slippery precipices, and the inward world with all its prickings and ticklings, its messings up and missings out, its throbbings and pulsings, its heavings and spasms, all that the mind whistled to him, all that the conscience clamped down upon him. (496)

This reinscription of Porius's mental life under the sign of death brings it into line with the novel that holds him, animating its digressive-evasive style and underwater lyricism with the dark fatality of history.

The extinction of the giants weights the novel's entropic fascination with 'reedy pools and moss-grown recesses wherein long-fallen, long-mouldering tree-trunks sank slowly, season after season, autumn after autumn, into ever softer and gentler dissolution' (155). These long lyric evocations of 'non-human silence and expectancy', forest 'avenues whose lights and shades were forever waiting for feet that had already become dust' (155), traduce late-Victorian and Edwardian-era fantasies of 'the old lost road through the woods' (Rudyard Kipling), those 'haunts of ancient peace' wherein imperial England readied herself 'for resolute action, should danger or difficultly call for it' (Alfred Austin).[55] Instead of Austin's 'ancient-ness' and 'abundance', *Porius* offers a moonlit river, its 'livid folornness ... the acme and epitome of desolation'.

> It suggested lost battles and the blood-frozen corpses of innumerable dead men. It suggested that just beyond the horizon lay the walls of deserted cities and the chilly wharves of ruined harbours, where great ships lay waterlogged and dismasted upon mud banks that were phosphorescent with the whiteness of death. (48)

Such descriptions record the world laid waste by human agency and position us on the far side of history's capacity to hurt. Porius in his contrite 'Cewri mood' imagines himself 'swimming round and round the solemn figureheads of a flotilla of ships' wrecked 'on a hidden reef' and there abandoned (561). In the meantime, the prose affords a sensuous response to bodies, whether animate or inanimate, understood in their physical vulnerability and susceptibility to pain.

Powys was proud of what he called his 'Bewick style', his 'little descriptions' of unremarkable creatures and 'inanimates like posts & stumps & stones' 'not so much poeticized as carefully noted'.[56] Familiar from his childhood, Bewick's *History of British Birds* (1797–1821) appealed to Powys for its illustrations that were 'brutal, grim, ghastly, terrible, exquisite, sad ... with such a sense of the mystery of

---

[55] Rudyard Kipling, *Rewards and Faeries* [1910] (London: Penguin, 1987), p.106; Alfred Austin, *Haunts of Ancient Peace* (London: Macmillan, 1902), p.184.

[56] John Cowper Powys to Louis Wilkinson, 21 January 1944; in *Letters to Louis Wilkinson*, p.195.

half-seen, half-felt passed-by things of no importance as you go about the country'.[57] *Porius* makes a point of attending to these ordinarily unattended to things, as when the poet Taliessin interrupts his composition to commune with a

> straw of wheat, dirty and split, crooked and crushed flat, with only a couple of empty husks adhering to its head end, and its tail end not only flattened out beyond all semblance of the hollow reed it had once been, but polished, in its enforced travels over the earth, to such a degree of thinness, smoothness, and whiteness, as to be almost transparent. (379)

Porius pauses after his massacre of the Saxon to watch

> with interest two tall reed stalks with feathery tops ... and there seemed to him to have detached itself from one or other of these swaying stalks a pair of seed husks that by some chance, possibly by a wandering gossamer thread, possibly by a weft of spiderweb, had got stuck together, and now made a hair's breadth bridge leading from one stalk to the other. By yet another chance this bridge of gossamer seed lifted up its twin angles of triune lines exactly in the centre of the moon's reflection, and once established there took on the appearance of a gallows.

A yet further 'accidental happening' occurs when a 'reckless breath of wind' causes 'a leaf or a twig, or it may even have been a tired and battered or possibly lifeless moth' to catch 'on that lunar-rippling horizontal bar' (517).

The impulse that drives these minute observations is as much ethical as it is aesthetic; the same 'pitiful fancy' would drive Powys to 'rescue bits of paper' from the covers of drains and the dryad Kleta in the late fantasy *Atlantis* (1954) to dedicate her 'garden' to the 'unruffled preservation of what is usually obliterated':

> bits of wood, bits of stalk, bits of fungus, bits of snail-shells, bits of empty birds' eggs, bits of animals' hair, bits of birds' feathers, bits of broken sheaths of long-perished buds and shattered insect-shards, strewn remnants of withered lichen-clusters, and scattered fragments of acorns and berries and oak-apples that have survived in these lonely trails and tracks to be scurf upon the skin of one world and the chaos-stuff for the creation of another world.[58]

Powys' 'Bewick style' is not 'the exquisite regard for common things' discovered in *The Prelude*, the compensatory 'green language' of a romantic withdrawal into nature, for it registers not only natural decomposition and Heraclitean flux

---

[57] Powys, *Petrushka and the Dancer*, pp.215–16; diary entry for 31 July 1936.
[58] John Cowper Powys to Louis Wilkinson, 16 August 1955; in *Letters to Louis Wilkinson*, p.295. John Cowper Powys, *Atlantis* (London: Macdonald, 1954), p.44.

(424) but also the damage done by humankind.[59] 'Stumps, logs, grasses, plant off-shoots, twigs and tussocks' are candidates for this kind of conscientious noticing, but so too are 'old gibbets, cruelties to dogs' and 'graves, graves, Graves!'[60] With vivisection, for Powys, the supreme instance of our modern, scientific depreciation of animal life and of the sadistic psychosexual impulse that shadows action on the stage of history, the Bewick style counters with compassion as the basis of a minimal morality: identifying with pain as that which should not be.[61]

From Myrddin Wyllt, the novel's mythological Merlin figure and an avatar of Saturn, we learn that 'nobody in the world, nobody beyond the world, can be trusted with power'. The goal should rather be 'to unmake' ourselves, to relinquish authority and leave others alone (260–1). What is true for gods and for governments applies also to novelists. Accordingly, Powys proceeds to divest himself of authorial craft and control, the apparatus of artistry. Against the modernist *mot juste*, Powys hones his deliberate '*slip-shod* style', his 'naïve unstylized wordiness', his 'method of writing at large and sans stint'.[62] As for 'the art of *the novel*', with its well-constructed plot, its 'mounting-up to an architectural dénouement' and 'rational "rounding off"', its '"notes"' all 'gathered up in one crashing crescendo at the close', Powys cries foul at what he imagines to be the costs of such closure.[63] He explained his decision in *Wolf Solent* (1929), for example, not to orchestrate 'a great crushing catastrophic King-Lear-like, Possessed-like finale', on the grounds that he took his characters 'so seriously': 'I can't bring myself to sacrifice them in cold blood to such an artistic' climax. He credits 'a queer conscientious scruple mixing in' with his own 'cowardice and natural timidity and shrinking from violence'.[64] Equating dramatic eventuality with collateral damage and the subordination of means to ends, Powys builds the case for a left-libertarian narrative praxis of divagation and delay. 'You see, my dear, *all* (without exception) of the talent, gift, eloquence, insight, clairvoyance I possess is always *digression*—never anything else.' Having built up what he calls

> a sort of foundation, and on top of that a sort of scaffolding, *both very simple*— including all the Main Characters & where they live, or all the main theses,

---

[59] William Wordsworth, *The Major Works*, edited by Stephen Gill (Oxford: Oxford University Press, 2000), p.584; Raymond Williams, *The Country and the City* (London: Chatto & Windus, 1973), pp.132–3.
[60] Powys, *Petrushka and the Dancer*, pp.215–16; diary entry for 31 July 1936.
[61] Cf. Felix Taylor, 'John Cowper Powys and the Anti-Vivisection Movement', *The Powys Journal* 29 (2019): pp.57–76.
[62] Powys, *Petrushka and the Dancer*, p.247; diary entry for 23 June 1937. Powys, *Obstinate Cymric*, p.156. John Cowper Powys to Llewelyn Powys, 5 June 1931; in *Letters of John Cowper Powys to his Brother Llewelyn, Volume 2: 1925–1939*, edited by Malcolm Elwin (London: Village Press, 1975), p.126.
[63] John Cowper Powys, *Dorothy Richardson* (London: Joiner & Steele, 1931), p.36; p.38.
[64] John Cowper Powys to Llewelyn Powys, 16 August 1928; in, *Letters to Llewelyn*, pp.83–4.

propositions & contentions ... *Then* I let *the chance moment* have its way—have its way with the characters, have its way with the ideas!⁶⁵

Digression is Powys' anti-art, its aesthetic keyed to the 'great *Anarchistic Taboo of Nature*', which works

> to break and lame and cramp and stiffen and distort and interrupt, yes! and even mutilate, those religious and moral and philosophical ideas, so much more consistent with their own first principles, so much more compact and premeditated, so much more hammered into shape and neatly riveted, so much more rounded off according to the claims of metaphysical satisfaction

than 'real life' ever is.⁶⁶ Against 'the artist's and poet's craving for shape, for form, for a definite issue, for a desired consummation', against the ideologue's craving for system, Powys asserts the virtue of non-interference and of letting '*the chance moment* have its way'.⁶⁷ As Porius at one point reflects, 'it was a mistake always to be making these rational efforts after order and uniformity, when the wisdom of every creature lay in reconciling itself as well as it could to that mysterious mingling of Nature's purposes with accident and chance, which is the only world we know' (116). *Porius* calls us instead—as a philosophy of life and in the texture of its prose—'to "tread water" in the flood of time as it rushes ... on and away', to step away from self and from our ambitions to bend history to our will 'into the general dissolution and rushing away of all things, organic and inorganic, chemical or structural, planetary or elemental, in the ceaseless flow of the vast centrifugal and centripetal currents of our corner of the multiverse'.⁶⁸

The most capacious of the metaphors that Powys offers to describe this dynamic is what *Owen Glendower* calls the Welsh 'mythology of escape', though contemporaneous essays afford it a more general application. According to this model, the soul that would escape co-optation, that would avoid and evade capture in the historical domain, makes a 'double flight. It flees into a circuitous *Inward*. It retreats into a circuitous *Outward*.'⁶⁹ Both lines of escape open onto absence. The sensuous embrace of the phenomenal world reveals, as we have seen, the 'nothing remains' of a Heraclitian flux, while our inward retreat discovers 'a dark and empty void': 'dead blackness and absolute negation' await us when we look from the 'inner window' of our consciousness.⁷⁰ The framing is philosophical, but *Porius* holds to the suggestion that this ontology of the self and the world might be historically contingent, a symptom of the sign Pisces and its baleful, two-thousand-year hold on

---

[65] John Cowper Powys to Louis Wilkinson, 5 October 1944; in *Letters to Louis Wilkinson*, p.160.
[66] John Cowper Powys, *Dostoievsky* [1946] (London: Village Press, 1974), p.98.
[67] Powys, *Dorothy Richardson*, p.31.
[68] Powys, *Obstinate Cymric*, p.157; p.145.
[69] Powys, *Owen Glendower*, p.889.
[70] Powys, *Obstinate Cymric*, pp.99–100

human affairs, a consequence of that constriction of possibility that began with the giants' extinction. Powys imagines this symmetry of 'nothingness' at the systole and diastole of the self as strangely sustaining: 'like you might use a battery or dynamo of inexhaustible and unfathomable power', Powys instructs us to draw on the void inside of ourselves to 'enjoy' all that is around us, 'dark' as it may be 'with fatality, and sprinkled with the foam of all that rushed away'.[71] Poised above a 'primordial abyss' in the novel's climactic closing scene, Porius will become aware of 'an unfathomable power within him, a power that was at once divine and human, animal and elemental, a power that could be drawn upon at will, not to create or to destroy, but simply to *enjoy*' (748–9).

This instinct drives a style of writing that, as Jerome McGann observes, 'seems energized rather than wearied by the emptiness it must transact. As the prose enters its belated and threadbare worlds, it springs to a nervous, strangely robust life, as if those worlds could never satisfy its curiosities, as if its own fascinations were themselves undiscovered countries'.[72] Fredric Jameson has called this 'the most authentic vocation of romance in our time', to register the disenchantment of the modern world, not to reinvent providence but to reveal, by silence and absence, its passing. Jameson's heroes of the twentieth-century fantastic—Julio Cortázar, Franz Kafka—'the last unrecognizable avatars of romance as a mode, draw their magical power from an unsentimental loyalty to those henceforth abandoned clearings across which the higher and lower worlds once passed'.[73] At the level of prose, Powys indeed sings the recessional of romance, recording a world evacuated of superhuman beings and transcendental meanings. At the level of the narrative, however, *Porius* makes one last equivocal move 'to tempt the impossible in fiction'—the phrase is McGann's—and to counter history with romance.

As the culmination of the novel's mythological plot, Powys rewrites the 'beguiling of Merlin' by the sorceress Nineue (Tennyson's Vivien) and his entrapment in her 'fatal esplumeoir' (738). Breaking with legend, Powys has Porius rescue Merlin from his mountaintop tomb that he may live to fight another day. Unlike his other great exertions in the novel, this act appears to escape historical irony because its outcome attends a future that is still not yet, a time in advance of our own when on the far side of the next cosmogonic age Merlin will inaugurate 'a second Age of Gold'. In the short term, meanwhile, the act enjoys the approbation of Nature: as Porius frees Merlin from his megalithic prison we hear 'the screaming of eagles', who as the tyrant's friend and symbol of empire fear Merlin's release, followed by 'a vast, indescribable, multitudinous murmur, groping up, fumbling up, like a mist among mists, from all the forests and valleys of Ynys Prydein, the response of innumerable weak and terrified and unbeautiful and unconsidered and unprotected

---

[71] Powys, *Obstinate Cymric*, p.100; Powys, *Owen Glendower*, p.750.
[72] McGann, 'Marvels and Wonders', p.5.
[73] Fredric Jameson, *The Political Unconscious: Narrative as a Socially Symbolic Act* (Ithaca, NY: Cornell University Press, 1981), p.135.

creatures' who look to Merlin as their champion. Porius's Herculean labour atop Snowdon looks set to reverse the curse of the giants' extinction, guaranteeing the survival of utopia and all its attendant marvels and wonders. It reads as a triumphant conclusion, its generosity to the world's 'weak' and 'unbeautiful' the very opposite of the kind of 'catastrophic King-Lear-like, Possessed-like finale' that would satisfy 'the art of *the novel*'. But this recovery of romance possibility falters in the face of what follows, as Porius once more recalls 'the floating blood and the strewn hair and the green water' of the giants' tarn:

> 'O Creiddylad! O Creiddylad!' he groaned within himself... And he thought how absolutely alone in this chaos of things was every single soul, whether of insect or worm or reptile or fish or beast or bird or man or god.
>
> 'There's nothing I can do,' he said to himself, 'but just accept this crazy loneliness in this unbounded chaos, and hope for the best among all the other crazy lonely selves! And why not? Such a chance-ruled chaos of souls, none of them without *some* fellow-feeling, *some* kindliness, at least to their offspring, at least to their mates, at least to their friends, is a better thing than a world of blind authority, a world ruled by one Caesar, or one God, or one—' (750)

With that, Porius falls asleep, the novel ends, and history resumes its grim dominion.

## IV. Communist Contraband

For Christmas in 1968, Sylvia Townsend Warner sent William Maxwell, her long-time editor at the *New Yorker*, an old copy of *The Corner That Held Them*. She instructed him to look out for the sweet-pea seeds she had smuggled into the spine and joked that, 'unless the customs have been there before you', he might also find 'some spores of anthrax, broomrape, rabies & Communism'.[74] As with all her dealings with the American magazine whose right of first refusal on Warner's short fiction was a main source of income, this allusion to politics is oblique and hedged about with humour. It allows us to laugh at the thought that a novel about nuns could be as invasive as chokeweed, as deadly as anthrax; only the paranoid

---

[74] Sylvia Townsend Warner to William Maxwell, 14 December 1948; in *Letters*, p.235, and *The Element of Lavishness: Letters of Sylvia Townsend Warner and William Maxwell*, edited by Michael Steinman (Washington, D.C.: *Counterpoint*, 2001), p.199. Earlier that summer, Warner had written asking whether he could grow sweet-peas in his 'stony garden in Yorktown Heights' and promised 'by hook or by crook' to smuggle him 'a packet of Unwin's Old Scented Sweet-Peas. The flowers are small, in bright Hundreds & Thousands colours. The smell is ravishing and so strong that half a dozen blooms will scent a room. I am enjoying mine so passionately, so carnally, that I can't bear it that you & Emmy should not have the same pleasure.' Sylvia Townsend Warner to William Maxwell, 29 July 1968; *Element of Lavishness*, p.193.

would test for spores. But customs officers are not always wrong, nor were all Cold War suspicions misplaced. Like the sweet-pea seeds secreted in the spine, Warner puts the reader on guard for a covert, contraband communism to be found, if not where we might expect to look, in the novel's conjugation of character and plot, then somewhere close by. The comment jokingly admits to a more radical intention than critics have often supposed, reconnecting the novel's obvious delight in the historical contingency and material specificity of its mediaeval lifeworld to a conception of politics as the extended temporal constitution of society, its production, reproduction, and transformation through struggle. The comment cuts against the common interpretation of *The Corner That Held Them* as a novel of retirement from activist politics and asserts, as Warner never ceased to do, the legitimacy of political violence in the service of social change.

*The Corner That Held Them* may seem an unlikely candidate for inclusion in a canon of mid-century communist historical fiction. Set in a remote fourteenth-century convent and told almost exclusively from the perspective of the 'professionally religious', the novel reconstructs the 'mortifying tranquillity' of a cloistered community.[75] It lavishes attention on the 'practical considerations' (196) of institutional life, the 'income and outgoing' (198) of Oby's accounts, the convent's internal politics and changes of post across a long, forty-year span. With a fine eye, it assesses the nuns' relative privilege in mediaeval society: their elite class status and social connections, the dowries downpaid on their religious careers, the gendered restrictions on their power and mobility. Meanwhile, the major events that bookend the narrative, the Black Death at mid-century and the Peasants' Revolt in June 1381, appear peripheral, their scale and relation obscure to the nuns who focalize the narrative and constrain its critical conception. In cleaving to the lifeworld and limited perspective of her cloistered women, honouring their experience as valid on its own terms, recording their prejudice without condescension and their ignorance without irony, Warner would seem to preclude a class-based history from below, a loving reconstruction of manorial life and labour, an empowering narrative of popular insurgency. In the absence of an alternative centre of authority, it is easy to assume that the nuns' experience of history is all that Warner has to say on that score. Even the novel's form seems to match itself to 'that epitome of humdrum, a provincial nunnery' (124). Wendy Mulford describes a novel 'without conventional plot development, crisis and dénouement', Claire Harman a narrative 'that loses itself in events', Melanie Micir a novel in which 'nothing really happens'.[76] But it is possible that others in Warner's fictional fourteenth century experience the time differently, and that we can learn to read for their experience.

---

[75] Sylvia Townsend Warner to Paul Nordoff, 9 April 1942; in *Letters*, p.79. Sylvia Townsend Warner, *The Corner That Held Them* (London: Virago, 1988), p.8; subsequent references are to this edition and given parenthetically in the body of the text.

[76] Mulford, *This Narrow Place*, p.199; Claire Harman, 'Introduction', to Warner, *The Corner That Held Them* (London: Virago, 1988), p. v; Melanie Micir, 'Not of National Importance: Sylvia Townsend

Warner claimed to have written the novel on 'the purest Marxian principles'. By this, she was not referring simply to the novel's materialist attitude to conventual history, her conviction that 'if you were going to give an accurate picture of the monastic life, you'd have to put in all their finances, how they made their money, how they dodged about from one thing to another and how very precarious it all was'.[77] The novel is indeed brilliantly attentive to the economic history and class composition of the convent at Oby. The influence of Eileen Power's landmark study of *Mediaeval English Nunneries* (1922) is readily apparent, with its long chapter on convents' 'financial difficulties', its caustic account of nuns' privileged backgrounds and their ordinary unsaintly lives, its wide 'allowance for human frailty' and silence on the subject of spiritual vocation.[78] Power's portraits of the female church builders and of the average prioress doing her best 'to make two ends of an inadequate income meet' required little elaboration, likewise a host of minor characters and incidents.[79] But Power's pioneering women's history was not the novel's starting point, which lies altogether beside the figure of the female religious and the spectre of insolvency. Warner's 'wish to write Marxianly of the ages of faith' supposed a wider canvas than the fortunes of a small religious house and the foibles of its women; it required a logic of structural transformation absent in Power's account and a parallel protagonist.[80]

For the US edition of the novel, Warner supplied a sophisticated 'Note on the Historical Background' that folds Oby's financial difficulties into the break-up of the feudal world.[81] This 'background' was not simply an afterthought, a mock-scholarly apparatus or primer for foreign readers; it was there from the beginning, as witness Warner's account of one of her wartime lectures, this one given in Weymouth to the women of the local Labour Party. 'We had great fun last week with the diseases of the Middle Ages, and how the Black Death, having killed off everything else, finally killed the feudal system.'[82] Here, in miniature, is the argument Warner spells out in her 'Note' about the 'economic consequences' of the Black Death, in whose aftermath 'the old cumbrous sleepy bargain of the manorial system ... was replaced by the more cut-throat bargain of capital and labour'. Told across the novel's *longue durée* is the transition from feudalism to capitalism, soon to become

---

Warner, 'Women's Work and the Mid-Century Historical Novel', in *Around 1945: Literature, Citizenship, Rights*, edited by Allan Hepburn (Montreal: McGill-Queens University Press, 2016), p.67.

[77] 'Sylvia Townsend Warner in Conversation', *PN Review* 8, no.3 (1981): p.36.

[78] Eileen Power, *Mediaeval English Nunneries, c.1275 to 1535* (Cambridge: Cambridge University Press, 1922), pp.161–236; p.473. Warner recalls sending 'to the L.L. [London Library] for Eileen Power's English nunneries for re-reading' mid-way through the writing, in 'Notes on *The Corner That Held Them*', edited by Peter Swaab, *The Journal of the Sylvia Townsend Warner Society* 20 (2020): p.4.

[79] Power, *Mediaeval English Nunneries*, pp.90–4.

[80] Warner, 'Notes on *The Corner That Held Them*', p.4.

[81] Sylvia Townsend Warner, 'A Note on the Historical Background', reprinted in *The Journal of the Sylvia Townsend Warner Society* 16 (2015): pp.9–13.

[82] Sylvia Townsend Warner to Elling Aanestad, 14 February 1942; D-TWA/A42; STW.2012.125.2267.

one of the great debates in Marxist historiography.[83] Warner's contribution is anchored in the reality of manorial labour and peasant struggle, resisting what was then the common impulse to abstract a narrative of self-propelling productive forces—trade and merchant capital, a nascent bourgeoisie—emerging alongside and external to the feudal agricultural mode to explain the subsequent take-off of capitalist development. Also important to Warner's account is the expropriated wealth congealed in the Church, a reservoir of capital ripe for one of the first great acts of primitive accumulation, the sixteenth-century dissolution of the monasteries, which abolished what Marx called 'the old conditions of landed property', powering the agricultural revolution and the rise of a rural gentry.[84] In the nearer term, Warner's historical note fastens on 'the exasperating richness' of the Church 'and its harshness in manorial administration' to explain the 'pressure of dissatisfied thinking' that exploded in 1381.[85]

As for a parallel protagonist, Warner recalled the novel's origins, its 'first bricks', in 'the feeling of how white Ely must have looked across the 14th-century fen, and how intimidatingly, tyrannically large, to the 14th-century peasant, coming out of his smoky hovel to stare over the fen'.[86] The lantern of Ely Cathedral from across the Cambridgeshire fens became the spire of Oby from across the Norfolk Broads; along the way, Warner thought also of setting the novel in the Somerset Levels, perhaps with the remains of Muchelney in mind.[87] These settings emphasize the separation of the religious house on its island from the wetlands round about; they underscore the elevation of its lantern, tower or spire from the peasants' lives below and position their perspective against that of the 'professionally religious'.[88] The contrast is moral and topographical; it is also theoretical, a literalization of the relationship in Marxist cultural analysis between material base and ideological superstructure, economic foundation—the means and relations of a given mode of production—and the corresponding forms of social consciousness.[89] Dame Alicia

---

[83] Maurice Dobb's *Studies in the Development of Capitalism* (1946) and Paul Sweezy's 1950 reply launched the so-called 'Transition Debate', which would ultimately embroil several generations of scholars in Britain and abroad.

[84] Karl Marx, *Capital. Volume 1*, translated by Ben Fowkes (London: Penguin, 1990), p.883.

[85] Warner, 'Note on the Historical Background', p.11.

[86] Warner, 'Notes on *The Corner That Held Them*', p.4.

[87] In her 1949 guidebook of the county, Warner described the ruined abbey as now comfortably ensconced in the modern village; but it was different in the fourteenth century, when the 'serfs and bordars' would have 'heard the Muchelney bells ringing across' the Sedgemoor 'swamp' and felt themselves apart. Sylvia Townsend Warner, *Somerset* (London: Paul Elek, 1949), p.83.

[88] Warner introduces Oby as 'perched on the little rise of ground which gave the place its old name' (6); 'the *ey* of Muchelney means *island*', she notes in *Somerset*, p.82. In *After the Death of Don Juan* (1938), it is both the church and the castle that sit upon a 'hillock' while the 'lime-washed hovels' of the village cower in their shadow. Sylvia Townsend Warner, *After the Death of Don Juan* (London: Virago, 1989), p.24; p.58.

[89] At the Third Congress of the League of American Writers in 1939, Warner instructed the historical novelist to include both 'the economic ground-base' and 'the social-economic variations which move above that ground base'. The talk appears in *Fighting Words*, edited by Donald Ogden Stewart (New York: Harcourt Brace, 1940), pp.50–3; p.52.

first envisions her spire, 'beautiful as art and money could make it', soaring up to be 'the glory of the countryside' (12); her cousin, the powerful Prior of Etchingdon, takes a no less aesthetic pleasure in picturing it rise 'out of the melancholy flatness of the moors' (47). But for the serfs of the manor, 'straightening up from their toil in their field' (51), the spire is only ever a symbol of their subjection. Theirs has been the heavy labour, digging the foundations (69), 'carting stone' for the masons, and later 'loading and carrying the hods' (107). In the feudal system it is time and effort they can ill afford, this 'extortion of cartage and labour dues' 'keeping them from their work' on the common fields that supply their scanty livelihood (107).

Peasant resentment runs as a refrain through *The Corner That Held Them*. The establishment of a nunnery at Oby is an ill day for the nuns who arrived in a 'batch' from France and 'felt that they had come a long way to worsen their lot' (6), but it is even more 'unwelcome' for the serfs already there. Long years of 'an absentee landlord and a careless bailiff' had accustomed the manor to 'a kind of scrambling devil-take-the-hindmost independence' (8), which it is sorry to lose. They make their disaffection felt with an infrapolitics of everyday resistance: foot-dragging excuses (8), shirked or careless labour, 'tithes and duties paid grudgingly or not at all' (11); occasionally, it erupts into open confrontation. In 1300, the 'bondwomen of the manor broke through the reed fence into the orchard where the nuns were at recreation and mobbed them'; for a long while thereafter, the nuns 'going along the cloisters to sing the night office ... would strain their ears for the footsteps of marauders or the crackle of a fired thatch' (11). In the aftermath of the Black Death, the manor's children run 'wild, thieving, maiming and destroying'; they vent their hostility by marching up and down 'during office hours ... singing lewd choruses to an accompaniment of bird-rattles and old cauldrons' (38). A year or two later it is their fathers' turn; angry at the spire, they ransack the masons' encampment before marching on the convent 'singing at the tops of their voices' (107). By 1377, the peasants are organizing; we learn of one vigilante group that calls itself 'the Twelve Apostles' (212), giving a practical edge to the doctrine of apostolic poverty which, as Warner notes, was 'in the wind' in the fourteenth century and popular with 'the laity' (40). By 1380, 'rebellions' are 'jumping up here, there, and everywhere, like a fire in the stubble' (243). The nuns have grown accustomed to 'threats of destruction' (250); the following year it comes.

It is characteristic of *The Corner That Held Them*, however, that the episodes Warner devotes to the Peasants' Revolt centre the lives and perspectives of the convent. 'A Green Staff' draws its gentle humour from the death of Ralph Kello, the nuns' fraudulent priest. For twenty years, Sir Ralph has sat on a promise to publicize a poem in his possession called 'The Lay of Mamillion', a para-Chaucerian vernacular epic. At last, in June 1381, he sets off for London, his mission coinciding with the great mobilization of rebel peasants marching on the capital. He falls by the way, and the women who attend to his dying mistake him for one of their own, a priest 'of our way of thinking' (279). Ralph's career has been a cheat from the start, his clerical appearance deceiving; this deathbed likeness to 'the poor man's priest' (281) John Ball is both of a piece and a fond farewell. In the following chapter, Oby's experience of the rebellion is real enough: it suffers the death of a bailiff and the loss of its plate, nor could anything have prevented 'Dame Joan from being raped, her fears were so implacably bent on that catastrophe' (292). But Warner's telling privileges instead the play of rumour and rationalization among the nuns, the psychological incentives to demonize the rebels and misconstrue their cause, to falsify a screen memory the better to forget.

> It went against the grain to identify such familiar useful shapes, figures at the plough's tail or at sheep-shearing, with the actors in these stories of wild and efficient vengeance, and to think of those wind-bitten red hands as reddened with blood. It was easier to listen to the stories from the other side: stories of reprisals, executions by scores, miraculous escapes, and the immense popularity of the young king, whom one and the same breath reported as loved for his clemency and dreaded for his ruthlessness. On the whole, the most comforting rumour, and the most pervading, was that the rebels were powerless because no one supported them, that they were riven by internal jealousies, had neither weapons nor leadership, and were dying in thousands from hunger, thirst, and exposure. (288–9)

This is the novel's last word on 1381 and a far cry from the agitational forms in which, as we saw in chapter two, Warner's fellow communists had taken up the story: Hyman Fagan's *Nine Days That Shook England* (1938), Charles Poulsen's *English Episode* (1946), Alan Bush's *Wat Tyler* (1951). No rebel widow's vow closes out *The Corner That Held Them* promising to raise her unborn son with 'two thoughts for ever in his mind', freedom and revenge.'[90] No 'evening glow' illuminates the stage as the chorus sings: 'Who once puts forth his strength for right sets free his spirit from its chain, looks on the world with altered eyes. All that is great in Man still lives and once again, and once again shall rise.'[91] Warner records instead the nuns' gentle relaxation into ruling-class consciousness.

This pivot of perspective from the vantage and moral compass of the '14th-century peasant' to those who live upon their labour and regard them, when at all, as 'shapes' in the landscape, may seem perverse, given the intensity of Warner's rural activism in the 1930s and her lifelong antipathy to the Church. But the common interpretation takes it in its stride, collapsing any distance between the author and her nuns to read the novel biographically as an allegory of retirement.[92] Late

---

[90] Charles Poulsen, *English Episode: A Tale of the Peasants' Revolt of 1381* (London: Progress Publishing, 1946), p.279.
[91] Bush, *Wat Tyler*, pp.248–50; Nancy Bush wrote the libretto.
[92] For claims that *The Corner That Held Them* was Warner's farewell to activist politics, see J. Lawrence Mitchell, 'In Another Country: Sylvia Townsend Warner at Large', in *Writers of the Old*

in life, Warner herself seemed to encourage this analogy, likening the situation of the novel's nuns to that of her comrades on the Left: as she told Arnold Rattenbury in the 1970s, 'who that one has ever loved was not in retreat in 1948?'[93] Certainly, by 1949 Warner was declining Nancy Cunard's invitation to attend the World Peace Congress in Paris that year and pleading a 'centrifugal' mood: 'I can't believe that anything will come of congressing and gathering just now. A sitting on already boiled eggs, a clucking of past hatchings. No, a quiet dust-bath is more to my mind, a dust-bath and a minding my own business.'[94] But the novel itself is of an earlier conception. She began it in early 1942 at a time when, as she confided in her diary, 'the defence of USSR was the defence of my deepest concerns'.[95] She wrote it with a portrait of Stalin by her desk.[96] Its publication in 1948 coincided with her powerfully pro-Soviet parable, 'The Jungle Blossom', as well as a fawning statement in praise of Stalin's wartime speeches.[97] Even in 1949, with her mood 'centrifugal', she was participating in Party literary debates, urging writers to 'be on our guard against decadence' in the English language: 'Let our English be our own and not a re-export from the U.S.A.'[98] To the extent that *The Corner That Held Them* is, as Rattenbury reported her saying, about 'women devoting themselves to an ideal even when palpably it [is] not working' and 'the cause seems false', the reference is not to communism but to Britain's prosecution of the war.[99]

I read *The Corner That Held Them* as instead a virtuoso performance by a writer who liked to play games with herself and the reader. Warner embarked on *The True Heart* (1929), for example, with the notion that it would be 'a good exercise' for a practising novelist 'to take a folk song or a fairy story and re-tell it'; the novel's classical pastiche—a rewriting of Apuleius—gave free rein to her wit,

School: *British Novelists of the 1930s*, edited by Rosemary Colt and Janice Rossen (London: Macmillan, 1992), p.136; and Mulford, *This Narrow Place*, p.196.

[93] Rattenbury, 'Plain Heart, Light Tether', p.47.
[94] Sylvia Townsend Warner to Nancy Cunard, 19 January 1949; in *Letters*, p.108.
[95] Warner, *Diaries*, p.113; entry for 23 January 1942.
[96] Harman, *Sylvia Townsend Warner*, p.195.
[97] Sylvia Townsend Warner, 'The Jungle Blossom', *Our Time* 7, no.11 (August 1948): pp.287–92; *Soviet Writers Reply to English Writers' Questions*, edited by Edgell Rickword (London: The Writers Group, Society for Cultural Relations with the U.S.S.R., 1948), p.48. Warner later recalled hearing Stalin's voice on the radio in 1943, 'a voice so living, so warm, so sturdy, that I would like to remember it on my deathbed as an assurance of the spirit of man'; quoted in Harman, *Sylvia Townsend Warner*, p.253.
[98] Sylvia Townsend Warner, open letter to the Communist Party Writers' Group, June 1949; D-TWA/A24; STW.2012.125.1333. In April 1951, the Party staged its third 'Battle of Ideas' conference on 'The American Threat to British Culture'.
[99] Rattenbury, 'Literature, Lying and Sober Truth', pp.231–2. Even after Germany's invasion of the Soviet Union in 1941 and the Communist Party's pivot to support the war, Warner remained persuaded by its original line, that Britain's interest in the war was not anti-fascist and that the fascism at home was going unfought. When later she watched footage of the Liberation of Paris in 'draggle-tailed' Dorchester, it only pointed the contrast in how the two countries had gone about their wars. The French had exerted 'mind and body to the limit of capacity' in the task of 'rooting out fascism'; the British had muddled through, attempting no such confrontation with the enemy within. Sylvia Townsend Warner, 'Love of France', *Our Time* 5, no.1 (August 1945): p.6. Sylvia Townsend Warner to Nancy Cunard, 11 November 1944; in *Letters*, p.88.

and she delighted in engineering so 'efficient' a fit of modern detail to mythic pretext that 'no reviewer saw what I was up to. Only my mother recognised the basis of my story'.[100] Other texts seem similarly designed to exercise Warner's talents as a writer, including a large corpus of narratives that defy traditional fiction's exemplary or heroic characterology, its modelling of moral development and privileging of individual perspectives and powers of response. Warner's animal fables and elfin tales differently decentre the human, looking for ways to 'abate the human smell', to cauterize 'the human heart'.[101] Other stories compete to inhabit the human lifeworld most removed from Warner's politics and person. The wartime short story collection, *A Garland of Straw* (1943), for example, contains two intimate portraits of fascists: the sentimental German soldier Kurt Winkler sent to Spain to rid the country of communists, and the flaxen-haired Lili, sadistic child of a German brothel in occupied Poland.[102] Both characters come to us unchaperoned: free indirect discourse draws us into their worlds, their actions and reactions go largely uncaptioned. With the ten-year-old Lili, it is up to the reader to register as irony Warner's deadpan description of the pleasures of power; and if we recoil too readily at Lili's deadly hunger games—she tortures starving Jewish children for fun—we may miss the ways in which Lili is herself a victim, already groomed and surely doomed to join her mother in the trade.

Warner's portrait of a mediaeval religious community may seem more benign than these studies in the psychology of fascism, but it too is a venture behind enemy lines and an experiment in form. Its women may have analogues on the wartime Home Front and among Warner's comrades on the Left; they may even, in their own way, be victims. Certainly, they are the products of their historical moment and milieu. The novel thematizes their lack of individuality, their serial formation and succession. Dame Alicia likens her sisters in Christ to 'a tray of buns':

> In some the leaven has worked more than in others, some are a little under-baked, some a little scorched, in others the spice has clotted and shows like a brown stain; but one can see that they all come out of the same oven and that one hand pulled them apart from the same lump of dough. A tray of buns, a tray of nuns ... (34)

The analogy is ingenious, not least for its secular conception: it is not God who has baked His nuns this way, but the rule and routine of religious life. The prioress arrives at her conceit by reflecting on how little she knows the women she has spent her life alongside; but for there to be 'intimacy', she reasons, there must first be 'the

---

[100] Sylvia Townsend Warner, 'Preface' to *The True Heart* (London: Penguin, 2021), pp. vii–viii.

[101] Sylvia Townsend Warner, *Kingdoms of Elfin* (New York: Viking Press, 1977), p.1. 'Bother the human heart, I'm tired of the human heart ... I want to write something entirely different', she explained; 'Sylvia Townsend Warner in Conversation', *PN Review* 8, no.3 (1981): p.36.

[102] Sylvia Townsend Warner, 'A Red Carnation' and 'Apprentice', in *A Garland of Straw* (New York: Viking, 1943).

option to approach or to move away'. Such freedom is impossible in a cloister (24). Warner boasted that her characters were 'innumerable and insignificant', but she meant no particular animus by this multiplication and flattening of her cast; she meant rather to suggest that even character has a history.[103] Warner's mediaeval convent, dedicated to St Leonard, the patron saint of prisoners, takes us to a time before the novel's Richardsonian rendezvous with psychological depth and before the modernist inward turn, moments soon to be canonized in Cold War literary criticism for their discovery of the individual and the freedoms of market democracy. In *The Corner That Held Them*, subjectivity is a function of social formation, and though beguiling, Warner's discrimination of nun from nun does not distract from her emphasis on the social type. Oby's nuns embody a class and institution she condemns.

That a reader may miss the condemnation returns us to Warner's success with *The True Heart* and how only her mother had recognized her ploy. This ability to fly under the radar and evade critical capture had only become more convenient as Warner's political convictions hardened. 'The reviews of *Summer Will Show* are all very spotless so far', she joked with the communist proletarian poet Julius Lipton in 1936: 'just another bourgeois stylist'.[104] The joke was on the British critical establishment, for *Summer Will Show* was at the same time 'in Moscow, being read with a possibility of coming out in *International Literature*. Oh if it would and could, how pleased I should be.'[105] Warner was perfecting the art of a dual address, balancing economic necessity and political expediency with what she called 'the writer's sense of responsibility to the subject chosen'.[106] It was a balance she praised Arnold Rattenbury for discerning in the rhetorical posture of Chaucer. In 1944, Rattenbury had written an article in *Our Time* explaining 'where the cash came in', for Chaucer, and how, 'like it or lump it, the poet had to write for two audiences at once' if he wanted to get paid and escape censure, the city and the court.[107] 'I wish more writers about writers would remember to put in the circumstances of their economics', Warner wrote in response: 'It might help to dissipate the notion that we sing like birds and pick up a few worms.'[108] Warner could not afford to be a songbird, as witness the 'First Reading Agreement' she signed 'with that eminent statuette of liberty', *The New Yorker*.[109] The magazine took 144 of her short stories and paid her handsomely, but it was not a neutral venue in the Cold War as her mocking reference to Lady Liberty makes clear. 'I plant little traps and

---

[103] Sylvia Townsend Warner to Paul Nordoff, 5 January 1946; in *Letters*, p.91.
[104] Sylvia Townsend Warner to Julius Lipton, 13 September 1936; D-TWA/A39; STW.2012.125.2387.
[105] Sylvia Townsend Warner to Julius Lipton, 24 February 1936; D-TWA/A39; STW.2012.125.2387.
[106] Warner, open letter, June 1949.
[107] Arnold Rattenbury, 'Geoffrey Chaucer. The Poet in Society', *Our Time* 4, no.1 (August 1944): p.7.
[108] Sylvia Townsend Warner to Arnold Rattenbury, 24 August 1944; cited in Rattenbury, 'Plain Heart', pp.47–8 and 'Literature, Lying and the Sober Truth', p.231.
[109] Sylvia Townsend Warner to Arnold Rattenbury, 5 November 1969; D-TWA/A41; STW.2012.125.2472.

hope the quickness of the hand deceives the eye' is how she later explained her 'method'.[110] Like Chaucer, Warner saw herself writing 'for two audiences at once', affording each their pleasures while coding her politics to those in the know. Tailoring her address in this way, Warner could keep her 'pinafore ... presentable' and her 'petticoats' clean.[111] But it would be a mistake to therefore minimize the radical intention, however coded its cues and covert its communication; Warner's communism sharpens the judgement and the generosity she visits on her portraits of Kurt and Lili, and of Dames Alice and Alicia, Salome and Susanna, among the mildly more memorable sisters of Oby.

This dual legibility is not quite identical with the 'bi-location' some critics have claimed as a hallmark of Warner's style. In 1959, Warner delivered a lecture to the Royal Society of Arts in which she traced the 'immediacy' she observed in some women's writing back to an ability to be 'in two places at once'. From having to juggle household responsibilities and the life of the mind women had learned to multitask, to 'follow an intricate train of thought, remember what it was [they] had to tell the electrician, answer the telephone, keep an eye on the time, and not forget about the potatoes'. For the woman writer, what thus began as a literal ability to be 'at her desk and at her washing machine' evolved into a technical ability to step aside, to absent herself from the page. In writing like this, Warner observed, no 'lecturer's little wand' 'intervenes between us and the presentation', no 'author's anxious hand' propels us.[112] The temptation has been to read Warner as similarly standing to one side and taking her politics off with her. Claire Harman thus praises the 'immediacy' of *The Corner That Held Them*: spared the teleology of a plot or any 'pressure to significance', Warner felt at liberty to 'absent herself from the writing ... and create [her] realistic illusions'.[113] Maud Ellmann likewise invokes Warner's 'art of bi-location' to separate the Party-line communist whose positions 'tended towards absolutism' from the creative artist whose fictions delight in human variety.[114] This is to assume, however, that Warner identified with her own theory, that she acknowledged herself a 'woman writer' ('an implication I might or might not resent') and understood 'immediacy' as an end in itself, absent a standpoint epistemology, a project of disalienation, and a science of the social whole.[115] It is to assume a contradiction between a politics of absolute values and a literature tolerant of difference, between the ability to name and frame the system and to record and value the particular. For her part, Warner believed

---

[110] Warner to Rattenbury, 16 September 1974; cited in Rattenbury, 'Literature, Lying and the Sober Truth', p.216.
[111] Warner to Lipton, 13 September 1936; Warner to Rattenbury, 16 September 1974.
[112] Sylvia Townsend Warner, 'Women as Writers', *Journal of the Royal Society of Arts* 107, no.5034 (1959): pp.380–4.
[113] Harman, 'Introduction' to *The Corner That Held Them*, pp. vii–viii.
[114] Maud Ellmann, 'The Art of Bi-Location: Sylvia Townsend Warner', in *The History of British Women's Writing, 1920–1945*, edited by Maroula Joannou (London: Palgrave Macmillan, 2013), p.84.
[115] Warner, 'Women as Writers', p.378.

that communism helped her to do both, or in the idiom she preferred, to hate and love together. A poem from the mid-1930s likens her communism to her own two hands, the one 'a fist' 'made tougher' by 'hate', while 'my heart's hand the other / Is opened by love / To give and to receive'.[116] A contemporaneous poem written as a valentine 'For Valentine' recalls their first visit to Spain in September 1936 and lists the partisans they befriended there:

> These stretched our hearts. We should be vilely their debtor
> If we do not love further henceforth, and hate better.[117]

This commitment informs all Warner's incursions into enemy territory, *The Corner That Held Them* among them.

## V. 'Spain is the heart'

Warner would sometimes make light of her hatred of religion, but in private, and in the communist press, she could be savage, and nowhere more so than in her writing on Spain. In 'The Drought Breaks', a 1937 short story, Warner makes a church in a Nationalist-controlled town a site of execution. In a scene recalling the Badajoz massacre from the year before, trades unionists are being rounded up and shot, but the church doesn't skip a beat. With the bloodstains still fresh, the building is reconsecrated and its furnishings refreshed; 'the religious people came clustering and buzzing back as fast as bluebottles, as though they too came wherever there was a smell of blood'—priests, gentlefolk, and soldiers all feeling themselves at home.[118] This is the fascist coalition Warner assembles in *After the Death of Don Juan* (1938), with its memorable portrait of the sacristan, Don Gil, who 'more than money or position or security or crayfish with saffron or a cigar in the summer dusk ... loved the sense of power'. His vision of the Church is of a 'hierarchy of bullying' with God at its head, an authoritarian apparatus with God 'like a heart eternally pumping fear into the universe'.[119] Meanwhile, for Celestina, the unscrupulous miller's daughter, it is an appetite for cold hard cash that draws her to a nunnery: she wants an 'easy life' free from labour ('for lay-sisters would see to that'), where 'money' would forever be 'amassing and never to lose'.[120]

---

[116] Sylvia Townsend Warner, 'Love by my left hand', in *New Collected Poems*, edited by Claire Harman (Manchester: Carcanet, 2008), pp.254–5.
[117] Sylvia Townsend Warner and Mercedes Aguirre, 'Sylvia Townsend Warner's Spanish Civil War Love Poems', *The Journal of the Sylvia Townsend Warner Society* 19, no.1 (2020): pp.66–7.
[118] Sylvia Townsend Warner, 'The Drought Breaks', *The Fight* 4, no.7 (May 1937): pp.16–17; *Life and Letters To-Day* 16, no.8 (June 1937): pp.68–71.
[119] Warner, *After the Death of Don Juan*, pp.154–5.
[120] Warner, *After the Death of Don Juan*, p.163. Warner's antipathy towards the Catholic Church did not stop with her advocacy for Republican Spain; in 1948, a year before Pope Pius XII approved the

Warner's conviction of the 'inherent vileness of religion' did not preclude a humanist solicitude for what Feuerbach called its 'true or anthropological essence'.[121] Religion, for Warner, was only ever an alienated form of human fear and desire, its gods forged by us in our image. When Ackland began backsliding to Catholicism in the late 1940s, she observed in her diary how Warner could be 'interested' in the 'various faiths', 'and sometimes charmed by the outward trappings: but *always* because of their association with Man as a creative artist … the imagination that conceived the idea, the fancy that contrived the ritual, the social forces of the time, which conditioned this or that form of Faith or worship'.[122] In *The Corner That Held Them*, that 'association with Man as a creative artist' is on loving display, most memorably in a scene that draws on Warner's training as a historian of Church music.

Henry Yellowlees, the custos of Oby, has been tasked with collecting arrears on one of the convent's more distant inland properties when he breaks his journey at an out-of-the-way leper house. After a meagre supper, the chaplain invites him to join in some music-making. Laying out a manuscript 'among the mutton bones and the bread-crumbs' (203), the chaplain introduces the custos to *ars nova*, the new rhythmic language and notational style associated with the fourteenth-century French composer Guillaume de Machaut.[123] They 'begin with an easy one' called 'Triste loysir' and Yellowlees soon gets the hang, holding on 'though he felt himself astray, bewildered by the unexpected progressions, concords so sweet that they seemed to melt the flesh off his bones. Coming to the *mors de moy*, where the chaplain's voice twittered in floriations high above his tolling longs, he could hardly contain himself for excitement' (204). If the 'Triste loysir' is 'astonishing' and a 'foretaste of paradise', the Machaut Kyrie is 'paradise itself'. For this they need a third voice, and John, a leper who trained in the Chapel of the Duke of Burgundy, is summoned to supplement their number.

This was how the blessed might sing, singing in a duple measure that ran as nimbly on its four feet as a weasel running through a meadow, with each voice in turn enkindling the others, so that the music flowed on and was continually renewed. (204–5)

---

'Decree Against Communism' and the same year that *The Corner That Held Them* came out, Warner published 'The Jungle Blossom', a Cold War fable in which the Holy See has relocated from St Peter's in Rome to Petrusville, Utah to better serve the new North Atlantic alliance.

[121] Warner, *Diaries*, p.100; Ludwig Feuerbach, *The Essence of Christianity*, translated by Marian Evans [George Eliot] (London: John Chapman, 1854), p.32.

[122] Ackland, diary entry for 19 January 1952; quoted in Harman, *Sylvia Townsend Warner*, p.249.

[123] Warner contributed the chapter on 'Notation: The Growth of a System' to *The Oxford History of Music. Introductory Volume*, edited by Percy C. Buck (Oxford: Oxford University Press, 1929), pp.66–84. The chapter closes with a discussion of Philippe de Vitry, author (attributed) of the 1322 treatise, *Ars nova notanda*, from whence the new music took its name.

The music is a revelation to the custos, who spends a restless night fantasizing of a life lived entirely 'in the fifth element of sound' (205). But there is a sting to this scene, as there is to all the novel's celebrations of religious artistry.

'Such music, and such squalor!' Warner has Yellowlees exclaim to himself: 'never had he seen a house so dirty, or slept in a more tattered bed. But out came the music as the kingfisher flashes from its nest of stinking fishbones' (205). The striking analogy resolves itself into an uneasy question: 'What did the other lepers think of it, those who could not sing, sitting in their straw, mumbling their sour bread (for if the food given to a guest were so bad the food given to the lepers must be worse), and hearing the music go on and on?' (204). A week later, returning to the lazar-house having failed in his mission to Esselby, Yellowlees receives his answer. The lepers have leagued with a roving band of vigilantes to take vengeance and make their escape. They kill the chaplain, torch his chapel, and take especial care to burn the music-books. The singer John they leave behind, and from him we learn their grievance, that the chaplain had 'spent all on music-books that should have been spent on them' (212), that they had starved so that he could sing. Yellowlees takes John to a nearby priory, and before they part, the leper helps him to memorize 'Triste loysir'. They sing it through three times together. The first time, Yellowlees is distracted by the memory of the chaplain's burned and beaten body; by the third, 'nothing remained but the delight of the two voices answering and according' (213). Yellowlees may thus forget this reminder of the class politics of mediaeval art; the art may even help us to forget; but Warner does not mean that we should.

However gentle its tread, this episode in *The Corner That Held Them* walks a line on the legitimacy of iconoclastic and anticlerical violence that Warner had learned to draw in the Spanish Civil War. Visiting Barcelona in 1936, Warner described how she had never before seen 'churches so heavy and hulking and bullying', so obviously 'reactionary fortresses', and she praised the thoroughness with which the Spanish had set about their sacking.[124] She described churches that once stood as 'Giant Popes' reduced 'to Giant Pagans', their 'gutted interiors, their unglazed windows, their broken boarded-up doorways' giving them a 'dissolute resemblance' to the ruined temples of antiquity. She dwelt lovingly on the 'peculiar litter which arrives to every derelict building': 'mortar and rubble, scraps of paper, scraps of clothing, pigeon's dung and pigeon's feathers.'[125] As for their furnishings, she noted that while anything of artistic value had been removed to museums lesser objects were getting the treatment they deserved. One anecdote described the demolition of a Madonna and Child, 'a vile pottery plaque' in the garden of a grand house that had somehow 'escaped notice' during the first round of reprisals. Two men arrived with hammers and 'seriously, without a vestige of either rage or contempt,

---

[124] Sylvia Townsend Warner to Elizabeth Wade White, 14 November 1936; in *Letters*, p.42.
[125] Sylvia Townsend Warner, 'Barcelona', *Left Review* 2, no.15 (1936): p.814.

they smashed it to bits'.[126] Warner was insistent: the violence in Spain had a popular mandate. 'It was the people themselves who, deliberately and systematically, put the churches out of action.' They had not been put up to it by outside elements or had it 'imposed' on them 'by a Marxist leadership'.[127] Spontaneous, sincere, the violence visited upon the fabric of religion was born of a justified resentment. This same discrimination returns with the leper-house chaplain and his charges: 'they had hated him for a long time', we are told, and it was they who killed him and burned his music, not the rebel peasants who aided their escape (212–13).

In other ways as well, the world of Oby recalls Warner's Spanish Civil War writing. In Spain, she had found an aristocracy and a church oddly unmodern in its relationship to money. She described the 'mediaeval brag of possessions' that still characterized the nobility, the desire to trap 'money in gold and jewels' and keep 'the gold and jewels for display'. The Spanish Church was equally conspicuous with its wealth and equally ignorant of the 'beauties'—and securities—'of a bank balance'. Unprepared for the Revolution, the Church had hurried to hide its hoards, 'burying its gold beneath the flagstones, lining its tapestries with banknotes', where the rebels duly found them.[128] This 'mediaeval' attitude to money explains the fate of the altar-ware in *The Corner That Held Them*. It is 1381 and the peasants are abroad; rumours of pillage and the plunder of religious houses have reached Oby, and two nuns conspire with their bailiff to remove the convent's silver and gold. Warner has fun with what follows. Having buried the treasure off-site in a far-off field where only he knows the place, the bailiff is promptly killed in an altercation and the knowledge of its location dies with him (293). Reduced to the use of a pewter paten and cup, the nuns feel themselves fallen in the world, 'and the words of Jeremy, *How is the fine gold become dim*, wailed through their minds' (294). The reader, however, may entertain thoughts less congenial to the mediaeval mind. Dame Amy, one of the unloved Dunford nuns, a dowerless transplant and a bastard to boot (194), chooses a bad moment 'to wander into modernistic speculations and to ask why the rite of mass could not be as efficaciously celebrated with pewter vessels as with gold and silver ones' (290).

Amy briefly breaks ranks in this moment, having, as Warner suggests, a surer appreciation than her better born peers of the real advantages of religious life; she does not need the show of gold to be grateful for not 'scrubbing trenchers, clacking at a loom, and bearing great hordes of hungry children' (195). But her dissident thought is as nothing compared with Dame Adela's deranged thinking when she elopes with the altar-hanging the nuns have been sewing to win favour with their new bishop, a Fleming who cares only 'for Our Lady, works of art, ritual, and foreign cheeses' (240). It is a work of *opus anglicanum,* an expensive embroidery of

---

[126] Sylvia Townsend Warner, 'Catalonia in Civil War', *New Masses* 21, no.9 (24 November 1936): p.4.
[127] Warner, 'Barcelona', p.816.
[128] Warner, 'Barcelona', p.815.

silk and gold thread, rich spangles and pearls. However mercenary their motive, the nuns' needlework briefly transfigures the life of the convent, touching the 'creative artist' in all of them and giving each 'the sense of something in the making' (244). But when a beggar at the gate unleashes a tirade about white-fingered nuns who lavish gold on 'God's altar' that would be better spent clothing and feeding 'God's poor', it is Oby's misfortune that Dame Adela should hear. Of all Warner's nuns, only Adela—'so lovely, so stupid' (173)—would see herself implicated in the alms-seeker's indictment; only she would mistake the invective for an ethical claim on her person and act to avert the charge. This she does, stealing the unfinished altar-cloth to give its proceeds to the poor.

The episode of the Oby altar cloth recalls another incomplete embroidery that Warner encountered in Republican Spain. In 1936, she visited an expropriated apartment whose 'fascist owners' had left in a hurry, leaving behind them 'a large frame of unfinished *petit point*'. Accompanying her on the tour was Asuncíon, communist cook and general factotum with Warner's British Red Cross unit. Warner watched as Asuncíon appraised the tapestry, 'respecting the industry' but 'deploring the idleness' that went into it (terms that return in *The Corner That Held Them*).[129] Asuncíon was much in Warner's thoughts as she worked on the novel. Warner had last heard from her before the war, and in 1945 she found herself wondering 'how long dead, my darling, and how?'[130] In all her correspondence with interned Spanish Republicans after the war, Warner enquired after her friend.[131] Warner admired her goodness, her 'sense of absolute values', and her ability to think systemically, to read even trivial things in their 'true light as a part, small but integral, of the political situation'.[132] She also delighted in Asuncíon's 'habit, if she wanted to express disapproval, of turning herself into a machine gun and saying, "*Poum, poum, poum, poum!*"' It is not inconceivable that Asuncíon, understanding its part—'small but integral'—in the history of capitalism, would have 'epitaphed' the Oby altar-hanging 'with a few *poum, poum, poum, poums*'.[133]

*The Corner That Held Them* has no Asuncíon to caption its chronicle, and Warner herself holds back. We sense her restraint, for instance, when she stages a conversation among the nuns about how to defuse the rising class tensions between the convent and the manor. It is 1380, a year before the great revolt, and the nuns have begun to think that perhaps some concession might be wise:

---

[129] Warner, 'Catalonia in Civil War', p.3.
[130] Warner, *Diaries*, p.127; entry for 13 January 1945.
[131] Gregorio Segunda to Sylvia Townsend Warner and Valentine Ackland, 17 September 1945; D-TWA/A38; STW.2012.125.2067. Segunda writes from the 'Hall o' th' Hill Camp' near Chorley in Lancashire, where Spanish prisoners of war were interned until 1946. He thanks his 'Comrades' for their aid parcel of books and of onions and garlic from their garden, but he adds: 'Although there are a lot of Catalans here, I am very sorry but no one knows Asuncíon Lou Fleta, to give you satisfaction.'
[132] Sylvia Townsend Warner to Steven Clark, 25 March 1939; D-TWA/A84; STW.2012.125.5008–5009. Sylvia Townsend Warner, 'A Castle in Spain', *The New Yorker*, 2 January 1937, pp.22–4.
[133] Warner, 'A Castle in Spain', p.24.

'Anything is better than being burned out or murdered in one's bed', they reason. But no solution proves acceptable. It will cost too much to placate the peasants with food and clothing, or to rethatch their huts, or to ring the gleaning bell sooner, or to allow a remission of dues. The cheaper alternative—a school—is also unthinkable: though it will cost them only 'time and trouble', the nuns worry that the children will have fleas, that they will be hard to discipline and loath to leave.

> And if we teach them they will all go off the manor to become friars and clerks, nuns and jugglers, they will never stay at work once they begin to think themselves scholars. Besides, how are we to teach children when our hands are full of the altar-hanging?

'Such were the answers', Warner drily reports, and 'the project got no further' (243). But some readers will register as justified the repossession of this altar cloth and the violence of the following year. And when, as the novel draws to its close, the 'more sophisticated' of Warner's nuns anticipate the collapse of their world (250), those readers may not shed a tear.[134] On his final visit as custos, Henry Yellowlees finds the convent smelling 'of dejection and incompetence' (294); this too we can surely stomach. But where does that leave the '14th-century peasant' whose 'feeling' of injustice was the novel's inspiration?

One answer may lie in an anecdote Warner recounted to Edgell Rickword in 1937 after hosting the exiled Chinese radical Wang Lixi on a tour of local Left Book Club groups. Wang was speaking on behalf of the China Campaign Committee, part of the Aid China movement formed in the wake of the Japanese invasion of Manchuria.[135] 'We loved him very much', Warner told Rickword, 'but I'm afraid his Dorchester audience found him perplexing.'

> He told them stories of the Chinese revolutionary spirit, but did not make it clear that the stories dated, many of them, from 3000 BC, and had, naturally, become stylised in course of time.
>
> One of the stories I saved for you, it was so beautifully Marxian. A Chinese dictator, determined to have peace in his dominions, took away all their weapons from the peasants. The metal thus collected he had melted down and cast into the shapes of twelve massive religious figures which adorned his palace. In the end the peasants overthrew him with sharpened bamboos.
>
> You will see that this all seemed rather odd to the Dorchester Labour Party.[136]

---

[134] These nuns foresee a future 'within the reach of speculation' when the smaller religious houses 'perish for lack of means' (250). The flipside of this story, untold in the novel but legible in its absence, is that the remaining religious establishments got 'so rich that everyone wanted their money': 'That's why the monastic houses were dissolved in England ... It's a strictly capitalist story', Warner later explained. 'Sylvia Townsend Warner in Conversation', p.36.

[135] 'China's Struggle for Freedom: Professor Shelley Wang at Dorchester', *Western Gazette*, 12 November 1937, p.7.

[136] Sylvia Townsend Warner to Edgell Rickword, 10 September 1937; in *Letters*, p.50.

Warner's portrait plays up Wang's unworldliness as a professor and classical poet, his stories charmingly vague about chronology; it downplays his historical and revolutionary credentials. But Wang had been a prominent figure in Chinese radical politics, working with Mao Zedong at the Peasant Movement Training Institute in 1926–27 and, following the collapse of the United Front, playing a leading role in the subsequent 'social history controversy', which looked to explain the setback through a critical revaluation of Chinese historical development.[137] At issue was the extent to which China remained a feudal society, with both Nationalist and Communist Party activists and intellectuals largely affirming this analysis against a rival, Trotskyite interpretation of China as a modern capitalist society with an established bourgeoisie.[138] Wang's fable about a despot overthrown by his subjects traffics in the timeless, but it touches what were then live debates about Chinese rural society, state power, and the agricultural masses. Warner found it 'beautifully Marxian', no doubt appreciating the fable's association of religion with oppressive state power and its parable of subaltern patience and cunning. But in its contemporary application the story played into a present sense of peasants on the march, with events in the Soviet Union and in China and Spain the hopeful horizon for Warner and Ackland's 'rustic diggings and delvings', as Warner described their attempts to organize country workers in Dorset.[139]

Writing in *The Countryman* in 1939, Warner compared her rural radicalization to the successive pleasures she had gotten from her cottage garden. A 'townee' by birth and to begin with only a 'weekender' in the Dorset village of Chaldon Herring, Warner's first interest in gardening had been to grow 'flowers and herbs'; her attachment to village life was likewise aesthetic, a pleasure in 'the traditions, the racy speech, the idiomatic quality of the English country worker' and, alongside these predictably pastoral 'flowers', the more pungent '*fleurs du mal*, the twists and patiently wrought vices that develop under thatch, the violent dramas that explode among green pastures'.[140] It took a 'year or so' to realize that 'it was harder, and more interesting, to grow vegetables'; harder, and more interesting, because 'the pursuit of more serious cabbages' required research, a disciplined approach

---

[137] On Wang, cf. Ke Ren, 'A "Chinese Shelley" in 1930s Britain: Wang Lixi's Transnational Activism and Transcultural Lyricism', in *Chiang Yee and His Circle: Chinese Artistic and Intellectual Life in Britain, 1930–1950*, edited by Paul Bevan, Ann Witchard, and Da Zheng (Hong Kong: Hong Kong University Press, 2022), pp.158–80. On the Peasant Movement Institute, cf. Roy Hofheinz, *The Broken Wave: The Chinese Communist Peasant Movement, 1922–1928* (Cambridge, MA: Harvard University Press, 1977), pp.78–92. On the Chinese history debates, cf. Arif Dirlik, *Revolution and History: The Origins of Marxist Historiography in China, 1919–1937* (Berkeley, CA: University of California Press, 1978), pp.207–12; and Xiaorong Han, *Chinese Discourses on the Peasant, 1900–1949* (Albany, NY: SUNY Press, 2005), pp.73–116.

[138] In the 'Study Magazine' [*Dushu zazhi*] he edited with Hu Qiuyuan in the early 1930s, Wang laid out his own position, framing Chinese imperial history in transitional terms, residually feudal but now thoroughly despotic, with the enemy a bureaucratic state apparatus evolved to serve an absolute monarchy.

[139] Warner to Lipton, 24 February 1936.

[140] Sylvia Townsend Warner, 'My Village Life', the fourth in a series titled 'The Way by Which I Have Come', *The Countryman* 19, no.2 (1939), p.472; p.481; p.483.

to finding the 'facts' about country life.[141] She studied the wages of workers and the state of rural water supplies, writing about them for the communist *Country Standard*; she reckoned costs and profits under the Milk Marketing Scheme for an appendix to *Country Conditions* (1936), a collection of Ackland's reportage for *Left Review*.[142] But by 1939, Warner had learned a third way of thinking about her garden. She still grew flowers and vegetables, still enjoyed 'the goings-on of my neighbours' and felt 'fury at the conditions they have to endure', but it was the 'soil' she now saw as 'the essential thing'. She had discovered that 'a plot of earth, clean, and well dug, and raked fine, and in good heart, is the deepest gratification' a garden can afford.[143] Warner's allegory of the garden equates soil improvement to the transformation of the material base, the knowledge that modes of production can be made to change.

Spain had taught Warner the difference a revolution could make. There she had seen peasants harvesting corn with sickles. It was the same 'beautiful gesture', 'tireless, identical', repeating itself 'mile after mile' as it had since time immemorial, but in 1937 it did so with a difference.[144] This was the 'first in a new lineage of harvests, the first these peasants have reaped for themselves'; it was also, 'if things go as they should', the 'last ... of the old lineage of harvests', won by hand from a rotten soil.[145] Though the crop was their own, it was a poor one, 'short in straw, light in the ear', the product of a 'shallow tilth' on stony ground.[146] What Spain needed now was tractors: 'deep-ploughing', 'a stronger technique of agriculture'. Warner predicted that when the Republicans won and beat their 'swords into ploughshares', they would transform the countryside: electricity pylons would bring 'power and light ... to the darkened and exploited', heavy machinery would raise the peasants from their age-old bondage to the soil.[147] The blueprint for this vision was the Soviet Union with its network of tractor stations serving the nearby collective farms.[148]

Franco's victory in 1939 did not dim Warner's faith in the politics of land redistribution and heavy machinery; she still hoped to persuade the British country

---

[141] Warner, 'My Village Life', 483; 485.

[142] Sylvia Townsend Warner, 'Underpayment of Agricultural Workers: Black Figures from Blue Books', *Country Standard* 1, no.2 (April 1936): p.5; Sylvia Townsend Warner, 'Unofficial Drought', *Country Standard* 1, no.6 (August 1936): pp.6–7; Sylvia Townend Warner, 'Appendix II. The Milk Marketing Scheme', in Valentine Ackland, *Country Conditions* (London: Lawrence & Wishart, 1936), pp.95–7.

[143] Warner, 'My Village Life', p.483; p.485.

[144] Sylvia Townsend Warner, 'Harvest in Spain', *New Statesman & Nation* n.s. 19, no.336 (July 1937): p.184.

[145] Sylvia Townsend Warner, 'Soldiers and Sickles in Spain', *The Countryman* 14, no.1 (October 1937): p.79.

[146] Warner, 'Harvest in Spain', p.184.

[147] Warner, 'Soldiers and Sickles', pp.79–80.

[148] In 1936, Warner had helped Ackland hand-produce a series of booklets on Soviet agriculture for distribution in Dorset villages; they drew up the stencils and duplicated them at home, using statistics from the Soviet trade delegation in London.

worker that 'the defeat of those peasants in Spain, defending their olive and orange co-operatives, is their loss, and that the new tractors swinging over the U.S.S.R. collective farms are their gain'.[149] But she knew also that 'to put things right, that have so long and so intricately been going wrong', would be 'a long job, must be a wide-span job'.[150] It is a job whose temporal and geographical 'span' invites that we coordinate the several moments of agricultural resistance in Warner's fiction—the 'insolence' of the limekiln man in *Summer Will Show* that puts Sophia Willoughby in mind of the 'Labourers' Rising of 1830', the rebellion in Tenorio Viejo in *After the Death of Don Juan*, the Peasants' Revolt in *The Corner That Held Them*—against a revolutionary horizon whose time is still to come.[151] Five thousand years is a long time to be sharpening bamboo, but Warner remained hopeful 'that these people I know, and their fellows in other countries, other continents, can do it'. She was also unillusioned, adding that 'unless they put their skilled hard hands to it', no-one can: without a revolution in the countryside, 'we can whistle for a remedy'.[152] The humility is striking. Warner arrogates to herself no outsize role for the writer in raising rural insurrection. The struggle in the countryside is of a different order, and on a different timeline, to the urgencies of anti-fascism, for which Warner clearly understood the need for cultural interventions in civil society, rallying to the defence of the national heritage and the people's culture, their '*patrimoine*', as she had told her audience in French at the Writers Congress in Valencia. In this more winnable '*croisade*', Jack Lindsay fought by her side.[153]

---

[149] Warner, 'My Village Life', pp.485–6.
[150] Warner, 'My Village Life', p.486.
[151] Warner, *Summer Will Show*, p.97.
[152] Warner, 'My Village Life', p.486.
[153] Sylvia Townsend Warner, typescript address to the Second International Congress of Writers for the Defence of Culture, 4 July 1937; D-TWA/A05; STW.2012.125.0931.

# 4

# Jack Lindsay, Socialist Humanism, and the Communist Historical Novel

## I. 'then came 1956 with its shattering effect'

In late autumn 1956, when within days of each other Soviet tanks invaded Budapest and British troops the Suez, the symmetries of violence structuring the Cold War world forced the British Left to account. For an older generation of communists, the refusal of their Party to brook discussion of Khrushchev's 'Secret Speech' in February and, in November, to denounce the Soviet response to Hungary brought to a head a long-simmering crisis of credibility and commitment: over the next several months, fully a fifth of the Party would resign or allow their membership to lapse. Meanwhile, for a generation of young people on the move 'out of apathy', the Anglo-French adventure in Egypt clarified the contradiction of a welfare state possessed of imperial ambitions and the H-bomb. With Hungary and Suez, as Stuart Hall recalled, the 'liminal, boundary-marking experiences' that brought about the beginning of the Cold War thaw, the search was on for a new direction in socialist politics.[1] In journals of opinion launched in the spring and summer of 1957, these two groupings of intellectuals and activists argued the definition of a socialism that would restore the moral conviction of the Left.

In its opening editorial, the student generation's *Universities & Left Review* declared its 'informing belief' 'that the moral imagination can still intervene creatively in human history'.[2] In the same issue, ex-communist historian and activist E.P. Thompson suggested 'socialist humanism' as a term to describe the desired 'rekindling of moral and intellectual passion'.[3] An extended article in the first number of his co-edited journal *The New Reasoner* further refined the idea. Socialist humanism means 'a *return to man*', Thompson explained:

> It is humanist because it places once again real men and women at the centre of socialist theory and aspiration ... It is socialist because it re-affirms the revolutionary perspectives of Communism, faith in the revolutionary potentialities not

---

[1] Stuart Hall, 'Life and Times of the First New Left', *New Left Review*, n.s. no.61 (2010): p.177.
[2] 'Editorial', *Universities & Left Review*, no.1 (Spring 1957): p.2.
[3] E.P. Thompson, 'Socialism and the Intellectuals', *Universities & Left Review*, no.1 (Spring 1957): p.35.

only of the Human Race or of the Dictatorship of the Proletariat, but of real men and women.[4]

Invoked in antiphon across the two journals, socialist humanism became 'the agreed basis' upon which the two generations began to chart their way between an embarrassed social democracy and the discredited socialism of communist allegiance.[5] The two groups had their differences, but when, in the last days of the decade, the ex-communist old guard joined forces with the young student Left to launch a combined journal called *New Left Review*, they did so to develop 'the humanist strengths of socialism' together.[6]

These intellectual debates set the terms of British cultural Marxism, but their practical intent was to support a social movement. They took inspiration from the news that filtered back from Hungary of the short-lived workers' councils and from the mobilization in Britain of the Campaign for Nuclear Disarmament (CND); but they also looked back across the mid-century, summoning the first-hand experience of the British Popular Front and 'People's War', or the same at one remove. Particularly important for the student Left was the example of Charles Bourdet, the former resistance leader whose weekly newspaper *France-Observateur* was coordinating a similar 'third way' or *nouvelle gauche* on the French political scene.[7] In these early years of the British New Left, the Old Left was still a powerful presence. With their choices of title, for example, *Universities & Left Review* and *New Left Review* both staked a claim on the precedent of the 1930s Cultural Front and its leading periodical, *Left Review*, launched in 1934 by the British section of what was then the International Union of Revolutionary Writers. This chapter will trace another line of connection from the Old Left to the New as it recovers a forgotten voice in these debates of the late 1950s; in so doing, I hope to bring my history of the mid-century historical novel in Britain to another kind of close. I take my cue from a letter Thompson wrote in 1961 to his former comrade, Jack Lindsay. Thompson concludes the letter as follows:

> P.S. In the past three or four years, when the 1844 MSS and 'alienation' have been all the rage, I sometimes laugh and think of wartime discussions—usually sparked off by the latest deviation of J.L.—and wonder how long you will have to wait before someone 'discovers' you as a premature socialist humanist.[8]

---

[4] E.P. Thompson, 'Socialist Humanism: An Epistle to the Philistines', *The New Reasoner. A Quarterly Journal of Socialist Humanism* 1 (Summer 1957): p.109.
[5] 'Notes for our Readers', *Universities & Left Review*, no.6 (Spring 1959): n.p. [73].
[6] Stuart Hall, 'Introducing NLR', *New Left Review*, no.1 (1960): p.1.
[7] The first issue of *Universities & Left Review* included an article by Claude Bourdet connecting the 'appearance of a *third* socialist current, the New Left', back to 'the social, internationalist and anti-colonial ideals of the Resistance'. Bourdet, 'The French Left: Long-Run Trends', *Universities & Left Review*, no.1 (Spring 1957): pp.13–16.
[8] E.P. Thompson to Jack Lindsay, 8 May 1961, NLA, 7168, Box 30, Folder 167.

A subsequent section will reconstruct the wartime discussions to which Thompson refers and 'discover' Lindsay as Thompson remembers him, but for my purpose what matters is that Lindsay's socialist humanism should find its 'mature' form in a historical novel.

*Thunder Underground: A Novel of Nero's Rome* was typed in its first full draft on the verso of letters received in mid-1957, including several of its pages on the back of Harry Hanson's 'Open Letter to Edward Thompson', later published in *The New Reasoner*.[9] But though fully intended as an intervention in these efforts to define a post-Stalinist socialism for the British Left, the novel missed its moment entirely. Lindsay's then publishers, Bodley Head, rejected the manuscript in the summer of 1958, reminding him that 'many a potentially good novel has been swamped by too much argument'.[10] When *Thunder Underground* finally did appear seven years later, it disappeared without a trace. By 1965, the social movement of the 'first' New Left was in disarray: *New Left Review*'s joint editorial board had been disbanded in 1962 and the journal transferred to the hands of a new New Left interested in sociology and the sterner strains of Western Marxism; the CND lay stalled; the socialist humanisms of *Universities & Left Review* and *The New Reasoner* were making their exits in defeat into the works and institutions of academic scholarship—the preface and practice of Thompson's *The Making of the English Working Class* (1963), the Birmingham Centre for Contemporary Cultural Studies (founded 1964)—and gearing themselves for the long haul.

*Thunder Underground* appeared amid the rout of the movement it had been written to serve. But if, as measured by its timing and impact, *Thunder Underground* must count as a failure, it is a kind of failure which it is itself interested to address, and it joins with a wider body of work by British Marxist historians in which the non-coincidence of an empowering socialist vision and the social movement to advance it is a key narrative device. Written in the slipstream of 1956 and published in 1965, just as the first shots were being fired in the so-called 'Arguments within English Marxism' over whether to develop or reject the legacy of mid-century communism, Lindsay's novel looks back upon this moment and attempts its own settling of accounts. Formally, as well, the novel is retrospective: the last historical novel by Britain's leading theorist and practitioner of the genre, *Thunder Underground* reads as a defence and valediction to the communist historical novel. Lastly, it is a very personal novel, and a point of access to an exemplary mid-century and Communist Party life.

---

[9] Jack Lindsay, 'Thunder Underground', n.d. [1957–58], NLA, 7168, Box 49, Folder MS86. Harry Hanson, 'An Open Letter to Edward Thompson', *The New Reasoner*, no.2 (Autumn 1957): pp.79–91. Here, Hanson accused Thompson of applying 'William Morrisy' balm to salve the 'sore consciences' of the Left. Lindsay responded in the following issue, identifying himself 'wholeheartedly' with Thompson and rejecting Hanson's suggestion that 'socialist humanism and scientific socialism' were wholly incompatible. Jack Lindsay, 'Socialism and Humanism', *The New Reasoner*, no.3 (Winter 1957–58): pp.95–102.

[10] Norman Denny to Jack Lindsay, 3 May 1958, NLA, 7168, Box 75.

## II. 'mad colonial'

From his first arrival in London in 1926 to launch an 'Australian Renaissance' of world culture that would stop metropolitan modernism dead in its tracks, an air of excess and improbability has hung over Jack Lindsay's career. A cameo appearance in Aldous Huxley's satire of 1920s literary London, *Point Counter Point* (1928), sets the trope. There we meet Lindsay as Willie Weaver, 'a little man perpetually smiling ... bubbling with good humour and an inexhaustible verbiage'.[11] Huxley's comparison of Weaver to a simmering tea-kettle returns in later recollections, as when Eric Hobsbawm recalls how Lindsay's 'encyclopaedic erudition and constantly simmering kettle of ideas let off steam' during meetings of the post-war Communist Party Historians' Group, or when the poet Charles Hobday remembers Lindsay's 'learning, and his capacity to turn out theories about anything' at meetings of the Party Writers' Group.[12] The portrait of Robert Midwinter in Roy Fuller's 1954 psychological thriller, *Fantasy and Fugue*, again catches Lindsay in full spate, speaking 'rapidly, his ideas rising so thickly in his mind that he never had time to develop them with any lucidity, or even give his speech grammatical coherence'. That Midwinter writes as he speaks is suggested by the 'battery of fountain pens' he carries in his pocket, 'as though he used them all simultaneously ... to accommodate the flood of ideas'.[13]

Lindsay's list of publications is indeed long; as he would later admit, 'there is no getting away from the number of books with my name on.'[14] That number exceeds one hundred and fifty books as sole author, with Lindsay the editor of another twenty titles, the editor also of six literary magazines and three book series. He wrote a huge number of articles and occasional pieces, and several book-length typescripts remain unpublished among his papers. The range is as remarkable as the number; it includes poetry, fiction, and sketches for the stage and street, anthologies, translations, as well as studies in archaeology, comparative anthropology, biography, literary and art history, the history of science and technology, philosophy and theory.[15] Lindsay had often to defend the 'multifariousness' of his works from the 'assumption that anyone who tries a lot of themes, genres, methods,

---

[11] Aldous Huxley, *Point Counter Point* (London: Chatto & Windus, 1928), p.168.

[12] Huxley, *Point Counter Point*, p.170. Eric Hobsbawm, 'The Communist Party Historians' Group', p.25; Charles Hobday, quoted in Andy Croft, 'Writers, The Communist Party and the Battle of Ideas, 1945–50', *Socialist History*, no.5 (1994): p.7.

[13] Roy Fuller, *Fantasy and Fugue* [1954], reprinted in Fuller, *Crime Omnibus* (Manchester: Carcanet, 1988), p.386.

[14] Jack Lindsay, 'Preface', in *Jack Lindsay. A Catalogue of First Editions*, p. i.

[15] Cf. John Arnold, 'Jack Lindsay: Towards a Bibliography', *Overland*, no.83 (1981): pp.50–5; and John Arnold, 'A Checklist of Jack Lindsay's Books', in *Culture & History: Essays Presented to Jack Lindsay*, edited by Bernard Smith (Sydney: Hale & Iremonger, 1984), pp.394–406. Ralph Dumain has a 'Bibliographic Addendum' of books not included on Arnold's checklist on his website, http://www.autodidactproject.org/bib/lindbib.html [accessed 30 August 2019]. Victor N. Paananen has compiled an annotated bibliography, including some of Lindsay's articles, in *British Marxist Criticism* (New York: Garland, 2000), pp.57–100.

cannot be master of any of them; and that only by specialization, by ringing out the small changes on a limited set of themes', can a writer become adequate to their subject.[16] But Lindsay rejected the adage that 'a Jack-of-all-trades must be shallow and ineffective at each of them', claiming instead to have taken to heart 'Hegel's definition of the educated man as one who can do anything.'[17] For Lindsay, 'multifariousness' stood in service to 'Marx's *human* goal: the breaking-down of the limits set up by the division of labour.' He considered the professionalization of knowledge production, the separation of those who make it from those who live with its effects, the further division between mental and manual labour, all symptoms of 'the alienating process (in Marx's sense)'. In naming alienation 'and the struggle against it' the common thread of his life's work, Lindsay insisted on a 'concentrated unity' to 'what at a glance may seem a scattering of interests and impulses', as well as two quite separate phases of activity.[18]

Lindsay would sometimes write his life as the two chapters of an Oedipal drama: an abandoned son reunited with his artist father and submitting with near total abandon to the father's reactionary philosophy of 'Life'; ten years of that 'surrender', 'and then the son's revolt, all the more violent for its damning up'.[19] Two phases, one of submission to Norman Lindsay's doctrine of 'Creative Effort', elitist, individualist, masculinist, a cult of art and the absolute; another of its inversion, a recovered materialism, the conversion to communism and socialist realism.[20] Two periods, poles apart, yet stages in what he came to call his 'dialectic', an evolving intellectual biography reaching forward from his first infatuation with Plato and the romantics to his late-career salvos in the arguments within English and Western Marxism. A 1984 'Note on my Dialectic' concludes: 'Despite all the changes, the many confusions as well as steady efforts to integrate afresh my ideas in order to tackle ever larger issues, I feel a deep and living continuity between my positions as set out in 1981', when he published his last big work of theory, 'and those with which I was struggling sixty years ago in my responses to Keats, Plato, Blake'.[21] An unpublished autobiography likewise underscores 'the element of continuity in

---

[16] Jack Lindsay, 'My Multifarious Works', talk delivered at the Norwich Public Library, 14 September 1967, NLA, 7168, Box 116 Odds; see also, Lindsay, *Life Rarely Tells*, p.809.

[17] Lindsay, 'My Multifarious Works'; Jack Lindsay, 'The Fullness of Life: Autobiography of an Idea' (unpublished typescript, c.1971), p.229; Jack Lindsay Collection, University of Technology Sydney Library; digitized by Anne Cranny-Francis at https://jacklindsayproject.com/the-fullness-of-life/ [accessed 30 August 2019]. Cf. G.W.F. Hegel, *Philosophy of Right*, translated by T.M. Knox (Oxford: Oxford University Press, 1952), p.268; p.197.

[18] Lindsay, *Life Rarely Tells*, p.783; Lindsay, 'My Multifarious Works'.

[19] Lindsay, *Life Rarely Tells*, p.175.

[20] Lindsay characterizes his father's intellectual trajectory as 'a sort of Nietzschean individualism, plus Rabelaisian Abbey-of-Thelema idea of free-living, Theocritan image of earthly paradise: turned through shock of the war into a Neoplatonism, the artist as demiurge descending through space-time to form matter, create man: set out in *Creative Effort*. He died late 1969, aged 90, by far the most potent character and influence in Australian culture.' Jack Lindsay, 'Political Autobiography', NLA, 7168, Box 116, Odds 29.

[21] Jack Lindsay, 'A Note on my Dialectic', in *Culture & History*, p.373.

my positions as well as the movement, erratic but constant, into a fully Marxist aesthetic'.[22]

This 'element of continuity' requires that we read Lindsay's discovery in 1936 of Marx and the proletarian cause in ways other than as a complete break with the platforms and polemics he had orchestrated in the 1920s to advance the art and opinions of his father. It floats the possibility that something of Lindsay's early Australian vitalism may have survived, at once cancelled and preserved, its dialectical sublation. This becomes significant when we follow Lindsay's lead in crediting the limited edition Fanfrolico Press (1923–30) and the little magazines *Vision* (1923–24) and *The London Aphrodite* (1928–29) as instruments of 'a particular brand of modernism, Australian Nietzscheanism'.[23] The label is not intuitive: throughout the 1920s, Norman Lindsay and his disciples inveighed against modernism as the 'absolute antithesis' of their programme, calling instead for a revival of the tradition of European high art reaching forward from Homer and Praxiteles.[24] 'We wish no traffic with that disintegrating condition of mind that is obsessed with physical decay', Jack Lindsay had written in *Vision*'s opening editorial, indicting thereby the 'physical tiredness, jaded nerves', and 'complex superficiality' that 'are the stigmata of Modernism': these are 'the exact antithesis of the youthfulness that affirms the eternality of all things, that does not submit to the dictation of physical conditions, but out of them builds the undying and ever youthful body of the Imagination'.[25] Twenty-five years later, however, when Lindsay embarked on writing his autobiography, he could admit the ways in which the Fanfrolico project, for all its obvious 'idiosyncrasies' and 'oddities', had also been 'typical' of its time.[26]

*Fanfrolico and After* (1962) asks that we read Lindsay's cultural activism of the 1920s as a modernism in its own right, albeit rearguard, revanchist, its stated opposition notwithstanding.[27] Certain formal similarities are immediately obvious: the

---

[22] Lindsay, 'The Fullness of Life', p.247.

[23] Jack Lindsay to Georg Lukács, 7 February 1963, NLA, 7168, Box 32, Folder 182. An excellent history of Lindsay's activities in these years is to be found in John Arnold, *The Fanfrolico Press: Satyrs, Fauns and Fine Books* (Pinner, Middlesex: Private Libraries Association, 2009). On 'Australian Nietzscheanism', cf. Jack Lindsay, 'Zarathustra in Queensland', *Meanjin* 7, no.4 (1948): pp.211–25; Noel Macainsh, *Nietzsche in Australia: A Literary Enquiry into a Nationalistic Ideology* (München: Verlag für Dokumentation und Werbung, 1975), pp.137–42; and John Docker, *Australian Cultural Elites: Intellectual Traditions in Sydney and Melbourne* (Sydney: Angus & Robertson, 1974), pp.22–41.

[24] James Cunninghame [Jack Lindsay], 'France the Abyss', *Vision*, no.2 (1923): p.39.

[25] [Jack Lindsay], 'Foreword', *Vision*, no.1 (1923): p.2. I consider Lindsay's changing relationship to modernism in 'Fanfrolico and After: The Lindsay Aesthetic in the Cultural Cold War', *Modernist Cultures* 15, no.3 (2020): pp.276–94.

[26] Lindsay, *Life Rarely Tells*, pp.683–4. Lindsay had encountered the idea of the literary 'type' from his reading of Lukács in the late 1930s, and in the early 1960s they discussed together the challenges of writing a Marxist autobiography: how to capture the typicality of one's own lived experience without succumbing, as Lukács would later put it, to 'vanity', the 'vice' that nails people to their particularity. Georg Lukács, *Record of a Life: An Autobiographical Sketch*, translated by Rodney Livingstone (London: Verso, 1983), p.169.

[27] Recent criticism concurs. David Carter notes the disjunction of anti-modernist 'argument' and modernist 'style' in *Vision*; in Carter, *Always Almost Modern: Australian Print Cultures and Modernity* (North Melbourne, Victoria: Australian Scholarly Publishing, 2013), p.89. Tim Armstrong cites

coterie formation, the little magazine, the manifesto with zest to inflame; even the fine press and the decorated book have a place in the material cultures of modernism. The fabulous investment in tradition and the individual talent, the contradictory recoil from the market and the mass, these too are familiar features. For my purposes, however, another common element deserves notice. The Fanfrolico aesthetic rejected all local content, all national specificity, as what it called a 'short-sighted Naturalism'. Its 'Vision' was trained on the universal: true poets, claimed Lindsay, have no 'nationality', or if they are citizens of any nation it is 'one that has no name upon the maps of the world, but lies with Pindar's Hyperboreans' beyond the North Wind.[28] To mark Lindsay as a 'typical' modernist of the 1920s as well as a leading theorist and practitioner of the communist historical novel in the 1930s and for two decades thereafter is to reflect again on the power of the mid-century national turn. He offers an example to compare with that of Hope Mirrlees and Virginia Woolf of the drawing of an elite, cosmopolitan aesthetic into the gravitational field of the national-popular.

Lindsay provides an excruciating account of this process in the third volume of his autobiography. In 1930, the Fanfrolico Press had gone into liquidation and Lindsay embarked on a radical settling of accounts with his father's reactionary politics and aesthetic ideology. It began as an intense bout of Freudian autoanalysis laced with ideas from Otto Rank, whose interest in the origins of anxiety returned him, by way of a footnote in Freud's *On the Interpretation of Dreams*, to 'the trauma of birth'. Under their tutelage, Lindsay found himself remembering his own birth 'in terrible spasms of fear and cloudy wrack of maddened sense', and in the lingering pain of forceps on flesh. He combined his 'ruthless Freudian method' with fortnight-long fasts and experienced strange visions as a result. In this period, Lindsay was also caring for a partner, the poet Elza de Locre, whose 'desperate anxieties' and 'neurosis' became his 'own—a complex of fears which precipitated all feared things'.[29] The Fanfrolico ethos of lyric gaiety and carefree sensual pleasure could not survive this contact with primal anxiety unchanged. It did not, however, disappear entirely: shorn of its aristocratic radicalism and masculine entitlement, the Lindsay aesthetic's arcadian pastoral and sexual license would form a horizon of social justice where equality in all things would transform not only our relations with each other but also with the natural world.[30]

---

Lindsay's *The London Aphrodite* as an instance of 'micromodernism', his term of art for the sometimes eccentric 'local effects' artists produced as they traversed the 'shifting' and 'uncertain' field of modernism during the 'open period of its production'; 'Micromodernism: Towards a Modernism of Disconnection', in *Moving Modernisms: Motion, Technology and Modernity*, edited by David Bradshaw, Laura Marcus and Rebecca Roach (Oxford: Oxford University Press, 2016), p.27.

[28] Jack Lindsay, 'Australian Poetry and Nationalism', *Vision*, no.1 (1923): pp.33–4.

[29] Lindsay, *Life Rarely Tells*, p.736; pp.704–6; Jack Lindsay to Ernest Martin, n.d. [January 1938], NLA 7168, Box 120, Odds 1–3.

[30] Lindsay writes in a late-career appreciation of his father, how after 1930 they parted ways and 'I turned back to the earth. The return was difficult and painful, but was in no simple sense a discarding of the Blakean theurgic world we had imagined. I think the dialectics I had brought in from Blake and Plato now found themselves much enriched; the concept of integration was not dropped but related

An early index of the new orientation was the desire 'to grow roots'; though he and Elza were living a peripatetic life at the time in the West of England, a prey to her 'restlessness' and fear of the city, Lindsay felt an urgent need 'to burrow in'. 'Within a week at any new place I had ransacked the public library for histories, records, and so on, and had begun to feel a local patriotism'.[31] Lindsay's writing had to support them both, and though he tried his hand at experimental fiction and a book on psychoanalytic theory, his brother Philip, a newly successful historical novelist, suggested he try his hand at the genre: Lindsay's Roman trilogy (1934–35) was the result, and with it a growing appreciation of the 'organic connection' between the individual and 'the deepest conflicts of the age—the conflicts between all that was most human and integrative, and all that was most inhuman, corrupted and divisive'.[32] The 'arrival' at Marxism came in January 1936, and in its train a firm belief 'that the Soviet Union and the C.P.s of the world' stood for the abolition of class and of 'all that Marx had gathered under the term, though I did not know it yet, alienation'.[33]

The 'C.P.' to which Lindsay pledged his allegiance in 1936 was the party of the Popular Front, fighting 'the demagogy of fascism' in all the ways Georgi Dimitrov had outlined the previous year.[34] At its Seventh World Congress in August 1935, Dimitrov had told the national sections of the Comintern to 'acclimatise' international communism in their home countries by naming it the telos of their traditions of domestic struggle. 'National forms of the proletarian class struggle and of the labour movement' were to be celebrated and socialist revolution refigured not as the abolition but as the *'saving of the nation'*. Lindsay was perfectly primed to heed Dimitrov's call for 'clear popular arguments' that would 'enlighten the masses on the past of their people', for powerful stories that would *'link up their present struggle with its revolutionary traditions and past'*.[35] His first contribution to the cause was a 'mass declamation' for May Day, a roll-call of radical movements from the fourteenth century to the present day that set out to redefine what it meant to be 'English'.[36] When later that year the London District Party's March of History came under criticism for marshalling on its banners 'a heterogeneous

---

afresh to history and to organic process ... I was going in the opposite direction to Norman, and yet the link remained.' Jack Lindsay, 'Norman Lindsay: Problems of his Life and Work', *Meanjin Quarterly* 29, no.1 (1970): p.47.

[31] Lindsay, *Life Rarely Tells*, p.723.

[32] Lindsay, *Life Rarely Tells*, pp.741–2. *Rome for Sale* (1934), *Caesar is Dead* (1934), and *Last Days with Cleopatra* (1935) comprise the trilogy; two further historical novels belong to this moment just prior to his Marxist conversion: *Despoiling Venus* (1935) and *The Wanderings of Wenamen* (1936), the latter probing the parallel between ancient Egypt and contemporary Europe as new civilizations rise to replace them. Lindsay wrote a cluster of short stories at this time—*Storm at Sea* (1935) and the collection *Come Home at Last* (1936)—also set in classical antiquity.

[33] Lindsay, *Life Rarely Tells*, p.763.

[34] Lindsay formally joined the Party five years later, in 1941, after he had been called up for war service and had Elza placed in a home.

[35] Dimitrov, *The Working Class against Fascism*, pp.69–73.

[36] Jack Lindsay, 'not english? A Reminder for May Day', *Left Review* 2, no.8 (1936): pp.353–7. The poem was so popular that, within days of the May issue selling out, *Left Review* republished it as a penny pamphlet.

collection of Englishmen, who down the ages for one reason or another fought against this or that form of authority', Lindsay rose to its defence: 'We must not judge past fighters by the test of whether they fought for a classless society' but rather by the test of what was then possible.

> The whole problem has been settled ... by Dimitrov in his magnificent *The Working Class Against Fascism* [as the British edition of his Comintern speech was called]. There he shows that the abandonment of the national slogans and names of the great past fighters to fascist propaganda is one of the cardinal errors that a Communist Party can commit. Congratulations to the London Party for a most magnificent step in the right direction.[37]

By January 1937, Lindsay was arguing in print that there was no need more pressing than for 'Communists in each country' to demonstrate 'that they stand for the true completion of the national destiny ... and what can do it better than adequate historical novels?'[38]

He followed prescription with practice: *1649* (1938) chronicled a year of the English Revolution; *Lost Birthright* (1939) followed the 'Wilkes and Liberty' riots of the 1760s; and *Men of Forty-eight* (written in the winter of 1939–40, published in 1948) dealt with English Chartism and the revolutions abroad. These novels, he later explained, were 'the first attempt made in English to define, in creative literature, the revolutionary traditions of our country'. They were begun at a time when the 'notion of revolutionary nationhood was hardly developed and when the whole problem of rooting the party in our national tradition and culture ... had scarcely even been formulated'.[39] For readers of the 1951 Polish translation of *1649*, Lindsay reflected further on the trilogy's intention: 'to clarify what happened in these great moments of national change; to judge them from the angle of the final liberation of nationhood which we call the proletarian revolution; to restore to the people their national revolutionary tradition'. Lindsay saw himself working directly in the tradition of Sir Walter Scott, who had pioneered the representation 'of historical struggle in the Novel', and of Scott's heirs, more abroad than at home, who had used the genre 'to express the aspirations of their people, to make the Novel a weapon in the fight for national liberation'.[40] The trilogy is, however, a

---

[37] Lewis Day, 'England Expects', *Discussion*, no.10 (November 1936): p.26; Jack Lindsay, 'Non-Dialectical', *Discussion*, no.11 (December 1936): p.31.

[38] Jack Lindsay, 'The Historical Novel', *New Masses* 22, no.3 (12 January 1937): p.16.

[39] Jack Lindsay, 'Autobiography', 12 June 1950, NLA, 7168, Box 77, File 4. Lindsay's 'absolutely central' role in articulating the cultural dimension of the Party's national turn is the subject of an important article by Ben Harker: '"Communism Is English": Edgell Rickword, Jack Lindsay and the Cultural Politics of the Popular Front', *Literature & History*, 3rd series, 20, no.2 (2011): p.17. See also Taylor, *The Popular Front Novel in Britain*, pp.93–140.

[40] Jack Lindsay, 'Note', NLA, 7168, Box 122; Jack Lindsay, *Opowieść o roku 1649*, translated by Krystina Tarnowska (Warsaw: Czytelnik, 1951). Czytelnik had published *Men of 48* in 1949; *Lost Birthright* followed in 1951.

fraction of Lindsay's total output in the genre: of the seventeen historical novels written after 1936, only a slim plurality inhabit an English setting and not all of these reach for the 'great moments of mass-upheaval in English history' to apprise the people of their heroic past.[41] There is a variety of method and ambition, and many were written at speed. In the winter of 1939–40 while he was waiting to be called up, Lindsay not only wrote the third volume in his English trilogy but no fewer than five other historical novels: *Hannibaal Takes a Hand* (1941) and *The Barriers Are Down* (published after the war in 1945) mined classical and late antiquity for parables of the fall of France; *Light in Italy* (1941) folded an English art student into the struggle for national independence in 1816; *The Dons Sight Devon* (1941) recounted the defeat of the Spanish Armada as a rousingly patriotic 'story for boys', while *The Stormy Violence* (1941) traversed the same terrain in a psychological study of one man's alienation and recovery to self-mastery and common cause.

Lindsay liked to think of himself as 'an odd man out' in the British literary establishment. 'First I was a mad colonial, throwing bricks at T.S. Eliot and the respectable', he recalled of his Fanfrolico years in the 1920s; then 'I went Left ... and ever since then I have gone from bad to worse as far as that world'—'the accepted world of b. [bourgeois] values'—is concerned.[42] Even on the Left, however, he could find himself exposed, his work accused of harbouring 'all sorts of unorthodox elements', of being 'over-complex and subtle, over-psychological, mystical, over-lyrical, lewd, over-naturalistic or psychopathological, over concerned with sex, etcetera'.[43] I will expand on Lindsay's relative eccentricity with respect to the intellectual culture of post-war communism in Britain; but it is against the cartoon portrait of Lindsay as kettle spout, of Lindsay the little man 'perpetually smiling' who wrote his height in books, that I have wanted in this section, while introducing a still largely unfamiliar mid-century writer, to underscore his typicality as an architect of the national turn who underwent that turn first in himself and who found in the romantic-era historical novel the perfect form with which to proselytize the politics of revolutionary nationalism.

This tension, between the eccentric and the social type, between dissidence and obedience, structures the story of Lindsay's Party allegiance. When Charles Hobday recalled Lindsay's erudition and facility with theory in meetings of the Party writers' group, he added this caveat: 'we had some difficulty taking him seriously'.

---

[41] Jack Lindsay, 'A Note on the Writing of BS [*Betrayed Spring*]', NLA, 7168, Box 3.
[42] Jack Lindsay to Sam Aaronovitch, n.d. (April 1955), NLA, 7168, Box 145, Self 21. Cf. the following self-descriptions: 'odd man out, a continuing outsider', 'my role as total outsider', 'always the outsider', the Fanfrolico Press was 'the 'the primary step to the position of odd-man out which I have managed to maintain (I trust with more validity in the revolts) until this day'. Lindsay, *Life Rarely Tells*, p.782; Lindsay, 'Political Autobiography'; *Meetings with Poets: Memories of Dylan Thomas, Edith Sitwell, Louis Aragon, Paul Eluard, Tristan Tzara* (London: Frederick Muller, 1968), p.124; 'Expatriate Publishing II', *Meanjin Quarterly* 33, no.2 (1974): p.176.
[43] Lindsay, *Life Rarely Tells*, p.783.

Andy Croft glosses the remark with reference to Lindsay's 'prolific' publication record but also to his proximity in the period Hobday is recalling to the Party's cultural apparatus. In the late 1940s, Lindsay was a member of its National Cultural Committee, which had been established in 1947 to 'support and encourage', as well as to supervise, the intellectual and creative work of Party members. Hobday's 'we' may not speak for all the Party's writers and his imputation of complicity is not immune to charges of hypocrisy (Hobday was himself a member of an 'editorial commission' which, at the Party's behest, took over the popular wartime cultural magazine, *Our Time*, ousting the veterans of the 1930s Cultural Front who had raised it to national prominence and remaking it as an instrument of the early cultural Cold War).[44] But any identification with the Party's King Street headquarters, especially at a time when it was staging a sterile and self-isolating assault on the intellectual freedom of its writers, must raise some concern. The Party's resumption of a policy of workerist anti-intellectualism after the positive cultural engagement of the Popular Front and People's War had a chilling effect that explains, in part, the exodus of so many writers, historians, and other cultural workers after 1956.[45] This moment, in the late 1940s and 1950s, represents a low ebb for a Party that, as Croft observed, sometimes went 'out of its way to appear as unattractive as possible to everyone'. 'There were long periods', Croft continues, 'when intellectuals were expected to sublimate their professional identities within a self-lacerating Communist one'.[46] That Lindsay was willing to do so is a part of the story he will tell in *Thunder Underground*; it is not, however, the whole story.

## III. 'Wartime discussions'

'Long before "1956"', as E.P. Thompson later recalled, 'there were centres of premature revisionism among the Communist intellectuals and others, who resisted the didactic methods of the Party's officers, the wooden economism of its policies

---

[44] E.P. Thompson recalled the Party's takeover of *Our Time* as 'a shameful episode and I shared in the shame', for along with Hobday, David Holbrook, and Arnold Rattenbury, he was 'part of the team of uncultured yobbos and musclemen' who 'allowed' themselves 'to be made use of' in the Party's move to wrest control of the magazine. Thompson, 'Edgell Rickword', *Poetry Nation Review* 6, no.1 (1979), Supplement, p. xxvi; see also Croft, 'Writers, The Communist Party and the Battle of Ideas, 1945–50', pp.14–16.

[45] Ben Harker chronicles this cultural realignment in 'Politics and Letters: The "Soviet Literary Controversy" in Britain', *Literature & History* 24, no.2 (2015): pp.43–58. Communist writers, artists, and intellectuals did, of course, break with the Party before 1956, as for example did Raymond Williams when in 1945 he returned to Cambridge and refused to renew his membership, or Harry Hanson (author of the 'Open Letter to E.P. Thompson' and a lecturer in public administration at the University of Leeds) in 1954. John Saville explains why the British Communist Party lost so 'few of its intellectuals before 1956' in 'The Communist Experience: A Personal Appraisal', *The Socialist Register* 27 (1991): p.20.

[46] Andy Croft, 'Authors Take Sides: Writers and the Communist Party', in *Opening the Books: Essays on the Social and Cultural History of British Communism*, edited by Geoff Andrews, Nina Fishman and Kevin Morgan (London: Pluto Press, 1995), p.86.

and the correct pabulum offered as Marxism.' Jack Lindsay was one such centre, his 'deviations' of a piece with the 'incipient heresy' and 'revisionist resistance' Thompson saw elsewhere at work in the Party. Against 'the déraciné uniformity and abstracted internationalist lingua franca of the Stalinist zenith', intellectuals like Lindsay represented 'the struggle for vitality and actuality'.[47] For Thompson, who came always to defend culture as 'a whole way of struggle', the 'complex and contradictory character of the Communist movement' was its saving grace; figures like Lindsay represented 'the forces within Communism making for its transformation', forces that against all the odds affirmed 'the possibility of *hope* within the pattern of social change'.[48]

To call Lindsay, as did Thompson, a 'premature' socialist humanist is to place him squarely within the complexity and contradictions of this struggle; it identifies a drama of personal integrity and mental fight that textures with lived experience the history of ideas. For it has been easy to read the Marxist humanisms that gained prominence in the late 1950s and 1960s as though they were simply a new mixture of philosophical ingredients (the discovery of the early Marx and reappraisal of his debt to Hegel, the recombination of Marxism with insights drawn from existentialism and psychoanalysis). To do so and no more, however, is to slight the conflict and confusion that for many attended the process. Lindsay's intellectual biography is here exemplary, the sheer difficulty of his 'deviations' from Party orthodoxy in the 1940s and 1950s a salutary correction to the frictionless narrative more commonly told of the discovery, in the late 1950s, of Marx's humanism. For the students who helped to form the British first New Left, that moment came in 1958 when the philosopher Charles Taylor returned from Paris with a new French translation of the *1844 Manuscripts*. But this myth of transmission from abroad and of the philosophical fresh start with Marx obscures many a messier story of how these same texts and ideas had circulated in the years before.[49] Lindsay had been working with a German edition of the Marx manuscripts from the early 1940s, and in 1947 he obtained a mimeographed translation by Ria Stone (pen name of the Chinese-American activist and scholar Grace Lee Boggs), who together

---

[47] Thompson, 'Edgell Rickword', p. xxvii.
[48] E.P. Thompson, 'Commitment in Politics', *Universities & Left Review*, no.6 (1959): p.54; E.P. Thompson, 'Outside the Whale', in *Out of Apathy*, edited by E.P. Thompson (London: Stevens and Sons, 1960), p.163. But see also John McIlroy's revisionist account of Thompson's own widely ascribed 'premature revisionism', with its conclusion that, from what we can tell, 'during the postwar decade [Thompson] poured his formidable intellectual abilities, his impressive energies, his passion for humanity and his longing for a better world—the qualities so many appreciated in the later Thompson—into prosecuting the cause of Stalinism which he identified with human progress.' McIlroy, 'Another Look at E.P. Thompson and British Communism, 1937–1955', *Labor History* 58, no.4 (2017): p.531.
[49] Stuart Hall, 'Life and Times', p.188; the first widely documented encounter of the British Left with Marx's *1844 Manuscripts* was that of the Christian Left group around Karl Polanyi and John Macmurray in 1936–37; see Fred Block, 'Karl Polanyi and the writing of *The Great Transformation*', *Theory and Society* 32, no.3 (2003): p.277 and p.303 fn.12; see also Tim Rogan, 'Karl Polanyi at the Margins of English Socialism, 1934–1947', *Modern Intellectual History* 10, no.2 (2013): pp.333–4.

with C.L.R. James and Raya Dunayevskaya formed the minority Johnson-Forest Tendency, first outside, and then within, the US (Trotskyite) Socialist Workers' Party.[50] Mobilizing the concept of alienation inside the British Communist Party laid Lindsay open to charges of revisionism, but during the sharpest of the cultural Cold War's 'mental frosts', when as Thompson recalls, 'Vitalities shrivelled up and books lost their leaves', the 'return to Marx's early works' was for Lindsay a lifeline, 'helping [him to] resist [the] sectarianism in those years'.[51]

Lindsay's post-war intellectual development informs the plot of *Thunder Underground* and for that reason I rehearse it here, but I do so also to describe a milieu. Lindsay had emerged from his war service eager to build a progressive 'cultural upsurge' out of what he and others on the Left saw as a wartime popular renaissance of the arts.[52] For five years, Lindsay threw himself into furious cultural and political activity, helping to found a stage production company, a modern dance theatre, and a script-writing centre for the Labour movement; working on Soviet and satellite state friendship committees, organizing and writing for the international peace and democracy movements; serving on the steering committee of the Society for Cultural Relations with the USSR Writers' Group, the Writers' and Historians' Groups of the British Communist Party, as well as on the Party's National Cultural Committee; co-directing the progressive publishing house, Fore Publications, and serving as a director for the magazine *Our Time*. All the while, he was publishing a steady stream of novels, translations, and works of history. Already in 1945, Lindsay's house in St John's Wood had come to seem a rival 'cultural centre' to the Communist Party's headquarters on King Street, and Lindsay himself a 'self-appointed "theoretical" guiding genius' or 'cultural fuehrer'. So, at least, it

---

[50] What Lindsay calls the 'difficult German text' in which he first encountered the *1844 Manuscripts* was Part 1 Vol.3 of the original *Historish-kritische Gesamtausgabe*, edited by David Riazanov and Vladimir Adoratsky (1932); Lindsay, *Meetings with Poets*, p.79. Riazanov had overseen the first publication of Marx's manuscripts in Russian in 1927; a French translation of Riazanov's text appeared in 1929 in *La Revue Marxiste* and 1932 saw the publication of two German-language editions, with Siegfried Landshut and Jacob Peter Mayer including the manuscripts in their edition of Marx's *Frühschriften* alongside the authoritative *Marx-Engels Gesamtausgabe* first mentioned. In her autobiography, Boggs recalled the 'exciting discoveries' she and Raya Dunayevskaya made in the New York Public Library in the mid-to-late-1940s: 'I will never forget the day that Raya came back from the library with the news that she had found a Russian translation of the *Economic and Philosophic Manuscripts*'. Boggs did her translation from the German edition and it circulated as a short pamphlet titled *Three Essays by Karl Marx, Selected from the Economic-Philosophical Manuscripts* (New York: Johnson-Forest Tendency, 1947). See Boggs, *Living for Change* (Minneapolis: University of Minnesota Press, 1998), pp.58–9.

[51] E.P. Thompson, 'Edgell Rickword', p. xxvi; Lindsay, 'Political Autobiography'.

[52] For his comments on the post-war 'cultural upsurge', see Jack Lindsay, *British Achievement in Art and Music* (London: Pilot Press, 1945). Andy Croft adopts the title of the first of Lindsay's contemporary-set 'Novels of the British Way' to chronicle this moment in 'Betrayed Spring: The Labour Government and British Literary Culture', in *Labour's Promised Land? Culture and Society in Labour Britain 1945–51*, edited by Jim Fryth (London: Lawrence & Wishart, 1995), pp.197–223. Croft has argued that it was 'during these years, rather than in the 1930s, that Communist writers made their most profound impact' on British cultural life; Croft, 'Writers, The Communist Party and the Battle of Ideas, 1945–50', p.2. Cf. also, Geoffrey Field, *Blood Sweat and Toil: Remaking the British Working Class, 1939–1945* (Oxford: Oxford University Press, 2011), pp.217–50; and Harker, 'Jack Lindsay's Alienation', pp.85–6.

appeared to Ted Willis, with whom Lindsay had collaborated at Unity Theatre and his own Script Centre.[53] There was, to be sure, bad blood between the two, in part over Willis' failed attempt in 1945 to turn Unity from an amateur into a professional theatre.[54] But Willis was not the only one to think Lindsay at risk of going rogue. When Lindsay finally came into collision with the leadership, Emile Burns, the Party's cultural policeman, could draw on a 'long memory' of Lindsay's infractions of the Party line.[55]

Lindsay's post-war 'heresies' made their first public appearance in a discussion document, distributed in the summer of 1945 to the Communist Party Writers' Group and fiercely disputed over three subsequent sessions.[56] In it, Lindsay criticized mechanical applications of the base-superstructure model of cultural production and made appeal to the early Marx. Lindsay often recalled this meeting, and how a young E.P. Thompson was the only member of the audience to stand in his defence.[57] 'Deviation' surfaced again in a 'Talk on Coloured Unity' with George Padmore, Richard Wright, and others, in which Lindsay called for 'a more human Marxism' able to think race with class, and again in his editorial

---

[53] Ted Willis to Jack Lindsay, 19 March 1945, NLA, 7168, Box 77, File 4.

[54] Described in detail in Colin Chambers, *The Story of Unity Theatre* (London: Lawrence & Wishart, 1989), pp.265-72. Lindsay describes Unity as having been 'captured by Ted Willis who turned it into a professional co., wholly to suit his own personal ambitions. After he had wrecked Unity, he passed on over its ruins to good jobs in the film world.' Jack Lindsay, 'Notes on Developments in Popular Culture during the War and After' [n.d.], NLA, 7168, Box 141, Self 3. Arnold Rattenbury recalls Willis in this period as 'the only bloke I ever met in the Communist Party who was a fully paid-up Zhdanovite'; quoted in Andy Croft, 'The Boys Round the Corner: The Story of Fore Publications', in *A Weapon in the Struggle: The Cultural History of the Communist Party in Britain*, edited by Andy Croft (London: Pluto Press), p.161. Willis's role in the popular TV series *Dixon of Dock Green* earned him a life peerage in 1963.

[55] Emile Burns to Jack Lindsay, 5 October 1949, NLA, 7168, Box 77, File 4.

[56] The paper appears to have circulated widely among communist and sympathetic Left intellectuals in the autumn of 1945, though some confusion exists as to when the actual meetings took place. According to a report on the activities of the CP Writers' Group presented to the National Cultural Committee the following year, Lindsay's paper was presented at the group's second monthly meeting in July 1945, with John Lewis for the Party rebutting it in a subsequent meeting, and Alick West convening two further sessions on the issues raised. 'Report of Writers' Group', 30 August 1946; Archive of the Communist Party of Great Britain, Labour History Archive and Study Centre, Manchester (LHASC), Betty Reid Papers, CP/CENT/CULT/1/1. E.P. Thompson was present at one of these meetings, from which he recalls 'the immense shaggy head of the anthropologist V. Gordon Childe, just in front of me, shaking in fury at the general scene of dogmatism'; Thompson, 'Edgell Rickword', p. xxvi. This could not, however, have been the first meeting in July, as in a postcard from Edinburgh Childe apologized to Lindsay for having missed it ('I am sure I should have enjoyed your discussion of superstructure had I been able to get up.') V. Gordon Childe to Jack Lindsay, 19 July 1945, NLA, 7168, Box 3, Letters Folder 11b. Miscellaneous correspondence from October suggests that discussion of the paper was live at this time. Many years later, however, Lindsay would date the controversy to early November, and in a foreword to Sally Green's 1981 biography of Childe, he claims that his original presentation, though slated for July, got postponed, and that 'Childe was able to attend after all.' Jack Lindsay, 'List of Activities' (1980), NLA, 7168, Box 24, Folder 31; Jack Lindsay, 'Foreword' to Sally Green, *Prehistorian: A Biography of V. Gordon Childe* (Bradford on Avon: Moonraker, 1981), p. xii.

[57] Jack Lindsay, 'Marxist Theory of Culture', LHASC, CP/CENT/CULT/4/11. For Lindsay's recollections of the occasion, cf. *Life Rarely Tells*, p.801; *Meetings with Poets*, p.151; and *The Crisis in Marxism* (Totowa, NJ: Barnes & Noble, 1981), p.126. Ben Harker reconstructs the arguments of Lindsay's paper and the Party's response in 'Jack Lindsay's Alienation', pp.85-91.

appeal on the launch of the journal *Arena* for a 'give-and-take between Marxism in its critical aspects and the free play of creative elements' in the culture at large.[58] Lindsay defended Sartre when British communism was attacking him and attacked Zhdanov when British communism was defending him. But it was his full-scale, book-length foray into cultural theory, *Marxism and Contemporary Science* (1949), that brought the 'heresies' to a head.

Lindsay had written the book in what he called a 'pioneer' spirit and had kept the Party at arm's length during the writing.[59] Such independence was not to be tolerated. Emile Burns led the attack with a savage review for the *Daily Worker*; a more systematic demolition followed in the *Communist Review*. In November 1949, Lindsay was hauled before a special meeting of the National Cultural Committee to explain himself. He would later recall 'the awful night' of that meeting, the 'nightmare feeling that to be thrown out of the party was the end of everything, my mind going round in circles trying to estimate correctly where the main errors of the book lay ... To feel the whole weight of the Party on one is a most distressing thing, and helps one to understand the confessions of the innocent'.[60] Under orders from the Committee and under the close supervision of Burns, Lindsay published 'A Note of Self Criticism' and retracted the book.[61] He stood chastened. In the self-report he submitted the following year, he acknowledged 'the anarchic element' in his personal development thus far and confessed his failure 'to come with all the force I can muster in the party-line'. He now expressed his hope 'every month to put my talents, such as they are, more effectively at the Party's disposal'.[62] This he did, becoming a public champion of Soviet aesthetics and explaining to all who would listen how the struggle for socialist realism is 'bound up at every point with the function of leadership by the communist party', how no writer 'is going to master socialist realism who does not understand what communist leadership is, who is not playing his part in development of that leadership, helping to change our people politically as well as culturally, seeing no division between politics and culture, and daily embodying in his own experience the experience of the Party'.[63]

---

[58] Jack Lindsay, 'Talk on Coloured Unity', with Cedric Dover, Richard Wright, Maung Ohm, M.A. Mahgoub, and George Padmore, n.d. [1946], NLA, 7168, Box 120, Odds 1–3; 'Editorial Note', *Arena: A Literary Magazine* 1, no.1 (1949): p.3.

[59] Jack Lindsay, *Marxism and Contemporary Science, or The Fullness of Life* (London: Dennis Dobson, 1949), p.7.

[60] Jack Lindsay to Alick West, n.d. (January 1965), NLA, 7168, Box 34, Folder 191.

[61] Jack Lindsay, 'A Note of Self Criticism', *Communist Review*, (March 1950), pp.93–5.

[62] Jack Lindsay, 'Autobiography'.

[63] Jack Lindsay, 'Socialist Realism and the British Tradition', n.d. (early 1950s), NLA, 7168, Box 75. For several British communist intellectuals, the controversies surrounding Lindsay's 'heresies' came to symbolize the worst effects of the Cold War communist brain chill. Alick West wrote to Lindsay in 1956: 'I've felt ashamed. For I've been thinking that an instance of my share in the so-called Stalin business is that I didn't fight hard enough in the controversy around your "Marxism and Contemporary Science."' Alick West to Jack Lindsay, 14 April 1956, NLA, 7168, Box 141, Self 3. Dona Torr recalled the controversy surrounding Lindsay's 1945 position paper as a time when 'as a *Party* we were too weak

What followed the 1949 National Cultural Committee meeting was, as Lindsay later confessed, a loss of 'nerve'. The attacks left him uncertain whether he was in fact, and as Emile Burns had charged, 'mistaking personal wilfulness for intellectual conviction', 'personal vanity and my intellectual pride for a superior grasp of the truth'.[64] A period of accommodation followed. These were the years in which Doris Lessing knew Lindsay, recalling him in her autobiography as 'perhaps the purest example of a good writer done in by the Party'.[65] These were also the years of Lindsay's highest cultural visibility, both at home and abroad. His 1952 history, *Byzantium into Europe*, prompted an anonymous reviewer in the *Times Literary Supplement* to call for the expulsion of Marxist historians from their university positions.[66] In the ensuing controversy, the *TLS* stood by its reviewer in a leading article by the conservative journalist and later prophet of the New Right, T.E. Utley. To the question 'whether it is legitimate for authorities in a university to exclude from teaching posts persons who repudiate western standards of scholarly integrity', Utley for the *TLS* answered yes.[67] Three years later, it was Lindsay's fiction that drew the paper's fire, another leading article reminding readers that Marxism was as antithetical to the novel as it was to 'the canons of Western scholarship'.[68]

Behind the Iron Curtain, by contrast, Lindsay was fêted. He was invited to attend the Pushkin anniversary celebrations in 1949 and the second and third Soviet Writers' Congresses in 1954 and 1959. He toured the 'new democracies' on several trips in the early 1950s and wrote glowingly of what he saw.[69] His works, translated into Russian and the languages of the communist Second World sold more than a million copies.[70] He was listed in the Soviet Union among 'the great foreign authors', hailed for his services to Russian Literature, and in 1966 awarded the Badge of Honour for his translations of Soviet poetry.[71] As a young British communist confided to Lindsay on his return from the USSR: 'They really know you

---

to help you & that any mistakes were much more our fault than yours.' Dona Torr to Jack Lindsay, 31 December 1951, NLA, 7168, Box 123, Odds 10.

[64] Lindsay, *Meetings with Poets*, pp.151–2.

[65] Doris Lessing, *Walking in the Shade: Volume Two of My Autobiography 1949–1962* (New York: Harper Collins, 1997), p.92.

[66] [Henry Moss], 'A Marxist view of Byzantium', review of Jack Lindsay, *Byzantium into Europe*, *Times Literary Supplement*, no.2654 (12 December 1952): p.816.

[67] [T.E. Utley], 'Freedom and Integrity', *Times Literary Supplement*, no.2657 (2 January 1953): p.9.

[68] [Richard Ollard], 'Marxism and the Novel', review of Jack Lindsay, *The Moment of Choice*, *Times Literary Supplement*, no.2774 (29 April 1955): p.253; 'A Marxist View of Byzantium', p.816.

[69] Lindsay writes of his visit to the 1949 Pushkin Celebrations in *A World Ahead: Journal of a Soviet Journey* (London: Fore Publications, 1950), and of his travels in Romania (with Maurice Cornforth) in *Rumanian Summer: A View of the Rumanian People's Republic* (London: Lawrence & Wishart, 1953).

[70] *Publishing in the Soviet Union*, translated by David Skvirsky (Moscow, 1967), p.12.

[71] Maurice Friedberg, *A Decade of Euphoria: Western Literature in Post-Stalin Russia, 1954–1964* (Bloomington: Indiana University Press, 1977), p.210. Jack Lindsay, *Russian Poetry, 1917–1955* (London: The Bodley Head, 1957), and Jack Lindsay, *Modern Russian Poetry* (London: Vista Books, 1960).

everywhere. In Tajikistan I was continually asked, "What is Jack Lindsay doing?"[72] Lindsay recounts a similar anecdote told him by his friend Alick West from a visit to the People's Republic of Bulgaria. West had been touring the monastery at Rila in the mountains south of Sofia when he saw a Bulgarian family making their way around the complex. The daughter was carrying a book. It was in Russian, but West recognized Lindsay's photo on the cover. '*Moy drug, moy drug*', he exclaimed, coming up to them—['My friend, my friend']—'and they were almost equally excited!'[73] In 1968, Lindsay learned from a local poet that the 1958 Chinese translation of *Betrayed Spring* (1953) had made him 'the favourite English novelist in Mongolia'.[74]

Such public recognition and apparent popularity existed alongside the deep distrust with which the Soviet Union and its satellites treated all intellectuals, whether foreign or domestic. Two years after his return to Hungary in 1947, the communist journalist and wartime British SOE agent George Paloczi-Horvath was arrested by Rakosi's security police, imprisoned, and tortured. Lindsay's was among the names on which he was forced to give information. According to Paloczi-Horvath's interrogators, the British Party leadership was 'full of intellectuals ... in the pay of the intelligence services. When the party gets power there, they will have to be liquidated, like all of you [Hungarian intellectuals] have been liquidated here.'[75]

With prestige abroad went neglect at home and a deep sense of isolation within the Party. Lindsay confessed in letters what he called 'the depressive factors' of the communist writing life, the 'particular vulnerability of the artist when he really throws in his lot wholeheartedly with the Party'. Though 'calloused' to criticism from the anti-communist establishment, he was painfully sensitive when it came from fellow members. To Alick West he described how criticism both from 'the party in general' and from 'comrades in the same field' can 'really strike home deadeningly behind' a writer's 'guards'. 'This puts a special responsibility on the party which is not always appreciated—eg the sectarianism and philistinism that drove Mayakovsky to suicide. A while ago I found that suicide hard to understand. Now I don't feel it quite so dark an enigma.'[76] As the 1950s wore on, Lindsay felt himself increasingly 'misliked and felt-jealously about among the party writers and round 'em'. In statements of 'semi-despair'—'Now don't think I'm becoming paranoiac! But I don't think I exaggerate my isolation'—Lindsay revealed the darker side of the Party writer's life.[77] From 1949 to 1956, this was the path he chose.

---

[72] Jack Lindsay to Alick West, n.d. (1953), NLA, 7168, Box 34, Folder 191.
[73] Jack Lindsay to Oksana Krugerskaya, 1960; original in Archive of the Muses (RGALI), Moscow. I am grateful to Henry Stead for the reference.
[74] Jack Lindsay, interviewed by Hazel de Berg, 6 April 1970; Hazel de Berg collection, NLA, DeB 478; Lindsay, 'Fullness of Life', p.190A.
[75] George Paloczi-Horvath, *The Undefeated* (London: Secker and Warburg, 1959), p.219.
[76] Jack Lindsay to Alick West, n.d. (1955), NLA, 7168, Box 34, Folder 191.
[77] Jack Lindsay to Alick West, n.d. (1957), NLA, 7168, Box 34, Folder 191.

Championing socialist realism as the expression of unanimity between vanguard party and party intellectual and bringing its prescriptions to bear in a series of nine contemporary novels 'of the British Way' (1953–64), designed to do for England what Aragon's six-volume *Les Communistes* had done for France, Lindsay claimed that he 'lost interest' in his critical agenda.[78] This is not entirely true. In fact, he continued his investigation of culture in two substantial projects: one, an evolving study of Marx, alienation, and the commodity fetish; the other, an epic history of British poetry from the seventeenth century to the present that he called 'The Starfish Road'.[79] Taken together, these two desk-drawer and ultimately abandoned works align with major developments in Western Marxism. It is from their pages that Lindsay drew for his contributions to *The New Reasoner* and from their arguments that he fashioned the novel, *Thunder Underground*.

Lindsay later described the 'shock' in 1956 of Khrushchev's revelations and the Soviet invasion of Hungary as 'shattering'.[80] He signed his name to a public letter condemning the Party's 'uncritical support' of the 'Soviet action in Hungary', which it framed as 'the undesirable culmination of years of distortion of fact, and failure by British Communists to think out political problems for themselves'.[81] For this, he received official censure.[82] In the spirit of self-criticism, he now looked for 'weaknesses' in himself and began to 'find certain elements of compromise' in his writings, especially in his novels of 'the British Way'. These 'elements' he blamed on his decision 'to write for the Party'. 'I see there the beginning of all corruption—that which has devastated Soviet culture.' Whether or not the 'English situation [had been] such that the surrender of responsibility could go so far', Lindsay had now to take stock.[83] He took back up the manuscript of his autobiographical trilogy, *Life Rarely Tells*, and revised it for publication (1958–62). And he returned to writing historical fiction. Feeling the need to write something 'simply heroic', he revisited a manuscript he had written in the late 1940s.[84] In the summer of 1957, and with the publisher's proofs of *The Great Oak: A Story of 1549* in front of him, he felt

---

[78] Lindsay, *Meetings with Poets*, p.151.
[79] The study of Marx went through various titles between 1951 and the mid-to-late 1960s, including 'Man and Nature' and 'The Whole Man and the Alien Thing'. 'The Starfish Road' was to have comprised seven books with titles like 'Rant and Rapture' and 'Prophesy and Passion'; for the last in the series, Lindsay toyed with the title 'Waste Land or Sleeping Beauty', so named after the poems by T.S. Eliot and Edith Sitwell he thought exemplified the choice to affirm or deny our socialist humanist potential.
[80] Lindsay, 'The Fullness of Life', p.210; Lindsay, 'Political Autobiography'.
[81] Eric Hobsbawm et al., *New Statesman and Nation*, 1 December 1956, p.701. The letter was initially intended for the *Daily Worker* and published in the *New Statesman* and *Tribune* when that paper refused to print it.
[82] John Gollan to Jack Lindsay, 19 November 1956, NLA, 7168 Box 5 Folder 26. Lindsay was also told off for his contributions to *The New Reasoner*; General Organization Department to Neville Carey, 21 March 1958; CP/CENT/DISC/14, LHASC.
[83] Jack Lindsay to Alick West, n.d. (May 1957, not sent), NLA, 7168, Box 34, Folder 191.
[84] Jack Lindsay, list of 'Books in the Press', n.d. (1957), NLA 7168, Box 123, Odds 11.

once again 'right back on my own centre'.[85] He then began work on the novel that would be his last, an extraordinary coming to terms with the project of revolution betrayed and a reprisal of his most firmly held convictions about alienation and experience, socialist humanism, and the artist's revolutionary vocation.[86]

## IV. 'A Novel of Nero's Rome'

In 1935, Georgi Dimitrov had instructed communists to 'link up the present struggle with the people's revolutionary traditions and past', and Lindsay had thrown himself into the task.[87] But if his first response to 1956 was a return to this model of heroic history-writing, his second was a calculated displacement of action from home soil to ancient Rome, and from the national-popular to the role and predicament of the individual artist. 'Why turn back to the shattered past', Lindsay asks in the novel's dedicatory poem,

> when in the present we can find
> more than enough to tease the mind
> confusion and the threatening claim
> of problems piling up to blind
> all life with foul atomic blast?[88]

The question is on point. The imputation of escapism hangs heavy on the historical novel as a genre, as it does on the historical imagination of the mid-century Left. For whether mobilized to domesticate the Soviet example (as in the 1930s) or to dissociate from it (as increasingly thereafter, discovering in the domestic tradition a socialism untainted by its Soviet instantiation), these radical rewritings of the national story were always also romances of the people, projections of popular agency, initiative, and the possibility of social justice through struggle. From the second New Left would come the charge that the whole undertaking had been a distraction. Writing in 1974 to recall socialist theory to the radical internationalism of Lenin, Luxemburg, and Trotsky, Perry Anderson mounted what became the standard criticism of Western (and English) Marxism when he framed its characteristic idioms and areas of study—philosophy and cultural study on the

---

[85] Jack Lindsay to Alick West, n.d. (May 1957).
[86] In the seven years between first drafting and finally publishing *Thunder Underground*, Lindsay wrote six more novels in his 'British Way' series; their character, however, changes significantly after 1956. Simpler in construction and shorter, with none of the earlier epic ambition, these later novels diagnose what Lindsay would later call 'the breakdown of struggle in the English scene' and 'the regression into the hectic frustrations of a consumer society'. Lindsay, 'The Fullness of Life', p.215.
[87] Dimitrov, *The Working Class against Fascism*, p.70.
[88] Jack Lindsay, *Thunder Underground: A Novel of Nero's Rome* (London: Muller, 1965), p.5. Subsequent references to this edition will be given parenthetically in the body of the text.

Continent, history in Britain—as 'hidden hallmarks' of '*defeat*', indices of the Left's 'unending detour from any revolutionary political practice'.[89]

*Thunder Underground: A Novel of Nero's Rome* is not what Anderson prescribed instead, a return to those 'areas most central to the classical traditions of historical materialism: scrutiny of the economic laws of motion of capitalism as a mode of production, analysis of the political machinery of the bourgeois state, strategy of the class struggle necessary to overthrow it'; but neither is it quite an evasion.[90] Lindsay answers his poem's rhetorical question:

> Wisdom perhaps at last begins
> when we can grasp the origins
> of our aspiring attainted plight.
> Then from the distance a deepening light
> can reach the present, clarifying
> what lives defiantly and what's dying
> in our strange world. (5)

Not, then, a flight from historical implication but rather a control-experiment in mapping the social totality, Lindsay's Roman detour is designed to recalibrate those cognitive instruments by which the novelist locates his characters in time and therewith his own position in the pattern of social change.

In the communist historical novel, political defeat had often been recuperated as an occasion for renewed intellectual work. Lindsay's English trilogy chronicles the emergence in defeat of a theory adequate to the developing struggle. *1649* ends with one of its heroes resolving to 'study hard'.[91] *Lost Birthright* concludes with its protagonist setting up a school for weavers in the East End of London and himself attending meetings of the Robin Hood Club in Butchers Row, where 'a keen body of workers and tradesmen' debated contemporary events, 'going right to the heart of political and social problems'.[92] But it is only in *Men of Forty-Eight* that the theory has begun to catch up with the events of that year of revolutions. The novel closes, not with the wasteful death of Richard Boon on the barricades of Vienna (a romantic sacrifice which affords no more than a personal solution to a life divided), but with his friend Tom Scamler pledging in defeat his renewed commitment to get 'the theory right'. We first meet Tom at the novel's start, his pockets bulging with books bought on the Continent, including one book, 'a book I especially don't want to lose ... by a fellow called Marx'; we leave him at the novel's end studying 'statistics', foretelling a future 'big clash' of class interests 'accompanied with vast wars', and blaming the present check to the revolutionary cause on the immaturity

---

[89] Perry Anderson, *Considerations on Western Marxism* (London: New Left Books, 1976), p.42.
[90] Anderson, *Considerations*, pp.44–5.
[91] Lindsay, *1649*, p.559.
[92] Lindsay, *Lost Birthright*, p.530.

of 'developments in industry' and 'the total lack of theory'.[93] The events of 1956 gave this fictional trope renewed application and urgency. Charged with reporting to the National Cultural Committee his impressions of the Party's 24th Congress in April 1956, Lindsay reproduced in his remarks the resolutions-in-defeat of his historical fictions. Now was the time to 'Clean up our own house. Get the theory of it all clarified and our own practice [sic].' Khrushchev's secret speech and the hesitations of the Party's political leadership presented its intellectuals, Lindsay argued, with the opportunity to articulate 'a creative Marxism', not in deference to a Party line but in solidarity with 'our people in this actual moment of deep-going change'.[94]

*Thunder Underground* is the narrative exposition of this 'creative Marxism'; it is also, and painfully, an acknowledgement of Lindsay's own credulity and of the 'elements of compromise' that had entered his work. Its hero, Lucius Cassius Firmus, arrives in Rome from his native Spain wide-eyed and willing to believe the best of its empire and its emperor—of 'the onward march of Roman power' (49), of 'Law now incarnated in one man ... who stood above all factions and racial distinctions, all social divisions', of Rome's 'great destiny, a power fountaining up from the valleys between these hills and flowing all over the world in an eternal dispensation. Bringing peace to warring peoples, drawing barbarians into the circle of civilization, spreading everywhere a creed of liberty through law' (46). In terms such as these Lindsay had described his own visits to the Soviet Union and the new democracies in Eastern Europe.[95] 'Of course, things were not yet perfected', but Lucius trusts in a 'pattern of unfolding reconciliation' that will spread 'the rule of liberty' and 'break through all the limiting factors' (46). Of the 'crimes imputed to the Emperor', Lucius has been willing to write them off as 'matters of the closed intrigues and conflicts of the Divine House. Even if the worst of them was true, was the imperial rule itself affected?' (68) But the longer he remains in Rome, the more he sees that it was: 'all was astray, twisted against itself, given over to fear, the supreme evil' (86). This grim reality issues in an analysis of Neronian Rome as at once 'a universal civilizing force and a mechanism of incalculable greed' (295). Here, in miniature, is Lindsay's reading of the Soviet Union under Stalin— the betrayal of the Russian revolutionary project, the subordination of all aspects of Soviet society to what the novel calls a 'State-machine which in the last resort controlled also the Emperor himself' (435)—and yet, in that image of a 'civilizing force', something still worthy of allegiance.

Lindsay's submission to *The New Reasoner* had made the same effort to seize the contradictions of Stalin's Russia dialectically, to understand 'the duality of the epoch, its vast constructive achievement both through and despite its evils'. He

---

[93] Jack Lindsay, *Men of Forty-Eight* (London: Methuen, 1948), p.50; pp.445–6.
[94] Jack Lindsay, 'Notes for Report Back of 24th Congress to Cult. Comm.', n.d. (1956), NLA, 7168, Box 5, Folder 25.
[95] Cf. Lindsay, *A World Ahead* and *Rumanian Summer*.

argued, as he would again in the novel, that any partial or only local explanation of the Stalinist epoch—in terms, for example, of 'the entangled factors that we can group under the heading of Russian backwardness, of the limitations of socialism in one country, of personal intrigues and ambitions, of secret-police controls, and so on'—must fail unless it is 'made in the wider perspective made possible by Marx's concept of alienation'. Taken by themselves and apart from the ongoing 'struggle to "unthingify" man' and to realize 'the whole man of a brotherly earth', the recitation of Stalinist crimes and Soviet betrayals can 'beget only disillusion and despair, a fatalist acceptance of evil things' (as Lindsay charged Harry Hanson of doing in his 'Open Letter to E.P. Thompson'), 'or a retreat from all efforts to formulate scientific socialism and to understand our world as a whole'. This effort to understand the 'complex goodness and badness' of the Soviet experiment requires that Lindsay 'reprobate' the atrocities of Stalinism, 'denounce the epoch's thinking as a limited distortion of Marxism', and yet 'accept it all'. 'I accept it because I am convinced that I can fight uncompromisingly against all that was evil and humanly cramped in it; I fight against all that because I feel more intensely than ever what great liberations of spirit were then achieved—the liberations that now make possible the ending of the Stalinist epoch'.[96] In *Thunder Underground*, Lucius passes from believing the 'division between acceptance and rejection' to be 'absolute' (397), to finding in socialist humanism 'the unbetraying point where acceptance and rejection became one' (412).

For Lucius, this unity in division brings to mind the lines of Catullus' poem 85: '*I love and I hate: you ask how this can be so. I do not know, I know my agony*' (361). Lindsay's *Brief Light: A Novel of Catullus* (1939) had fixed on the writing of this couplet as an early discovery of the dialectic, with its poet explaining how 'only in cloven spasms of torment was it possible to see the whole thing, the hopeful and the hopeless as both aspects of the same urge'.[97] Twenty years later, the challenge remains how to go 'beyond the sheer division, [and reach] an acceptance which [overcomes] the division' (361). *Thunder Underground* poses this question of its young protagonist and charts, in schematic fashion, his pursuit of an answer. From political commitment and a minor role in the ill-conceived Pisonian conspiracy, through a variety of religious and philosophical alignments, Lucius arrives finally at an understanding of the world and his place in it. These successive way stations—political education through a senatorial plot, religious conversion to the worship of Isis and Osiris, discovery of brotherliness among the 'stript and stormtosst outcasts' (395) of Rome's outer slums, of community among a congregation of persecuted Christians, and ultimately of the virtues of labour and 'the way of Nature' (410)—belong to the ideological fabric of the first century,

---

[96] Lindsay, 'Socialism and Humanism', pp.96–9.
[97] In the novel's introduction, Lindsay introduces Catullus as 'the first modern poet', 'the first poet to reflect as a personally urgent and conscious matter the tragic issues which had previously appeared only in drama.' Lindsay, *Brief Light*, pp.219–20; p. x.

but their composite form is Lindsay's prescription for a twentieth-century politics that has lost its way.

Against 'the ravening maw, the insatiable heart, the blind greed' of a world awry, Lindsay asserts the dignity of the 'active life' (363) and the 'virtue of the earth' (414). The soldier Silvanus sees the people of Rome 'driven by alien needs, the needs begotten of fear, not of the body free and unashamed, the body accepting pleasure and unafraid'. But he understands also that 'all the things he named as alien in them, he had found in himself, he had struggled to root them out, he knew they were there, still in the unpurged darkness, ready to assert themselves the moment he lost his balance, the painfully-won, painfully-held acceptance of earth and its warm simplicities of growth' (86). Here, then, is the battle against alienation that Lindsay named in retrospect the common thread of his whole career, one that had begun in Sydney in the early 1920s in visionary Dionysian revolt and which in the conversion to Marxism preserved an element, however heterodox, of its original Australian vitalism. The influence of Marx's *1844 Manuscripts* is also clear. To release 'man's essential wholeness ... from the fettering forms and forces' of society, Lucius must overcome the artificial division between mental and manual labour; he must learn that only in 'the active life' and through 'the brotherhood of man' can 'the wholeness of each individual' be 'realized' (363).

In the 'patient earth' and the virtue of 'all that grappled with her and made her fruitful' (414), Lindsay names the promise of a socialist humanism—a time not only when will we be ourselves undivided but we will 'learn to rejoice in the earth and use its gifts aright' (5). This vision of a transformed ecology supplies the utopian horizon of Lindsay's literary project. It derives its terms from Lindsay's pre-Marxist vitalism and from Marx's early research into the 'metabolism' between nature and man, from Blake's prophetic books and the Goethean *Naturphilosophie* Lindsay learned from his friend, the physicist and philosopher Lancelot Law Whyte. It informs 'a general critique of science', of ideologies of economic growth, social progress, and material plenty, for to use the earth and its gifts 'aright' implies a fundamental reconsideration of our relationship with nature.[98] Lindsay had come to see 'practically all large-scale extensions of technology' as 'disastrous', listing among the consequences of a capitalist science that separates means from ends, benefits from costs, and knowledge from moral calculus: 'vast dam-projects which upset the whole ecology of regions and irritate the earth's surface into fractures and quakes, huge oil tankers that foul the seas, nuclear fission projects that beget incalculable hazards with their waste materials, insecticides, detergents and other chemicals that more or less permanently poison the soil', as well as 'vehicles and engines that send out toxic fumes'.[99]

---

[98] Jack Lindsay, *Blast-Power and Ballistics: Concepts of Force and Energy in the Ancient World* (London: Frederick Muller, 1974), p.13.

[99] Lindsay, 'The Fullness of Life', p.226. Lindsay's 'green' socialism of the 1960s and 1970s corrects a conventional, mid-century socialist belief in 'the infinite possibilities of man's mastery over nature', as

'Remember always that in yourself ... which is one with Nature and is truly human'. These words, uttered by a 'wandering Cynic, devoted to poverty', carry the novel's endorsement, but not so the choice the Cynic then offers, 'Between the way of Nature that brings us peace and brotherhood, and the way of Greed that leads us into the injustices of the Law and the defilements of the bloody Amphitheatre. That puts our neck into the Noose of the State and slowly strangles us all' (409–10). The Cynic frames as absolute the choice between necessity and freedom, expediency and moral imperative. Lucius, however, understands that 'as things were, it was impossible to get outside the net of buying and selling' (414), outside the place of complicity and compromised choice, unless by doing so one withdraw from society and from the possibility of changing it altogether. In *The New Reasoner*, Lindsay had warned of the dangers of isolating 'oneself in some cranky self-righteousness', reacting to the strain and stain of historical implication by cultivating one's own personal purity in defiance of the world. Lindsay's late-career intellectual autobiography, 'The Fullness of Life', responds to the events of 1956 in similar terms: 'The complexity of the moral problem, its endless casuistical contradictions, seemed insoluble. But there it was, inescapable. I could only contract out of it by contracting out of life altogether'.[100] But 'how' then, the novel asks, to 'go on living in such a world', 'how come to terms with the powers that ruled it, how ever find ... peace in its snares?' (361) Lindsay's answer to the dilemma is an appeal to the utopian imagination.

Lucius affirms that 'a man could be aware all the time how far he was being drawn in, he could fight ... against being drawn in', *and* 'he could keep before himself all the while a different set of values' (414). It matters for Lindsay that this uneasy equipoise between necessity and desire plays out in the present continuous tense. As he and Thompson both argued in *The New Reasoner*, in the quarrel between means and ends, realism and utopianism, the exercise of moral choice could not be postponed for some future time. For Thompson, though 'the transition to socialism' may be 'a necessary precondition for building a desirable and rational society', '*choices can and must be made along the way*'. To sustain a culture of democratic decision-making, socialism must vindicate 'the right of the moral imagination to project an ideal to which it is legitimate to aspire; and the right of the reason' to adjudicate 'aims and ends' as well as means, to ask both 'Why?' and 'How?'[101] Lindsay hailed what he saw as a renewal of Leninist traditions within the Soviet and international communist movement, noting signs of movement

---

hymned in Lindsay's historical novel of Giordano Bruno, *Adam of a New World* (London: Nicholson & Watson, 1936), p.356. By 1974, Lindsay had come to frame the problem as follows: nothing would be solved by simply scrapping 'science and technology as they have developed to date'; 'we must somehow achieve a new vital synthesis of man and nature', 'a radically new approach' that can liberate 'science and technology ... from the old obsessions with blast-power'. Lindsay, *Blast-Power and Ballistics*, p.406.

[100] Lindsay, 'Socialism and Humanism', p.96; Lindsay, 'The Fullness of Life', p.210.
[101] E.P. Thompson, 'Agency and Choice I: A Reply to Criticism', *The New Reasoner*, no.5 (1958): p.91.

'towards decentralisation and elementary democracy at lower levels', including 'the raising of the issue of workers' councils'.[102] But in stating his faith in the active life, Lindsay, like Thompson, doubled down on the pain of participation, how for those who pledge their lives to 'the gigantic task of creating an unalienated society of socialist freedoms' there can be no preliminary clearing up of problems 'before they accept the struggle'.

> To accept the struggle in all its complications, imperfections, confusions, and harshnesses must be the first and steadfast decision. After that one can proceed to do the best one can do to direct things along the most effective and humanly valid lines; and in the process one will make one's own mistakes as well as the others.[103]

Lucius accepts this awkward station. The novel adopts as its motto a line spoken first by the Pisonian conspirator, Flavius Scaevinus: 'Consciousness set against the grain of events, not running in accord with them' (251); it names at once the pain of implication—'the suffering mind' resolved to run 'against the grain of things, continually jarred, hurt, torn' (436)—and the insistence on an alternative.

## V. The Artist as Revolutionary

Embedded in Lindsay's propitiation of the 'encircling year' and the earth 'eternally reborn' (216) through labour and ritual practice is an aesthetic, by turns orthodox and suitably eclectic. It leans on the idea of revolutionary romanticism codified by Gorky and Zhdanov at the 1934 Soviet Writers Congress as one of the core components of the then new socialist realism: a faithful depiction 'of the most stern and sober practical work' in the context of 'magnificent future prospects' (Zhdanov); the representation of 'life' infused with a vision of 'mankind, united into a single family' and a world transformed by its labour (Gorky).[104] In the course of canvassing for a British socialist realism in the early 1950s, Lindsay had put his own spin on this elision of present and future tense when he argued that the novel's new attention 'to productive activity as the core of the life-process of man' must cast into sharp relief the 'crushing destructive effect' of alienation on people's ability to live at full capacity or fully express what Marx had called their 'species being'. What Lindsay calls 'the transformative role of literature' is then its ability to name the desirability and project the possibility of *dis*-alienation. As a token of what this might look like, Lindsay calls on socialist realism to encode 'a new

---

[102] Lindsay, 'Socialism and Humanism', p.100.
[103] Lindsay, 'The Fullness of Life', pp.240–240a.
[104] Andrei Zhdanov, 'Soviet Literature—Richest in Ideas, Most Advanced Literature' and Maxim Gorky, 'Soviet Literature', in Bukharin et al., *Problems of Soviet Literature*, p.22 and pp.65–6.

attitude to nature', a 'new lyrical sense of unity with nature ... a kind of emotional symbolism, free from all mysticism, which subtly realizes man's place on earth'.[105]

A sequence in Lindsay's 1957 historical novel, *The Great Oak*, gives an idea of what this 'new attitude to nature' might look like. One of the defeated rebels of the 1549 Norfolk Rising flees the battlefield at Dussindale, pushing his way through a thicket on the edge of a nearby wood to escape the massacre of his comrades. The tangle of brambles forces him down onto his hands and knees. As he squeezes through a 'passage-arch formed by suckers that had taken new root',

> he felt the whole noise and panic of the battle die away behind. There was no defeat. As though he had gone down into the earth, in a death and birth, and was at last himself, secure, knowing what he knew, knowing what a man need know. As though the past were the confused throes issuing only in this moment which gave them meaning and yet looked entirely to the future.

The struggle will continue, he understands, a continued 'grasping at a shadowy earth which yet was all things'—bodies 'in love and in labour, our solitude and our commonwealth'. Emerging from the wood, Ned starts walking 'arm in arm' with another escapee. 'And as they went, the earth opened up before them.' Night has fallen, and the path they follow rises up out of the dark to meet them, as though 'it were their quiet and resolute going which held the earth secure under their feet and opened up a way through the darkness.'[106] Through this densely symbolic sequence, Lindsay figures 'the patient earth' protecting her children and restoring their strength; patient because long-suffering, but patient also as an index of the 'not yet', a claim that nature awaits completion in a world without alienation and exploitation.[107]

In a lecture delivered to the Communist Party Historians' Group in January 1959, Lindsay identified this utopian strain as a necessary constituent of the novel. Postulating a variable combination of picaresque, romance, and pastoral elements, Lindsay explained his theory as follows:

> The picaresque is the critical and realistic attitude turned on to existent society, accepting the necessity of implication, yet exposing the discordant basis of that society, the divisive form of money. The romance sustains the heroic theme and lifts the picaresque from mere muck-raking, insists on the need for a different way

---

[105] Jack Lindsay, 'Aspects and Problems of Socialist Realism in Literature', in *Essays on Socialist Realism and the British Cultural Tradition* (London: Arena, n.d. [1953]), pp.76–7.

[106] Lindsay, *The Great Oak*, pp.300–1.

[107] In *The Principle of Hope* [written 1938–45, published 1954], Ernst Bloch elaborated on his concept of the '*Noch-Nicht*' and the politics of prefiguration; he did so in service to a socialist humanism whose romance of 'a right world' and of a nature in balance bears comparison with Lindsay's. Cf. Bloch, *The Principle of Hope*, translated by Neville Plaice, Steven Plaice, and Paul Knight (Cambridge, MA: MIT Press, 1986), Vol.3, pp.1375–6.

of life, and lays stress on struggle. The pastoral completes by giving an ultimate direction, an ultimate criterion to the critical faculty, by holding fast to the belief that men can live without the divisive forces that dominate actuality.[108]

Across the long history of the modern novel, the pastoral has not always been equally prominent, Lindsay concedes, but 'however confused and continually submerged', it is this that provides the 'imagery and ideas' that look 'beyond all class limitations to a free, equal and brotherly society'. Without it, 'the leaven is missing', the future foreclosed.[109] For Lindsay, the novel's 'triadic basis' captures the world it narrates as an integrated social totality in which inequalities of power, forces of exploitation, division and dissent play out against a horizon of their ultimate transformation.

In Lindsay's hands, the novel becomes no longer a symbolic meditation on the political emancipation of the privileged individual but a form of cultural production that has as its object the problem of community; specifically, it associates with pastoral the semantic potential of primitive religion as the symbolic enactment, displaced truth, and utopian anticipation of the collective agency of the people. As the revolutionary protagonist in *The Barriers Are Down* (1945) explains, the peasants 'had their dreams of unity, of a changed world, as much as he had—in fact their dreams were more firmly rooted and purposive than his. The difficulty [was] to learn their idiom', to read their symbols of accomplished collectivity in the 'rituals of sowing and harvest' 'embedded deep in the productive life of the country'.[110] In this, Lindsay anticipates the move Fredric Jameson will make in *The Political Unconscious* (1981), when he recruits Northrop Frye and Emile Durkheim to serve as signposts to the reparative hermeneutic that would shadow the work of ideology critique. It is by way of Frye's theory of romance and of Durkheim's sociology of religion that Jameson locates the operation of utopian desire. And it is for the sake of utopian thinking that Lindsay himself looks back, as Frye and Durkheim had themselves both done, to the classical anthropology of the Cambridge Ritualists, chief among them Jane Harrison. As Lindsay many times acknowledged, Harrison's neo-romantic conviction that the origins of art lay in ritual praxis helped prepare for the mid-century Left a labour theory of culture, one that privileged function over form and collective wish fulfilment over private pleasure.[111]

---

[108] Jack Lindsay, 'The Nature of the Historical Novel', *Our History*, no.13 (1959): p.2.
[109] Lindsay, 'The Historical Novel', pp.9–10.
[110] Jack Lindsay, *The Barriers Are Down: A Tale of the Collapse of a Civilisation* (London: Victor Gollancz, 1945), p.390. To learn their idiom: I hear in this the historiographical challenge later theorized by the British Marxist historians, as when Christopher Hill explained the need to transcode the language of the Civil War's 'lunatic fringe' and E.P. Thompson the need to pause with even the 'deluded follower of Joanna Southcott'.
[111] 'I feel that I owe to her, far more than to anyone else, such understanding as I have ever gained into the nature of culture.' Jack Lindsay, 'Scholarly and Kindly', review of *Jane Ellen Harrison: A Portrait from Letters* by Jessie Stewart, *Daily Worker*, 13 August 1959: p.2. Lindsay first read Harrison as an undergraduate in Australia; returning to her work twenty years later, while working on his first *Short*

What Lindsay calls the 'pastoral element' in his theory of the novel parallels his thinking on the poetic symbol. The groundwork for this theory lies in the manuscripts of 'The Starfish Road', worked at over two decades from the mid-1940s to the mid-1960s, and though never published, memorialized in a long essay on Edith Sitwell who was this work's one devoted reader. 'The Starfish Road' takes its title from a poem by Tristan Tzara, recounting a morning walk he took upon a beach in the Basque country in 1936 after a storm had washed ashore a galaxy of sea stars. Treading his way carefully through the casualties of the night, the poet reflects on the recent murder of Garcia Lorca and on the wider war in Spain, and he resolves to

> make the road of starfish penetrate
> deep into life
> as countless as the sand
> and the sea's joy
> and make it hold the sun
> within the breast
> where shines tomorrow's man[112]

Lindsay hails this resolution as the model of a committed poetry that acknowledges 'the omnipresent and immeasurable violence of the life that surrounds us today' and yet still comes down on 'the vanguard side of life'.[113]

For Lindsay, 'The Starfish Road' exemplifies and names a tradition of radical poetics reaching forward from the sixteenth century to the present day. Lindsay first discovers his poet hero in the anonymous sixteenth-century authors of the Tom o' Bedlam ballads, in whose poetry of derangement he finds 'the hint of a sanity and harmony, a fuller rationality, which lies the other side of the existing set-up—which looks to different centres of living, in which the ruling logic is transcended by a deeper grasp of truth and its processes and the false-face [of existing social relations] is torn away'. The early-modern fascination with 'states of mind, which at first glance seem to express the alienating process in its worst triumph' but which 'are retorted back on the disintegrative world, and are made to yield the clues of a higher sanity and union, a revolutionary vision', anticipates romanticism, as it then anticipates Baudelaire, Lautréamont and Rimbaud, Verhaeren and Whitman, Apollinaire, Tzara and Dada, Gorky and Mayakovsky, Aragon and

---

*History of Culture*, Lindsay found 'passage after passage' come 'so home to my business and bosom that it seemed whatever had been sound in my wanderings was derived from them, and whatever had been unsound was the result of failing to follow their signposts.' Jack Lindsay, *A Short History of Culture* (London: Victor Gollancz, 1939), p.12.

[112] Tristan Tzara, 'On the Starfish Road. To Frederico Garcia Lorca', translated by Lindsay in *Meetings with Poets*, pp.227–31.

[113] Lindsay, *Meetings with Poets*, p.222.

Eluard, Edgell Rickword and Edith Sitwell.[114] But this is also, and bravely, a literary history from below, as Lindsay follows Tom's descendants in popular ballad and antinomian religion, through such eighteenth-century visionaries as Smart and Blake, to Joanna Southcott and the visionary excess of the Spasmodic and Chartist poets. Taken together, they comprise a symbolist tradition defined not by formal concerns but by radical politics. As such and for its time, 'The Starfish Road' represents a remarkable revaluation of terms, a counterblast to the New Critical fetish of the autotelic lyric and to conventional Cold War declensions of modernism's romantic and symbolist roots.[115]

In *Thunder Underground*, Lucius is a poet. In Rome he has come into contact with a variety of possible artforms, from the praise poetry of Nero and the coded coterie-verse of Lucan to the biting epigrams of Martial; but it is from the popular and artisanal arts of a dancer (234–7), an architect (259–60), and a sculptor (266) that he gains 'the passing intuitions of a new poetry' (260), one which would 'grasp the elusive point in experience where the accepted terms of the world broke down and a quite new pattern of relationships began tentatively assembling. Feeling out like the tendrils of an unknown plant, with colours for which there were as yet no words' (236). From art such as theirs, 'how could anyone fail to believe that human life might be changed, changed from within with lucid and universal harmonies?' (266) Lucius is Lindsay's type of the revolutionary poet whose lines hold in mind the images of alienation and of utopia. Lindsay's 'pastoral' and 'symbol' come together as one in a picture of 'the patient earth into which all forms were compacted, from which they broke loose and to which they returned', an image of 'Circular movements swung into spirals, broken, reforming, climbing again, changing, unchanging', and through it all 'the Face of Man looking out … itself broken and renewed, assuming a radiance that made it supreme' (363).

Amid a cast of famous historical figures, Lucius is the one fictional character. His name, however, is real: Martial addresses a poem to a Lucius whose verses sang his native Spain.[116] Although posterity preserves none of his poems, the novel imagines the circumstances of their composition, supplying the silence of the historical record with the story of a young Spanish poet who went to Rome and thence returned 'to work the stony fields and hills', resolved that were he to write 'any poems, the earth of [his] birth would underlie them all' (437). These poems are unwritten at the novel's end but promissory of the 'new poetry' that is the criterion

---

[114] Jack Lindsay, 'The Starfish Road', unpublished typescript, NLA, 7168, Box 145, Self 21, p.15.

[115] Cf. Charles Feidelson, *Symbolism and American Literature* (Chicago: University of Chicago Press, 1953). Lindsay's closest analogue might be Frank Kermode's dissident classic, *Romantic Image* (1957), insofar as Kermode also writes against the tyranny of two complementary beliefs: 'in the Image as a radiant truth out of space and time, and in the necessary isolation or estrangement of men who can perceive it'. Kermode calls instead for a 'liberation of Milton', a return to the long poem and a reconciliation of the symbol with 'the ordinary syntax of the daily life of action'. Kermode, *Romantic Image* (London: Routledge and Kegan Paul, 1957), p.2; pp.165–6.

[116] Martial, *Epigrams*, Book IV, poem 55.

of judgement in 'The Starfish Road'. In 1968, and with that work finally abandoned, Lindsay felt the need to defend his 'faith in poetry': 'In the darkest night of society and the spirit, if one believes in poetry, one believes also in the possibility and inevitability of renewal, in the revolt of the young, in the miraculous gift of sight for the nation of the blind, in the return of the consuming hunger for wholeness.'[117] That same year, in a lecture in New York, E.P. Thompson had felt likewise compelled to defend the poet's revolutionary vocation, quoting lines from the US communist poet Tom McGrath, first published in *The New Reasoner*:

> Though every battle, every augury,
> Argue defeat, and if defeat itself
> Bring all the darkness level with our eyes—
> It is the poem provides the proper charm
> Spelling resistance and the living will,
> To bring to dance a stony field of fact
> And set against terror exile or despair
> The rituals of our humanity.[118]

For McGrath, as for Thompson and Lindsay, this is 'the proper aura for the poem': 'the charm which the potential has'.[119]

By the second half of the 1960s, many of Lindsay's and Thompson's core tenets, cornerstones of their mid-century communism, had been called into question. The 'people's history' of the Old and first New Left was being assailed in articles by Perry Anderson and Tom Nairn that framed Britain in a critical, comparative perspective and held its 'peculiarities'—the 'components' of its national culture, the trajectory of its national story—to blame for 'the present crisis'.[120] For the intellectuals of this second New Left, whose formative experience was not the 'popular élan' of the anti-fascist struggle and the 'afterglow' of the People's War but rather the national-imperial chauvinism of British culture in the 1950s, their relationship to 'nationalism of whatever stripe was one of hostility rather than harmony'.[121] The whole framework of ideological struggle mapped out by Georgi Dimitrov in 1935—appealing to the legitimate 'national sentiments' of the people, linking up 'the present struggle with the people's revolutionary traditions and past', finding 'national forms' and local idioms for the insights of international socialism—was anathema. Their histories would be theoretical, totalizing 'theses' on the structural

---

[117] Lindsay, *Meetings with Poets*, p.235.

[118] Tom McGrath, 'Against the False Magicians', *The New Reasoner*, no.1 (1957): p.60.

[119] E.P. Thompson, 'Disenchantment or Default: A Lay Sermon' [1968], in *The Romantics: England in a Revolutionary Age* (New York: New Press, 1997), p.73.

[120] The Nairn-Anderson theses were first elaborated in a series of essays in *New Left Review*: these included Anderson's 'Origins of the Present Crisis' (1964), 'Socialism and Pseudo-Empiricism' (1966), 'Components of the National Culture' (1968), and Nairn's 'The English Working Class' (1964).

[121] Perry Anderson, *Arguments within English Marxism* (London: New Left Books, 1980), pp.47–9.

composition and dominant tendencies of British society rather than sympathetic reconstructions of individual and collective agency and aspiration. Instead of finding points of positive comparison with other countries' radical traditions, they insisted on 'the differential formation and development of British capitalist society' and the consequent anomalies and pathologies of its socialist tradition.[122] In particular, the failure of Britain's mid-century Left to either mobilize as a revolutionary mass party or generate a capable critical theory required, they now argued, the importation of Marxisms from those movements that had.

Ultimately, however, even the demystifying insights of mid-century French and Italian communism would come to seem insufficient for the tasks at hand. By the mid-1970s, Anderson was framing the whole Western Marxist tradition as an aberration of historical materialism, a falling away from its claim to be a 'universal science—no more amenable to merely national or continental ascriptions than any other objective cognition of reality'.[123] Characterized by its *'lack of internationalism'*, Western Marxism shared the history and the hallmarks ('narrowing of focus', 'generalized parochialism and blankness towards extra-national bodies of thought') of the mid-century national turn: concludes Anderson, 'The failure of the socialist revolution outside Russia, cause and consequence of its corruption inside Russia, is the common background to the entire theoretical tradition of this period.'[124] There were signs, however, that 'the prolonged, winding detour of Western Marxism' from its properly universal horizons of theory and internationalist revolutionary praxis had at last run its course. With its 'senior theorists' now dead or lapsing into 'repetition or exhaustion', Anderson called for a return to the 'classical Marxism' of an earlier generation, a present reconnection with the legacy of Lenin and Luxemburg and above all, of Trotsky, 'the dimensions of [whose] internationalism overtop any before or since'.[125] It was a call to move on from the mid-century by recovering what Stalinism and socialism in one country had stalled.

A further challenge, this time to the very concept of the human in whose name the moral critique of capitalism and the socialist defence of popular agency and initiative had been framed, was developing both in the rarefied worlds of French philosophy and psychoanalysis and on the anticolonial frontline, where figures like Franz Fanon drove home the hypocrisy of the Western discourse of 'Man'. *Thunder Underground* does not respond to the force of these critiques; only in his eighties would Lindsay again engage directly, publishing *The Crisis in Marxism* (1981) to counter the anti-humanist turn of Althusser and Lacan, and to restate his faith in alienation as Marxism's central problematic. By then he had come to know the work of Gramsci and found in his conception of anti-hegemonic struggle

---

[122] Perry Anderson, 'Origins of the Present Crisis', *New Left Review*, no.23 (1964): p.28.
[123] Anderson, *Considerations*, p.94.
[124] Anderson, *Considerations*, pp.68–9; p.94.
[125] Anderson, *Considerations*, pp.102–3; Anderson, *Arguments within English Marxism*, p.156.

a theory of revolutionary cultural work compatible with his own understanding of the role poets and novelists should play in figuring alienation and prefiguring its end.[126]

True to its first-century social world as well as to its moment of inscription in the late 1950s and early '60s, *Thunder Underground* makes no appeal, in closing, to what Gramsci had called the 'war of manoeuvre'; the novel states no faith in the intentions of history or the rising tides of revolution, but rather sends its protagonist 'home', resolved to model in his conduct and in his art the disalienated world he desires. Lucius will run his farm with free labour, working the land himself and treating every person as an equal. His family's 'frenzy ... for worldly security and success, for conformity, for money and power over others' he will wear down with the same capacity for 'endurance', the same ability 'to hang on and resist', he has learned from 'the common people' (441). His poetry, when it comes, will share a quality he first encountered in Martial—a national-popular inflection he identifies as 'Spanish', a simplicity and 'earth-rooted[ness]' that counters cynicism and disillusionment with the conviction that it is 'possible, after all, to live among men' (414).

What the novel cannot imagine, and does not project, is the readership for Lucius' 'new poetry' (260), the social movement that might be moved by its 'tendrils of intuition' (236), the dissident formation ready to share its belief that 'human life' can be 'changed from within with lucid and universal harmonies' (266). For Lindsay, as for others of the Old and first New Left, socialist humanism named the attempt to match the 'proper aura' of this poetry with what Thompson had called 'the living, indomitable agents of that potential'.[127] In the process, they worked to rehabilitate the principle of hope, reclaiming the category of utopia from the strictures of scientific Marxism and moving the education of desire to the centre of the socialist project. They stressed that the whole point of 'utopianism' was 'political action', that its 'value' lay 'not in raising banners in the wilderness, but in confronting people with an image of their own potential life, in summoning up their aspirations so that they challenge the old forms of life and in influencing such social choices as there are in the direction that is desired'. Romance and realism, desire and necessity, must learn to 'quarrel in a constructive way in the heart of the same movement', rather than splitting off into 'rival contingents'.[128] It was this belief that inspired the premature revisionism within the post-war Communist Party and that after 1956 brought dissident communists and left socialists together in reasserting the moral agency and imagination of 'real men and women' against the status quo.

---

[126] On Lindsay's reading of Gramsci, see Harker, 'Jack Lindsay's Alienation', pp.94–6.
[127] E.P. Thompson, 'An Open Letter to Leszek Kolakowski', in *The Poverty of Theory and other Essays* (New York: Monthly Review Press, 1978), p.304.
[128] Thompson, 'Commitment in Politics', p.55.

Transposed into the register of history, however, the narrative was more often one of rival contingents and of a poetry of the revolution out of step with its people. *The Making of the English Working Class* (1963), for example, narrated a missed connection between the radical political culture of the emergent working class and the moral voice of the period's poets and visionaries. 'In the failure of these two traditions to come to a point of junction, something was lost. How much we cannot be sure, for we are among the losers.'[129] It was the same refrain in Thompson's 1976 'Postscript' to *William Morris: Romantic to Revolutionary* (1955), as he told the story of an 'orthodox Marxism' that 'turned its back upon a juncture' with Morris, whose ideas 'it neglected to its own peril and subsequent disgrace'. 'Morris's "conversion" to Marxism offered a juncture which Marxism failed to reciprocate'; this failure represents for us 'a *continuing* failure', a continuing impoverishment of 'the imaginative utopian faculties'.[130] Christopher Hill's *The World Turned Upside Down* (1972) narrated another near miss—how, during the English Civil War the radical 'revolt within the Revolution' missed its moment of purchase and the 'poetic insights' of those who 'foresaw and worked for—not our modern world, but something far nobler, something yet to be achieved—the upside down world' 'disappeared, leaving hardly a trace'.[131] Hill with his ranting tradition, Thompson with his romantics, Lindsay with his starfish road of revolutionary poets: the historians and historical novelists of the Old and first New Left developed a myth of what the communist historian A.L. Morton, writing of William Blake, called the 'Everlasting Gospel', a repository of radical symbolism and utopian desire to attend in passing victory and long defeat the revolution which 'is always beginning and never ends'.[132]

It was the misfortune of Lindsay's last historical novel to reproduce this narrative of the missed conjuncture, its delayed publication in 1965 a testament to the frequent asynchrony of social movement insurgency and emancipatory visions. The space *Thunder Underground* had hoped to enter was by then closed to it, that point of contact and conversation between different generations and critical formations—between a dissident communist impulse still in some way loyal to the Soviet project, the young men and women who massed on the march to Aldermaston and flocked to the Left Clubs and London's Partisan café, and the wider labour movement. This is a note in the minor key on which to close a history of the mid-century historical novel, but a note that should sound alongside the story told in chapter two of the genre's role as incubator for habits of historical attention that found their full vocation in the practice of history from below and in the historical

---

[129] Thompson, *The Making of the English Working Class*, p.832.

[130] E.P. Thompson, *William Morris: Romantic to Revolutionary* (London: Merlin, 1976), p.779; p.786; p.792.

[131] Hill, *The World Turned Upside Down*, p.11; p.310–11; p.306.

[132] A.L. Morton, *The Everlasting Gospel: A Study in the Sources of William Blake* (London: Lawrence & Wishart, 1958); Hill, *The World Turned Upside Down*, p.310.

consciousness of the new world novel. There, the communist historical novel was read as a vanishing mediator in the making of radical social history and magical realism; here, I have pressed pause at one of the moments of its disappearance; my epilogue will look to the way Raymond Williams in the 1980s tried to reverse the vanishing of mid-century socialist culture, reviving a Popular Front historical novel by Gwyn Thomas to guide him in writing his own late-career trilogy, *People of the Black Mountains*. But the last word on Lindsay should be given to one of his friends and fellow activists in the 1950s 'Battle for Realism', the young art critic and later novelist of peasant labour and poet of the patient earth, John Berger. On the first day of the New Year, 1958, Berger wrote to Lindsay fresh from reading his 'Socialism and Humanism' essay in *The New Reasoner*: 'I admire it and argue with it so much that I had to just write you these few lines to say so. With such a vision we become invincible. Thank you.'[133]

---

[133] John Berger to Jack Lindsay, 1 January 1958, NLA, 7168, Box 30, Folder 167.

# Epilogue
## Parables of Survival

In one of his last public lectures before his death in 1988, Raymond Williams instructed his audience to revisit the mid-century.[1] Left intellectuals, he argued, should 'search out and counterpose an alternative tradition' to the canon of modern literature.[2] He had in his sights the modernism that had been canonized in the Anglo-American academy, disseminated as cultural diplomacy in the cultural Cold War, and vernacularized, as he saw it, in capitalist advertising and popular entertainment. It was a modernism that had become stripped of its original dissenting dynamism, 'stabilized' as a hostile, '"modernist" and "postmodernist" establishment'.[3] Williams was troubled, moreover, by how this modernism, its norms and values codified in opposition to the realist aesthetics of the socialist Second World, had become domesticated in the culture of the New Left, shaping its definitions of radical art and responsible theory. He objected to what he called modernism's 'extension' across an 'undifferentiated twentieth century' and the transposition of its particular (if in many places continuing) articulation of metropolitan alienation into 'what is beyond question and for all time the "modern absolute", the defined universality of a human condition which is effectively permanent'.[4] In order to exit 'the long and bitter impasse of a once liberating Modernism' and discover 'a present beyond "the modern"'—a present of possibility, a present in play—Williams urged his listeners to seek out inspiration among the 'neglected works left in the wide margin of the century'.[5]

Williams had begun mining the mid-century margins himself. In 1986, he oversaw the reissue of Gwyn Thomas's historical novel *All Things Betray Thee* (1949). In his introduction, Williams suggested placing it 'within the broader course of Welsh writing from the 1930s', looking to the novel's Welshness to explain its difference 'from the ordinary shape of a historical novel' and from 'that dominant

---

[1] Williams, 'When Was Modernism?' [1987], in *Politics of Modernism*, pp.31–5. The script of this famous lecture was for a long time known only through a short composite text, compiled by Fred Inglis from his own notes and from Williams' speaking notes. Philip O'Brien has since edited a transcription of the full recorded lecture, in Raymond Williams, *Culture and Politics: Class, Writing, Socialism* (London: Verso, 2022), pp.203–20. I will refer, however, to the well-known short form of this text and the essays and lectures that accompany it in *The Politics of Modernism*.
[2] Williams, 'When Was Modernism?', p.35.
[3] Raymond Williams, 'Culture and Technology' [1983], in *Politics of Modernism*, p.130
[4] Raymond Williams, 'Metropolitan Perceptions and the Emergence of Modernism' [1985], in *Politics of Modernism*, p.38.
[5] Williams, 'Culture and Technology', p.139; 'Metropolitan Perceptions', p.39; 'When Was Modernism?', p.35.

English pressure, now crude, now subtle', to reserve literature for what is 'said to be its true deep concern with private lives and private feelings'.[6] But Williams could as easily and more correctly have placed Thomas's novel in the context of British and international communism. Certainly, this was its contemporary reception. In 1950, Howard Fast hailed *All Things Betray Thee* as 'one of the best achievements in socialist realism that we know in modern Western literature'.[7] Fast was a leading US communist writer with a massive global reach; in the 1950s he could plausibly boast of being 'the most widely read author of this century'.[8] He was also a historical novelist and, for Thomas, a friend. In November 1948, having just finished Fast's tale of the Maccabean Revolt, *My Glorious Brothers*, Thomas wrote to share his sense of common purpose with the Jewish-American author. 'We need to reinvigorate the wonderful creative legends of the people that first made socialism, the legends of irreducible valour, humanity and friendliness.' 'Our struggle gains wings and a splendid face as artists sing out the hymns of the common folk in the torment of their growth.'[9] Fast was a hero for Thomas, and his fiction an inspiration in finishing *All Things Betray Thee*. For it is from his own novel that Thomas took this metaphor of socialist struggle as a music in the making.

Thirty years later, this metaphor lies at the heart of Raymond Williams' response. *All Things Betray Thee* may be 'epic ... in outline', Williams explains in his introduction, but 'the substance is consciously different'.[10] Its fictional history of the 1831 Merthyr Rising does not end when the rebellion ends; instead, it renders 'the full experience of struggle: not only its causes and its courage, but its defeats and the slow music of is renewal'.[11] That 'slow music' is key. The novel's protagonist is in hiding when he learns of the workers' foiled resistance, the murder and capture of their leaders. But the innkeeper who brings him the news frames this defeat in terms that he, a travelling harpist, will understand: the politics of struggle as a stating of facts, a speaking that becomes a singing.

> We state them now softly, now loudly. The next time it will be softly for our best voices will have ceased to speak. The silence and the softness will ripen. The lost blood will be made again. The chorus will shuffle out of its filthy aching corners and return. The world is full of voices, harpist, practicing for the great anthem, but

---

[6] Raymond Williams, 'Introduction', to Gwyn Thomas, *All Things Betray Thee* [1949] (London: Lawrence & Wishart, 1986), pp. iv–v.
[7] Howard Fast, *Literature and Reality* (New York: International Publishers, 1950), p.51.
[8] Howard Fast, interviewed by Martin Agronsky on NBC television, 13 October 1957. Rossen Djagalov takes this comment, recorded in Fast's FBI file, for the title of his article on Fast and mid-century Left literary culture, '"I don't boast about it, but I'm the most widely read author of this century"', pp.40–55.
[9] Gwyn Thomas to Howard Fast, 6 November 1948; cited in Victor Golightly, '"We who speak for the workers:" The Correspondence of Gwyn Thomas and Howard Fast', *Welsh Writing in English* 6 (2000): p.71.
[10] Williams, 'Introduction', p. v.
[11] Williams, 'Introduction', p. x.

hardly ever heard. We've been privileged. We've had our ears full of the singing. Silence will never be absolute for us again.[12]

The novel ends with Alan Hugh Leigh walking away from this scene of defeat, 'full of a strong, ripening, unanswerable bitterness, [and] feeling in [his] fingers the promise of a new enormous music'.[13] Williams glosses the line: 'The music can be felt in the fingers because the singing has been heard and silenced but also remembered; it is there to be practiced and developed for the next time'. Pointing to a future beyond its frame, *All Things Betray Thee* undoes the terms of its title, for 'what comes through' is not betrayal but the 'promise of that music'. Beyond victory and defeat there is 'the certainty of the composition: not only the remaking of the lost blood, but the memory of voices which is also a finding of voices: the vast struggle out of silence into a chorus which is at once being practiced and composed'.[14]

For Williams, this musical conceit lifts Thomas's novel from the run of the generic mill, what he calls 'period fictions', novels that convey the past 'enclosed in its time' without meaningful connection to the present. At best, the 'period novel' lends itself to a simple contrast—'what it was like yesterday; not like today'—at worst, it offers the past as 'an object—often colourful—of spectacle'.[15] *All Things Betray Thee* escapes the corral of period fiction because the events it relays, 'though vividly described, are in effect themes for what is the real movement of the novel: a pattern, a composition of voices, in which what is being said is both of and beyond its time'.[16] The novel's 'immediate location is [1831], but the connection is beyond it: to 1986 if we can hear it'. Thomas's novel is a bridge between the past and the future, 'but in the intricacy of its own movement it is always primarily of the present: that endlessly repeated present in which the issues and the choices are personally active'.[17] With these references to practice and performance, to movement and connection both within and beyond the novel, Williams offers *All Things Betray Thee* as an antidote to the forms of cultural and political fixity he saw as defining his late-century moment. This sense of immobility was not limited to the nostalgia novel or to the emerging metafictional forms of postmodernism, nor was the legacy of a 'once liberating modernism' solely to blame for the culture of disconnection and detachment, of social disengagement, Williams saw as widespread. The impasse extended to modes of cultural production closer to home, to the practice of realism and radical social history.

[12] Gwyn Thomas, *All Things Betray Thee* (London: Lawrence & Wishart, 1986), p.311.
[13] Thomas, *All Things Betray Thee*, p.318.
[14] Williams, 'Introduction', pp. viii–ix.
[15] Raymond Williams, 'Working-Class, Proletarian, Socialist: Problems in Some Welsh Novels' [1982], in *Who Speaks for Wales? Nation, Culture, Identity*, edited by Daniel Williams (Cardiff: University of Wales Press, 2003), pp.156–7.
[16] Williams, 'Introduction', p. iv.
[17] Williams, 'Introduction', p. viii.

By the late 1970s, Williams had grown critical of what he saw as a tendency in Left social history to rest content with the rescue of history's losers and lost causes, a tendency to narrate 'the making, the struggles, the defeats of a class', without then framing those defeats 'as springboards for new struggles or as lessons for final victory'.[18] He worried that the mid-century repossession of the radical-popular past had become a kind of substitute for political action in the present. 'For there is a sense in which the reproduction of struggle is not primarily, whatever may be claimed, a production of struggle.'[19] These terms—'reproduction' and 'production'—map onto the contrast in Williams' long-standing defence of realism between what he called its 'indicative' and 'subjunctive' modes. For there will always be 'social realities that cry out' for realism's 'serious detailed recording and diagnostic attention', its 'challenging selection of the crises, the contradictions, the unexplored dark areas' of the social: 'our central commitment ought always to be to those areas of hitherto silenced or fragmented or positively misrepresented experience.'[20] This is what realism in its 'indicative' mode can do. But what if 'the mere reproduction of an existing reality' becomes 'a passivity, even an acceptance of the fixed and immobile?'[21] Realism can indeed state powerfully 'that this is what reality is like, these were the impulses that emerged and these were the impulses that were thwarted'; it can bear witness to 'a social situation in which at one level or another all roads have been blocked'.[22] But we have then to move beyond 'the more bystanding and incidental versions of realism' towards a more dynamic mode of aesthetic and political 'production'.[23]

Williams grappled with how to take this step beyond the merely mimetic. Soviet-style socialist realism, with its infusion of labour and struggle with a vision of their ultimate reward, was no longer an option. For much of Williams' writing life, the 'magnificent future prospects' A.A. Zhdanov invoked at the 1934 Soviet Writers' Congress had seemed questionable at best.[24] But by the 1980s, it was not simply the socialist horizon that now felt in doubt. Williams wrote of a 'widespread loss of the future', 'the loss of hope; the slowly settling loss of any acceptable future'.[25] The failures of the Soviet experiment and the colonial liberation movements, the rise of the New Right and 'the terrible disintegration of what was once a labour movement': all these had worn down the power of temporal protension, depleting a sense of

---

[18] Williams, 'Working-Class, Proletarian, Socialist', p.154.
[19] Raymond Williams, 'Afterword to *Modern Tragedy*' [1979], reprinted in *Politics of Modernism*, p.104.
[20] Raymond Williams, 'Cinema and Socialism' [1985], in *Politics of Modernism*, pp.115–16; Raymond Williams, 'Theatre as a Political Forum' [1988], in *Politics of Modernism*, p.85.
[21] Williams, 'Cinema and Socialism', p.116.
[22] Raymond Williams, *Politics and Letters: Interviews with the New Left Review* (London: New Left Books, 1979), p.218.
[23] Raymond Williams, 'The Welsh Industrial Novel' [1978], in *Who Speaks for Wales?*, p.108.
[24] Zhdanov, 'Soviet Literature', p.22.
[25] Williams, 'Afterword to *Modern Tragedy*', pp.96–7.

plausible futurity.[26] The socialist project was in retreat, but figurations of catastrophe were also now encroaching on Fordism's fantasy-bribes of personal happiness, social mobility, and 'managed affluence'. Williams pointed to mass unemployment, environmental collapse, 'the millennium as apocalypse; the final crisis as nuclear holocaust'.[27] He concluded that the Left could not now rely on utopian prefiguration to educate desire and 'move [us] beyond the present paralysing sense of loss'.[28] Writers must work instead to recuperate 'the generative immediacy' of 'the true social present', that inch of existence that is always 'emergent'.[29] 'What has now to be proved ... is indeed possibility': possibility, 'not as what with luck might happen', but as 'what we can believe in enough to want, and then by active wanting, make possible'.[30] For socialist writers, 'the celebration of possibility' had become the 'most profound need'.[31]

Across the final decade of his life, Williams maintained that a literature of the Left must learn to include 'the production and the practice of possibility', and that a selective tradition of mid-century writing could show it the way.[32] He saw traces of this tendency in Brecht, especially in the proletarian 'teaching plays' of the early 1930s, and in some of the radical television drama of the 1960s. In Jim Allen's *The Big Flame* (1969), produced by Tony Garnett and directed by Ken Loach, he hailed a scenario 'which is not realist in the indicative sense of recording contemporary reality, but in the subjunctive sense of supposing a possible sequence of actions beyond it'.[33] *The Big Flame* opens with Liverpool's dockworkers out on strike in protest at the 1965 Devlin Report, with its call to modernize the ports, decasualizing dock labour with redundancies to follow. But after six weeks on the picket, the men are losing steam. It's then that the strike committee meets with an old hand, Jack Reagan, who suggests a change of strategy. Instead of the 'hit-and-run' of serial strikes for small concessions, why not 'think big': 'Let's have a workers' control now.' 'All I say is, let's give it a try; at least, let's make the attempt. Let's try and get out of this straitjacket.'[34] For five days, the workers occupy the port and run the docks themselves; although they are then evicted by subterfuge and force, they prove the possibility of democratic self-management. As Williams observes, the hypothesis has been defeated 'in terms of the local action' but not 'defeated as an idea': and when the film closes with a nod to that 'remaking of lost blood' we met

---

[26] Williams, *Politics and Letters*, pp.294–5.
[27] Raymond Williams, 'Walking Backwards into the Future' [1985], in *Resources of Hope: Culture, Democracy, Socialism*, edited by Robin Gable (London: Verso, 1989), p.282.
[28] Williams, 'Afterword to *Modern Tragedy*', p.104.
[29] Raymond Williams, *Marxism and Literature* (Oxford: Oxford University Press, 1977), pp.132–4.
[30] Raymond Williams, 'Beyond Actually Existing Socialism' [1980], in *Culture and Materialism*, p.252.
[31] Raymond Williams in conversation; in *Talking Films: The Best of* The Guardian *Film Lectures*, edited by Andrew Britton (London: Fourth Estate, 1991), p.129.
[32] Williams, 'Beyond Actually Existing Socialism', p.273.
[33] Williams, *Politics and Letters*, p.219.
[34] *The Big Flame*, directed by Ken Loach (British Broadcasting Corporation, 1969).

with in Thomas, it does so 'within a teaching perspective that the working-class must understand and learn from its defeats as well as its victories'.[35]

These are the threads that Williams combined in *People of the Black Mountains*, a planned trilogy of historical novels unfinished at his death and posthumously edited by his wife Joy and published in two volumes (1989, 1990). Raymond Williams came no stranger to the genre. His first attempt at publication had been a Popular Front historical novel, sent to Victor Gollancz in 1937 when he was sixteen and politely declined.[36] The long struggle with what became *Border Country* (1960) included a historical novel among its seven or more full drafts.[37] With *People of the Black Mountains*, Williams knew exactly what he had to do: devise a form of working-class fiction to include 'defeats and failures', but also 'the relations between these and subsequent adaptations', the 'learning from defeat', 'the actual learning of lessons, the attainment of a new consciousness by analysis of what has happened'.[38] Improving on his own past practice and the subjunctive-mode precedent of his mid-century countercanon of Brecht and Thomas, Allen and Loach, Williams moved to multiply their scenes of lesson-learning within and between generations. 'Twenty-five thousand years, a thousand generations', is the trilogy's vast chronological sweep, all told within the tightest of spatial frames.

Each volume begins with a lesson on place:

See this layered sandstone in the short mountain grass. Place your right hand on it, palm downward. See where the summer sun rises and where it stands at noon. Direct your index finger midway between them. Spread your fingers, not widely. You now hold this place in your hand.[39]

With our fingers pressed 'close on this lichened sandstone', our hand becomes a map of the Black Mountains, their ridges and rivers; we 'hold their shapes and their names' in our hand, becoming the point of contact with a history that reaches back millennia. This rock is our first introduction to the trilogy's conjugation of time and space, a place 'received and made and remade' across countless generations.[40] The novels' chronotope is no longer national. Since the 1970s, Williams had come to think 'the nation-state, in its classical European form', as 'at once too large and too small for the range of real social purposes'.[41] Too large to thicken solidarity

---

[35] Raymond Williams, 'A Lecture on Realism', *Screen* 18, no.1 (1977): p.69.
[36] Williams recalled 'Mountain Sunset' as a novel of the English Civil War in Wales, culminating in the rout of the Royalist forces at the Battle of Montgomery in 1644; *Politics and Letters*, p.30. The novel is now lost.
[37] Raymond Williams, 'Between Two Worlds', unpublished typescript dated 8 March 1955; Raymond Williams Collection, Richard Burton Archives, Swansea University; WWE/2/1/1/3/1.
[38] Williams, 'A Lecture on Realism', p.70.
[39] Raymond Williams, *People of the Black Mountains. 1: The Beginning* (London: Paladin, 1990), p.1. The prefaces recycle material from Williams' contribution to *Places: An Anthology of Britain*, edited by Ronald Blythe (Oxford: Oxford University Press, 1981), pp.215–22.
[40] Williams, *People of the Black Mountains*, pp.1–2.
[41] Raymond Williams, *Towards 2000* (Harmondsworth: Penguin, 1983), p.197.

and cohere a common purpose, too small to secede from or significantly counter the 'powerfully extending and profoundly interacting para-national political and economic system'.[42] Instead, the novels begin as Williams would have socialist theory do, in a tangibly material place, and then scale up, scale out, translate, and transpose. To this 'militant particularism' corresponds a temporal regime which radically foreshortens the braided biographical plots of the national-historical novel, their trajectories of individual hero and class collective fused in an allegory of becoming. Instead of the singular narrative arc, *People of the Black Mountains* unfolds as a series of more and less discontinuous episodes, beginning in 23,000 BCE and ending, had Williams lived to complete the trilogy, 'in the 20th century, or a bit ahead'.[43] The stories converge on, and are interwoven with, a present in which a young man called Glyn, searching for his grandfather fallen in the hills, retraces the old man's steps and the history that lies beneath them.

This episodic structure takes aim at the epic conception of the mid-century historical novel, with its tropism towards the hot chronology of crisis. Williams was the first to acknowledge that his own lived history had been one of 'moving crises', of 'victories' and 'defeats'. But he countered this eventful history with an ethos he marked as 'one of the peculiar qualities of the socialist', that these ups and downs 'can be looked at as they are: not in the brief enthusiasms or despairs of mere supporters, but in the unalterable commitment, in and through any argument or diagnosis, to the lives of the working people who continue, as real men and women, beyond either victory or defeat'.[44] However studiously the communist historical novel had reflected on the continuity of radical-popular traditions, insisting, as Thomas had done, on the 'certainty of the composition' and the succession of voices practising for the great anthem, its narratives had always gravitated towards moments of high drama. Lukács, for example, had urged the 'faithful artistic reproduction of the great collisions, the great crises and turning-points of history'.[45] He claimed that it was only in these 'big occasions', these 'crisis periods' and 'deep disturbances', that history made its presence felt, triggering the 'vast heroic, human potentialities which are always latently present in the people'.[46] But if history is indeed 'what hurts', as Fredric Jameson had just recently contended in 1981, the argument of Williams' trilogy is that it can hurt without the state of exception, without war as such and as a proxy for revolution.[47] Radical militancy and collective mobilization cannot be the Left's only narrative: survival, the process of maintaining and repairing solidarity, has also to be told, because it too, and crucially, has always happened.

---

[42] Raymond Williams, 'Wales and England' [1983], in *Who Speaks for Wales?*, p.24.
[43] Williams, *Politics and Letters*, p.302.
[44] Williams, 'Cinema and Socialism', p.116.
[45] Lukács, *The Historical Novel*, p.166.
[46] Lukács, *The Historical Novel*, p.52.
[47] Jameson, *The Political Unconscious*, p.102.

Rather than project a possible future to motivate political desire, *People of the Black Mountains* suggests that we draw our conclusions from 'the sheer duration of the struggle for alternatives; the repeated postponements of hope'.[48] 'The defeats have occurred over and over again, and what my novel is then trying to explore is simply the condition of anything surviving at all.'[49] The fact and the feat of survival is the trilogy's true theme, a statement of faith in our ability to invent, and continually to reinvent, from within the scene of survival, new idioms of the social. It is perhaps a bleak lesson to draw from the past and from our own blocked present: a rethinking of revolution as 'long, hard, contentious and untidy—its criterion of success, for as far as we can see, being a possible majority of successes over its many failures'.[50]

Williams would have us remember that 'the moment of transition to an idea of socialism' 'comes not once and for all but many times; is lost and is found again; has to be affirmed and developed, continually, if it is to stay real'.[51] *People of the Black Mountains* commits to this labour of affirmation and development, where with each new defeat it is not the pain of loss that comes to the fore but rather the assurance that despite it, and at whatever minimum, some of us have survived and so preserved the possibility of social change. It is this 'shared belief and insistence that there are practical alternatives' that 'has been, from the beginning, the sense and impulse of the long revolution.'[52]

One episode takes place some five and a half millennia before the Common Era and tells of a boy, too frail to hunt with his tribe, who conceives instead the plan to trap a wild piglet and to feed it up for food in the winter months when the hunting is lean. He is foiled, and the story ends with his failure. Had he succeeded, we are to understand, the Neolithic Revolution would have come early to the Black Mountains. As Glyn then reflects, 'What had happened, and failed, in the case of Aaron and his pig, must have happened, failing or briefly and intermittently succeeding, many hundreds of times. Two thousand years were to pass, eighty generations, before another hunter ... saw the decisive change from hunting to herding and cultivation.'[53] 'Many hundreds of times': we hear in this Williams' one 'criterion of success' in living the long revolution, the possible preponderance of victories over defeats.[54] At stake in the episode, then, is less the domestication of livestock than its drama of improvisation, and the assurance, within what Williams calls 'the endlessly repeated present', of 'subsequent adaptations'. Against the once-and-for-all revolutionary conjuncture with its providential teleology, Williams argues for a

---

[48] Williams, 'Afterword to *Modern Tragedy*', p.98.
[49] Raymond Williams in conversation with Terry Eagleton, 'The Practice of Possibility' [1987], in *Resources of Hope*, p.322.
[50] Williams, 'Beyond Actually Existing Socialism', p.272.
[51] Raymond Williams, 'The Forward March of Labour Halted?' [1981], in *Resources of Hope*, p.249.
[52] Williams, *Towards 2000*, pp.268–9.
[53] Williams, *People of the Black Mountains*, Vol.1, p.83.
[54] Williams, 'Beyond Actually Existing Socialism', p.272.

change of pace and scale, a sort of devolution from the destiny-driven grand narrative of the great collective project to the moments of small drama that constitute the interleaved episodes of the trilogy. 'The true pace, always, was local and day by day', Glyn concludes of the story of Aaron's pig.[55]

This change of pace and scale resonates with recent attempts in practice and theory to inhabit a socialism without guarantees, a politics of direct action, of local process and becoming in place. A variety of new anarchist, autonomist, and neo-communitarian projects now occupy the space vacated by a traditional communist politics organized around waged labour and the point of production, scaled to the nation and the capture of state power. They have drawn on dissident traditions in socialist theory and anti-systemic praxis from the council communism of the 1920s to the anti-nuclear campaigns and punk subculture of the 1970s. David Graeber, for example, describes how contemporary anarchism scrambles insights from French situationism and from quaker and second-wave feminist organizational theory. Sharing the situationist ambition to disalienate the imagination and revolutionize everyday life, anarchists have nevertheless given up on organizing towards some revolutionary conjuncture that would finally commandeer the state, 'neutralize the entire apparatus of structural violence', and so open the field 'for an untrammelled outpouring of revolutionary creativity'. It is in 'the here and now' that anarchism looks to create its 'liberated territories', little pockets of alternative reality, temporary laboratories in which to improvise other ways of being.[56] Lauren Berlant echoes the 'counternoise' of the global anti-capitalist movements when she heralds a desire 'to revitalize political action ... not first by mapping out the better good life but by valuing political action as the action of not being worn out by politics'.[57] It is an important discrimination, a weak-theoretical defence of immanent activity and the kind of prefigurative politics that would do without the first articulation of ultimate ends, and it has found a place in new-millennium historical fiction.

'Do not advance the action according to a plan', concludes *Q* (1999), the first of several historical novels by the Italian writers' collective Luther Blissett/Wu Ming.[58] From Luther's ninety-five theses in 1517 to the Peace of Augsburg in 1555, *Q* follows its name-shifting protagonist as he travels across Europe from one insurgency to the next: in Mühlhausen, he joins with Thomas Müntzer's Peasants' Revolt; in Münster, he joins the Anabaptist rebellion; in the Low Countries with Jan van Batenburger's *Zwaardgesten*; and in Antwerp with the Loists. 'A different faith each time, always the same enemies, one defeat.'[59] The novel's third section takes him to Venice and Constantinople, and its sequel *Altai* (2009) to Mokha on

---

[55] Williams, *People of the Black Mountains*, Vol.1, p.83.
[56] David Graeber, *Direct Action: An Ethnography* (Oakland, CA: AK Press, 2009), pp.527–34.
[57] Lauren Berlant, *Cruel Optimism* (Durham, NC: Duke University Press, 2011), pp.261–2.
[58] Luther Blissett, *Q*, translated by Shaun Whiteside (London: Arrow, 2004), p.635.
[59] Blissett, *Q*, p.452.

the coast of Yemen and thence to Cyprus. It is his destiny, he reflects, despite 'half a century of defeats', 'to survive, always, to go on living in defeat, taking it a little at a time'.[60] This resilience is based, in part, on archetype: like the Anansi of Akan folktale or the coyote of Native American lore and the Looney Tunes cartoon, he is 'a "trickster with a thousand faces", a golem made of the clay of three rivers—the agit-prop tradition, folk mythology, and pop culture'.[61] Through his power of survival, he becomes a living memorial to his fallen comrades and a cipher for their many names, which history will soon forget. Above all, his ability 'to go on living', always loyal to the cause and ready to rejoin the fray, reflects a commitment to permanent revolution, to challenging 'the world order' wherever and whenever the opportunity presents.[62] In Thomas and Williams, as now in Wu Ming, there is the same investment in the present tense, a present the imagination holds open to what it may yet become.

In an influential essay from 2011, Perry Anderson set out to prescribe what role the historical novel should play. In the age of new nations, he argued, the genre had flattered a bourgeoisie that believed 'it bore the wind of the future within it'. Now came the reckoning: 'In Joycean terms, history as a nightmare from which we cannot wake up', or in thematic terms, 'the ravages of empire: not progress as emancipation but impending or consummated catastrophe'.[63] Anderson leant on Lukács to characterize the nineteenth-century historical novel, and for its contemporary iteration—in the literary culture of postmodernism and at 'the upper ranges of fiction' since—he called on Walter Benjamin, invoking his famous angel, blown backwards out of paradise as the wreckage of human history piles up at his feet. Anderson pictured the historical novel clinging to the angel's wings, crucified in the wind and likewise powerless to help.[64] Ample vocation may doubtless be found in this task, as witness to the violence and pain of capitalist modernity. But there remains a role for romance to play, as what distinguishes fiction from history, as what cuts against the recognition of our blighted world. Signpost to the place of desire and to the optimism of the will, to narrative as a principle of emergence from the flat facticity of the real, romance is one of our 'resources for a journey of hope'.[65] Raymond Williams believed, as did others in this study, that it was 'in making hope practical, rather than despair convincing, that we must resume and change and extend our campaigns'.[66]

---

[60] Blissett, Q, p.399.
[61] Henry Jenkins, 'How Slapshot Inspired a Cultural Revolution (Part One): An Interview with the Wu Ming Foundation', *Confessions of an Aca-Fan*, 5 October 2006, http://henryjenkins.org/2006/10/how_slapshot_inspired_a_cultur.html [accessed 10 July 2023].
[62] Blissett, Q, p.626.
[63] Anderson, 'From Progress to Catastrophe', p.24.
[64] Anderson, 'From Progress to Catastrophe', p.28.
[65] Williams, *Towards 2000*, p.268.
[66] Williams, 'The Politics of Nuclear Disarmament' [1980], in *Resources of Hope*, p.209.

# Works Cited

## Archival Material

Dorset History Centre, Dorchester. Sylvia Townsend Warner and Valentine Ackland Collection.
Hungarian Academy of Sciences, Budapest. Georg Lukács Archive.
King's College Archives, University of Cambridge. Papers of E.M. Forster.
Labour History Archive & Study Centre, Manchester. Archive of the Communist Party of Great Britain.
National Archives, Kew. The Security Service: Personal Files.
National Library of Australia, Canberra. Papers of Jack Lindsay.
Swansea University, Richard Burton Archive. Raymond Williams Collection.
University of Durham Library, Archives and Special Collections. Harold Heslop Papers.
University of Sussex Library, The Keep. Monks House Papers. Papers of Virginia Woolf and Related Papers of Leonard Woolf.
University of Technology, Sydney, Special Collections. Jack Lindsay Collection.
Victoria and Albert Museum, London. Unity Theatre Archive.

## Books and Other Publications

### A

Abrams, M.H. 'English Romanticism: The Spirit of the Age'. In *Romanticism Reconsidered: Selected Papers from the English Institute*, edited by Northrop Frye (New York: Columbia University Press, 1963), pp. 26–72.
Abrams, M.H. *Natural Supernaturalism: Tradition and Revolution in Romantic Literature* (New York: W.W. Norton, 1971).
Adorno, Theodore. 'Extorted Reconciliation: On Georg Lukács' *Realism in Our Time*' [1958]. In *Notes to Literature*, edited by Rolf Tiedemann, translated by Shierry Weber Nicholsen (New York: Columbia University Press, 1991), pp. 216–40.
Alexis, Jacques Stephen. 'Du réalisme merveilleux des Haïtiens' [1956]. Reprinted in *Présence Africaine*, n.s. nos.165/6 (2002): pp. 91–112.
Amado, Jorge. *The Violent Land* [1943], translated by Samuel Putnam (New York: Alfred A. Knopf, 1945).
Anand, Mulk Raj. *The Village* (London: Jonathan Cape, 1939).
Anand, Mulk Raj. *Across the Black Waters* (London: Jonathan Cape, 1940).
Anand, Mulk Raj. *The Sword and the Sickle* (London: Jonathan Cape, 1942).
Anderson, Amanda. 'Character and Ideology: The Case of Cold War Liberalism'. *New Literary History* 42, no.2 (2011): pp. 209–29.
Anderson, Benedict. *Imagined Communities: Reflections on the Origin and Spread of Nationalism*, second edition (London: Verso, 2006).
Anderson, Perry. 'Origins of the Present Crisis'. *New Left Review*, no.23 (1964): pp. 26–53.
Anderson, Perry. 'Socialism and Pseudo-Empiricism'. *New Left Review*, no.35 (1966): pp. 2–42.
Anderson, Perry. *Considerations on Western Marxism* (London: New Left Books, 1976).
Anderson, Perry. *Arguments within English Marxism* (London: New Left Books, 1980).
Anderson, Perry. 'Internationalism: A Breviary'. *New Left Review*, n.s. no. 14 (2002): pp. 5–25.

Anderson, Perry. 'From Progress to Catastrophe'. *London Review of Books* 33, no.15 (28 July 2011): pp. 24–28.
Aragon, Louis. 'About "The Massacres of Paris"'. *International Literature*, no.9 (1936): pp. 107–08.
'Argo'. 'Idee d'oltre confine'. *Educazione fascista* 11, no.3 (March 1933): pp. 264–68
Arnold, John. 'Jack Lindsay: Towards a Bibliography'. *Overland* 83 (1981), pp. 50–55.
Arnold, John. 'A Checklist of Jack Lindsay's Books'. In *Culture & History: Essays Presented to Jack Lindsay*, edited by Bernard Smith (Sydney: Hale & Iremonger, 1984), pp. 394–406.
Arnold, John. *The Fanfrolico Press: Satyrs, Fauns and Fine Books* (Pinner, Middlesex: Private Libraries Association, 2009).
Arrighi, Giovanni, Terrence K. Hopkins, and Immanuel Wallerstein. *Antisystemic Movements* (London: Verso, 1989).
Arrighi, Giovanni. 'Marxist Century, American Century: The Making and Remaking of the Labour Movement'. *New Left Review*, no.179 (1990): pp. 29–64.
Arrighi, Giovanni. *The Long Twentieth Century: Money, Power and the Origins of our Times* (London: Verso, 1994).
Arrighi, Giovanni. 'The Winding Paths of Capital. Interview with David Harvey'. *New Left Review*, n.s. no.56 (2009): pp. 61–94.
Arthur, Dave. *Bert: The Life and Times of A.L. Lloyd* (London: Pluto Press, 2012).
Asor Rosa, Alberto. *Scrittori e popolo. Saggio sulla letteratura populista in Italia* (Rome: Samonà e Savelli, 1965).
Austin, Alfred. *Haunts of Ancient Peace* (London: Macmillan, 1902).
*Authors Take Sides on the Spanish War*, edited by Nancy Cunard (London: Left Review, 1937).
Ayers, David. *Modernism, Internationalism and the Russian Revolution* (Edinburgh: Edinburgh University Press, 2020).

# B

Baer, Brian James. 'From International to Foreign: Packaging Translated Literature in Soviet Russia'. *The Slavic and East European Journal* 60, no.1 (2016): pp. 49–67.
Bakhtin, Mikhail. *Rabelais and His World*, translated by Hélène Iswolsky (Cambridge, MA: MIT Press, 1968).
Bakhtin, Mikhail. 'Forms of Time and of the Chronotope in the Novel'. In *The Dialogic Imagination: Four Essays*, edited by Michael Holquist, translated by Caryl Emerson and Michael Holquist (Austin: University of Texas Press, 1981), pp. 84–258.
Bakhtin, Mikhail. *Problems of Dostoevsky's Poetics*, edited and translated by Caryl Emerson (Minneapolis: University of Minnesota Press, 1984).
Bakhtin, Mikhail. 'The *Bildungsroman* and Its Significance in the History of Realism'. In *Speech Genres and Other Late Essays*, edited by Caryl Emerson and Michael Holquist, translated by Vern W. McGee (Austin: University of Texas Press, 1986), pp. 10–59.
Baldick, Chris. *The Oxford English Literary History, Volume 10. 1910-1940: The Modern Movement* (Oxford: Oxford University Press, 2004).
Banfield, Ann. *The Phantom Table: Woolf, Fry, Russell and the Epistemology of Modernism* (Cambridge: Cambridge University Press, 2000).
Barga, Corpus. 'El II Congreso Internacional de Escritores. Su Significacíon'. *Hora de España*, no.8 (August 1937): pp. 5–10.
Barke, James. *The Land of the Leal* [1939] (Edinburgh: Canongate, 1987).
Barke, James. *The Wind That Shakes the Barley: A Novel of the Life and Loves of Robert Burns* (London: Collins, 1946).
Barke, James. *The Song in the Green Thorn Tree: A Novel of the Life and Loves of Robert Burns* (London: Collins, 1947).
Barke, James. *The Wonder of All the Gay World: A Novel of the Life and Loves of Robert Burns* (London: Collins, 1949).

Barke, James. *The Crest of the Broken Wave: A Novel of the Life and Loves of Robert Burns* (London: Collins, 1953).
Barke, James. *The Well of the Silent Harp: A Novel of the Life and Loves of Robert Burns* (London: Collins, 1954).
Barnhisel, Greg. *Cold War Modernists: Art, Literature and American Cultural Diplomacy* (Columbia University Press, 2015).
Bauer, Otto. *The Question of Nationalities and Social Democracy*, edited by Ephraim Nimni, translated by Joseph O'Donnell (Minneapolis, MN: University of Minnesota Press, 2000).
Beard, Mary. *The Invention of Jane Harrison* (Cambridge, MA: Harvard University Press, 2000).
Beer, Gillian. 'Hume, Stephen, and Elegy in *To the Lighthouse*'. In *Arguing with the Past: Essays in Narrative from Woolf to Sydney* (London: Routledge, 1989), pp. 183–202.
Bell, Daniel. *The End of Ideology: On the Exhaustion of Political Ideas in the Fifties* (Glencoe, IL: Free Press, 1960).
Benda, Julien. *La trahison des clercs* (Paris: Grasset, 1927).
Beneš, Jakub. *Workers & Nationalism: Czech and German Social Democracy in Habsburg Austria, 1890–1918* (Oxford: Oxford University Press, 2017).
Benjamin, Walter. *The Arcades Project*, translated by Howard Eiland and Kevin McLaughlin (Cambridge, MA: Harvard University Press, 1999).
Benjamin, Walter. 'On the Concept of History'. In *Walter Benjamin: Selected Writings, Volume 4: 1938–1940*, edited by Howard Eiland and Michael Jennings (Cambridge, MA: Harvard University Press, 2003), pp. 389–400.
Bentley, Phyllis. *Freedom, Farewell!* [1936] (Harmondsworth: Penguin, 1950).
Bentley, Phyllis. *O Dreams, O Destinations* (New York: Macmillan, 1962).
Berard, Ewa. 'The "First Exhibition of Russian Art" in Berlin: The Transnational Origins of Bolshevik Cultural Diplomacy, 1921–1922'. *Contemporary European History* 30, no.2 (2021): pp. 164–80.
Berens-Totenohl, Josefa. *Der Femhof* (Jena: Eugen Diederichs Verlag, 1934).
Berlant, Lauren. *Cruel Optimism* (Durham, NC: Duke University Press, 2011).
Beumelburg, Werner. *Mont Royal: Ein Buch von himmlischen und vom irdischen Reich* (Oldenburg: Stalling Verlag, 1936).
Beumelburg, Werner. *Geschichten vom Reich*, edited by Karl Plenzat (Leipzig: Hermann Eichblatt Verlag, 1941).
Beumelburg, Werner. *Jörg* (Stuttgart: Deutsche Volksbücher, 1943).
Blissett, Luther. *Q*, translated by Shaun Whiteside (London: Arrow, 2004).
Bloch, Ernst. *The Principle of Hope*, translated by Neville Plaice, Stephen Plaice, and Paul Knight, 3 volumes (Cambridge, MA: MIT Press, 1986).
Bloch, Ernst. *Heritage of Our Times*, translated by Neville and Stephen Plaice (Berkeley, CA: University of California Press, 1990).
Bloch, Ernst. *The Spirit of Utopia*, translated by Anthony Nassar (Stanford, CA: Stanford University Press, 2000).
Block, Fred. 'Karl Polanyi and the Writing of *The Great Transformation*'. *Theory and Society* 32, no.3 (2003): pp. 275–306.
Bloom, Harold. 'The Internalization of Quest Romance'. *Yale Review* 58 (1969): pp. 526–36.
Bloom, Harold. *The Ringers in the Tower: Studies in Romantic Tradition* (Chicago: University of Chicago Press, 1971).
Boggs, Grace Lee. *Living for Change* (Minneapolis: University of Minnesota Press, 1998).
Bourdet, Charles. 'The French Left: Long-Run Trends'. *Universities & Left Review* 1, no.1 (1957): pp. 13–16.
Braudel, Fernand. *Civilization and Capitalism, 15th–18th Century III: The Perspective of the World*, translated by Siân Reynolds (New York: Harper & Row, 1984).
Brennan, Timothy. 'Postcolonial Studies between the European Wars: An Intellectual History'. In *Marxism, Modernity and Postcolonial Studies*, edited by Crystal Bartolovich and Neil Lazarus (Cambridge: Cambridge University Press, 2002), pp. 185–203.
Brennan, Timothy. 'Cosmotheory'. *South Atlantic Quarterly* 100, no.3 (2001): pp. 659–91.

Briggs, Julia. 'The Wives of Herr Bear'. Review of *The Invention of Jane Harrison* by Mary Beard. *London Review of Books* 22, no.18 (21 September 2000): pp. 24–25.

Briggs, Julia. '"Almost Ashamed of England being so English": Woolf and Ideas of Englishness'. In *At Home and Abroad in the Empire: British Women Write the 1930s*, edited by Robin Hackett, Freda Hauser, and Gay Wachman (Newark: University of Delaware Press, 2009), pp. 97–118.

Brown, Homer. 'Why the Story of the Origin of the (English) Novel is an American Romance (If Not the Great American Novel)'. In *Cultural Institutions of the Novel*, edited by Deidre Lynch and William B. Warner (Durham, NC: Duke University Press, 1996), pp. 11–43.

Bullivant, Joanna. *Alan Bush, Modern Music, and the Cold War: The Cultural Left in Britain and the Communist Bloc* (Cambridge: Cambridge University Press, 2017).

Burke, Edmund. *Selected Letters*, edited by Harvey C. Mansfield Jr. (Chicago: University of Chicago Press, 1984).

Burke, Edmund. *Reflections on the Revolution in France*, edited by Conor Cruise O'Brien (Harmondsworth: Penguin, 1986).

Burton, Robert. *The Anatomy of Melancholy*, edited by Thomas Faulkner, Nicholas Kiessling, and Rhonda Blair, with J.B. Bamborough and Martin Dodsworth, 6 vols. (Oxford: Clarendon Press, 1989–2000).

Bush, Alan. *Wat Tyler: An Opera in Two Acts with a Prologue* (London: Novello, 1959).

## C

Calder-Marshall, Arthur. 'The Works of Graham Greene'. *Horizon* 1, no.5 (1940): pp. 367–75.

*Campaigning Culture and the Global Cold War: the Journals of the Congress for Cultural Freedom*, edited by Giles Scott-Smith and Charlotte Lerg (London: Palgrave Macmillan, 2017).

Carpentier, Alejo. *The Kingdom of This World* [1949], translated by Harriet B. Onís (Harmondsworth: Penguin, 1975).

Carpentier, Alejo. 'On the Marvellous Real in America' [1967], translated by Tanya Huntington and Lois Parkinson Zamora. In *Magical Realism: Theory, History, Community*, edited by Zamora and Wendy B. Faris (Durham, NC: Duke University Press, 1995), pp. 75–88.

Carpentier, Alejo. *Bajo el Signo de la Cibeles: Crónicas sobre España y los españoles, 1925–1937*, edited by Julio Rodríguez Puértolas (Madrid: Editorial Nuestra Cultura, 1979).

Carpentier, Alejo. 'La evolución cultural de América Latina'. In *Alejo Carpentier: Crónicas Caribeñas*, edited by Emilio Jorge Rodríguez, translated by Rafael Rodríguez Beltrán (Havana: Instituto Cubano del Libro, 2012), pp. 107–23.

Carrington, Dora. *Carrington: Letters and Extracts from her Diaries*, edited by David Garnett (New York: Holt, Reinhart and Winston, 1970).

Casanova, Pascale. *The World Republic of Letters*, translated by M.B. DeBevoise (Cambridge, MA: Harvard University Press, 2004).

Casanova, Pascale. 'Literature as a World'. *New Left Review*, n.s. no.31 (2005): pp. 71–90.

Cassou, Jean. *Les Massacres de Paris* (Paris: Gallimard, 1935).

Cassou, Jean. 'The Massacres of Paris'. Translated by H.O. Whyte, *International Literature*, no.9 (1936): pp. 36–65.

*Ceddo* ['The Outsiders'], directed by Ousmane Sembène (Dakar: Filmi Doomireew, 1977).

Chambers, Colin. *The Story of Unity Theatre* (London: Lawrence & Wishart, 1989).

Chase, Richard. *Herman Melville: A Critical Study* (New York: Macmillan, 1949).

Chuvoksky, Kornei. *The Art of Translation: Kornei Chukovsky's A High Art*, translated by Lauren Leighton (Knoxville: University of Tennessee Press, 1984).

Clark, Katerina. *Moscow: The Fourth Rome. Stalinism, Cosmopolitanism and the Evolution of Soviet Culture, 1931–1941* (Cambridge, MA: Harvard University Press, 2011).

Clark, Katerina and Evgeny Dobrenko. *Soviet Culture and Power: A History in Documents, 1917–1953* (New Haven: Yale University Press, 2007).

Clark, Katerina and Galin Tihanov. 'Soviet Literary Theory in the 1930s: Battles Over Genre and the Boundaries of Modernity'. In *A History of Russian Literary Theory and Criticism: The Soviet*

*Age and Beyond*, edited by Evgeny Dobrenko and Galin Tihanov (Pittsburgh: University of Pittsburgh Press, 2011), pp. 109–43.

Clark, Katerina. *Eurasia without Borders: The Dream of a Leftist World Literature* (Cambridge, MA: Harvard University Press, 2021).

Cleary, Joe. *Modernism, Empire, World Literature* (Cambridge: Cambridge University Press, 2021).

Coleridge, Samuel Taylor. *Lay Sermons*, edited by R.J. White (Princeton, NJ: Princeton University Press, 1972).

*Comintern Aesthetics*, edited by Amelia Glaser and Steven Lee (Toronto: University of Toronto Press, 2020).

Connor, John. 'Fanfrolico and After: The Lindsay Aesthetic in the Cultural Cold War'. *Modernist Cultures* 15, no.3 (2020): pp. 276–94.

Craig, Cairns. 'Coleridge, Hume and the Romantic Imagination'. In *Scotland and the Borders of Romanticism*, edited by Leith Davis, Ian Duncan, and Janet Sorensen (Cambridge: Cambridge University Press, 2004), pp. 20–37.

Craig, Cairns. *Associationism and the Literary Imagination: From the Phantasmal Chaos* (Edinburgh: Edinburgh University Press, 2007).

Croft, Andy. *Red Letter Days: British Fiction in the 1930s* (London: Lawrence & Wishart, 1990).

Croft, Andy. 'Writers, The Communist Party and the Battle of Ideas, 1945–50'. *Socialist History* 5 (1994): pp. 2–25.

Croft, Andy. 'Betrayed Spring: The Labour Government and British Literary Culture'. In *Labour's Promised Land? Culture and Society in Labour Britain 1945–51*, edited by Jim Fryth (London: Lawrence & Wishart, 1995), pp. 197–223

Croft, Andy. 'Authors Take Sides: Writers and the Communist Party'. In *Opening the Books: Essays on the Social and Cultural History of British Communism*, edited by Geoff Andrews, Nina Fishman, and Kevin Morgan (London: Pluto Press, 1995), pp. 83–101.

Croft, Andy. 'The Boys Round the Corner: The Story of Fore Publications'. In *A Weapon in the Struggle: The Cultural History of the Communist Party in Britain*, edited by Croft (London: Pluto Press, 1998), pp. 142–62.

Croft, Andy. *Comrade Heart: A Life of Randall Swingler* (Manchester: Manchester University Press, 2003).

Croft, Andy. 'The Ralph Fox (Writer's) Group'. In *And in Our Time: Vision, Revision, and British Writing of the 1930s*, edited by Anthony Shuttleworth (Cranbury, NJ: Associated University Press, 2003), pp. 163–80.

Cunningham, Valentine. *British Writers of the Thirties* (Oxford: Oxford University Press, 1988).

## D

David-Fox, Michael. *Showcasing the Great Experiment: Cultural Diplomacy and Western Visitors to Soviet Russia, 1921–1941* (Oxford: Oxford University Press, 2012).

Denning, Michael. *The Cultural Front: The Laboring of American Culture in the Twentieth Century* (London: Verso, 1997).

Denning, Michael. 'The Novelists' International'. In *Culture in the Age of Three Worlds* (London: Verso, 2004), pp. 51–72.

Denny, Norman and John Cowper Powys. 'Letters on the Publication of *Porius*', edited by Michael Ballin. *Powys Notes* 7, no.2 (1992): pp. 25–37.

DeSola, Ralph and Frederica. 'For Young Revolutionists'. *New Masses* 16, no.8 (20 August 1935): pp. 24–25.

Deutscher, Isaac. *Marxism in Our Time* (London: Jonathan Cape, 1972).

Dewald, Jonathan. *Lost Worlds: The Emergence of French Social History, 1815–1970* (University Park: Penn State University Press, 2006).

Dimitrov, Georgi. *The Working Class against Fascism* (London: Martin Lawrence, 1935).

Dirlik, Arif. *Revolution and History: The Origins of Marxist Historiography in China, 1919–1937* (Berkeley, CA: University of California Press, 1978).

Djagalov, Rossen. '"I don't boast about it, but I'm the most widely read author of this century": Howard Fast and International Leftist Literary Culture, ca. Mid-Twentieth Century'. *Anthropology of East Europe Review* 27, no.2 (2009): pp. 40–55.

Djagalov, Rossen. *From Internationalism to Postcolonialism: Literature and Cinema between the Second and Third Worlds* (Montreal: McGill-Queen University Press, 2020).

Dobb, Maurice. *Studies in the Development of Capitalism* (London: George Routledge and Sons, 1946).

Döblin, Alfred. *Wallenstein* (Berlin: S. Fischer Verlag, 1920).

Dobrenko, Evgeny. *The Making of the State Reader: Social and Aesthetic Contexts of the Reception of Soviet Literature*, translated by Jesse M. Savage (Stanford: Stanford University Press, 1997).

Docker, John. *Australian Cultural Elites: Intellectual Traditions in Sydney and Melbourne* (Sydney: Angus & Robertson, 1974).

Dorson, Richard. 'Folklore or Fake Lore'. *The American Mercury* 70, no.315 (1950): pp. 335–43.

Drew, Elizabeth. *The Modern Novel. Some Aspects of Contemporary Fiction* (London: Jonathan Cape, 1926).

Du, Pengcheng. *Baowei Yan'an* ['Guarding Yan'an'] (Beijing: The People's Literature Publishing House, 1956).

Dumain, Ralph. 'Bibliographic Addendum', to John Arnold. 'A Checklist of Jack Lindsay's Books'. http://www.autodidactproject.org/bib/lindbib.html

Duncan, Ian. *Modern Romance and Transformations of the Novel: The Gothic, Scott, Dickens* (Cambridge: Cambridge University Press, 1992).

Duncan, Ian. 'The Mythology of Escape: *Owen Glendower* and the Failure of Historical Romance'. *Powys Notes* 8 (1992): pp. 53–81.

Duncan, Ian. 'Supernatural Narration: *A Glastonbury Romance*, Modernity and the Novel'. *Western Humanities Review* 57, no.1 (2003): pp. 78–111.

Duncan, Ian. *Scott's Shadow: The Novel in Romantic Edinburgh* (Princeton, NJ: Princeton University Press, 2007).

Duncan, Ian. 'The Trouble with Man: Scott, Romance, and World History in the Age of Lamarck'. In *Romantic Frictions*, edited by Theresa Kelley (*Romantic Circles: Praxis Series*, 2011): https://romantic-circles.org/praxis/frictions/HTML/praxis.2011.duncan.html

E

Elistratova, E. 'The Work of Harold Heslop'. *International Literature*, no.1 (1932): pp. 99–102.

Ellmann, Maud. 'The Art of Bi-Location: Sylvia Townsend Warner'. In *The History of British Women's Writing, 1920–1945*, edited by Maroula Joannou (London: Palgrave Macmillan, 2013), pp. 78–93.

*Emitaï*, directed by Ousmane Sembène (Dakar: Filmi Domireew, 1971).

*Essays on John Cowper Powys*, edited by Belinda Humfrey (Cardiff: University of Wales Press, 1972).

Esty, Jed. *A Shrinking Island: Modernism and National Culture in England* (Princeton, NJ: Princeton University Press, 2004).

Esty, Jed. 'Global Lukács'. *Novel* 42, no.3 (2009): pp. 366–72.

Esty, Jed. *Unseasonable Youth: Modernism, Colonialism and the Fiction of Development* (Oxford: Oxford University Press, 2012).

F

Fagan, Hyman. *Nine Days That Shook England: An Account of the English People's Uprising in 1381* (London: Victor Gollancz, 1938).

Fast, Howard. *Literature and Reality* (New York: International Publishers, 1950).
Feidelson, Charles. *Symbolism and American Literature* (Chicago: University of Chicago Press, 1953).
Feuchtwanger, Lion. 'Vom Sinn und Unsinn des historischen Romans'. In *Paris 1935: Erster internationaler Schriftstellerkongreß zur Verteidigung der Kultur. Reden und Dokumente*, edited by Wolfgang Klein (Berlin: Akademie Verlag, 1982), pp. 293-98.
Feuerbach, Ludwig. *The Essence of Christianity*, translated by Marian Evans [George Eliot] (London: John Chapman, 1854).
Field, Geoffrey. *Blood Sweat and Toil: Remaking the British Working Class, 1939-1945* (Oxford: Oxford University Press, 2011).
Flores, Angel. 'Magical Realism in Spanish American Fiction'. *Hispania* 38, no.2 (1955): pp. 187-92.
Forster, E.M. 'Mr Wells' "Outline"', review of *The Outline of History* Vol.2 by H.G. Wells, *The Athenaeum*, no.4725 (19 November 1920): pp. 690-91.
Forster, E.M. *Aspects of the Novel*, edited by Oliver Stallybrass (Harmondsworth: Penguin, 1976).
Foucault, Michel. *Madness and Civilization: A History of Insanity in the Age of Reason*, translated by Richard Howard (New York: Vintage, 1988).
Friedberg, Maurice. *A Decade of Euphoria: Western Literature in Post-Stalin Russia, 1954-1964* (Bloomington: Indiana University Press, 1977).
Fuller, Roy. *Fantasy and Fugue* [1954]; in *Crime Omnibus* (Manchester: Carcanet, 1988).


# G

Garside, Peter. 'Essay on the Text'. In Sir Walter Scott, *Waverley*, edited by Peter Garside (Edinburgh: Edinburgh University Press, 2007), pp. 367-83.
Glebov, Sergey. *From Empire to Eurasia: Politics, Scholarship and Ideology in Russian Eurasianism, 1920s-1930s* (DeKalb: Northern Illinois University Press, 2017).
Glendinning, Victoria. *Vita: The Life of V. Sackville-West* (New York: Knopf, 1983).
Golightly, Victor. '"We who speak for the workers": The Correspondence of Gwyn Thomas and Howard Fast'. *Welsh Writing in English* 6 (2000): pp. 67-88.
Goodway, David. *Anarchist Seeds Beneath the Snow: Left Libertarian Thought and British Writers from William Morris to Colin Ward* (Liverpool: Liverpool University Press, 2006).
Gorky, Maxim. 'Soviet Literature'. In Nikolai Bukharin, Maxim Gorky, Karl Radek, Andrey Zhdanov et al., *Problems of Soviet Literature* (London: Martin Lawrence, 1934), pp. 27-69.
Gorokhov, F. 'An Anti-Marxist Theory of History'. Translated by S. Altschuler, *International Literature*, no.9 (1937): pp. 73-77.
Graeber, David. *Direct Action: An Ethnography* (Oakland, CA: AK Press, 2009).
Gramsci, Antonio. *Selections from the Prison Notebooks*, edited and translated by Quintin Hoare and Geoffrey Nowell Smith (London: Lawrence & Wishart, 1971).
Gramsci, Antonio. *Selections from the Cultural Writings*, edited by David Forgacs and Geoffrey Nowell-Smith, translated by William Boelhower (Chicago: Haymarket, 2012).
Greene, Graham. 'Introduction', to *The Man Within* [1929] (London: Heinemann and the Bodley Head, 1976), pp. v-x.
Greene, Graham. *The Ministry of Fear* [1943] (London: Penguin, 1978).
Greene, Graham. 'The Third Man' [1949]. In *The Portable Graham Greene*, edited by Philip Stratford (London: Penguin, 1994), pp. 306-81.
Greene, Graham. *Collected Essays* (Harmondsworth: Penguin, 1970).
Greene, Graham. *A Sort of Life* (Harmondsworth: Penguin, 1972).
Greene, Graham. *Ways of Escape* (Harmondsworth: Penguin, 1981).
Grose, Francis. *A Classical Dictionary of the Vulgar Tongue* [1785], second edition (London: Hooper, 1788).
Gualtieri, Elena. *Virginia Woolf's Essays: Sketching the Past* (Basingstoke: Palgrave, 2000).

Guilbaut, Serge. *How New York Stole the Idea of Modern Art: Abstract Expressionism, Freedom, and the Cold War*, translated by Arthur Goldhammer (Chicago: University of Chicago Press, 1983).

# H

Hall, Stuart. 'Introducing NLR'. *New Left Review*, no.1 (1960): p. 1.
Hall, Stuart. 'Life and Times of the First New Left'. *New Left Review*, n.s. no.61 (2010): pp. 177–96.
Han, Xiaorong. *Chinese Discourses on the Peasant, 1900–1949* (Albany: SUNY Press, 2005).
Hanson, Harry. 'An Open Letter to Edward Thompson'. *The New Reasoner*, no.2 (1957): pp. 79–91.
Harker, Ben, '"Communism is English": Edgell Rickword, Jack Lindsay and the Cultural Politics of the Popular Front'. *Literature & History* 20, no.2 (2011): pp. 23–40.
Harker, Ben. '"Workers' Music": Communism and the British Folk Revival'. In *Red Strains: Music and Communism Outside the Communist Bloc*, edited by Robert Adlington (Oxford: Oxford University Press, 2013), pp. 89–104.
Harker, Ben. 'Politics and Letters: The "Soviet Literary Controversy" in Britain'. *Literature & History* 24, no.2 (2015): pp. 43–58
Harker, Ben. 'Jack Lindsay's Alienation'. *History Workshop Journal* 82 (2016): pp. 83–103.
Harman, Claire. 'Introduction', to Sylvia Townsend Warner, *The Corner That Held Them* (London: Virago, 1988), pp. v–viii.
Harman, Claire. *Sylvia Townsend Warner: A Biography* (London: Chatto & Windus, 1989).
Harper, Frederick. *Tilewright's Acre* (London: Lawrence & Wishart, 1959).
Harper, Frederick. *Joseph Capper* (London: Lawrence & Wishart, 1962).
Harris, Alexandra. *Romantic Moderns: English Writers, Artists and the Imagination from Virginia Woolf to John Piper* (London: Thames & Hudson, 2010).
Harrison, Jane. *Prolegomena to the Study of Greek Religion* (Cambridge: Cambridge University Press, 1905).
Harrison, Jane. *Themis: A Study in the Social Origins of Greek Religion* (Cambridge: Cambridge University Press, 1912).
Harrison, Jane. *Ancient Art and Ritual* (London: Williams and Norgate, 1913).
Harrison, Jane. *Unanimism: A Study of Conversion and Some Contemporary French Poets* (Cambridge: 'The Heretics', 1913).
Harrison, Jane. *Aspects, Aorists and the Classical Tripos* (Cambridge: Cambridge University Press, 1919).
Harrison, Jane. *Rationalism and Religious Reaction* (London: Watts & Co., 1919).
Harrison, Jane. *Epilegomena to the Study of Greek Religion* (Cambridge: Cambridge University Press, 1921).
Harrison, Jane and Hope Mirrlees. *The Book of the Bear* (London: Nonesuch, 1926).
Hauser, Kitty. *Shadow Sites: Photography, Archaeology & the British Landscape 1927–1955* (Oxford: Oxford University Press, 2007).
Hegel, G.W.F. *Philosophy of Right*, translated by T.M. Knox (Oxford: Oxford University Press, 1952).
von Heiseler, Bernt. 'Segen und Unsegen des historischen Romans'. *Das deutsche Wort*, no.11 (1935): pp. 6–11.
Henig, Suzanne. 'Queen of Lud: Hope Mirrlees'. *Virginia Woolf Quarterly*, no.1 (1972): pp. 8–27.
Henry, David. *Life on Air: A History of Radio Four* (Oxford: Oxford University Press, 2007).
Heslop, Harold. 'Ten Thousand Men'. *International Literature*, no.2 (1933): pp. 32–40
Heslop, Harold. *Last Cage Down* [1935] (London: Lawrence & Wishart, 1984).
Heslop, Harold. 'Sunnybank'. *International Literature*, nos.8–9 (1939): pp. 28–52.
Heslop, Harold. *The Earth Beneath* (London: T.V. Boardman & Co., 1946).
Hill, Christopher. 'Historians on the rise of British Capitalism'. *Science and Society* 14, no.4 (1950): pp. 307–21.

Hill, Christopher. *The World Turned Upside Down: Radical Ideas during the English Revolution* (London: Temple Smith, 1972).

Hilton, Rodney. 'Peasant Movements in England before 1381'. *Economic History Review* 11 (1949): pp. 117–36.

Hobday, Charles. 'Charles Poulsen: A Study in Loyalties'. In *Whitechapel Spring: Poems and Stories by Charles Poulsen*, edited by Hobday (Belfast: Lapwing Publications, 2005).

Hobsbawm, Eric et al. Letter, *New Statesman and Nation*, 1 December 1956, p. 701.

Hobsbawm, Eric. *Primitive Rebels: Studies in Archaic Forms of Social Movements in the 19th and 20th Centuries* (New York: Norton, 1965).

Hobsbawm, Eric. 'The Communist Party Historians' Group'. In *Rebels and their Causes: Essays in Honour of A.L. Morton*, edited by Maurice Cornforth (London: Lawrence & Wishart, 1978), pp. 21–48.

Hobsbawm, Eric. 'Comments' on Peter Burke, 'Reflections on the Historical Revolution in France: The *Annales* School and British Social History'. *Review (Fernand Braudel Center)* 1, nos.3/4 (1978): pp. 157–62.

Hobsbawm, Eric. *Nations and Nationalism since 1780*, second edition (Cambridge: Cambridge University Press, 1992).

Hobsbawm, Eric. *Bandits* (London: Weidenfeld and Nicholson, 2000).

Hobson, Harold. 'Mr Ustinov, Enchanted', *The Sunday Times*, 29 April 1962, p. 41.

Hobson, J.A. *Imperialism: A Study* (London: James Nisbet, 1902).

Hofheinz, Roy. *The Broken Wave: The Chinese Communist Peasant Movement, 1922–1928* (Cambridge, MA: Harvard University Press, 1977).

Holmes, Richard. 'A Strange Kingdom'. *The Times*, 20 December 1973: p. 10.

Hume, David. *The Letters of David Hume. Volume 1: 1727–1765*, edited by J.Y.T. Greig (Oxford: Oxford University Press, 1932).

Hume, David. *A Treatise of Human Nature: Being an Attempt to Introduce the Experimental Method of Reasoning into Moral Subjects*, edited by Ernest Campbell Mossner (London: Penguin, 1985).

Hume, David. *An Enquiry Concerning Human Understanding*, edited by Peter Millican (Oxford: Oxford University Press 2007).

Hurd, Richard. *Letters on Chivalry and Romance* (London: A Millar, 1762).

Huxley, Aldous. *Point Counter Point* (London: Chatto & Windus, 1928).

Huyssen, Andreas. *After the Great Divide: Modernism, Mass Culture, Postmodernism* (Bloomington: Indiana University Press, 1986).

# I

*'If I had a song': A Song Book for Children Growing Up*, edited by Alan Gifford (London: Workers' Music Association, 1954).

# J

*Jack Lindsay. A Catalogue of First Editions Extensively Annotated by the Author, together with Letters, Manuscripts and Association Items*, edited by Harry Chaplin (Sydney: The Wentworth Press, 1983).

Jackson, T.A., Georg Lukács, and Sylvia Townsend Warner. 'Points from Letters'. *International Literature*, no.9 (1938), pp. 100–01.

Jackson, T.A. 'Walter Scott and His Historical Significance'. *International Literature*, nos.8–9 (1939): pp. 68–76.

James, Mervyn. *Society, Politics and Culture: Studies in Early Modern England* (Cambridge: Cambridge University Press, 1986).

Jameson, Fredric. 'The Vanishing Mediator: Narrative Structure in Max Weber'. *New German Critique*, no.1 (1973): pp. 52–89.
Jameson, Fredric. *The Political Unconscious: Narrative as a Socially Symbolic Act* (Ithaca, NY: Cornell University Press, 1981).
Jameson, Fredric. 'Introduction', to Georg Lukács, *The Historical Novel*, translated by Hannah and Stanley Mitchell (Lincoln: University of Nebraska Press, 1983), pp. 1–8.
Jameson, Fredric. *A Singular Modernity: Essay on the Ontology of the Present* (London: Verso, 2002).
Jellinek, Frank. 'The Way to Do It. The Albert Hall Murals for the Communist Manifesto Centenary'. *Our Time* 7, no.7 (1948): pp. 174–75.
Jenkins, Henry. 'How Slapshot Inspired a Cultural Revolution (Part One): An Interview with the Wu Ming Foundation'. *Confessions of an Aca-Fan*, 5 October 2006: http://henryjenkins.org/2006/10/how_slapshot_inspired_a_cultur.html
Joannou, Maroula. 'Sylvia Townsend Warner in the 1930s'. In *A Weapon in the Struggle: The Cultural History of the Communist Party in Britain*, edited by Andy Croft (London: Pluto Press, 1998), pp. 89–105.
Jones, Clara. *Virginia Woolf: Ambivalent Activist* (Edinburgh: Edinburgh University Press, 2016).
Joyce, James. *Finnegans Wake* [1939] (London: Penguin, 1999).

# K

Kalliney, Peter. *The Aesthetic Cold War: Decolonization and Global Literature* (Princeton, NJ: Princeton University Press, 2022).
Kenner, Hugh. *The Pound Era* (Berkeley: University of California Press, 1971).
Kenner, Hugh. 'The Making of the Modernist Canon'. *Chicago Review* 34, no.2 (1984): pp. 49–61.
Kermode, Frank. *Romantic Image* (London: Routledge and Kegan Paul, 1957).
Kerridge, Eric. 'The Revolts in Wiltshire against Charles I'. *Wiltshire Archaeological and Natural History Society Magazine* 57 (1958): pp. 64–75.
Kerzhentsev, Platon. 'Falsification of the Historical Past'. Translated by S. Altschuler, *International Literature*, no.5 (1937): pp. 76–83.
Kipling, Rudyard. *Rewards and Faeries* [1910] (London: Penguin, 1987).
Knipovich, E. 'Problems of the Historical Novel'. *International Literature*, no.9 (1937): pp. 55–69.
Krissdóttir, Morine. *Descents of Memory: The Life of John Cowper Powys* (New York: Overlook Duckworth, 2007).

# L

Langenbucher, Hellmuth. 'Deutsches Schrifttum 1937—politisch gesehen'. *Nationalsozialistische Bibliographie* 3, no.3 (1938): pp. i–xx.
Lansing, Robert. *The Peace Negotiations: A Personal Narrative* (Boston: Houghton Mifflin 1921).
Latham, Sean. *Am I a Snob? Modernism and the Novel* (Ithaca, NY: Cornell University Press, 2003).
Lauren, Paul Gordon. *Diplomats and Bureaucrats: The First International Responses to Twentieth-Century Diplomacy in France and Germany* (Stanford, CA: Hoover Institution Press, 1976).
Lawrence, D.H. *Selected Critical Writings*, edited by Michael Herbert (Oxford: Oxford University Press, 1998).
Leavis, F.R. *The Great Tradition: George Eliot, Henry James, Joseph Conrad* (London: Chatto & Windus, 1948).
Leavis, F.R. *Scrutiny. A Retrospect* (Cambridge: Cambridge University Press, 1963).
Le Sueur, Meridel. 'Cacao Rush'. *New Masses* 56, no.11 (11 September 1945): p. 28.
Lee, Hermione. *Virginia Woolf* (New York: Vintage, 1999).

Lehmann, John. *Prometheus and the Bolsheviks* (London: Cresset Press, 1937).
Lenin, V.I. *Imperialism, The Highest Stage of Capitalism*. In *Collected Works. Volume 22: December 1915–July 1916*, translated by Yuri Sdobnikov (Moscow: Progress Publishers, 1964), pp. 185–304.
Lenin, V.I. 'The State and Revolution'. In *Collected Works. Volume 25: June–September 1917*, edited by Stepan Apresyan and Jim Riordan (Moscow: Progress Publishers, 1964), pp. 385–498.
Lenin, V.I. 'Address to the Second All-Russia Congress of Communist Organisations of the Peoples of the East' [22 November 1919]. In *Collected Works. Volume 30: September 1919–April 1920*, translated by George Hanna (Moscow: Progress Publishers, 1965), pp. 151–62.
Lessing, Doris. *Walking in the Shade: Volume Two of My Autobiography 1949–1962* (New York: Harper Collins, 1997).
Lindsay, Jack. 'Australian Poetry and Nationalism'. *Vision*, no.1 (1923): pp. 30–35.
Lindsay, Jack [unsigned]. 'Foreword'. *Vision*, no.1 (1923): pp. 2–3.
Lindsay, Jack [as James Cunninghame]. 'France the Abyss'. *Vision*, no.2 (1923): pp. 35–39.
Lindsay, Jack. *Caesar is Dead* (London: Nicholson & Watson, 1934).
Lindsay, Jack. *Rome for Sale* (London: Elkin Matthew and Marrot, 1934).
Lindsay, Jack. *Come Home at Last* (London: Nicholson & Watson, 1935)
Lindsay, Jack. *Last Days with Cleopatra* (London: Nicholson & Watson, 1935).
Lindsay, Jack. *Runaway* (Oxford: Oxford University Press, 1935)
Lindsay, Jack. *Storm at Sea* (London: Golden Cockerel Press, 1935).
Lindsay, Jack. *Adam of a New World* (London: Nicholson & Watson, 1936).
Lindsay, Jack. 'Non-Dialectical'. *Discussion*, no.11 (1936): p. 31.
Lindsay, Jack. 'not english? A Reminder for May Day'. *Left Review* 2, no.8 (1936): pp. 353–57.
Lindsay, Jack. *Rebels of the Goldfields* (London: Lawrence & Wishart, 1936).
Lindsay, Jack. *The Wanderings of Wenamen, 115–114 B.C.* (London: Nicholson & Watson, 1936).
Lindsay, Jack. 'The Historical Novel'. *New Masses* 22, no.3 (12 January 1937): pp. 15–16.
Lindsay, Jack. *John Bunyan: Maker of Myths* (London: Methuen, 1937).
Lindsay, Jack. *1649. A Novel of a Year* (London: Methuen, 1938).
Lindsay, Jack. *To Arms! A Story of Ancient Gaul* (Oxford: Oxford University Press, 1938).
Lindsay, Jack. *A Short History of Culture* (London: Gollancz, 1939).
Lindsay, Jack. *Brief Light: A Novel of Catullus* (London: Methuen, 1939).
Lindsay, Jack. *England My England: A Pageant of the English People* (London: Fore Publications, 1939).
Lindsay, Jack. *Lost Birthright* (London: Methuen, 1939).
Lindsay, Jack. *Hannibaal Takes a Hand* (London: Andrew Dakers, 1941).
Lindsay, Jack. *Light in Italy* (London: Gollancz, 1941).
Lindsay, Jack. *The Dons Sight Devon. A Story of the Invincible Armada* (London: Oxford University Press, 1941).
Lindsay, Jack. *The Stormy Violence* (London: Andrew Dakers, 1941).
Lindsay, Jack. *British Achievement in Art and Music* (London: Pilot Press, 1945).
Lindsay, Jack. *The Barriers Are Down: A Tale of the Collapse of a Civilisation* (London: Gollancz, 1945).
Lindsay, Jack. *Men of Forty-Eight* (London: Methuen, 1948).
Lindsay, Jack. 'Zarathustra in Queensland'. *Meanjin* 7, no.4 (1948): pp. 211–25.
Lindsay, Jack. 'Editorial Note'. *Arena: A Literary Magazine* 1, no.1 (1949): p. 3.
Lindsay, Jack. *Marxism and Contemporary Science, or The Fullness of Life* (London: Dennis Dobson, 1949).
Lindsay, Jack. 'A Note of Self Criticism'. *Communist Review* (March 1950): pp. 93–95.
Lindsay, Jack. *A World Ahead: Journal of a Soviet Journey* (London: Fore Publications, 1950).
Lindsay, Jack. *Fires in Smithfield: A Novel of Mary Tudor's Days* (London: Bodley Head, 1950).
Lindsay, Jack. *The Passionate Pastoral. An 18th Century Escapade* (London: Bodley Head, 1951).
Lindsay, Jack. 'Aspects and Problems of Socialist Realism in Literature'. In *Essays on Socialist Realism and the British Cultural Tradition* (London: Arena, n.d. [1953]), pp. 60–77.

Lindsay, Jack. [No title]. In *Georg Lukács zum siebzigsten Geburtstag* (Berlin: Aufbau Verlag, 1955), pp. 130–32.
Lindsay, Jack. *Russian Poetry, 1917–1955* (London: Bodley Head, 1957).
Lindsay, Jack. *The Great Oak* (London: Bodley Head, 1957).
Lindsay, Jack. 'Socialism and Humanism'. *The New Reasoner*, no.3 (1957–58): pp. 95–102.
Lindsay, Jack. 'The Nature of the Historical Novel'. *Our History*, no.13 (1959): pp. 1–13.
Lindsay, Jack. 'Scholarly and Kindly', review of *Jane Ellen Harrison: A Portrait from the Letters* by Jessie Stewart. *Daily Worker*, 13 August 1959, p. 2.
Lindsay, Jack. *Modern Russian Poetry* (London: Vista Books, 1960).
Lindsay, Jack. *Fanfrolico and After* (London: Bodley Head, 1962).
Lindsay, Jack. *The Clashing Rocks: A Study of Early Greek Religion and Culture and the Origins of Drama* (London Chapman & Hall, 1965).
Lindsay, Jack. *Thunder Underground: A Novel of Nero's Rome* (London: Muller, 1965).
Lindsay, Jack. *Meetings with Poets: Memories of Dylan Thomas, Edith Sitwell, Louis Aragon, Paul Eluard, Tristan Tzara* (London: Muller, 1968).
Lindsay, Jack. 'Norman Lindsay: Problems of his Life and Work'. *Meanjin Quarterly* 29, no.1 (1970): pp. 39–48.
Lindsay, Jack. *Blast-Power and Ballistics: Concepts of Force and Energy in the Ancient World* (London: Frederick Muller, 1974).
Lindsay, Jack. 'Expatriate Publishing II'. *Meanjin Quarterly* 33, no.2 (1974): pp. 176–79.
Lindsay, Jack. 'The Life and Art of Norman Lindsay'. *Meanjin Quarterly* 33, no.1 (1974): pp. 27–41.
Lindsay, Jack. 'The Part and the Whole: The Achievement of Georg Lukács'. In *Decay and Renewal: Critical Essays on Twentieth Century Writing* (London: Lawrence & Wishart, 1976), pp. 11–52.
Lindsay, Jack. 'Foreword', to Sally Green, *Prehistorian: A Biography of V. Gordon Childe* (Bradford on Avon: Moonraker, 1981), pp. ix–xvii.
Lindsay, Jack. *The Crisis in Marxism* (Totowa, NJ: Barnes & Noble, 1981).
Lindsay, Jack. *Life Rarely Tells: An Autobiography in Three Volumes* (Ringwood, Victoria: Penguin, 1982).
Lindsay, Jack. 'Preface', to *Jack Lindsay. A Catalogue of First Editions extensively annotated by the author*, edited by Harry Chaplin (Sydney: Wentworth Press, 1983), pp. i–v.
Lindsay, Jack. 'A Note on my Dialectic'. In *Culture & History: Essays Presented to Jack Lindsay*, edited by Bernard Smith (Sydney: Hall & Iremonger, 1984), pp. 363–73.
Lindsay, Jack and Maurice Cornforth. *Rumanian Summer: A View of the Rumanian People's Republic* (London: Lawrence & Wishart, 1953).
Lindsay, Norman. *Creative Effort: An Essay in Affirmation* (Sydney: Art in Australia, 1920).
Lloyd, A.L. 'The People's Own Poetry'. *Daily Worker*, 10 February 1937, p. 7.
Lloyd, A.L. 'The Revolutionary Origins of English Folksong' [1943]. Reprinted in *Folk: Review of People's Music, Part One*, edited by Max Jones (London: Jazz Music Books, 1945), pp. 13–15.
Lloyd, A.L. *The Singing Englishman: An Introduction to Folksong* (London: Workers' Music Association, 1945).
Lloyd, A.L. *Folk Song in England* (London: Lawrence & Wishart, 1967).
Lovejoy, A.O. 'On the Discrimination of Romanticisms'. *PMLA* 39, no.2 (1924): pp. 229–53.
Lukács, Georg. 'Tendency or Partisanship?' [1932]. In *Essays on Realism*, edited by Rodney Livingstone, translated by David Fernbach (London: Lawrence & Wishart, 1980), pp. 33–44.
Lukács, Georg. 'Walter Scott and the Historical Novel [1]'. *International Literature*, no.4 (1938): pp. 61–77.
Lukács, Georg. 'Walter Scott and the Historical Novel [2]'. *International Literature*, no.12 (1938): pp. 73–84.
Lukács, Georg. *Rekishi bungakuron*, translated by Fusaji Yamamura (Tokyo: Mikasa Shobo, 1938).
Lukács, Georg. *The Historical Novel*, translated by Hannah and Stanley Mitchell (London: Merlin Press, 1962).

Lukács, Georg. 'Interview: Lukács on his Life and Work'. *New Left Review*, no.68 (1971): pp. 49–58.
Lukács, Georg. 'Die Widersprüche des Fortschritts und die Literatur'. In *Moskauer Schriften zur Literaturtheorie und Literaturpolitik 1934–1940*, edited by Frank Benseler (Frankfurt am Main: Sendler Verlag, 1981), pp. 79–86.
Lukács, Georg. *The Process of Democratization*, translated by Susanne Bernhardt and Norman Levine (Albany, NY: SUNY Press, 1991).
Luo, Gangbin and Yang Yiyan. *Red Crag* [1961], translated by Hong Yan (Peking: Foreign Languages Press, 1978).

# M

Macainsh, Noel. *Nietzsche in Australia: A Literary Enquiry into a Nationalistic Ideology* (München: Verlag für Dokumentation und Werbung, 1975).
Mahfouz, Naguib. *Khufu's Wisdom* [1939], translated by Raymond Stock (Cairo: American University in Cairo Press, 2003).
Mahfouz, Naguib. *Rhadopis of Nubia* [1943], translated by Anthony Calderbank (Cairo: American University in Cairo Press, 2003).
Mahfouz, Naguib. *Thebes at War* [1944], translated by Humphrey Davies (Cairo: American University in Cairo Press, 2003).
Mandler, Peter. *The Fall and Rise of the Stately Home* (New Haven: Yale University Press, 1997).
Manela, Erez. *The Wilsonian Moment: Self-Determination and the International Origins of Anticolonial Nationalism* (Oxford: Oxford University Press, 2007).
Mao Tse-tung. *On New Democracy* (Peking: Foreign Languages Press, 1954).
Marks, Peter. 'Art and Politics in the 1930s: *The European Quarterly* (1934–5), *Left Review* (1934–8), and *Poetry and the People* (1938–40)'. In *The Oxford Critical and Cultural History of Modernist Magazines. Volume 1, Britain and Ireland 1880–1955*, edited by Peter Brooker and Andrew Thacker (Oxford: Oxford University Press, 2009), pp. 623–46.
Martin, Benjamin. *The Nazi-Fascist New Order for European Culture* (Cambridge, MA: Harvard University Press, 2016).
Martin, Terry. *The Affirmative Action Empire: Nations and Nationalism in the Soviet Union, 1923–1939* (Ithaca, NY: Cornell University Press, 2001).
Marx, Karl. *Capital. Volume 1*, translated by Ben Fowkes (London: Penguin, 1990).
Marx, Karl and Friedrich Engels. *The Communist Manifesto*, edited by Phil Gasper (Chicago: Haymarket, 2005).
Mason, Michael. 'The Long March of Everyman'. *The Listener* 86, no.2225 (18 November 1971): pp. 683–84.
Maxwell, Richard. 'Inundations of Time: A Definition of Scott's Originality'. *ELH* 68 (2001): pp. 419–68.
Maxwell, Richard. *The Historical Novel in Europe, 1650–1950* (Cambridge: Cambridge University Press, 2009).
Mayer, Arno. *Political Origins of the New Diplomacy, 1917–1919* (New Haven: Yale University Press, 1959).
McGann, Jerome. *The Romantic Ideology: A Critical Investigation* (Chicago: University of Chicago Press, 1983).
McGann, Jerome. 'Marvels and Wonders: Powys, *Porius* and the Attempt to Revive Romance in the Age of Modernism'. *Times Literary Supplement*, no.4835 (1 December 1995): pp. 4–6.
McGrath, Tom. 'Against the False Magicians'. *The New Reasoner*, no.1 (1957): p. 60.
McGurl, Mark. *The Novel Art: Elevations of American Fiction after Henry James* (Princeton, NJ: Princeton University Press, 2001).
McIlroy, John. 'Another Look at E.P. Thompson and British Communism, 1937–1955'. *Labor History* 58, no.4 (2017): pp. 506–39.

McKeon, Michael. *The Origins of the Eighteenth-Century Novel, 1600–1740* (Baltimore, MD: Johns Hopkins University Press, 1987).
McMurry, Ruth Emily and Muna Lee. *The Cultural Approach: Another Way in International Relations* (Chapel Hill: University of North Carolina Press, 1947).
Merrill, Michael. 'An Interview with E.P. Thompson'. *Radical History Review* 3, no.4 (1976): pp. 4–25.
Merson, A.L. 'The Writing of Marxist History'. *Communist Review* (July 1949): pp. 590–96.
Micir, Melanie. 'Not of National Importance: Sylvia Townsend Warner, Women's Work and the Mid-Century Historical Novel'. In *Around 1945: Literature, Citizenship, Rights*, edited by Allan Hepburn (Montreal: McGill-Queens University Press, 2016), pp. 66–83.
Mills, Jean. 'The Writer, the Prince and the Scholar: Virginia Woolf, D.S. Mirsky, and Jane Harrison's Translation from the Russian of *The Life of the Archpriest Avvakum, by Himself*—a Revaluation of the Radical Politics of the Hogarth Press'. In *Leonard and Virginia Woolf, the Hogarth Press and the Networks of Modernism*, edited by Helen Southworth (Edinburgh: Edinburgh University Press, 2010), pp. 150–75.
Mirrlees, Hope. *Madeleine: One of Love's Jansenists* (London: Collins, 1919).
Mirrlees, Hope. *Paris: A Poem* (London: Hogarth Press, 1919).
Mirrlees, Hope. *The Counterplot* (London: Collins, 1924).
Mirrlees, Hope. 'Quelques aspects de l'art d'Alexis Mikhailovitch Rémizov'. *Le Journal de Psychologie Normale et Pathologique* 23 (1926): pp. 148–59.
Mirrlees, Hope. *Lud-in-the-Mist* [1926] (Doylestown, PA: Wildside Press, n.d.).
Mirrlees, Hope. *Collected Poems*, edited by Sandeep Parmar (Manchester: Carcanet, 2011).
Mitchell, J. Lawrence. 'In Another Country: Sylvia Townsend Warner at Large'. In *Writers of the Old School: British Novelists of the 1930s*, edited by Rosemary Colt and Janice Rossen (London: Macmillan, 1992), pp. 120–37.
Mitchison, Naomi. *The Moral Basis of Politics* (London: Constable, 1938).
Mitchison, Naomi. *The Kingdom of Heaven* (London: Heinemann, 1939).
Mitchison, Naomi. *You May Well Ask. A Memoir, 1920–1940* (London: Fontana, 1986).
Mitchison, Naomi. *The Blood of the Martyrs* [1939] (Edinburgh: Canongate, 1988).
Moriarty, Michael. *The Age of Suspicion: Early Modern French Thought* (Oxford: Oxford University Press, 2003).
Moriarty, Michael. *Fallen Nature, Fallen Selves: Early Modern French Thought II* (Oxford: Oxford University Press, 2006).
Morley, Iris. *Cry Treason* (London: Peter Davies, 1940).
Morley, Iris. *We Stood for Freedom* (New York: William Morrow & Co., 1942).
Morley, Iris. *The Mighty Years* (London: Peter Davies, 1943).
Morton, A.L. 'The Norfolk Rising'. *Communist Review* (July 1949): pp. 602–08.
Morton, A.L. *The Everlasting Gospel: A Study in the Sources of William Blake* (London: Lawrence & Wishart, 1958).
[Moss, Henry]. 'A Marxist view of Byzantium'. Review of Jack Lindsay, *Byzantium into Europe*, *Times Literary Supplement*, no.2564 (12 December 1952): p. 816.
Mulford, Wendy. *This Narrow Place. Sylvia Townsend Warner and Valentine Ackland: Life, Letters and Politics, 1930–1951* (London: Pandora, 1988).

# N

Namcheon, Kim. *Scenes from the Enlightenment: A Novel of Manners* [1939], translated by Charles La Shure (Champaign, IL: Dalkey Archive Press, 2014).
Nelson, Truman. *The Sin of the Prophet* (Boston: Little, Brown and Company, 1952).
Nelson, Truman. *The Passion by the Brook* (New York: Doubleday, 1953).
Nelson, Truman. *The Surveyor* (New York: Doubleday, 1960).
Nelson, Truman. 'On Creating Revolutionary Art and Going Out of Print'. *Triquarterly* 23 (1972): pp. 92–110.

Ngũgĩ wa Thiong'o, *Petals of Blood* [1977] (London: Penguin, 2002).
Ngũgĩ wa Thiong'o, interviewed by Maureen Warner-Lewis. In *Ngũgĩ wa Thiong'o Speaks: Interviews with the Kenyan Writer*, edited by Reinhard Sander and Bernth Lindfors (Oxford: James Currey, 2006), pp. 219–24.
Nicole, Pierre. 'Of Charity and Self-Love' [1674]. In Bernard Mandeville, *The Fable of the Bees and Other Writings*, edited by E.J. Hundert (Indianapolis, IN: Hackett, 1997), pp. 1–8.
Nizan, Paul. 'Littérature révolutionnaire en France'. *La revue des vivants* 6, no.9 (September–October 1932): pp. 393–400.

## O

Oinas, Felix. 'Folklore and Politics in the Soviet Union'. *Slavic Review* 32, no.1 (1973): pp. 45–58.
[Ollard, Richard]. 'Marxism and the Novel'. Review of Jack Lindsay, *The Moment of Choice*, *Times Literary Supplement*, no.2774 (29 April 1955): p. 209.
Orwell, George. 'The Frontiers of Art and Propaganda'. In *The Complete Works of George Orwell. Volume 12: A Patriot Above All, 1940–1941*, edited by Peter Davison (London: Secker and Warburg, 1998), pp. 483–86.

## P

Paananen, Victor. *British Marxist Criticism* (New York: Garland, 2000).
Paloczi-Horvath, George. *The Undefeated* (London: Secker and Warburg, 1959).
Park, Sunyoung. *The Proletarian Wave: Literature and Leftist Culture in Colonial Korea, 1910–1945* (Cambridge, MA: Harvard University Press, 2015).
Parnell, Michael. *Laughter from the Dark: A Life of Gwyn Thomas* (London: John Murray, 1988).
Percy, Thomas. *Reliques of Ancient English Poetry: Consisting of Old Heroic Ballads, Songs, and other Pieces of our earlier Poets*, 3 vols. (London: J. Dodsley, 1765).
Percy, Thomas. *Bishop Percy's Folio Manuscript: Ballads and Romances*, edited by John W. Hales and Frederick J. Furnivall (London: Trübner, 1867), 4 vols.
Pike, David. *German Writers in Soviet Exile, 1933–1945* (Chapel Hill: University of North Carolina Press, 1982).
[Pinkerton, John]. Review of *Scottish Song* by Joseph Ritson. *Critical Review, or Annals of Literature* 13, no.1 (1795): pp. 49–58.
Pocock, J.G.A. *The Ancient Constitution and the Feudal Law: A Study of English Historical Thought in the Seventeenth Century* (Cambridge: Cambridge University Press, 1957).
Polanyi, Karl. *The Great Transformation: The Political and Economic Origins of Our Time* (Boston, MA: Beacon, 2001).
Popescu, Monica. *At Penpoint: African Literatures, Postcolonial Studies, and the Cold War* (Durham, NC: Duke University Press, 2020).
Poulsen, Charles. *English Episode: A Tale of the Peasants' Revolt of 1381* (London: Progress Publishing, 1946).
Poulsen, Charles. *Scenes from a Stepney Youth* (London: Tower Hamlet Arts Project Books, 1988).
Poulsen, Charles. *Whitechapel Spring: Poems and Stories by Charles Poulsen*, edited by Charles Hobday (Belfast: Lapwing Publications, 2005).
Power, Eileen. *Mediaeval English Nunneries, c.1275 to 1535* (Cambridge: Cambridge University Press, 1922).
Powys, John Cowper. *Dorothy Richardson* (London: Joiner & Steele, 1931).
Powys, John Cowper. *A Glastonbury Romance* (New York: Simon and Schuster, 1932).
Powys, John Cowper. 'The Creation of Romance'. *The Modern Thinker and Author's Review* 1, no.1 (1932): p. 75.
Powys, John Cowper. *The Pleasures of Literature* (London: Cassell, 1938).

Powys, John Cowper. 'The Real and the Ideal'. *Spain and the World* 2, no.34 Supplement (May 1938): p. 3.
Powys, John Cowper. *Owen Glendower* [1941] (London: Picador, 1978).
Powys, John Cowper. *Dostoievsky* [1946] (London: Village Press, 1974).
Powys, John Cowper. *Obstinate Cymric: Essays 1935-47* [1947] (London: Village Press, 1973).
Powys, John Cowper. *Rabelais: His Life, The Story Told by Him, Selections Therefrom Here Newly Translated, and an Interpretation of His Genius and His Religion* (London: Bodley Head, 1948).
Powys, John Cowper. *In Spite Of: A Philosophy for Everyman* (London: Macdonald, 1953).
Powys, John Cowper. *Atlantis* (London: Macdonald, 1954).
Powys, John Cowper. *The Brazen Head* [1956] (London: Picador, 1978).
Powys, John Cowper. *The Letters of John Cowper Powys to Louis Wilkinson* (London: Macdonald, 1958).
Powys, John Cowper. '"Preface" or anything you like to *Porius*'. In 'The Matter of *Porius*', edited by R.L. Blackmore, *Powys Newsletter* 4 (1974): pp. 7-13.
Powys, John Cowper. *Letters of John Cowper Powys to his Brother Llewelyn, Volume 2: 1925-1939*, edited by Malcolm Elwin (London: Village Press, 1975).
Powys, John Cowper. *Petrushka and the Dancer: The Diaries of John Cowper Powys, 1929-1939*, edited by Morine Krissdóttir (Manchester: Carcanet, 1995).
Powys, John Cowper. *Powys to Sea Eagle: The Letters of John Cowper Powys to Philippa Powys*, edited by Anthony Head (London: Cecil Woolf, 1996).
Powys, John Cowper. *Porius: A Romance of the Dark Ages*, edited by Judith Bond and Morine Krissdóttir (New York: Overlook Duckworth, 2007).
Powys, John Cowper. *The Letters of John Cowper Powys and Emma Goldman*, edited by David Goodway (London: Cecil Woolf, 2008).
Pramoedya Ananta Toer. *The Girl from the Coast* [1962], translated by Willem Samuels (New York: Hyperion, 2003).
Pramoedya Ananta Toer. 'My Apologies, in the Name of Experience'. Translated by Alex G. Bardsley, *Indonesia* 61 (1996): pp. 1-14.
Prichard, Katherine Susannah. *The Roaring Nineties* [1946] (London: Virago, 1983).
Prichard, Katherine Susannah. *Golden Miles* [1948] (London: Virago, 1984).
Prichard, Katherine Susannah. *Winged Seeds* [1950] (London: Virago, 1984).
*Publishing in the Soviet Union*, translated by David Skvirsky (Moscow: Progress Publishers, 1967).

# Q

# R

Radek, Karl. 'Contemporary World Literature and the Tasks of Proletarian Art'. In A. Zhdanov, M. Gorky, N. Bukharin, K. Radek A. Stetsky et al., *Problems of Soviet Literature* (London: Martin Lawrence, 1934), pp. 73-182.
Ransome, John Crowe. 'Criticism as Pure Speculation', in *The Intent of the Critic*, edited by Donald Stauffer (Princeton, NJ: Princeton University Press, 1941), pp. 89-124.
Rattenbury, Arnold. 'Geoffrey Chaucer. The Poet in Society'. *Our Time* 4, no.1 (1944): p. 7, p.18.
Rattenbury, Arnold. 'Plain Heart, Light Tether'. *PN Review* 8, no.3 (1981): pp. 46-48.
Rattenbury, Arnold. 'Literature, Lying and Sober Truth: Attitudes to the Work of Patrick Hamilton and Sylvia Townsend Warner'. In *Writing and Radicalism*, edited by John Lucas (London: Longman, 1996), pp. 201-44.
Ren, Ke. 'A "Chinese Shelley" in 1930s Britain: Wang Lixi's Transnational Activism and Transcultural Lyricism'. In *Chiang Yee and His Circle: Chinese Artistic and Intellectual Life in Britain, 1930-1950*, edited by Paul Bevan, Ann Witchard and Da Zheng (Hong Kong: Hong Kong University Press, 2022), pp. 158-80.

Rimbaud, Arthur. *Œuvres complètes*, edited by André Guyaux with Aurélia Cervoni (Paris: Bibliothèque de la Pléiade, 2009).

[Ritson, Joseph]. 'A Historical Essay on the Origin and Progress of National Song'. In *A Select Collection of English Songs*, 3 vols. (London: Joseph Johnson, 1783), vol.1, pp. i–lxxii.

[Ritson, Joseph]. *Robin Hood: a Collection of all the Ancient Poems, Songs, and Ballads, now extant, relative to that Celebrated English Outlaw*, 2 vols. (London: T. Egerton and J. Johnson, 1795).

Rogan, Tim. 'Karl Polanyi at the Margins of English Socialism, 1934–1947'. *Modern Intellectual History* 10, no.2 (2013): pp. 317–46.

Rolland, Romain. 'Au-dessus de la mêlée'. *Journal de Genève*, 22 September 1914, Supplement: n.p.

Rolland, Romain. *Au-dessus de la mêlée* (Paris: Librarie Paul Ollendorff, 1915).

Rubin, Andrew. *Archives of Authority: Empire, Culture and the Cold War* (Princeton, NJ: Princeton University Press, 2012).

## S

Salton-Cox, Glyn. *Queer Communism and the Ministry of Love: Sexual Revolution in British Writing of the 1930s* (Edinburgh: Edinburgh University Press, 2019).

Samuel, Raphael. 'British Marxist Historians, 1880–1980: Part One'. *New Left Review*, no.120 (1980): pp. 21–96.

Samuel, Raphael. *Island Stories: Unravelling Britain. Theatres of Memory, Volume II*, edited by Alison Light (London: Verso, 1998).

Sankrityayan, Rahul. *From Volga to Ganga. A Picture in Nineteen Stories of the Historical, Economic and Political Evolution of the Human Society from 6000 B.C. to 1922 A.D.* [1943], translated by Victor Kiernan (Bombay: People's Publication House, 1947).

Sankrityayan, Rahul. *From Volga to Ganga*, edited by Kanwal Dhaliwal and Maya Joshi, translated by Victor Kiernan and Kanwal Dhaliwal (New Delhi: Left World Books, 2021).

Saunders, Frances Stonor. *Who Paid the Piper? The CIA and the Cultural Cold War* (London: Granta, 1999).

Schmitt, Carl. *Political Theology: Four Chapters on the Concept of Sovereignty*, translated by George Schwab (Chicago: University of Chicago press, 2005).

Scott, Walter. *The Antiquary*, edited by David Hewitt (Edinburgh: Edinburgh University Press, 1995).

*Second International Conference of Revolutionary Writers. Reports. Resolutions. Debates*, special issue of *Literature of the World Revolution* (n.d.) [1931].

Sembène, Ousmane. *God's Bits of Wood* [1960], translated by Francis Price (London: William Heinemann, 1962).

Shapiro, David and Cecile Shapiro. 'Abstract Expressionism: The Politics of Apolitical Painting'. *Prospects* 3 (1978): pp. 175–214

Sherry, Norman. 'Obituary: Graham Greene'. *The Independent*, 4 April 1991: Gazette 3.

Sillen, Samuel. 'History and Fiction'. *New Masses* 27, no.12 (14 June 1938): pp. 22–23.

Silver, Beverly. *Forces of Labor: Workers' Movements and Globalization Since 1870* (Cambridge: Cambridge University Press, 2003).

Silver, Beverly and Eric Slater. 'The Social Origins of World Hegemonies'. In *Chaos and Governance in the Modern World System*, edited by Beverly Silver and Giovanni Arrighi (Minneapolis, MN: University of Minnesota Press, 1999), pp. 151–216.

Silver, Brenda R. '"Anon" and "The Reader": Virginia Woolf's Last Essays'. *Twentieth-Century Literature* 25, nos.3/4 (1979): pp. 356–441.

Sim, Loraine. *Virginia Woolf: The Patterns of Ordinary Experience* (Farnham: Ashgate, 2010).

Smith, G.S. 'Jane Ellen Harrison: Forty-Seven Letters to D.S. Mirsky'. *Oxford Slavonic Papers* n.s. 28 (1995): pp. 62–97.

Smith, G.S. *D.S. Mirsky: A Russian-English Life, 1890–1939* (Oxford: Oxford University Press, 2000).

Smith, James. 'The Radical Literary Magazine of the 1930s and British Government Surveillance: The Case of *Storm* Magazine'. *Literature & History* 19, no.2 (2010): pp. 69–86.
Smith, Jeremy. *The Bolsheviks and the National Question, 1917–23* (London: Macmillan, 1999).
Smith, Marilyn Schwinn. '"Bergsonian Poetics" and the Beast: Jane Harrison's Translations from the Russian'. *Translation and Literature* 20, no.3 (2011): pp. 314–33.
Snowman, Daniel. 'Daniel Snowman writes about the series as history'. *The Listener* 86, no.2225 (18 November 1971): p. 685.
Soler, Manuel Aznar. *Républica literaria y revolución* (Sevilla: Editorial Renacimiento, 2014).
*Soviet Writers Reply to English Writers' Questions*, edited by Edgell Rickword (London: The Writers' Group, Society for Cultural Relations with the U.S.S.R., 1948).
[Spender, Stephen and Irving Kristol]. 'After the Apocalypse'. *Encounter* 1, no.1 (1953): p. 1.
Startsev, A. 'The Civil War and the Contemporary American Historical Novel'. *International Literature*, no.9 (1937): pp. 70–72.
Stead, Christina. 'The Writers Take Sides. Report on the First International Congress of Writers for the Defence of Culture, held in the Salle de la Mutualité at Paris, 21st–25th June, 1935'. *Left Review* 1, no.11 (1935): pp. 453–62.
Steiner, George. 'The Difficulties of Reading John Cowper Powys'. *Powys Review*, no.1 (1977): pp. 7–11.
Stevenson, R.L. *Familiar Studies of Men and Books* (New York: Charles Scribner, 1895).
Stiker-Métral, Charles-Olivier. *Narcisse contrarié: L'amour propre dans le discours moral en France, 1650–1715* (Paris: Honoré Champion, 2007).
Strutt, Joseph. *Queenhoo-Hall, A Romance*, 4 vols. (London: John Murray, 1808).
Sutherland, John. *Fiction and the Fiction Industry* (London: Athlone Press, 1978).
Swanwick, Michael. 'Hope-in-the-Mist'. *Foundation* 87 (2003): pp. 14–49.
Sziklai, László. *After the Proletarian Revolution: Georg Lukács's Marxist Development 1930–1945*, translated by Iván Sellei (Budapest: Akadémiai Kiadó, 1992).


T

Taunton, Matthew. *Red Britain: The Russian Revolution in Mid-Century Culture* (Oxford: Oxford University Press, 2019).
Taylor, Elinor. *The Popular Front Novel in Britain, 1934–1940* (Leiden: Brill, 2018).
Taylor, Felix. 'John Cowper Powys and the Anti-Vivisection Movement'. *The Powys Journal* 29 (2019): pp. 57–76.
Taylor, Philip. *The Projection of Britain Abroad: British Overseas Publicity and Propaganda 1919–1939* (Cambridge: Cambridge University Press, 1981).
*The Big Flame*, directed by Ken Loach (London: British Broadcasting Corporation, 1969).
Thein Pe Myint. *Thabeik-hmauk kyaung-tha* ['The Student Boycotter', 1938] (Rangoon: Pagan Publishing House, 1967).
Thein Pe Myint. *Ashei-ga nay-wun htwet-thi-pama* ['As Sure as the Sun Rising in the East', 1958] (Rangoon: Kyaw Lin, 1960).
*The Long March of Everyman 1750–1960*, edited by Theo Barker (Harmondsworth: Penguin, 1978).
'The Matter of *Porius*', edited by R.L. Blackmore. *Powys Newsletter* 4 (1974): pp. 4–21.
*The Second Congress of the Communist International, as Reported by the Official Newspapers of Soviet Russia* (Washington, D.C.: Government Printing Office, 1920).
Thomas, Gwyn. *All Things Betray Thee* [1949] (London: Lawrence & Wishart, 1986).
Thomas, Gwyn. *A Few Selected Exits* (London: Hutchinson, 1968).
Thomas, Gwyn. *Sorrow For Thy Sons* (London: Lawrence & Wishart, 1986).
Thompson, E.P. 'Socialism and the Intellectuals'. *Universities & Left Review* 1, no.1 (1957): pp. 31–36.
Thompson, E.P. 'Socialist Humanism: An Epistle to the Philistines'. *The New Reasoner*, no.1 (1957): pp. 105–43.

Thompson, E.P. 'Agency and Choice I: A Reply to Criticism'. *The New Reasoner*, no.5 (1958): pp. 89-106.
Thompson, E.P. 'Commitment in Politics'. *Universities & Left Review*, no.6 (1959): pp. 50-55.
Thompson, E.P. 'Outside the Whale'. In *Out of Apathy*, edited by E.P. Thompson (London: Stevens and Sons/New Left Books, 1960), pp. 141-94.
Thompson, E.P. *The Making of the English Working Class* (London: Gollancz, 1963).
Thompson, E.P. 'Disenchantment or Default: A Lay Sermon'. In *Power & Consciousness*, edited by Conor Cruise O'Brien and William Dean Vanech (London: University of London Press, 1969), pp. 149-82.
Thompson, E.P. *William Morris: Romantic to Revolutionary*, revised edition (London: Merlin, 1976).
Thompson, E.P. 'Romanticism, Moralism and Utopianism: The Case of William Morris'. *New Left Review*, no.99 (1976): pp. 83-111.
Thompson, E.P. 'An Open Letter to Leszek Kolakowski'. In *The Poverty of Theory and other Essays* (New York: Monthly Review Press, 1978), pp. 303-402.
Thompson, E.P. 'Edgell Rickword'. *PN Review* 6, no.1 Supplement (1979): pp. xxvi-xxviii.
Thompson, E.P. 'Homage to Tom Maguire'. In *Making History: Writings on History and Culture* (New York: New Press, 1994), pp. 23-65.
Thompson, E.P. *The Poverty of Theory, or An Orrery of Errors* (London: Merlin, 1995).
Thomson, George. *Marxism and Poetry* (London: Lawrence & Wishart, 1945).
Tihanov, Galin. *The Master and the Slave: Lukács, Bakhtin and the Ideas of their Time* (Oxford: Oxford University Press, 2000).
Tihanov, Galin. 'Viktor Shklovskii and Georg Lukács in the 1930s'. *Slavonic and East European Review* 78, no.1 (2000): pp. 44-65.
Tihanov, Galin. 'Cosmopolitans without a Polis: Towards a Hermeneutics of the East-East Exilic Experience (1929-1945)'. In *The Exile and Return of Writers from East-Central Europe: A Compendium*, edited by John Neubauer and Borbála Zsuzsanna Török (Berlin: De Gruyter, 2009), pp. 123-43.
Timasheff, Nicholas. *The Great Retreat: The Growth and Decline of Communism in Russia* (New York: Dutton, 1946).
Tönnies, Ferdinand. *Zur Kritik der öffentliche Meinung* (Berlin: Julius Springer, 1922).
Trease, Geoffrey. *Bows against the Barons* (London: Martin Lawrence, 1934).
Trease, Geoffrey. *Comrades for the Charter* (London: Martin Lawrence, 1934).
Trease, Geoffrey. *Pfeile gegen Barone*, translated by Willi Schulz (Moscow: Verlagsgenossenschaft ausländischer Arbeiter in der UdSSR, 1935).
Trease, Geoffrey. 'Revolutionary Literature for the Young'. *International Literature*, no.7 (1935): pp. 100-02.
Trease, Geoffrey. *Cue for Treason: A Tale of Shakespearean England* (Oxford: Basil Blackwell, 1940).
Trease, Geoffrey. *Bows against the Barons*, revised edition (Leicester: Bockhampton Press, 1966).
Trease, Geoffrey. *A Whiff of Burnt Boats. An Early Autobiography* (Macmillan: London and Basingstoke, 1971).
Trease, Geoffrey. 'A Lifetime of Storytelling: The Author Takes Stock of Writing Books for Children since 1933'. In *The Cool Web: The Pattern of Children's Reading*, edited by Margaret Meek, Aidan Warlow, and Griselda Barton (London: The Bodley Head, 1977), pp. 145-56.
Trilling, Lionel. 'Wordsworth and the Rabbis', in *The Opposing Self: Nine Essays in Criticism* (London: Secker and Warburg, 1955), pp. 118-50.
Trory, Ernie. *Between the Wars: Recollections of a Communist Organiser* (Brighton: Crabtree Press, 1974).
Trotsky, Leon. *The Revolution Betrayed: What is the Soviet Union and Where is it Going?*, translated by Max Eastman (New York: Doubleday, Doran and Co., 1937).
Trubetzkoy, Nikolai Sergeevich. *The Legacy of Genghis Khan and Other Essays on Russia's Identity*, edited by Anatoly Liberman (Ann Arbor: Michigan Slavic Publications, 1991).

Trumpener, Katie. *Bardic Nationalism: The Romantic Novel and the British Empire* (Princeton, NJ: Princeton University Press, 1997).
Tylor, E.B. *Primitive Culture: Researches into the Development of Mythology, Philosophy, Religion, Language, Art and Custom* (London: John Murray, 1871).

## U

Unsigned. 'China's Struggle for Freedom: Professor Shelley Wang at Dorchester'. *Western Gazette*, 12 November 1937: p. 7.
Unsigned. 'Three Authors at Dorchester'. *Western Gazette*, 30 July 1937: p. 16.
Unsigned. 'Writers and History'. *International Literature*, no.9 (September 1937): pp. 51–52.
Unsigned. 'Howard Fast'. In *Current Biography: Who's News and Why 1943*, edited by Maxine Block (New York: H.W. Wilson Company, 1944), pp. 200–02.
Unsigned. 'New Play is by Taxi Driver'. *Daily Worker*, 2 May 1951: p. 3.
Unsigned. 'Ritorna Spartaco eroe popolare'. *l'Unità*, 4 January 1952: p. 3,
Unsigned. 'Editorial'. *Universities & Left Review* 1, no.1 (1957): pp. i–ii.
Unsigned. 'Notes for our Readers'. *Universities & Left Review*, no.6 (1959): n.p. [73].
[Utley, T.E.]. 'Freedom and Integrity'. *Times Literary Supplement*, no.2657 (2 January 1953): p. 9.

## V

Vanita, Ruth. '"Uncovenanted Joys": Catholicism, Sapphism, and Cambridge Ritualist Theory in Hope Mirrlees' *Madeleine: One of Love's Jansenists*'. In *Catholic Figures, Queer Narratives*, edited by Lowell Gallagher, Frederick Roden, and Patricia Juliana Smith (Basingstoke: Palgrave Macmillan, 2006), pp. 85–96.
*Virginia Woolf: The Critical Heritage*, edited by Robin Majumdar and Allen McLaurin (London: Routledge & Kegan Paul, 1975).

## W

Wallerstein, Immanuel. *After Liberalism* (New York: The New Press, 1995).
Wallerstein, Immanuel. *Utopistics, or Historical Choices of the Twenty-First Century* (New York: The New Press, 1998).
Wallis, Mick. 'Pageantry and the Popular Front: Ideological Production in the Thirties'. *New Theatre Quarterly* 10, no.38 (1994): pp. 132–56.
Wallis, Mick. 'The Popular Front Pageant: Its Emergence and Decline'. *New Theatre Quarterly* 11, no.41 (1995): pp. 17–32.
Wallis, Mick. 'Heirs to the Pageant: Mass Spectacle and the Popular Front'. In *A Weapon in the Struggle: The Cultural History of the Communist Party in Britain*, edited by Andy Croft (London: Pluto Press, 1998), pp. 48–67.
Walpole, Hugh. *The Waverley Pageant: The Best Passages from the Novels of Sir Walter Scott* (London: Eyre and Spottiswoode, 1932).
Wang, David Der-wei. *The Monster that is History: History, Violence, and Fictional Writing in Twentieth-Century China* (Berkeley: University of California Press, 2004).
Warner, Sylvia Townsend. 'Notation: The Growth of a System'. In *The Oxford History of Music. Introductory Volume*, edited by Percy C. Buck (Oxford: Oxford University Press, 1929), pp. 66–84.
Warner, Sylvia Townsend. *The True Heart* [1929] (London: Penguin, 2021).
Warner, Sylvia Townend. 'Appendix II. The Milk Marketing Scheme'. In Valentine Ackland, *Country Conditions* (London: Lawrence & Wishart, 1936), pp. 95–97.
Warner, Sylvia Townsend. 'Barcelona'. *Left Review* 2, no.15 (1936): pp. 812–16.

Warner, Sylvia Townsend. 'Catalonia in Civil War'. *New Masses* 21, no.9 (24 November 1936): pp. 3–4.
Warner, Sylvia Townsend. *Summer Will Show* [1936] (London: Virago, 1987).
Warner, Sylvia Townsend. 'Underpayment of Agricultural Workers: Black Figures from Blue Books'. *Country Standard* 1, no.2 (April 1936): p. 5.
Warner, Sylvia Townsend. 'Unofficial Drought'. *Country Standard* 1, no.6 (August 1936): pp. 6–7.
Warner, Sylvia Townsend. 'A Castle in Spain'. *The New Yorker*, 2 January 1937: pp. 22–24.
Warner Sylvia Townsend. 'The Drought Breaks'. *The Fight* 4, no.7 (1937): pp. 16–17.
Warner, Sylvia Townsend. 'The Drought Breaks'. *Life and Letters To-Day* 16, no.8 (1937): pp. 68–71.
Warner, Sylvia Townsend. 'Harvest in Spain'. *New Statesman & Nation*, n.s. 19, no.336 (1937): pp. 184.
Warner, Sylvia Townsend. 'Soldiers and Sickles in Spain'. *The Countryman* 14, no.1 (1937): pp. 78–80.
Warner, Sylvia Townsend. 'Women of Yesterday—2: Rosa Luxemburg'. *Woman To-Day* (April 1937): p. 5; p.12.
Warner, Sylvia Townsend. *After the Death of Don Juan* [1938] (London: Virago, 1989).
Warner, Sylvia Townsend. 'My Village Life'. *The Countryman* 19, no.2 (1939): pp. 472–86.
Warner, Sylvia Townsend. 'The Historical Novel'. In *Fighting Words*, edited by Donald Ogden Stewart (New York: Harcourt Brace and Company, 1940), pp. 50–53.
Warner, Sylvia Townsend. *A Garland of Straw* (New York: Viking, 1943).
Warner, Sylvia Townsend. 'Love of France'. *Our Time* 5, no.1 (1945): pp. 5–6.
Warner, Sylvia Townsend. *The Corner That Held Them* [1948] (London: Virago, 1988).
Warner, Sylvia Townsend. 'The Jungle Blossom'. *Our Time* 7, no.11 (1948): pp. 287–92.
Warner, Sylvia Townsend. *Somerset* (London: Paul Elek, 1949).
Warner, Sylvia Townsend. 'Women as Writers'. *Journal of the Royal Society of Arts* 107, no.5034 (1959): pp. 380–84.
Warner, Sylvia Townsend. *Kingdoms of Elfin* (New York: Viking Press, 1977).
Warner, Sylvia Townsend. 'Sylvia Townsend Warner in Conversation'. *PN Review* 8, no.3 (1981): pp. 35–37.
Warner, Sylvia Townsend. *Letters*, edited by William Maxwell (London: Chatto & Windus, 1982).
Warner, Sylvia Townsend. *The Diaries of Sylvia Townsend Warner*, edited by Claire Harman (London: Chatto & Windus, 1994).
Warner, Sylvia Townsend. *The Element of Lavishness: Letters of Sylvia Townsend Warner and William Maxwell*, edited by Michael Steinman (Washington, D.C.: Counterpoint, 2001).
Warner, Sylvia Townsend. *New Collected Poems*, edited by Claire Harman (Manchester: Carcanet, 2008).
Warner, Sylvia Townsend. 'A Note on the Historical Background'. Reprinted in *The Journal of the Sylvia Townsend Warner Society* 16 (2015): pp. 9–13.
Warner, Sylvia Townsend. 'Notes on *The Corner That Held Them*'. Edited by Peter Swaab, *The Journal of the Sylvia Townsend Warner Society* 20 (2020): pp. 3–7.
Warner, Sylvia Townsend and Mercedes Aguirre. 'Sylvia Townsend Warner's Spanish Civil War Love Poems'. *The Journal of the Sylvia Townsend Warner Society* 19, no.1 (2020): pp. 64–69.
Weitz, Eric. 'Self-Determination: How a German Enlightenment Idea Became the Slogan of National Liberation and a Human Right'. *American Historical Review* 120, no.2 (2015): pp. 462–96.
Wellek, René. 'The Concept of "Romanticism" in Literary History: II. The Unity of European Romanticism'. *Comparative Literature* 1, no.2 (Spring 1949): 147–72.
Wells, H.G. *Outline of History* (London: Cassell, 1920).
Wesker, Arnold. 'The Nottingham Captain: A Moral for Narrator, Voices and Orchestra'. In *Six Sundays in January* (London: Jonathan Cape, 1971), pp. 41–60.
Wesker, Arnold. *Chips With Everything and Other Plays* (Harmondsworth: Penguin, 1980).
Wilford, Hugh. 'The Cultural Cold War: Recent Scholarship and Future Directions'. *Cahiers Charles V*, no.28 (2000): pp. 33–47.

Williams, Raymond. *The Country and the City* (London: Chatto & Windus, 1973).
Williams, Raymond. 'A Lecture on Realism'. *Screen* 18, no.1 (1977): pp. 61–74.
Williams, Raymond. *Marxism and Literature* (Oxford: Oxford University Press, 1977).
Williams, Raymond. *Politics and Letters: Interviews with the New Left Review* (London: New Left Books, 1979).
Williams, Raymond. *Culture and Materialism* [1980] (London: Verso, 2005).
Williams, Raymond. *Towards 2000* (Harmondsworth: Pelican, 1985).
Williams, Raymond. 'Introduction', to Gwyn Thomas, *All Things Betray Thee* (London: Lawrence & Wishart, 1986), pp. iii–x.
Williams, Raymond. *Resources of Hope: Culture, Democracy, Socialism*, edited by Robin Gable (London: Verso, 1989).
Williams, Raymond. *The Politics of Modernism: Against the New Conformists*, edited by Tony Pinkney (London: Verso, 1989).
Williams, Raymond. *People of the Black Mountains. 1: The Beginning* (London: Paladin, 1990).
Williams, Raymond. 'Raymond Williams'. In *Talking Films: The Best of The Guardian Film Lectures*, edited by Andrew Britton (London: Fourth Estate, 1991), pp. 103–32.
Williams, Raymond. *People of the Black Mountains. 2: The Eggs of the Eagle* (London: Paladin, 1992).
Williams, Raymond. *Who Speaks for Wales? Nation, Culture, Identity*, edited by Daniel Williams (Cardiff: University of Wales Press, 2003).
Williams, Raymond. *Culture and Politics: Class, Writing, Socialism*, edited by Philip O'Brien (London: Verso, 2022).
Witt, Susanna. 'Between the Lines: Totalitarianism and Translation in the USSR'. In *Contexts, Subtexts, Pretexts: Literary Translation in Eastern Europe and Russia*, edited by Brian James Baer (Amsterdam: John Benjamins, 2011), pp. 149–70.
Woolf, Virginia. *Jacob's Room* [1922], edited by Kate Flint (Oxford: Oxford University Press, 1992).
Woolf, Virginia. *Mrs Dalloway* [1925], edited by Bonnie Kime Scott (Orlando, FL: Harcourt, 2005).
Woolf, Virginia. *To the Lighthouse* [1927], edited by Stella McNichol (London: Penguin, 1992).
Woolf, Virginia. *Orlando* [1928], edited by Maria DiBattista (New York: Harcourt, 2006).
Woolf, Virginia. *The Waves* [1931], edited by David Bradshaw (Oxford: Oxford University Press, 2015).
Woolf, Virginia. *The Years* [1937], edited by Hermione Lee (Oxford: Oxford University Press, 1999).
Woolf, Virginia. *Between the Acts* [1941] (Harmondsworth: Penguin, 1972).
Woolf, Virginia. *The Letters of Virginia Woolf*, edited by Nigel Nicholson and Joanne Trautmann, 6 vols. (London: Hogarth Press, 1975–1980).
Woolf, Virginia. *The Diaries of Virginia Woolf*, edited by Anne Oliver Bell with Andrew McNeillie. 5 vols. (London: Hogarth Press, 1977–84).
Woolf, Virginia. '"Anon" and "The Reader": Virginia Woolf's Last Essays', edited by Brenda R. Silver. *Twentieth-Century Literature* 25, nos.3/4 (1979): pp. 356–441.
Woolf, Virginia. *The Essays of Virginia Woolf*, edited by Andrew McNeillie and Stuart N. Clarke, 6 vols. (London: Hogarth Press, 1986–2011).
Virginia Woolf. *The Complete Shorter Fiction of Virginia Woolf*, edited by Susan Dick, second edition (Orlando, FL: Harcourt, 1989).
Woolf, Virginia. *A Room of One's Own and Three Guineas*, edited by Morag Shiach (Oxford: Oxford University Press, 1992).
Woolf, Virginia. *Orlando: The Original Holograph Draft*, edited by Stuart Clarke (London: Stuart Nelson Clarke, 1993).
Woolf, Virginia. *Moments of Being: Autobiographical Writings*, edited by Jeanne Shulkind (London: Pimlico, 2002).
Wordsworth, William. *The Major Works*, edited by Stephen Gill (Oxford: Oxford University Press, 2000).

Wright, Patrick. *The Village That Died for England: The Strange Story of Tyneham*, revised edition (London: Faber, 2002).
Wu Ming. *Altai* [2009], translated by Shaun Whiteside (London: Verso, 2013).

X

Y

Yang, Mo. *Qingchun zhige* ['The Song of Youth'] (Beijing: Writers Publishing House, 1958).
Young, George. *Diplomacy Old and New* (London: Swarthmore Press, 1921).

Z

Zhdanov, A.A. 'Soviet Literature—Richest in Ideas, Most Advanced Literature'. In Nikolai Bukharin, Maxim Gorky, Karl Radek, Andrey Zhdanov et al., *Problems of Soviet Literature* (London: Martin Lawrence, 1934), pp. 15–24.

# Index

*For the benefit of digital users, indexed terms that span two pages (e.g., 52–53) may, on occasion, appear on only one of those pages.*

Abensour, Miguel, 26
Abrams, M.H., 20–21
Ackland, Valentine, 32–33, 124, 126–127, 152–154
Adorno, Theodor, 89–90 n.54
Afro-Asian Writers Conference (1958), 79–81
Aiken, Conrad, 35
Alexis, Jacques Stephen, 121–122
Allen, Harvey, 11, 129–130
Allen, Jim, 200–201
Amado, Jorge, 79–82
Anand, Mulk Raj, 79–81
Anderson, Amanda, 19–20 n.72
Anderson, Benedict, 27
Anderson, Perry, 3–4, 18–19, 34, 75–76 n.9, 180–181, 191–192, 205
Aragon, Louis, 97–98, 179, 189–190
Armstrong, Tim, 167 n.27
Arnold, John, 165–166 n.15, 167 n.23
Arrighi, Giovanni, 7–8, 9–10
Arthur, Dave, 104–105 n.111
Asor Rosa, Alberto, 75–76 n.9
Asturias, Miguel Ángel, 73–74
Auden Generation, 5–6
Auden, W.H., 103 n.107
Augustine, 42–43
Austin, Alfred, 138
Ayers, David, 37 n.16

Bakhtin, Mikhail, 4–5, 26, 85–86, 85–86 n.45, 87
Banfield, Ann, 68
Barga, Corpus, 124–125
Barke, James, 92–93, 101–102
Barnhisel, Greg, 16 n.59
Bataille, Georges, 122–123
Bauer, Otto, 9 n.32
Beard, Mary, 43–45 n.42
Bedny, Demian, 78–79
Beer, Gillian, 68
Bell, Daniel, 18–19
Benda, Julien, 14
Benjamin, Walter, 11–12, 39–40, 87, 122–123, 205

Bennett, Arnold, 35
Bentley, Phyllis, 95–96
Berard, Ewa, 15 n.55
Berens-Totenohl, Josefa, 11–12, 77 n.14
Berger, John, 194–195
Berlant, Lauren, 204
Beumelberg, Werner, 77
Bland, William, 109–110
Blissett, Luther (Wu Ming), 34, 204–205
Bloch, Ernst, 26–27, 122, 187 n.107
Bloom, Harold, 20–21
Blunck, Hans-Friedrich, 77 n.14
Boggs, Grace Lee, 173–174
Bourdet, Charles, 163
Brecht, Bertolt, 200–201
Brennan, Timothy, 122–123 n.176
Bresciani, Antonio, 28–29
Briggs, Julia, 43–45 n.40
Bullivant, Joanna, 107–108 n.124
Burke, Edmund, 56–57
Burns, Emile, 174–176
Burns, Robert, 101–102
Burton, Robert, 67
Bush, Alan, 106–108, 148
Byron, Lord, 116–117 n.154

Calder Marshall, Arthur, 1–2 n.2, 18
Campaign for Nuclear Disarmament, 163–164
Carpentier, Alejo, 74–75, 118–121, 122–123, 124–125
Carter, David, 167–168 n.27
Casanova, Pascale, 12–14
Cassou, Jean, 79, 97–98
Centre for Contemporary Cultural Studies, 164
Chase, Richard, 19–20
Chukovskii, Kornei, 17–18
Clark, Katerina, 13–14 n.47, 73–74 n.3, 116–117 n.154
Cleary, Joe, 13–14 n.47
Coleridge, Samuel Taylor, 67–68
*Comintern Aesthetics*, 73–74 n.3
Communist Party of Great Britain, 5–6, 106
  and 1956, 103, 162, 171–173

Communist Party of Great Britain (*Continued*)
Historians' Group, 32, 102–103, 117–118, 165, 174–175, 187
historical culture of, 32, 102–111
and intellectuals, 171–173
National Cultural Committee, 171–172, 174–176, 181–182
Writers' Group, 148–149, 165, 174–176
Communist International (Comintern), 5–6, 15–16, 17–18, 25–26, 27–28, 29–30, 32–33, 73–75, 83–84, 91, 122–123, 127, 169–170
see also Georgi Dimitrov, Popular Front, Third Period
Communist Party of the Soviet Union, 75–76
Congress of Black Writers and Artists (1956), 121
Congress for Cultural Freedom, 17–18
Cornford, John, 95–96
Cortazar, Julio, 142
cosmopolitanism, 4–5, 27–30, 29–30 n.123, 73–74 n.2
Cold War culture, 2–3, 13–20, 103, 115, 143–144, 151–152, 162, 171–172, 173–174, 196
and literary study, 18–21, 114–115, 122, 126–127, 150–151, 189–190
see also cultural diplomacy, modernism
Craig, Cairns, 68, 71–72
Croft, Andy, 29–30 n.122, 106–107 n.122, 108–109, 112 n.141, 165 n.12, 171–172
cultural diplomacy, 14–18, 196
see also Cold War culture, literary institutions, literary world-system, new diplomacy
Cunard, Nancy, 127–128 n.19, 148–149
Cunningham, Valentine, 97–98
'Cutty Wren, The', 102–111

Dane, Clemence, 43–45
Denning, Michael, 13–14 n.47, 19–20, 29–30 n.122, 73–75, 76–77, 79–81, 82–83, 92–93, 103–104 n.110, 122–123
Denny, Norman, 135–136
Derrida, Jacques, 114–115
DeSola, Ralph and Frederica, 94–95
Deutscher, Isaac, 83–84
Dewald, Jonathan, 25–26 n.104
Dimitrov, Georgi, 25–26, 32–33, 75–78, 82–83, 91, 96–97, 108, 115, 122–123, 127, 169–170, 180, 191–192
see also Communist International (Comintern), Popular Front
Djagalov, Rossen, 13–14 n.47, 73–74 n.3, 79–81 n.20
Dobb, Maurice, 145–146 n.83

Döblin, Alfred, 39–40
Docker, John, 167 n.23
Du Pengchen, 79–81 n.23
Dumain, Ralph, 165–166 n.17
Dumas, Alexandre, 28–29
Dunayevskaya, Raya, 173–174
Duncan, Ian, 23–24 n.90, 24–25, 87–88 n.48, 115–116, 132–134, 136–137
Durkheim, Emile, 188

Ehrenburg, Ilya, 82–83
Eliot, T.S., 5–6, 30, 35–37, 56, 115, 132–133, 179 n.79
Ellis, Bob, 15–16
Ellis, Clifford and Rosemary, 25–26
Ellmann, Maud, 152–153
Engels, Friedrich, 8–9, 85, 97–98, 106
Esty, Jed, 5–6, 30, 35–37, 86 n.46, 115
Eurasianism, 37–38, 52–53
*Europäischer Schriftsteller-Vereinigung*, 17–18

Fagan, Hyman, 105–106, 148
Fanon, Franz, 192–193
Fast, Howard, 79–81, 196–197
Feuchtwanger, Lion, 76–77
Feuerbach, Ludwig, 27, 154
Flaubert, Gustave, 87–88
Flores, Angel, 122
folk culture, 23–24, 26, 52–54, 64–66, 102–113, 115–116, 117–118, 119–120, 121–122, 204–205
see also romance
Forster, E.M., 5–6, 35–36, 39, 115
Foucault, Michel, 45
Fox, Ralph, 105–106
Frank, Bruno, 79
Frazer, J.G., 103
Freud, Sigmund, 137
Frye, Northrop, 188
Fuller, Roy, 165

Garnett, Tony, 200–201
Gifford, Alan, 109–110
Giovagnoli, Raffaello, 28–30
Goldmann, Emma, 128–129
Gollancz, Victor, 93–94, 201
Goodway, David, 126–127
Gorky, Maxim, 26, 115, 121, 186–187, 189–190
Graeber, David, 204
Gramsci, Antonio, 27–30, 75–76 n.10, 192–193
Greene, Graham, 1–2, 5, 18–19
Grose, Francis, 23–24
Guest, David, 95–96
Guilbaut, Serge, 16, 17–18 n.60

Hall, Stuart, 109–110 n.131, 162
Hanson, Harry, 164, 164 n.9, 171–172 n.45, 182–183
Harker, Ben, 106 n.118, 112, 170–171 n.39, 192–193 n.126
Harman, Claire, 144, 152–153
Harper, Frederick, 18, 100–101
Harris, Alexandra, 5–6
Harrison, Jane Ellen, 31–32, 43–45, 43–45 n.42, 46–49, 51, 98–99, 188, 188 n.111
Hauser, Kitty, 65–66 n.126
Heard, Gerald, 98–99
von Heiseler, Bernt, 77
Henry, David, 109–110 n.131
Henty, G.A., 94–95
Heslop, Harold, 15–16, 18, 92, 97, 100–101
Hill, Christopher, 32, 103, 105–106, 109–110 n.131, 111, 117, 194
Hilton, Rodney, 103, 109–110 n.131, 117–118 n.158
history from below, 4–5, 25–26, 32, 73, 111–123, 199
historical novel
 Antonio Gramsci on, 28–29
 communist, 32–34, 73, 127, 164, 180–182, 196–198
 decline of, 3–4, 38, 76–77, 86–88
 Georg Lukács on, 3–4, 11–12, 32, 40–41, 83–92, 202, 205
 Mikhail Bakhtin on, 85–86, 85–86 n.45
 and modernism, 2–6, 35, 38–41
 Nazi-fascist, 11–12, 32, 76–77
 Perry Anderson on, 3–4, 34, 205
 postmodern, 2–3, 198, 205
 romantic-era, 2–4, 3–4 n.11, 11–12, 40–41, 73, 83, 85–86, 88–89, 170–171, 205
Hobday, Charles, 108–109 n.128, 165, 171–172
Hobsbawm, Eric, 32, 103, 103 n.106, 111–112, 116–117, 165
Hobson, Harold, 75
Hobson, J.A., 35–36
Ho Chi Minh, 10
Hume, David, 60, 67–70
Hurd, Richard, 24–25
Huxley, Aldous, 165

Ian Campbell Folk Group, 103
Ilford New Era Film Society, 109–110
Ilin, M., 94–95
imperial realignment, 6, 13–14, 37, 115
International Association of Writers for the Defence of Culture, 15–16
 First Congress (1935),16, 76–77

 Second Congress (1937),122–123, 124–125, 160–161
*International Literature*, 17–18, 78–79, 90–91, 94–95, 151–152
International Union of Revolutionary Writers, 15–16, 17–18, 29–30, 163

Jackson, T.A., 90–91
James, C.L.R., 173–174
James, Henry, 24–25
Jameson, Fredric, 40–41, 73–74 n.1, 83 n.35, 188, 202
Jelusich, Mirko, 77 n.14
Joannou, Maroula, 126–127
Jones, Clara, 57–58 n.90
Joyce, James, 12–13, 39–40, 92–93

Kafka, Franz, 142
Kalliney, Peter, 13–14 n.47, 16 n.59
Kenner, Hugh, 18–19
Khrushchev, Nikita, 124, 181–182
Kiernan, Victor, 79–81 n.25, 103, 109–110 n.131
Kim Namcheon, 79–81, 90–91 n.55
Kino Films, 114 n.146
Kipling, Rudyard, 138
Kristol, Irving, 18–19

Langenbucher, Hellmuth, 11–12
Lautréamont, Comte de, 119–120, 189–190
Lawrence, D.H., 3
Leach, Edmund, 110
League of American Writers, 146–147 n.89
Leavis, F.R., 19–21
Lee, Hermione, 56–57, 66–67
Left Book Club, 93–94, 112, 124
*Left Review*, 15–16, 163
Lehmann, John, 115 n.151
Lenin, V.I., 9, 75–76 n.10, 180–181, 192
Lessing, Doris, 177
Lindsay, Jack, 5, 95, 109–110, 160–162
 *1649: A Novel of a Year*, 98–99, 112–113, 170–171, 181–182
 and 1956,179–180, 181–182
 *Adam of a New World*, 100–101, 184 n.99
 and alienation, 165–166, 169, 170–171, 173–174, 179, 179 n.79, 182–184, 186–187, 192–193
 *Barriers Are Down, The*, 97–98, 170–171, 188
 *Brief Light: A Novel of Catullus*, 100–101, 183–184
 British Way (novel sequence),177–178, 179–180, 179–180 n.86
 *Clashing Rocks, The*, 98–99

Lindsay, Jack, (*Continued*)
  and communism, 33–34, 95, 165–180, 182–183, 185–186
  *Crisis in Marxism, The*, 192–193
  and 'cultural upsurge', 174–175
  *Dons Sight Devon, The*, 94–95 n.73, 170–171
  *England, My England*, 114
  and E.P. Thompson, 163–164, 185–186, 190–191
  Fanfrolico Press, 167–168
  *Fires in Smithfield*, 81–82, 97–98
  'Fullness of Life, The', 166–167, 185
  and Georg Lukács, 91, 167 n.26
  *Great Oak, The*, 117–118, 179–180, 187
  *Hannibaal Takes a Hand*, 95–96, 170–171
  and Jane Harrison, 98–99
  *John Bunyan: Maker of Myths*, 98–99
  *Life Rarely Tells*, 179–180
  *Light in Italy*, 96–97, 170–171
  *London Aphrodite, The*, 167
  *Lost Birthright*, 97–99, 113–114, 170–171, 181–182
  *Marxism and Contemporary Science*, 175–176
  'Marxist Theory of Culture', 175–176, 175–176 n.56
  *Men of Forty-Eight*, 98–99, 170–171, 181–182
  and modernism, 33–34, 166–168
  and national turn, 33–34, 95, 167–168, 169–171
  'not english? A Reminder for May Day', 114, 114 n.146, 169–170
  'Note of Self Criticism, A', 176
  *Rebels of the Goldfields*, 95 n.73
  reception of, 81–82, 177–178
  relationship with Norman Lindsay, 166–168, 168 n.30
  reputation of, 18, 165–172, 177–178
  Roman Trilogy, 95, 169
  and romance, 193
  *Runaway: A Tale of Ancient Roman Days*, 95 n.73
  and science and technology, 184
  and Scott, 91–92, 162–171
  and socialist humanism, 33–34, 163–164, 172–174, 182–186, 191–193, 194–195
  and socialist realism, 166–167, 176, 179, 186–188
  *Short History of Culture*, 98–99, 112
  'Starfish Road', 179, 189–191, 194
  *Stormy Violence, The*, 97–98, 170–171
  and theory of the novel, 187–188
  and theory of poetry, 189–191
  *Thunder Underground*, 33–34, 96–98, 100–101, 164, 171–172, 179, 180–186, 190–191
  *Times Literary Supplement*, 177
  *To Arms! A Story of Ancient Gaul*, 95 n.73
  and utopia, 168, 184, 188, 193
  *Vision*, 167
  vitalism, 167, 184
Lindsay, Norman, 33–34, 166–168, 168 n.30
Lindsay, Philip, 95, 169
*Literaturnyi kritik*, 84, 89–91
literary institutions, 14–18, 73–74, 77 n.14, 146–147 n.89
literary world-system, 12–18, 37, 79–81
Lloyd, A.L. (Bert), 104–105
Loach, Ken, 200–201
Locre, Elza de, 168–169
Lovejoy, A.O., 20–21
Lukács, Georg
  and crisis of realism, 3–4, 40–41, 87–88
  and critical realism, 116–117
  *Historical Novel, The*, 3–4, 11–12, 32, 40–41, 83–91, 120–121, 202, 205
  and Jack Lindsay, 91, 91 n.57, 167 n.26
  and Marxism, 84–85
  and Mikhail Bakhtin, 85–86, 85–86 n.44
  and modernism, 40–41, 83, 85–86, 88
  in Moscow, 84–85, 89–90
  nation and empire in, 40–41, 85–89
  and national turn, 88–89
  and Popular Front, 83–84, 88–90
  and romanticism, 116–117, 116–117 n.154
  and Scott, 11–12, 41, 83, 88–91, 116–117 n.154
  and Sylvia Townsend Warner, 90–91, 127
  theory of history, 11–12, 89–90, 202
  and typicality, 41, 116–117 n.154, 167 n.26
Luo Guangbin and Yang Yiyan, 88 n.23
Luxemburg, Rosa, 100–101, 186

Macainsh, Noel, 167 n.23
MacCarthy, Desmond, 35
Machaut, Guillaume de, 154
magical realism, 4–5, 32, 73–75, 118–123
Mahfouz, Naguib, 73–74, 79–81
Maisky, Ivan, 15 n.55
Mandler, Peter, 60–61
Manzoni, Alessandro, 28–29
Mao Zedong, 9, 159
Marquez, Gabriel Garcia, 32, 73–74, 122–123
Martin, Benjamin, 13–14 n.47
Marx, Karl, 106, 145–146 n.84, 175–176, 186–187

*1844 Manuscripts*, 84, 163, 173–174, 173–174 n.50, 184
*Communist Manifesto* (with Friedrich Engels), 8–9, 97–98, 100–101, 181–182
Marxism, 99–101
　English, 164, 166–167, 180–181, 191–192
　and national question, 8–9, 204
　Western, 164, 166–167, 180–181, 191–192
　*see also* socialist humanism
Mason, Michael, 109–111
Maxwell, Richard, 3–4 n.11, 127 n.17
Maxwell, William, 143–144
Mayer, Arno, 14
McGann, Jerome, 20–21 n.75, 135–136, 142
McGrath, Tom, 190–191
McGurl, Mark, 24–25
McIlroy, John, 172–173 n.48
McKeon, Michael, 24–25
Micir, Melanie, 144
Mirrlees, Hope, 5, 30–32, 42–49, 115, 167–168
　and Alexei Remizov, 54
　and capitalist modernity, 42–43, 45–46, 49–50, 54–55
　*Counterplot, The*, 31–32, 38, 40, 45–46, 52
　and Eurasianism, 37–38, 52–53
　and Jane Harrison, 43–45, 43–45 n.42, 46–49, 51
　*Lud-in-the-Mist*, 31–32, 35, 41, 49–56
　*Madeleine: One of Love's Jansenists*, 31–32, 35, 41–49
　and modernism, 30–32, 38–39
　and national culture, 54–56
　and national identity, 55–56
　and national turn, 31–32, 49, 52
　*Paris: A Poem*, 30–31, 38, 52
　and publication of *Orlando*, 35
　and re-enchantment, 43–45 n.42, 48–49, 51–52, 54–55
　and religion, 50, 56
　and romance, 50, 52, 54–56
　and same-sex desire, 43–46
　and Scott, 31–32, 37–38, 54
Mirsky, D.S., 52–53
Mitchell, Lawrence, 148–149 n.92
Mitchell, Margaret, 11–12, 79
Mitchison, Naomi, 95–96, 98–99
Mo Yang, 79–81 n.23
modernism, 2–3, 4–5, 32–33, 127
　and Antonio Gramsci, 29–30
　Cold War, 16–19, 18–19 n.0, 34, 189–190, 196, 198
　and empire, 6, 35–37, 40–41, 85–86
　and Georg Lukács, 40–41, 83, 85–86, 88
　high, 19–20, 24–25, 29–30, 35–37, 39–40, 55–56, 65, 67–68, 132–133, 140, 150–151, 163, 167–168
　and historical novel, 2–3, 38, 40–41
　late, 5–6, 19–20, 27–28, 30, 35–37, 68, 115
　and literary world-system, 12–13, 37
　and national turn, 27–28, 30, 31–32, 35–37, 40–41, 115
　proletarian, 29–30, 73–74, 92–93, 92–93 n.64
　romantic, 5–6
　and Scott, 21–22
Moore, G.E., 68
Morley, Iris, 95, 97, 99–100
Morris, John, 105–106
Morton, A.L., 104–105, 117–118 n.158, 194
Mulford, Wendy, 126–127, 144, 148–149 n.92
Myers, L.H., 129–130
Myson, Mike, 106–107

Nairn, Tom, 191–192
national-popular, 27–30, 75–76 n.10, 78, 180–181
national turn, 4–12, 18–20, 27–32, 33–37, 73, 75–84, 85–86, 92, 96–97, 115, 167–170
nationalism
　and communism, 8–9, 75, 191–192
　Eurasian, 52–53
　anti-colonial, 4–5, 88–89, 121–122
　Cold War critique of, 18–20
　counter-revolutionary, 9–10
　cultural, 4–5, 20–21, 37–38, 41, 52–53, 55–56, 69–70, 71–72, 79–81
　mid-century, 4–6, 11–12, 71–73, 88–89, 115, 191–192
　and internationalism, 18–19, 37, 82–83, 180–181, 190–191
　National Socialism, 4–5, 76–77
　Popular Front, 4–5, 25–26, 75–76, 78–79, 82–83, 88–89, 91, 96–97, 127, 162—170, 191–192
　Soviet, 4–5, 75–76, 115–116
　romantic, 20–21, 37–38, 41, 69–70, 71–73, 115–117, 170–171
Nelson, Truman, 34 n.133
new diplomacy, 14
New Left, 8 n.27, 33–34, 75–76 n.9, 109–110, 162–164, 173–174, 180–181, 191–192, 196
*New Left Review*, 163–164
*New Reasoner, The*, 124–125, 164, 179, 185–186, 194–195
Ngũgĩ wa Thiong'o, 82–83
Nizan, Paul, 29–30

Oinas, Felix, 115 n.151
Orwell, George, 14, 17–18
*Our Time*, 171–172, 174–175

Padmore, George, 175–176
Paloczi-Horvath, George, 178
Park, Sunyoung, 90–91 n.55
People's Newsreels, 114 n.146
Percy, Thomas, 23–24
phonocentrism, 114–115
Pike, David, 73–74 n.3
Playter, Phyllis, 129–130
*Poetry and the People*, 112
Polanyi, Karl, 6, 39–40
Pokrovskii, M.N., 78–79
postmodernism, 2–3
Popescu, Monica, 13–14 n.47
Popova-Mutafova, Fani, 77 n.14
Popular Front (Comintern policy),4–6, 25–26, 28–29, 75–76, 78–79, 83–84, 88–90, 103–104, 106–107, 112–115, 117, 122–123, 126–127, 163, 169–170, 191–192
  see also Communist International (Comintern), Georgi Dimitrov
Poulsen, Charles, 18, 108–109, 148
Power, Eileen, 145
Powys, John Cowper, 5
  and anarchism, 32–33, 126–127, 128–129, 133–134, 141
  *Brazen Head, The*, 134
  and communism, 32–33, 125, 126–127, 133–134
  and Emma Goldman, 128–129
  *Glastonbury Romance, A*, 132–134
  late fiction, 134
  and modernism, 32–33, 127, 130–131
  *Owen Glendower*, 130, 133–134, 136–137
  *Porius*, 32–33, 129–143
  reputation of, 126–127
  return to Wales, 129–130, 133–134
  and romance, 129–130, 132–137
  and Scott, 127, 130, 132
  and Second World War, 127–129
  and Spanish Civil War, 32–33, 125, 127–128, 133–134
  and style, 130, 138–142
Powys, Philippa [Katie],128
Pramoedya Ananta Toer, 73–74, 79–81
Prichard, Katharine Susannah, 79–81
proletarian
  internationalism, 4–5, 27–28
  literature, 15–16, 29–30, 73–74, 82–83, 92–94

Radek, Karl, 13–14
Rank, Otto, 168
Rattenbury, Arnold, 126–127, 148–149, 151–152
realism, 1–2, 3–4, 16, 24–26, 40–41, 73–74, 85–86, 87–88, 116–117, 127, 186, 193, 194–195, 199–201
  see also magical realism, romance, socialist realism
Regler, Gustav, 79
Remizov, A.M., 52–54
Rickword, Edgell, 158, 189–190
Rimbaud, Arthur, 31, 189–190
Ritson, Joseph, 23–24
Roberts, Kenneth, 11
Robeson, Paul, 106–107
Rolland, Romain, 14
romance, 21–27, 31–32, 35–38, 45, 54, 71–72, 101–123, 129–130, 132–143, 193, 205
  see also magical realism, realism, socialist realism
romanticism, 2–3, 27, 28–29, 37–38, 41, 69–70, 71–72, 85–87, 139–140, 166–167, 171, 194
  Cold War study of, 18–21, 189–190
  revolutionary (socialist realism),26, 115–117, 121, 186–187
Rubin, Andrew, 13–14 n.47, 17–18
Rudé, George, 103, 109–110 n.131, 113
Russell, Bertrand, 68

Sackville-West, Vita, 35, 57–58, 60–61, 66–67, 124, 126–127
Salton-Cox, Glyn, 126–127
Samuel, Raphael 39–40 n.24, 103, 109–110 n.131, 116–117 n.155
Sankrityayan, Rahul, 79–81
Schiller, Friedrich, 115–116
Schmitt, Carl, 11–12
Scott, Sir Walter, 3–4, 11–12, 20–21, 24, 27–28, 31–32, 38, 39–40, 52–54, 60, 72, 79–81, 87–88 n.48, 91–92, 127
de Scudéry, Madeleine, 42–45
Sembène, Ousmane, 79–81
Sender, Ramon, 79
Shakespeare, William, 55–57, 64, 66–67, 70–71, 103
Shklovskii, Viktor, 89–90
Sholokhov, Mikhail, 82–83
Sillen, Samuel, 11
Silver, Beverly, 8
Sim, Loraine, 68
Sitwell, Edith, 179 n.79, 189–190
social history. *see* 'history from below'

socialist humanism, 33–34, 85, 120–121, 154, 162–164, 172–174, 179 n.79, 179–180, 182–184, 193
socialist realism, 16, 19–20, 26, 30, 75–76, 78–79 n.16, 79–81, 93–94 n.64, 115–117, 121, 176, 186–187, 196–197, 199–200
*see also* magical realism, realism, romance
Soler, Manuel Aznar, 122–123 n.177
Sommerfield, John, 95–96
Soviet Writers' Congress, 13–14, 16, 26, 93–94 n.64, 115, 177–178, 186–187, 199–200
Spender, Stephen, 18–19
Stalin, Joseph, 75–76, 79, 115–116
Stead, Christina, 16
Stead, Henry, 177–178 n.73
Steiner, George, 126–127
Stevenson, Robert Louis, 3
Stonor Saunders, Frances, 16
Strutt, Joseph, 24
Sue, Eugène, 28–29
le Sueur, Meridel, 81–82
Swanwick, Michael, 42–43
Swingler, Randall, 106–107

Taunton, Matthew, 114–115
Taylor, Charles, 173–174
Taylor, Elinor, 90–91 n.56, 92–93 n.64, 98–99
Thein Pe Myint, 82–83
Third Period (Comintern policy), 29–30, 75, 92–94, 106–107 n.118
*see also* Communist International (Comintern)
Thomas, Gwyn, 93–94, 101, 194–195, 196–198, 201, 204–205
Thompson, Dorothy, 103
Thompson, E.P., 20–21 n.77, 25–26, 32, 75–76 n.9, 81–82, 103, 111–113, 162–164, 171–172 n.44, 172–174, 175–176, 185–186, 188 n.110, 190–191, 193–194
Thomson, George, 112, 115 n.151
Tihanov, Galin, 85–86 n.44, 89–90
Timasheff, Nicholas, 75–76
Torr, Dona, 105–106
Trease, Geoffrey, 81–82, 94–95
Trory, Ernie, 114 n.146
Trotsky, Leon, 75–76, 180–181, 192
Trubetskoy, N.S., 53
Trumpener, Katie, 3–4 n.11
Tylor, E.B., 54–55
Tzara, Tristan, 189

de Unamuno, Miguel, 50
Unity Theatre, 108–110, 114 n.146, 174–175
*Universities & Left Review*, 162–164

Utley, T.E., 177
utopia, 24–26

Wallerstein, Immanuel, 8 n.27
Wallis, Mick, 114 n.146
Wang, David Der-wei, 79–81 n.23
Wang Lixi (Shelley), 158–159
Warner, Sylvia Townsend, 5, 95
  *After the Death of Don Juan*, 95–96, 127–128, 146–147 n.86, 153, 160–161
  and agrarian revolution, 127–128, 159–161
  and anti-clericalism, 127–128, 145–147, 150–151, 153, 155–156, 159
  and anti-fascism, 148–149 n.99, 149–150, 160–161
  and communism, 32–33, 126–127, 143–144, 148–149, 151–153, 159–160
  *Corner That Held Them, The*, 32–33, 95, 143–161
  'Drought Breaks, The', 153
  and feudalism, 127–128, 145–147, 159
  *Flint Anchor, The*, 95
  *Garland of Straw, A*, 149–150
  and Georg Lukács, 90–91, 127
  and humanism, 149–150, 154
  and iconoclasm, 155–156
  and modernism, 32–33, 127
  and music, 154–155
  *New Yorker, The*, 143–144, 151–152
  and peasantry, 145–147, 158–161
  and religion, 154, 159
  reputation of, 18, 126–127
  and rural activism, 32–33, 159–161, 160 n.149
  and Scott, 90–91, 127
  and Second World War, 127–128, 148–149 n.99, 150
  Second Congress of the International Association of Writers for the Defence of Culture, 124–125
  'Soap for Spain', 124–127
  Soviet Union, 148–149, 160–161
  and Spanish activism, 124–128, 127–128 n.19, 157, 157 n.132
  and Spanish Civil War, 32–33, 124–125, 126–128, 152–153, 155–157, 160–161
  and Stalin, 148–149, 148–149 n.97
  and style, 149–150, 151–153
  *Summer Will Show*, 18, 79, 95, 100–101, 151–152, 160–161
  *True Heart, The*, 95, 149–150, 151–152
  'Women as Writers', 152–153
Wellek, René, 20–21
Wells, H.G., 39
Wesker, Arnold, 103–104, 109–110

West, Alick, 177–178
Whyte, Lancelot Law, 184
Wilford, Hugh, 16 n.59
Williams, Joy, 201
Williams, Raymond, 34, 59, 109–110 n.131, 139–140 n.59, 171–172 n.45, 194–195
   *Border Country*, 201
   and communist historical novel, 34, 196–197, 201–202
   and Gwyn Thomas, 34, 194–195, 196–198, 201–202, 204–205
   and long revolution, 34
   and mid-century, 34, 196–197, 200–201
   and 'militant particularism', 201–202
   and modernism, 34, 196
   *People of the Black Mountains*, 34, 201–204
   and postmodernism, 34, 196, 198
   and social history, 198–199
   and realism, 198-199–200
   and survival, 202–204
Willis, Ted, 174–175, 174–175 n.54
Wilson, Woodrow, 10
Woolf, Virginia, 5–6, 30, 115, 167–168
   'Abbeys and Cathedrals', 57–58
   and ambivalence, 57–58, 60, 69–70, 72
   'Anon', 63–66
   *Between the Acts*, 35–36, 66–67 n.126, 70
   and class privilege, 41, 56–58, 60–61, 66–67
   and capitalist modernity, 57–58, 61–66
   and David Hume, 60, 67–70, 71–72
   and democracy, 57–61, 72
   and E.M. Forster, 21–22 n.85
   and historical change, 56–61
   and the individual, 59, 61–66
   *Jacob's Room*, 22, 56–57
   and literary history, 56–57, 61–66
   'Modern Fiction', 67
   and modernism, 21–22, 35–37, 61–62, 65, 68
   *Mrs Dalloway*, 22
   and national culture, 21–22, 56, 59–60, 67, 70–72
   and national identity, 56, 67, 69–70, 71–72
   and national turn, 31–32, 35–37, 56, 68
   *Orlando*, 31–32, 35, 41, 56–72
   and publication of *Paris: A Poem*, 38
   and Hope Mirrlees, 43–45
   and re-enchantment, 56, 65–66
   review of *Madeleine: One of Love's Jansenists*, 46–47, 49
   and romance, 70, 72
   and Scott, 21–22, 56, 72
   *To the Lighthouse*, 21–22, 67
   'This is the House of Commons', 57–60
   and tradition, 56–57, 70–72
   *Voyage Out, The*, 57–58
   *Years, The*, 70
   *Waves, The*, 57–58 n.86, 67, 70
Wordsworth, William, 139–140
Workers' Music Association, 106–107, 108–109 n.128, 112
Wright, Patrick, 126–127
Wu Ming. *see* Luther Blissett

Zhdanov, A.A., 79, 121, 175–176, 186–187, 199–200